THE BURNING CITY

LARRY NIVEN & JERRY POURNELLE

THE BURNING CITY

POCKET BOOKS

New York   London   Toronto   Sydney   Singapore

This book is a work of fiction. Names, characters, places and incidents are products of the authors' imagination or are used fictitiously. Any resemblance to actual events or locales or persons, living or dead, is entirely coincidental.

 POCKET BOOKS, a division of Simon & Schuster Inc.
1230 Avenue of the Americas, New York, NY 10020

Copyright © 2000 by Larry Niven and Jerry Pournelle

All rights reserved, including the right to reproduce
this book or portions thereof in any form whatsoever.
For information address Pocket Books, 1230 Avenue
of the Americas, New York, NY 10020

ISBN 978-1-4165-7508-5

First Pocket Books hardcover printing March 2000

10 9 8 7 6 5 4 3 2 1

POCKET and colophon are registered trademarks of
Simon & Schuster Inc.

Maps by Paul Pugliese

Printed in the U.S.A.

For Roberta and Marilyn

Editor's Acknowledgment

The editor would like to thank Larry Niven
and Jerry Pournelle for that rarest of all novels,
one with something to say.

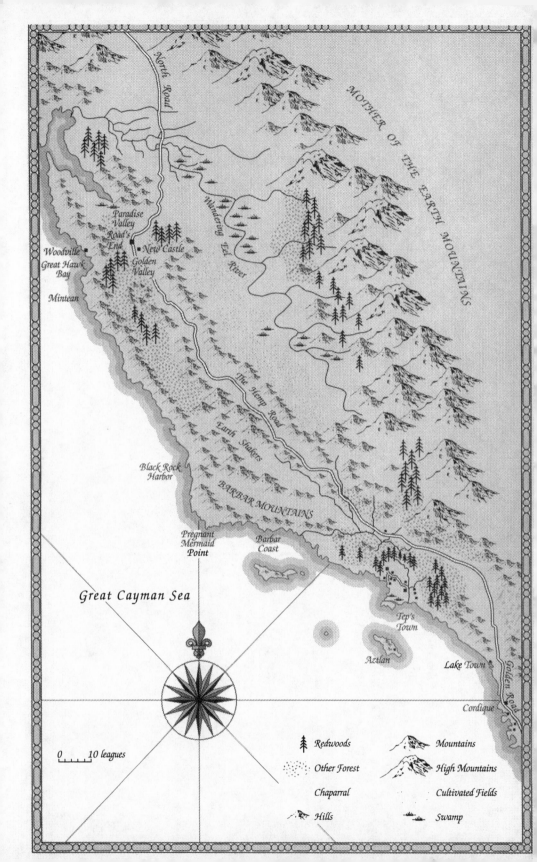

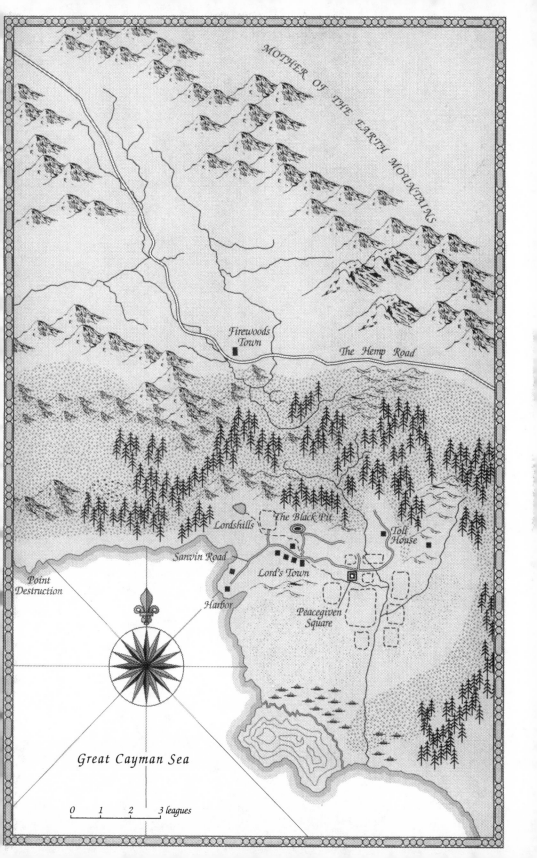

"It is not God who kills the children. Not fate that butchers them or destiny that feeds them to the dogs. It's us. Only us."

From *Watchmen* by Alan Moore

CAST

Gods

YANGIN-ATEP (TEP, FIREBRINGER)
ZOOSH
COYOTE
BEHEMOTH
LOKI
PROMETHEUS

Lordkin

Placehold

WHANDALL PLACEHOLD (Seshmarl)
POTHEFIT: Whandall's father
SHASTERN: Whandall's younger brother
SHIG: Whandall's younger brother
MOTHER'S MOTHER: Dargramnet
WANSHIG: Whandall's older half brother
RESALET: Whandall's father's brother and leader of the Placehold
WESS: a girl about Whandall's age
LENORBA
VINSPEL
ILYESSA: Whandall's sister
THOMER
TOTTO
TRIG: Whandall's brother
ELRISS

RUBYFLOWER
ILTHERN
SHARLATTA
FREETHSPAT

Serpent's Walk

LORD PELZED
GERAVIM
TUMBANTON
TRAZALAC
STANT CORLES
DUDDIGRACT
RENWILDS
COSCARTIN
SHEALOS
THE FORIGAFT BROTHERS
KRAEMAR
ROUPEND
CHAPOKA
MIRACOS
HARTANBATH

Other Bands

BANSH
ILTHER
ALFERTH
TARNISOS
ILSERN: a tough, athletic woman
CHIEF WULLTID
IDREEPUCT
FALCONS: called Dirty Birds by most but not to their faces
STAXIR

Kinless

KREEG MILLER
RIGMASTER
WILLOW ROPEWALKER
CARVER ROPEWALKER
CARTER ROPEWALKER
HAMMER MILLER
IRIS MILLER
HYACINTH MILLER
OPAL MILLER
DREAM-LOTUS INNKEEP

Lords

LORD CHIEF WITNESS SAMORTY
LORD CHANTHOR
LORD QIRINTY: a lord fascinated by magic
LADY RAWANDA: first lady of Lordshills
LORD JERREFF
SHANDA
RABBLIE (LORD RABILARD)
LORD QUINTANA: later becomes Lord Chief Witness
MORTH OF ATLANTIS
LORD QUIRINTHAL THE FIRST
ROWENA
LADY SIRESEE

Their Servants

SERANA: a cook; later, chief cook
ANTANIO
BERTRANA (MISS BATTY): governess
PEACEVOICE WATERMAN

Turf

PLACEHOLD
SERPENT'S WALK
PEACEGIVEN SQUARE
BULL PIZZLE
FALCON LAIR: generally called Dirty Bird
THE WEDGE: the meadow at the top of Deerpiss River
CONDIGEO
LORD'S TOWN
THE LORDSHILLS
WOLVERINES
TEP'S TOWN (VALLEY OF SMOKES, BURNING CITY)
WATER DEVILS
SANVIN STREET: winds over the low hills that separate Serpent's
    Walk from the harbor
THE BLACK PIT
ATLANTIS
BARBAR MOUNTAINS
TOROV
MAZE WALKERS
EASTERN ARC
GOOD HAND HARBOR
OWL BEAK
MARKET ROUND
SERPENT STREET
COLDWATER
DARK MAN'S CUP STREET
DEAD TOWN
THE TORONEXTI
LION'S ATTIC
STRAIGHT STREET
ANGLE STREET

Lookers

TRAS PREETROR
ARSHUR THE MAGNIFICENT

Seamen

JACK RIGENLORD
ETIARP
MANOCANE
SABRIOLOY

Water Devils

LATTAR

Beyond Tep's Town

Turf

FIREWOODS TOWN
WALUU PORT
THE HEMP ROAD
MOUNT JOY
PARADISE VALLEY
STONE NEEDLES
GORMAN
GOLDEN VALLEY
LAST PINES
MARSYL TOWN
ORANGETOWN
COYOTE'S DEN
GREAT HAWK BAY

Clan Members and Others

SPOTTED COYOTES
RORDRAY
BLACK KETTLE (KETTLE BELLY)
NUMBER THREE
NUMBER FOUR
HAJ FISHHAWK
RUBY FISHHAWK
ORANGE BLOSSOM
BISON CLAN
MIRIME
LONESOME CROW
GREATHAND: the blacksmith
HICKAMORE
FAWN
MOUNTAIN CAT
STARFALL
RUTTING DEER
TWISTED CLOUD
STAG RAMPANT

Book Two

Turf

ROAD'S END
DEAD SEAL FLATS
GRANITE KNOB
LONG AVENUE
NORTH QUARTER
NEW CASTLE
HIGH PINES
GREAT VALLEY
RORDRAY'S ATTIC
MOUNT CARLEM
WARBLER FLATS
DRYLANDS
FARTHEST LAND

STONE NEEDLES
MINTERL
CASTLE MINTERL
HIP HIGH SPRING
VEDASIRAS RANGE
FAIR CHANCE
THE ESTATES
CARLEM MARCLE
NEO WRASELN
QUAKING ASPEN
THE SPRINGS

Travelers

WHANDALL FEATHERSNAKE
GREEN STONE
LARKFEATHERS
SABER TOOTH
CHIEF FARTHEST LAND
HAWK IN FLIGHT
WOLF TRIBE
MOUNTAIN CAT
SESHMARLS THE BIRD
TERROR BIRDS
LILAC
WHITECAP MOUNTAIN
PUMA TRIBE
PASSENGER PIGEON
THONE
KING TRANIMEL
GLINDA
DREAM OF FLYING
WHITE LIGHTNING
STONE NEEDLES MAN (CATLONY, TUMBLEWEED, HERMIT)
HIDDEN SPICE
CLEVER SQUIRREL (SQUIRRELLY)
LURK (NOTHING WAS SEEN)
STARFALL ROPEWALKER

FIGHTING CAT FISHHAWK
BURNING TOWER
INSOLENT LIZARD
FALLEN WOLF

Returning

HALF HAND
EGON FORIGAFT
MASTER PEACEVOICE WATERMAN
LORD CHIEF WITNESS QUINTANA
WITNESS CLERK SANDRY
ADZ WEAVER
FUBGIRE
RONI
HEROUL
FIREGIFT
SILLY RABBITS
SADESP
LEATHERSMITH MILLER (SMITTY)
SAPPHIRE CARPENTER
SWABOTT
REBLAY OF SILLY RABBITS
HEJAK
LAGDRET

PREFACE

There was fire on Earth before the fire god came. There has always been fire. What Yangin-Atep gave to humankind was madness. Yangin-Atep's children will play with fire even after they burn their fingers.

It was only Yangin-Atep's joke, then and for unmeasured time after. But a greater god called down the great cold, and Yangin-Atep's joke came into its own. In the icy north people could not survive unless the fire god favored one of their number.

Cautious men and women never burned themselves twice; but their people died of the cold. Someone must tend the fire during the terrible winters. Twelve thousand years before the birth of Christ, when most of the gods had gone mythical and magic was fading from the world, Yangin-Atep's gift remained.

BOOK ONE

WHANDALL PLACEHOLD

PART ONE

Childhood

CHAPTER
1

They burned the city when Whandall Placehold was two years old, and again when he was seven.

At seven he saw and understood more. The women waited with the children in the courtyard through a day and a night and another day. The day sky was black and red. The night sky glowed red and orange, dazzling and strange. Across the street a granary burned like a huge torch. Strangers trying to fight the fire made shadow pictures.

The Placehold men came home with what they'd gathered: shells, clothing, cookware, furniture, jewelry, magical items, a cauldron that would heat up by itself. The excitement was infectious. Men and women paired off and fought over the pairings.

And Pothefit went out again with Resalet, but only Resalet came back.

Afterward Whandall went with the other boys to watch the loggers cutting redwoods for the rebuilding.

The forest cupped Tep's Town like a hand. There were stories, but nobody could tell Whandall what was beyond the forest where redwoods were pillars big enough to support the sky, big enough to replace a dozen houses. The great trees stood well apart, each guarding its turf. Lesser vegetation gathered around the base of each redwood like a malevolent army.

The army had many weapons. Some plants bristled with daggers; some had burrs to anchor seeds in hair or flesh; some secreted poison; some would whip a child across the face with their branches.

Loggers carried axes, and long poles with blades at the ends. Leather armor and wooden masks made them hard to recognize as men. With the poles they could reach out and under to cut the roots of the spiked or poisoned lesser plants and push them aside, until one tall redwood was left defenseless.

Then they bowed to it.

Then they chopped at the base until, in tremendous majesty and with a sound like the end of the world, it fell.

They never seemed to notice that they were being watched from cover by a swarm of children. The forest had dangers for city children, but being caught was not one of them. If you were caught spying in town you would be lucky to escape without broken bones. It was safer to spy on the loggers.

One morning Bansh and Ilther brushed a vine.

Bansh began scratching, and then Ilther; then thousands of bumps sprouted over Ilther's arm, and almost suddenly it was bigger than his leg. Bansh's hand and the ear he'd scratched were swelling like nightmares, and Ilther was on the ground, swelling everywhere and fighting hard to breathe.

Shastern wailed and ran before Whandall could catch him. He brushed past leaves like a bouquet of blades and was several paces beyond before he slowed, stopped, and turned to look at Whandall. *What should I do now?* His leathers were cut to ribbons across his chest and left arm, the blood spilling scarlet through the slashes.

The forest was not impenetrable. There were thorns and poison plants, but also open spaces. Stick with those, you could get through . . . it *looked* like you could get through without touching anything . . . almost. And the children were doing that, scattering, finding their own paths out.

But Whandall caught the screaming Shastern by his bloody wrist and towed him toward the loggers, because Shastern was his younger brother, because the loggers were close, because somebody would help a screaming child.

The woodsmen saw them—saw them and turned away. But one dropped his ax and jogged toward the child in zigzag fashion, avoiding . . . what? Armory plants, a wildflower bed—

Shastern went quiet under the woodsman's intense gaze. The woodsman pulled the leather armor away and wrapped Shastern's wounds in strips of clean cloth, pulling it tight. Whandall was trying to tell him about the other children.

The woodsman looked up. "Who are you, boy?"

"I'm Whandall of Serpent's Walk." Nobody gave his family name.

"I'm Kreeg Miller. How many—"

Whandall barely hesitated. "Two tens of us."

"Have they all got"—he patted Shastern's armor—"leathers?"

"Some."

Kreeg picked up cloth, a leather bottle, some other things. Now one of the others was shouting angrily while trying not to look at the children. "Kreeg, what do you want with those candlestubs? We've got work to do!" Kreeg ignored him and followed the path as Whandall pointed it out.

There were hurt children, widely scattered. Kreeg dealt with them. Whandall didn't understand, until a long time later, why other loggers wouldn't help.

Whandall took Shastern home through Dirty Birds to avoid Bull Pizzles. In Dirty Birds a pair of adolescent Lordkin would not let them pass.

Whandall showed them three gaudy white blossoms bound up in a scrap of cloth. Careful not to touch them himself, he gave one to each of the boys and put the third away.

The boys sniffed the womanflowers' deep fragrance. "Way nice. What else have you got?"

"Nothing, Falcon brother." Dirty Birds liked to be called Falcons, so you did that. "Now go and wash your hands and face. Wash hard or you'll swell up like melons. We have to go."

The Falcons affected to be amused, but they went off toward the fountain. Whandall and Shastern ran through Dirty Birds into Serpent's Walk. Marks and signs showed when you passed from another district to Serpent's Walk, but Whandall would have known Serpent's Walk without them. There weren't as many trash piles, and burned-out houses were rebuilt faster.

The Placehold stood alone in its block, three stories of gray stone. Two older boys played with knives just outside the door. Inside, Uncle Totto lay asleep in the corridor where you had to step over him to get in. Whandall tried to creep past him.

"Huh? Whandall, my lad. What's going on here?" He looked at Shastern, saw bloody bandages, and shook his head. "Bad business. What's going on?"

"Shastern needs help!"

"I see that. What happened?"

Whandall tried to get past, but it was no use. Uncle Totto wanted to hear the whole story, and Shastern had been bleeding too long. Whandall started screaming. Totto raised his fist. Whandall pulled his brother upstairs. A sister was washing vegetables for dinner, and she shouted too. Women came yelling. Totto cursed and retreated.

Mother wasn't home that night. Mother's Mother—Dargramnet, if you were speaking to strangers—sent Wanshig to tell Bansh's family. She put Shastern in Mother's room and sat with him until he fell asleep. Then she came into the big second-floor Placehold room and sat in her big chair. Often that room was full of Placehold men, usually playful, but sometimes they shouted and fought. Children learned to hide in the smaller rooms, cling to women's skirts, or find errands to do. Tonight Dargramnet asked the men to help with the injured children, and they all left so that she was alone with Whandall. She held Whandall in her lap.

"They wouldn't help," he sobbed. "Only the one. Kreeg Miller. We could have saved Ilther—it was too late for Bansh, but we could have saved Ilther, only they wouldn't help."

Mother's Mother nodded and petted him. "No, of course they wouldn't," she said. "Not now. When I was a girl, we helped each other. Not just kin, not just Lordkin." She had a faint smile, as if she saw things Whandall would never see, and liked them. "Men stayed home. Mothers taught girls and men taught boys, and there wasn't all this fighting."

"Not even in the Burnings?"

"Bonfires. We made bonfires for Yangin-Atep, and he helped us. Houses of ill luck, places of illness or murder, we burned those too. We knew how to serve Yangin-Atep then. When I was a girl there were wizards, real wizards."

"A wizard killed Pothefit," Whandall said gravely.

"Hush," Mother's mother said. "What's done is done. It won't do to think about Burnings."

"The fire god," Whandall said.

"Yangin-Atep sleeps," Mother's Mother said. "The fire god was stronger when I was a girl. In those days there were real wizards in Lord's Town, and they did real magic."

"Is that where Lords live?"

"No, Lords don't live there. Lords live in Lordshills. Over the hills, past the Black Pit, nearly all the way to the sea," Mother's Mother said, and smiled again. "And yes, it's beautiful. We used to go there sometimes."

He thought about the prettiest places he had seen. Peacegiven Square, when the kinless had swept it clean and set up their tents. The Flower Market, which he wasn't supposed to go to. Most of the town was dirty, with winding streets, houses falling down, and big houses that had been well built but were going to ruin. Not like Placehold. Placehold was stone, big, orderly, with roof gardens. Dargramnet made the women and children work to keep it clean, even bullied the men until they fixed the roof or broken stairs. Placehold was orderly, and that made it pretty to Whandall.

He tried to imagine another place of order, bigger than Placehold. It would have to be a long way, he thought. "Didn't that take a long time?"

"No, we'd go in a wagon in the morning. We'd be home that same night. Or sometimes the Lords came to our city. They'd come and sit in Peacegiven Square and listen to us."

"What's a Lord, Mother's Mother?"

"You always were the curious one. Brave too," she said, and petted him again. "The Lords showed us how to come here when my grandfather's father was young. Before that, our people were wanderers. My grandfather told me stories about living in wagons, always moving on."

"Grandfather?" Whandall asked.

"Your mother's father."

"But—how could she know?" Whandall demanded. He thought that Pothefit had been his father, but he was never sure. Not *sure* the way Mother's Mother seemed to be.

Mother's Mother looked angry for a moment, but then her expression softened. "She knows because I know," Mother's Mother said. "Your grandfather and I were together a long time, years and years, until he was killed, and he was the father of all my children."

Whandall wanted to ask how she knew that, but he'd seen her angry look, and he was afraid. There were many things you didn't talk about. He asked, "Did he live in a wagon?"

"Maybe," Mother's Mother said. "Or maybe it was his grandfather. I've forgotten most of those stories now. I told them to your mother, but she didn't listen."

"I'll listen, Mother's Mother," Whandall said.

She brushed her fingers through his freshly washed hair. She'd used three days' water to wash Whandall and Shastern, and when Resalet said something about it she had shouted at him until he ran out of the Placehold. "Good," she said. "Someone ought to remember."

"What do Lords do?"

"They show us things, give us things, tell us what the law is," Mother's Mother said. "You don't see them much anymore. They used to come to Tep's Town. I remember when we were both young—they chose your grandfather to talk to the Lords for the Placehold. I was so proud. And the Lords brought wizards with them, and made rain, and put a spell on our roof gardens so everything grew better." The dreamy smile came back. "Everything grew better; everyone helped each other. I'm so proud of you, Whandall; you didn't run and leave your brother—you stayed to help." She stroked him, petting him the way his sisters petted the cat. Whandall almost purred.

She dozed off soon after. He thought about her stories and wondered how much was true. He couldn't remember when anyone helped anyone who wasn't close kin. Why would it have been different when Mother's Mother was young? And could it be that way again?

But he was seven, and the cat was playing with a ball of string. Whandall climbed off Mother's Mother's lap to watch.

*   *   *

Bansh and Ilther died. Shastern lived, but he kept the scars. In later years they passed for fighting scars.

Whandall watched them rebuild the city after the Burning. Stores and offices rose again, cheap wooden structures on winding streets. The kinless never seemed to work hard on rebuilding.

Smashed water courses were rebuilt. The places where people died—kicked to death or burned or cut down with the long Lordkin knives—remained empty for a time. Everybody was hungry until the Lords and the kinless could get food flowing in again.

None of the other children would return to the forest. They took to spying on strangers, ready to risk broken bones rather than the terrible plants. But the forest fascinated Whandall. He returned again and again. Mother didn't want him to go, but Mother wasn't there much. Mother's Mother only told him to be careful.

Old Resalet heard her. Now he laughed every time Whandall left the Placehold with leathers and mask.

Whandall went alone. He always followed the path of the logging, and that protected him a little. The forest became less dangerous as Kreeg Miller taught him more.

All the chaparral was dangerous, but the scrub that gathered round the redwoods was actively malevolent. Kreeg's father had told him that it was worse in his day: the generations had tamed these plants. There were blade-covered morningstars and armory plants, and lordkin's-kiss, and lordkiss with longer blades, and harmless-looking vines and flower beds and bushes all called touch-me and marked by five-bladed red or red-and-green leaves.

Poison plants came in other forms than touch-me. Any plant might take a whim to cover itself with daggers and poison them too. Nettles covered their leaves with thousands of needles that would burrow into flesh. Loggers cut under the morningstar bushes and touch-me flower beds with the bladed poles they called severs. Against lordwhips the only defense was a mask.

The foresters knew fruit trees the children hadn't found. "These yellow apples *want* to be eaten," Kreeg said, "seeds and all, so in a day or two the seeds are somewhere else, making more plants. If you don't eat the core, at least throw it as far as you can. But these red death bushes you stay away from—far away—because if you get close you'll eat the berries."

"Magic?"

"Right. And they're poison. They want their seeds in your belly when you die, for fertilizer."

One wet morning after a lightning storm, loggers saw smoke reaching into the sky.

"Is that the city?" Whandall asked.

"No, that's part of the forest. Over by Wolverine territory. It'll go out," Kreeg assured the boy. "They always do. You find black patches here and there, big as a city block."

"The fire wakes Yangin-Atep," the boy surmised. "Then Yangin-Atep takes the fire for himself? So it goes out . . ." But instead of confirming, Kreeg only smiled indulgently. Whandall heard snickering.

The other loggers didn't believe, but . . . "Kreeg, don't you believe in Yangin-Atep either?"

"Not really," Kreeg said. "Some magic works, out here in the woods, but in town? Gods and magic, you hear a lot about them, but you see damn little."

"A magician killed Pothefit!"

Kreeg Miller shrugged.

Whandall was near tears. Pothefit had vanished during the Burning, just ten weeks ago. Pothefit was his father! But you didn't say that outside the family. Whandall cast about for better arguments. "You *bow* to the red-wood before you cut it. I've seen you. Isn't that magic?"

"Yeah, well . . . why take chances? Why do the morningstars and laurel whips and touch-me and creepy-julia all protect the redwoods?"

"Like house guards," Whandall said, remembering that there were always men and boys on guard at Placehold.

"Maybe. Like the plants made some kind of bargain," Kreeg said, and laughed.

Mother's Mother had told him. Yangin-Atep led Whandall's ancestors to the Lords, and the Lords had led Whandall's ancestors through the forest to the Valley of Smokes where they defeated the kinless and built Tep's Town. Redwood seeds and firewands didn't sprout unless fire had passed through. Surely these woods belonged to the fire god!

But Kreeg Miller just couldn't see it.

They worked half the morning, hacking at the base of a vast redwood, ignoring the smoke that still rose northeast of them. Whandall carried water to them from a nearby stream. The other loggers were almost used to him now. They called him Candlestub.

When the sun was overhead, they broke for lunch.

Kreeg Miller had taken to sharing lunch with him. Whandall had managed to gather some cheese from the Placehold kitchen. Kreeg had a smoked rabbit from yesterday.

Whandall asked, "How many trees does it take to build the city back?"

Two loggers overheard and laughed. "They never burn the whole city," Kreeg told him. "Nobody could live through that, Whandall. Twenty or thirty stores and houses, a few blocks solid and some other places scattered, then they break off."

The Placehold men said that they'd burned down the whole city, and all of the children believed them.

A logger said, "We'll cut another tree after this one. We wouldn't need all four if Lord Qirinty didn't want a wing on his palace. Boy, do you remember your first Burning?"

"Some. I was only two years old." Whandall cast back in his mind. "The men were acting funny. They'd lash out if any children got too close. They yelled a lot, and the women yelled back. The women tried to keep the men away from us.

"Then one afternoon it all got very scary and confusing. There was shouting and whooping and heat and smoke and light. The women all huddled with us on the second floor. There were smells—not just smoke, but stuff that made you gag, like an alchemist's shop. The men came in with things they'd gathered. Blankets, furniture, heaps of shells, stacks of cups and plates, odd things to eat.

"And afterward everyone seemed to calm down." Whandall's voice trailed off. The other woodsmen were looking at him like . . . like an enemy. Kreeg wouldn't look at him at all.

CHAPTER 2

The world had moved on, and Whandall had hardly noticed.

His brothers and cousins all seemed to have disappeared. Mostly the girls and women stayed home, but on Mother's Day each month the women went to the corner squares where the Lordsmen gave out food and clothing and shells, presents from the Lords. There were always men around that day and the next. Later, they might be around or they might be gone.

But boys appeared only for meals and sleep, and not always then. Where did they go?

He followed a cluster of cousins one afternoon. As in the forest, he took pride in being unseen. He got four blocks before four younger men challenged him. They'd beaten him half senseless before Shastern turned around, saw what was happening, and came running.

Shastern showed the tattoos on his hands and arms. Whandall had once asked about those, but Shastern had put off answering. They blended in with the terrible scars Shastern carried from the forest, but many of his cousins had them too. He never asked that kind of question of his cousins. Now Whandall did not quite hear what Shastern and his cousins said to them, but the strangers turned him loose and his cousins carried him home.

He woke hurting. Shastern woke around noon and sought him out. Shastern was barred from speaking certain secrets, but some things he could say . . .

Serpent's Walk wasn't just this region of the city.

Serpent's Walk was the young men who held it. These streets belonged to Serpent's Walk. Other streets, other bands. The region grew or shrank, streets changed hands, with the power of the bands. They put up signs on walls and other places.

Whandall had been able to read them for years. Serpent's Walk had a squiggle sign, easy to draw. Dirty Birds was a falcon drawn wild and sloppy. Shastern showed him a boundary, a wall with the Serpent's Walk squiggle at one end and a long thin phallus to mark Bull Pizzle territory at the other. Unmarked, one did not walk in Serpent's Walk, or in Bull Pizzle or Dirty Bird either, if one did not belong. As a child Whandall had wandered the streets without hindrance, but a ten-year-old was no longer a child.

"But there are places with no signs at all," Whandall protested.

"That's Lord territory. You can go there until one of the Lordsmen tells you not to. Then you leave."

"Why?"

"Because everyone is scared of the Lordsmen."

"Why? Are they so strong?"

"Well, they're big, and they're mean, and they wear that armor."

"They walk in pairs too," Whandall said, remembering.

"Right. And if you hurt one of them, a lot more will come looking for you."

"What if they don't know who did it?"

Shastern shrugged expressively. "Then a bunch of them come and beat up on everybody they can find until someone confesses. Or we kill someone and say he confessed before we killed him. You stay away from Lordsmen, Whandall. Only good they do is when they bring in the presents on Mother's Day."

Whandall found it strange to have his one-year-younger brother behaving as his elder.

He must have spoken to Wanshig too. Wanshig was Whandall's eldest brother. Wanshig had the tattoos, a snake in the web of his left thumb, a rattlesnake that ran up his right arm from the index finger to the elbow, a small snake's eye at the edge of his left eye. The next night Wanshig took him into the streets. In a ruin that stank of old smoke, he introduced his younger brother to men who carried knives and never smiled.

"He needs protection," Wanshig said. The men just looked at him. Finally one asked, "Who speaks for him?"

Whandall knew some of these faces. Shastern was there too, and he said, "I will." Shastern did not speak to his brothers, but he spoke of Whandall in glowing terms. When the rest fled the forest in terror, Whandall had stayed to help Shastern. If he'd learned little of the customs of Serpent's Walk, it was because he was otherwise occupied. When none of the boys would return to the wood but took to the streets instead, Whandall Placehold continued to brave the killer plants, to spy on the woodsmen.

The room was big enough to hold fifty people or more. It was dark outside now, and the only light in the room came from the moon shining through holes in the roof, and from torches. The torches were outside, stuck into holes in the windowsills. Yangin-Atep wouldn't allow fires inside, except during a Burning. You could build an outside cookfire under a lean-to shelter, but never inside, and if you tried to enclose a fire with walls, the fire went out. Whandall couldn't remember anyone telling him this. He just knew it, as he knew that cats had sharp claws and that boys should stay away from men when they were drinking beer.

There was a big chair on a low platform at one end of the room. The chair was wooden, with arms and a high back, and it was carved with serpents and birds. Some kinless must have worked hard to make that chair, but Whandall didn't think it would be very comfortable, not like the big ponyhair-stuffed chair Mother's Mother liked.

A tall man with no smile sat in that chair. Three other men stood in front of him holding their long Lordkin knives across their chests. Whandall knew him. Pelzed lived in a two-story stone house at the end of a block of well-kept kinless houses. Pelzed's house had a fenced-in garden and there were always kinless working in it.

"Bring him," Pelzed said.

His brothers took Whandall by the arms and pulled him to just in front of Pelzed's chair, then forced him down on his knees.

"What good are you?" Pelzed demanded.

Shastern began to speak, but Pelzed held up a hand. "I heard you. I want to hear him. What did you learn from the woodsmen?"

"Say something," Wanshig whispered. There was fear in his voice.

Whandall thought furiously. "Poisons. I know the poisons of the forest. Needles. Blades. Whips."

Pelzed gestured. One of the men standing in front of Pelzed's chair raised his big knife and struck Whandall hard across the left shoulder.

It stung, but he had used the flat of the blade. "Call him Lord," the man said. His bared chest was a maze of scars; one ran right up his cheek into his hair. Whandall found him scary as hell.

"Lord," Whandall said. He had never seen a Lord. "Yes, Lord."

"Good. You can walk in the forest?"

"Much of it, Lord. Places where the woodsmen have been."

"Good. What do you know of the Wedge?"

"The meadow at the top of the Deerpiss River?" What did Pelzed *want* to hear? "Woodsmen don't go there, Lord. I've never seen it. It is said to be guarded."

Pause. Then, "Can you bring us poisons?"

"Yes, Lord, in the right season."

"Can we use them against the enemies of Serpent's Walk?"

Whandall had no idea who the enemies of Serpent's Walk might be, but he was afraid to ask. "If they're fresh, Lord."

"What happens if they aren't fresh?"

"After a day they only make you itch. The nettles stop reaching out for anyone who passes."

"Why?"

"I don't know." The man raised his knife. "Lord."

"You're a sneak and a spy."

"Yes, Lord."

"Will you spy for us?"

Whandall hesitated. "Of course he will, Lord," Shastern said.

"Take him out, Shastern. Wait with him."

Shastern led him through a door into a room with no other doors and only a small dark window that let in a little moonlight. He waited until they were closed in before letting go of Whandall's arm.

"This is dangerous, isn't it?" Whandall asked.

Shastern nodded.

"So what's going to happen?"

"They'll let you in. Maybe."

"If they don't?"

Shastern shook his head. "They will. Lord Pelzed doesn't want a blood feud with the Placehold family."

Blood feuds meant blood. "Is he really a Lord—"

"He is here," Shastern said. "And don't forget it."

When they brought him back in, the room was dark except for a few candles near Pelzed's chair. Shastern whispered, "I knew they'd let you in. Now whatever happens, don't cry. It's going to hurt."

They made him kneel in front of Pelzed again. Two men took turns asking him questions and hitting him.

"We are your father and your mother," Pelzed said.

Someone hit him.

"Who is your father?" a voice asked from behind.

"You are—"

Someone hit him harder.

"Serpent's Walk," Whandall guessed.

"Who is your mother?"

"Serpent's Walk."

"Who is your Lord?"

"Pelzed. . . . Argh. Lord Pelzed. Aagh! Serpent's Walk?"

"Who is Lord of Serpent's Walk?"

"Lord Pelzed."

It went on a long time. Usually they didn't hit him if he guessed the right answer, but sometimes they hit him anyway. "To make sure you remember," they said.

Finally that was over. "You can't fight," Pelzed said. "So you won't be a full member. But we'll take care of you. Give him the mark."

They stretched his left hand out and tattooed a small serpent on the web of his thumb. He held his arm rigid against the pain. Then everyone said nice things about him.

After that it was easier. Whandall was safe outside the house as long as he was in territory friendly to Serpent's Walk. Wanshig warned him not to carry a knife until he knew how to fight. It would be taken as a challenge.

He didn't know the rules. But one could keep silent, watch, and learn.

Here he remembered a line of black skeletons of buildings. The charred remains had come down and been carried away. Whandall and others watched from cover, from the basement of a house that hadn't been replaced yet. Kinless were at work raising redwood beams into skeletons of new buildings. Four new stores stood already, sharing common walls.

You knew the kinless by their skin tone, or their rounder ears and pointed noses, but that was chancy; a boy could make mistakes. Better to judge by clothing or by name.

Kinless were not allowed to wear Lordkin's hair styles or vivid colors. On formal occasions the kinless men wore a noose as token of their servitude. They were named for things or for skills, and they spoke their family names, where a Lordkin never would.

There were unspoken rules for gathering. There were times when you could ask a kinless for food or money. A man and woman together might accept that. Others would not. Kinless men working to replace blackened ruins with new buildings did not look with favor on Lordkin men or boys. Lordkin at their gatherings must be wary of the kinless who kept shops or sold from carts. The kinless had no rights, but the Lords had rights to what the kinless made.

The kinless did the work. They made clothing, grew food, made and used tools, transported it all. They made rope for export. They harvested rope fibers from the hemp that grew in vacant lots and anywhere near the sluggish streams that served as storm drains and sewers alike. They built. They saw to it that streets were repaired, that water flowed, that garbage reached the dumps. They took the blame if things went wrong. Only the kinless paid taxes, and taxes were whatever a Lordkin wanted, unless a Lord said otherwise. But you had to learn what you could take. The kinless only had so much to give, Mother's Mother said.

Suddenly it was all so obvious, so embarrassing. Loggers were kinless! *Of course* they wouldn't help a Lordkin child. The loggers thought Kreeg Miller was strange, as the Placehold thought Whandall was strange, each to be found in the other's company.

Whandall had been letting a kinless teach him! He had carried water for them, working like a kinless!

Whandall stopped visiting the forest.

The Serpent's Walk men spent their time in the streets. So did the boys of the Placehold, but their fathers and uncles spent most of their time at home.
Why?

Whandall went to old Resalet. One could ask.

Resalet listened and nodded, then summoned *all* the boys and led them outside. He pointed to the house, the old stone three-story house with its enclosed courtyard. He explained that it had been built by kinless for themselves, two hundred years ago. Lordkin had taken it from them.

It was a roomy dwelling desired by many. The kinless no longer built houses to last centuries. Why should they, when a Lordkin family would claim it? Other Lordkin had claimed this place repeatedly, until it fell to the Placehold family. It would change hands again unless the men kept guard.

The boys found the lecture irritating, and they let Whandall know that afterward.

Mother never had time for him. There was always a new baby, new men to see and bring home, new places to go, never time for the older boys. Men hung out together. They chewed hemp and made plans or went off at night, but they never wanted boys around them, and most of the boys were afraid of the men. With reason.

Whandall saw his city without understanding. The other boys hardly realized there was anything to understand and didn't care to know more. It was safe to ask Mother's Mother, but her answers were strange.

"Everything has changed. When I was a girl the kinless didn't hate us. They were happy to do the work. Gathering was easy. They gave us things."

"Why?"

"We served Yangin-Atep. Tep woke often and protected us."

"But didn't the kinless hate the Burnings?"

"Yes, but it was different then," Mother's Mother said. "It was arranged. A house or building nobody could use, or a bridge ready to fall down.

We'd bring things to burn. Kinless, Lordkin, everyone would bring something for Yangin-Atep. *Mathoms,* we called them. The Lords came, too, with their wizards. Now it's all different, and I don't understand it at all."

One could keep silence, watch, and learn.

Barbarians were the odd ones. Their skins were of many shades, their noses of many shapes; even their eye color varied. They sounded odd, when they could talk at all.

Some belonged in the city, wherever they had come from. They traded, taught, doctored, cooked, or sold to kinless and Lordkin alike. They were to be treated as kinless who didn't understand the rules. Their speech could generally be understood. They might travel with guards of their own race or give tribute to Lordkin to protect their shops. A few had the protection of Lords. You could tell that by the symbols displayed outside their shops and homes.

Most barbarians avoided places where violence had fallen. But lookers sought those places out. The violence of the Burning lured them across the sea to Tep's Town.

Boys who gave up the forest had taken to spying on lookers instead. Whandall would do as they did: watch the watchers. But they were far ahead of him at that game, and Whandall had some catching up to do.

Watch, listen. From under a walk, from behind a wall. Lookers took refuge in the parts of the city where kinless lived, or in the harbor areas where the Lords ruled. Lordkin children could sometimes get in those places. Lookers spoke in rapid gibberish that some of the older boys claimed to understand.

At first they looked merely strange. Later Whandall saw how many kinds of lookers there were. You could judge by their skins or their features or their clothing. These pale ones were Torovan, from the east. These others were from the south, from Condigeo. These with noses like an eagle's beak came from farther yet: Atlantean refugees. Each spoke his own tongue, and each mangled the Lordkin speech in a different fashion. And others, from places Whandall had never heard of.

Serpent's Walk watched, and met afterward in the shells of burned buildings. They asked themselves and each other, *What does this one have that would be worth gathering?* But Whandall sometimes wondered, *Does that one come from a more interesting place than here? or more exciting? or better ruled? or seeking a ruler?*

CHAPTER
3

When he was eleven years old, Whandall asked Wanshig, "Where can I find a Lord?"

"You know where Pelzed lives—"

"A real Lord."

"Don't talk like that," Wanshig said, but he grinned. "Do you remember when those people came to the park? And made speeches? Last fall."

"Sure. You gathered some money in the crowd and bought meat for dinner."

"*That* was a Lord. I forgot his name."

"Which one? There were a lot of people—"

"Guards, mostly. And lookers, and storytellers. The one that stood on the wagon and talked about the new aqueduct they're building."

"Oh."

"The Lords live on the other side of the valley, in the Lordshills mostly. It's a long way. You can't go there."

"Do they have a band?"

"Sort of. They have guards, big Lordsmen. And there's a wall."

"I'd like to see one. Up close."

"Sometimes Lords go to the docks. But you don't want to go there alone," Wanshig said.

"Why not?"

"It's Water Devils territory. The Lords say anyone can go there, and the Devils have to put up with that, but they don't like it. If they catch you alone with no one to come back and tell what happened, they may throw you in the harbor."

"But Water Devils don't go into the Lordshills, do they?"

"I don't know. Never needed to find out."

How do you know what you need to find out until you know it? Whandall wondered, but he didn't say anything. "Is there a safe way to the harbor?"

Wanshig nodded. "Stay on Sanvin Street until you get past those hills." He pointed northwest. "After that there aren't any bands until you get to the harbor. Didn't used to be. Now, who knows?"

The forest had fingers: hilltop ridges covered with touch-me and lord-kin's-kiss that ran from the sea back into the great trees with their deadly guards. There were canyons and gaps through the hills, but they were filled with more poisonous plants that grew back faster than anyone could cut them. Only the hills above the harbor were cleared. Lords lived up there. When the winds blew hard so that the day was clear, Whandall could see their big houses. The adults called them palaces.

Whandall pointed toward the Lordshills. "Does anyone gather there during a Burning?"

Wanshig squinted. "Where? On Sanvin Street?"

"No, up there. The palaces."

"That's where the Lords live. You can't gather from Lords!"

"Why not?"

"Yangin-Atep," Wanshig said. "Yangin-Atep protects them. People who go up there to gather just don't come back. Whandall, they're Lords. We're Lordkin. You just don't. There's no Burning up there either. Yangin-Atep takes care of them."

At dawn he snatched half a loaf from the Placehold kitchen and ate it as he ran. The energy boiling in him was half eagerness, half fear. When it faded, he walked. He had a long way to go.

Sanvin Street wound over the low hills that separated Tep's Town from the harbor. At first there were burned-out shells of houses, with some of the lots gone back to thorns and worse. The plants gradually closed in on the old road. When he reached the top of the hills, all was thorns and chaparral and touch-me, just sparse enough to permit passage. It was nearly dark when he reached a crest of a ridge. There were lights ahead, the distance enough that he didn't want to walk farther. He used the dying twilight to find a way into the chaparral.

He spent the night in chaparral, guarded by the malevolent plants he knew how to avoid. It was better than trying to find a safe place among people he didn't know.

The morning sun was bright, but there was a thin haze on the ground. Sanvin Street led down the ridge, then up across another. It took him half an hour to get to the top of the second ridge. When he reached it, he could see a highlight sun glare, the harbor, off ahead and to the left.

He had reached the top. He knew of no band who ruled here, and that was ominous enough. He crouched below the chaparral until he was sure no eyes were about.

He stood on a barren ridge, but the other side of the hill was—different. Sanvin Street led down the hills. Partway down, it divided into two parallel streets with olive trees growing in the grassy center strip, and to each side of the divided street there were houses, wood as well as stone.

He was watching from the chaparral when a wagon came up from the harbor. He had plenty of time to move, but close to the road the chaparral was too sparse to hide him, and farther in were the thorns. He stood in the sparse brush and watched the wagon come up the hill. As it passed him the kinless driver and his companion exchanged glances with Whandall and drove on. They seemed curious rather than angry, as if Whandall were no threat at all.

Couldn't they guess that he might bring fathers or older brothers?

He went back to the road and started down the hill, openly now, past the houses. He guessed this was Lord's Town, where Mother's Mother used to go when she was a girl.

Each set of houses was banded around a small square, and in the center of each square was a small stone cairn above a stone water basin, like Peacegiven Square but smaller. Water trickled down the cairn into the basin, and women, Lordkin and kinless alike, came to dip water into stone and clay jars. Down toward the harbor was a larger square, with a larger pool, and a grove of olive trees. Instead of houses, there were shops around the square. Kinless merchants sat in front of shops full of goods openly displayed, free for the gathering, it seemed. In the olive grove people sat in the shade at tables and talked or did mysterious things with small rock markers on the tables. Shells—and even bits of gold and silver—changed hands.

Were these Lords? They looked like no one he had ever seen. They were better dressed than the kinless of Serpent's Walk, better dressed than most Lordkin, but few had weapons. One armed man sat at a table honing a big Lordkin knife. No one seemed to notice him; then a merchant spoke to him. Whandall didn't hear what was said, but the merchant seemed friendly, and the armed Lordkin grinned. Whandall watched as a girl brought a tray of cups to a table. She looked like a Lordkin.

No one paid him any attention as he walked past. They would glance at him and look away, even if he stared at them. He wasn't dressed like they were, and that began to bother him. Back of the houses, he could sometimes see clothes hanging on lines, but gathering those might be riskier than remaining as he was, and how could he know that he was wearing them right?

He went on to the bottom of the hills, nearer yet to the Lords' domain. Soon there was black, barren land in the distance to his right, with a gleam of water and a stench of magic. It had to be magic; it was no natural smell. Breathing through his mouth seemed to help.

The place drew him like any mystery.

Whandall knew the Black Pit by repute. Scant and scrawny alien scrub grew along the edges of black water a quarter of a mile on a side, and nobody lived there at all. He'd heard tales of shadowy monsters here. All he saw were pools that gleamed like water, darker than any water he'd ever seen.

A palisade fence surrounded the Pit, more a message than a barrier. A graveled wagon road led into it through a gate that Whandall was sure he could open. The fence was regular, flawless, too fine even for kinless work. Kinless working under the eyes of Lords might make such a thing.

Such offensive perfection made it a target. Whandall wondered why Lordkin hadn't torn it down. And why did Lords want people kept away? He saw no monsters, but he sensed a malevolent power here.

The distant harbor drew him more powerfully yet. He saw a ship topped by a forest of masts. That was escape, that was the way to better places, if he could learn of a way past the Water Devils.

Ahead and to the right was a wall taller than any man. Houses two and three stories tall showed above the wall. Palaces! They were larger than he'd dreamed.

The street went past an open gate where two armed men stood guarding a barrier pole. They looked strange. Their clothing was good but drab and they were dressed nearly alike. They wore daggers with polished handles. Helmets hid their ears. Spears with dark shafts and gleaming bronze spearheads hung on brackets near where they stood. Were they armed kinless? But they might be Lordkin.

A wagon came up from the harbor and went to the gate. The horses seemed different, taller and more slender than the ponies he saw in Tep's Town. When it reached the gate, the guards spoke to the driver, then lifted the barrier to let the wagon in. Whandall couldn't hear what they said to each other.

If the guards were kinless, they wouldn't try to stop a Lordkin. Would they? He couldn't tell what they were. They acted relaxed. One drank from a stone jar and passed it to the other. They watched Whandall without much curiosity.

The gate was near a corner of the wall. Whandall became worried when he saw the guards were looking at him. There was a path that led along the wall and around the corner out of sight of the guards, and he went along that, shuffling as boys do. The guards stopped watching him when he turned away from the gate, and soon he was out of sight around the corner.

The wall was too high to climb. The path wasn't much used, and Whandall had to be careful to avoid the weeds and thorns. He followed the path until it led between the wall and a big tree.

When he climbed into the tree he was glad he hadn't tried to get over the wall. There were sharp things, thorns and broken glass, embedded in its top. One bough of the tree not only grew over the wall but was low enough that it had scraped the top smooth. That must have taken a long time, and no one had bothered to fix it.

Mother's Mother had told him that kinless believed in a place they called Gift of the King, a place across the sea where they never had to work and no Lordkin could gather from them. The other side of the wall looked like that. There were gardens and big houses. Just over the wall was a pool of water. A big stone fish stood above the pool. Water poured from the fish's mouth into the pool and flowed out of the pool into a stream that fed a series of smaller pools. Green plants grew in those pools. There were both vegetable and flower gardens alongside the stream. They were arranged in neat little patterns, square for the vegetable gardens, complex curved shapes along curved paths for the flower beds. The house was nearly a hundred yards from the wall, two stories tall, square and low with thick adobe walls, as large as the Placehold. The Gift of the King, but this was no myth. The Lords lived better than Whandall could have imagined.

It was late afternoon, and the sun was hot. There was no one around. Whandall had brought a dried crabapple to eat, but he didn't have any way to carry water, and he was thirsty. The fountain and stream invited him. He watched while his thirst grew. No one came out of the house.

He wondered what they would do to him if they caught him. He was only a thirsty boy; he hadn't gathered anything yet. The people outside the walls had glanced at him, then glanced away, as if they didn't want to see him. Would the people in here do the same? He didn't know, but his thirst grew greater.

He crawled along the tree branch until he was past the wall, then dropped into the grass. He crouched there waiting, but nothing happened, and he crept to the edge of the fountain.

The water was sweet and cool, and he drank for a long time.

"What's it like outside?"

Whandall jumped up, startled.

"They don't let me go outside. Where do you live?"

The girl was smaller than he was. She'd be eight years old or so, where Whandall was already eleven. She wore a skirt with embroidered borders, and her blouse was a shiny cloth that Whandall had seen only once, when

Pelzed's wife had dressed up for a party. No one in Whandall's family owned anything like that, or ever would.

"I was thirsty," Whandall said.

"I can see that. Where do you live?"

She was only a girl. "Out there," he said. He pointed east. "Beyond the hills."

Her eyes widened. She looked at his clothing, at his eyes and ears. "You're Lordkin. Can I see your tattoos?"

Whandall held out his hand to show the serpent on the web of his thumb.

She came closer. "Wash your hands," she said. "Not there; that's where we get drinking water. Down there." She pointed at the basin below the fountain pool. "Don't you have fountains where you live?"

"No. Wells." Whandall bent to wash his hands. "Rivers after it rains."

"Your face too," she said. "And your feet. You're all dusty."

It was true, but Whandall resented being told that. She was only a girl, smaller than he, and there was nothing to be afraid of, but she might call someone. He would have to run. There wasn't any way out of here. The branch was too high to reach without a rope. The water felt cool on his face and wonderful on his feet.

"You don't need to be afraid of me," she said. "Now let me see your tattoo."

He held out his hand. She turned it in both her hands and pulled his fingers apart to bare his serpent tattoo to the sun.

Then she looked closely at his eyes. "My stepfather says that wild Lordkin have tattoos on their faces," she said.

"My brothers do," Whandall said. "But they carry knives and can fight. I haven't learned yet. I don't know what you mean by 'wild.' We're not wild."

She shrugged. "I don't really know what he means either. My name is Shanda. My stepfather is Lord Samorty."

Whandall thought for a moment, then said, "My name is Whandall. What does a stepfather do?"

"My father's dead. Lord Samorty married my mother."

She'd spoken of her father to a stranger, without hesitation, without embarrassment. Whandall tasted words on his tongue: *My father is dead; we have many stepfathers.* But he didn't speak them.

"Do you want something to eat?"

Whandall nodded.

"Come on." She led him toward the house. "Don't talk much," she said. "If anyone asks you where you live, point west, and say 'Over there, sir.' But no one will. Just don't show that tattoo. Oh, wait." She looked at him again. "You look like someone threw clothes at you in the dark."

Huh?

"Miss Batty would say that," she said, leading him south around the house. "Here." Clothes were hanging on long lines above a vegetable patch. The lines were thin woven hemp, not tarred. "Here, take this, and this—"

"Shanda, who wears this stuff?"

"The chief gardener's boy. He's my friend, he won't mind. Put your stuff in that vat—"

"Is anyone going to see me who knows who we gathered it from?"

She considered. "Not inside. Maybe Miss Batty, but she never goes to the kitchen. Wouldn't eat with the staff if she was starving."

A band of men carrying shovels came around the house. One waved to Shanda. They began digging around the vegetables.

The gardeners were kinless, but they were better dressed than Lordkin. They had water bottles, and one had a box with bread and meat. A lot of meat, more than Whandall got for lunch except on Mother's Day, and often not then. If kinless lived this well, how did Lordkin live here?

A Lordkin should have guile. Watch and learn . . .

Shanda led him into the back of the house.

CHAPTER

4

The house was cool. Shanda led him through corridors to a room that smelled of cooking. A fat woman with ears like a Lordkin's stood at a counter stirring a kettle. The kettle frothed with boiling liquid. Whandall stared. The smells went straight to his hunger.

The counter she stood over was a big clay box. The top was an iron grill, and flames licked up through it, under a copper pot.

A fire, *indoors,* that didn't go out. Squinting, he approached the yellow-white glare and lifted his hands to it. *Hot.* Yes, fire.

Shanda gave him the funniest look.

The fat woman looked at them with an expression that might have been menacing but wasn't. "Miss Shanda, I got no time just now. Your daddy is having visitors. There's a wizard coming to dinner, and we have to get ready."

A wizard! But Shanda didn't act surprised or excited. She said, "Serana, this is Whandall, and he's hungry."

The fat woman smiled. "Sure he's hungry. He's a boy, isn't he? A boy's nothing but an appetite and trouble," she said, but she was still smiling. "Sit over there. I'll get you something in a minute. Where do you live?"

Whandall pointed vaguely west. "Over there . . . ma'am."

Serana nodded to herself and went back to the stove, but then she brought out a bowl and a spoon. "Have some of my pudding," she said. "Bet your cook can't make pudding like that."

Whandall tasted the pudding. It was smooth and creamy. "No, ma'am," Whandall said.

Serana beamed. "Miss Shanda, this is a nice boy," she said. "Now scoot when you get done. I've got my work to do."

After he finished the pudding, he followed Shanda down another corridor. The house was built around an interior courtyard, and they went upstairs to a long outside balcony over the atrium. There was a small fountain in the center of the courtyard.

There were half a dozen doors along the balcony. Shanda led him to one of them. "This is my room." She looked up at the sun. "It won't be long until dark. Can you get home before night?"

"I don't think so," Whandall said.

"Where will you stay?"

"I can stay out in the chaparral."

"In the thorns?' She sounded impressed. "You know how to go into those?"

"Yes." He grinned slightly. "But I don't know how to get out of here. Will the guards stop me?"

"Why should they?" she asked. "But if you don't come home tonight, won't someone worry about you?"

"Who?"

"Your nurse . . . oh. Well, come on in."

The room was neat. There was a closet with a door, and there were more clothes hung up in it than any of Whandall's sisters had. There was a chest against one wall, and the bed had a wool blanket on it. Another blanket with pictures woven into it hung above the bed. There was a window that faced out on the balcony, and another on the opposite wall. That looked out on a smaller interior courtyard crisscrossed with clotheslines and drying clothes, more rope than Whandall had ever seen in one place. He eyed the clothesline with satisfaction. It looked strong, and there was so much they might not miss one piece. It would get him up to the tree branch. If he could take it home, it would make Resalet happy. They always needed rope at the Placehold. But he didn't know the rules here.

"Could you really sleep in the thorns?" she asked. "How?"

"Without leathers you can't go far into the chaparral," Whandall said. "There's a lot worse than thorn. You have to know what plants are safe. Most aren't."

"What are leathers? Where do you get them?"

"You need a leather mask and leggings, at least. Some kinless have them, and the foresters use sleeves and vests. I don't know where my uncles got them. They must have gathered them."

"But you don't have any with you. There's nobody in the room next to this. You can sleep there tonight."

They ate in the kitchen at a small table in the corner. Serana put food in front of them, then went back to her stove. Other servants came in and Serana gave them instructions on what to do. Everyone seemed to be in a hurry, but there was no shouting, and no one was frantic.

There were more *kinds* of food than Whandall had ever seen for one meal. Serana arranged trays of food, eyed them critically, sometimes changed the arrangements. When she was satisfied, the servants came and took the trays out to another room where the adults ate. It was like . . . the gardens here, and the neat little fence around the Black Pit . . . it was *orderly.* Serana was making *patterns* with her cooking.

Whandall couldn't take his eyes off the stove.

Once during dinner a tall woman with serious eyes and dark clothing looked into the kitchen. She nodded in satisfaction when she saw Shanda. "Did you study your lessons?" she demanded.

"Yes, ma'am," Shanda said.

She fixed Whandall with a critical eye. "Neighbor boy?" she asked.

"From down the road," Shanda said quickly.

"You behave yourself," the woman said. She turned to the cook. "Did she get a good dinner?"

"I always make a good dinner for Miss Shanda, even when I've got guests to cook for," Serana said huffily. "Don't you worry about that."

"All right. Good night."

After she left, Shanda giggled. "Miss Batty's not happy," she said. "She wants to eat with the family, but they didn't invite her tonight."

"That's as it may be," Serana said. "Miss Bertrana's all right. Not like that other nurse you had. You be nice to her."

Miss Batty was kinless. Whandall was certain of it. He wasn't quite as certain that Serana was Lordkin. And neither seemed to care much.

A servant came carrying a tray of dirty dishes. Some were piled high with uneaten food.

After dinner they went back to the balcony. The adults came out to the atrium to finish their own dinner. Whandall and Shanda lay on the balcony outside her room and listened to them.

The courtyard was lit by a central fire and by candles in vellum cylinders. There were four men and three women in the courtyard. Lazy wisps of steam curled up from the cups they were holding. One of the men said, "I thought that wizard was coming to dinner."

"He was invited, Qirinty. I don't know what happened to him."

"Stood you up, did he, Samorty?"

Samorty had a deep and resonant voice, and his chuckle was loud. "Maybe. I'd be surprised, but maybe."

When Placehold men talked in the evenings, there were usually fights. These men smiled, and if anyone was angry, it was well hidden. Whandall came to believe that he was watching a dance. They were dancing with the rhythm of speech and gestures.

It was a thing he could learn. A Lordkin should have guile.

Qirinty's voice was feeble; Whandall had to listen hard. "We need a wizard. The reservoir's getting low again. If it doesn't rain pretty soon we could be in trouble, Samorty."

Samorty nodded sagely. "What do you propose we do?"

"It's more your problem than mine, Samorty," the other man said. He picked up two cups, interchanged them, tossed them lightly in the air. The cups were chasing each other in a loop, and now he'd added a third cup.

"Lord Qirinty has such wonderful hands!" Shanda said.

It enchanted Whandall that Shanda already knew how to lurk. He asked, "Are those Lords?"

Shanda giggled. "Yes. The big man there at the end is Lord Samorty. He's my stepfather."

"Is that your mother with him?"

"Rawanda's not my mother! Stepmother," Shanda said. "My mother's dead too. She died when Rabblie was born."

"Rabblie?"

"My little brother. There. With her. He's five. She doesn't like him any more than she likes me, but he gets to eat with them because he's the heir. If she ever has a boy, he's dead meat, but I don't think she can have children. She had one, my sister, and that took a week. It was almost two years ago—"

Whandall tapped her arm to shut her up, because Lord Samorty was talking: ". . . Wizard. Can he do it again?"

"Would you want him to?" one of the others asked. "The iceberg damn near wiped out the city!"

The women shouted with laughter. The man with the clever hands said, "It did not, Chanthor! It crossed *your* farm."

Samorty chuckled. "Well, and mine too, and left nothing but a plowed line three hundred paces wide and longer than any man has traveled. That cost me, I admit, but it didn't cross much of the city, and it sure solved the water problem."

Chanthor snorted.

Qirinty snatched his cup and added it to the dance.

Samorty said, "A mountain of ice from the farthest end of the Earth. Don't you sometimes wish you could do that?"

"That, or *any* real magic. But he said he could do it only once," Lord Qirinty said.

"He said that after we paid him. Did you believe him? I'd say he wants a better price."

Qirinty set the cups down without spilling a drop. "I don't know if I believed him or not."

One of the servants came in. "Morth of Atlantis," he announced.

Morth? Whandall knew that name . . .

He stood tall and straight, but Morth was older than any of the Lords, fragile and perhaps blind. His face was all wrinkles; his hair was long and straight and thick but pure white. He tottered very carefully into the circle of firelight. "My Lords," he said formally. "You will have to forgive me. It has been twenty years since I was last here."

"I would think Lordshills is easy enough to find," Samorty said. "Even if you had never been here before."

"Yes, yes, of course," Morth said. "To find, yes. To get to, perhaps not so easy for one in my profession. I came by the back roads. The ponies I hired could not climb your hill, and as I walked up, this change came on me. But you must know all this."

"Perhaps we know less than you think. A dozen years ago a Condigeano wizard offered us a spell that would let cook fires burn indoors," Samorty said. "Cheap too. He didn't have to cast it himself. Sent an apprentice up to do it. It worked, but since then the only horses that can get up the hill are our big ones. The Lordkin ponies can't make it. We don't know why."

Morth nodded. He was amused without making a point of it. "But surely this—spell—has not lasted a dozen years?"

"No, he sends an apprentice to renew it. He's done that twice since. We've discussed having him cast it for other areas, but we decided not to."

"Oh, good," Morth said. "Very wise. May I be seated?"

"Yes, yes, of course. Dinner's finished, but would you like tea and dessert?" Samorty's wife said.

"Thank you, yes, my lady."

Rawanda waved to a servant as Morth sat with an effort.

The fourth Lord was older than the rest. The others had come out with women, but he reclined alone on his couch. The servants treated him with as much respect as they treated Samorty. He had been quiet, but now he spoke. "Tell us, Sage, why is it wise not to cast this spell in the other parts of the city? Why not in Tep's Town?"

"Side effects," Qirinty said. "The Lordkin need their ponies."

"Yes, that and the fires, Lord Jerreff," Morth said. His voice had changed slightly. There was less quaver.

"Could you cast such a spell if we asked you to?"

Morth cut off a laugh. "No, Lord. No wizard could do that. Only apprentices cast *that* spell, and I'll wager that it's never the same apprentice twice, either."

"You'd win that wager," Samorty said. "Is this spell dangerous?"

"Confined to a small area, no," Morth said. "Cast throughout Tep's Town? I am certain you would regret it."

"Fires," Lord Jerreff said. "There would be fires inside houses, anytime, not just during a Burning. That's what our Condigeano wizard told us. He wouldn't tell us what the spell was. Just that it would keep Yangin-Atep at a distance. Sage, I don't suppose you will tell us either?"

Morth solemnly shook his head. "No, Lord, I cannot."

"But you do know what the spell is."

"Yes, Lord, I know," Morth said. "And frankly I am concerned that a hedge wizard from Condigeo would know about—about that spell. I am also surprised that you would employ powerful magic you do not understand."

"Oh, we know what it does," Qirinty said. "It uses up the power in magic, the manna. Gods can't live where there's no manna."

"I didn't know that," Lord Chanthor said. "Did you know, Samorty?"

Lord Samorty shook his head. "All I bargained for was a way to let the cooks work inside. Does that mean the fountains aren't magic?"

"Just good plumbing, Samorty," Lord Qirinty said. "But there is magic in running water—I suppose that's why our Sage looks better now. He found some manna in the fountains."

"Astute, Lord. But very little, I fear." He chuckled mirthlessly. "I do not believe you need pay to renew the spell this year."

"Is that why the wizards can't bring rain?" Samorty demanded. "No manna?"

"Yes," Morth said. "The manna is dying all over the world, but especially here in Tep's Town. The void you have created here isn't helping."

"Where can we find more manna?" Chanthor asked.

"The water comes from the mountains," Qirinty said. "Look there, if we can find the way."

"There are maps," Chanthor said. "I recall my father telling me of an expedition to the mountains. They brought back manna—"

"Gold. Wild manna. Unpredictable," Samorty said. "Some of the effects were damned odd."

"Yes, Samorty, and anyway, they got all they could find," Chanthor said. "We wouldn't do better. But there was water. Can we get water from the mountains?"

"*We* can't. Maybe nobody can."

"We did once."

"Yes, Jerreff, and long ago the kinless were warriors," Chanthor said.

"Do you believe that?" Samorty asked.

"Oh, it's true," Jerreff said.

"My Lords, we are neglecting our guest," Samorty said. He turned to Morth. The wizard was quietly sipping tea. He looked less ill than when he had come to the table.

"Sage, if we don't have water, there'll be a Burning, sure as anything. How can we stop it?" Qirinty asked. "Can you bring more water?"

Morth shook his head. He spoke solemnly. "No, my Lords. There is not enough manna to bring rain. As for the gold in the mountains, you don't want it."

"Isn't it magic?"

"Wild magic. I've heard some very funny stories about gold's effect on men and magicians, but in any case, I would not survive the rigors of the trip."

"There are other mountains," Jerreff said. "The Barbar Mountains remain. Too far to go by land, but we could take ship."

Morth smiled thinly. "I fear I must decline that as well," he said.

"The ice. Can you bring more ice?" Qirinty demanded. "We will pay well. Very well, won't we, Samorty?"

"We would pay to have the reservoirs filled again, yes," Samorty said. "You would not find us ungenerous."

"Alas, as I told you then, I could do that only once. Loan me a charioteer and I could fill your reservoirs, but I do not believe you would care for salt water."

"Salt water?" Samorty demanded. "What would we want with reservoirs full of salt water?"

"I can't imagine," Morth said. "But it is the only kind I control just at the moment." His smile was thin and there was a tiny edge to his voice. "It would be difficult but not impossible to drown the city and even parts of the Lordshills, but the water would be sea water."

"Are you threatening to do that?" Samorty demanded.

"Oh no, Lord. I have worked for many years to prevent that," Morth said. Mother's Mother's humor sometimes matched this old man's: they laughed at things nobody else understood. "But do not be deceived, it could happen. For example, if you were to use in Tep's Town the spell that that idiot Condigeano used here, you might well find the sea walking across the city. May I have some more tea?"

"Certainly, but it is a long way back, Sage, and I perceive you are not comfortable here," Samorty said. "With your permission I will arrange transportation with our horses, and an escort of guards."

"Your generosity is appreciated," Morth said.

Morth. "He's too old," Whandall murmured.

The girl asked, "Too old for what?"

"He's not who I thought." *Too old to be the Morth who killed my father and put my uncle to flight.* But wasn't that also Morth of drowned Atlantis? Mother's Mother had told another tale. "The wizard who wouldn't bless a ship?"

"Yes, that's him," Shanda said.

Samorty clapped his hands for a servant. "Have the cooks prepare a traveler's meal for the wizard. We will need a team and wagon from the stables, and two guardsmen to accompany Morth of Atlantis to the city."

"At once, Lord," the servant said.

"He will see to your needs, Sage," Samorty said. "It has been our honor."

"My thanks, Lords." Morth followed the servant out. He leaned heavily on his staff as he walked. They watched in silence until he was gone.

This powerless wizard couldn't be the Morth who had killed Pothefit. Was it a common name in Atlantis?

"Well, he wasn't any use," Chanthor said.

"Perhaps. I want to think about what he *didn't* say," Jerreff said.

"What I learned is that he can't get us any water. So what do we do now?" Samorty demanded.

"The usual. Give out more. Increase the Mother's Day presents," Chanthor said.

Whandall's ears twitched. More Mother's Day presents was good news for the Placehold, for Serpent's Walk, for everyone! But Lord Qirinty said, "The warehouses are getting empty. We need rain!"

"There's a ship due with some sea dragon bones," Chanthor said. "Magic to make rain, if Morth is as good as he says he is."

"It won't happen," Jerreff said, "and you know it. Do you remember the last time you bought dragon bones? Ebony box, lined with velvet, wrapped in silk, and nothing but rocks inside."

"Well, yes, but that merchant is crab dung now," Chanthor said, "and I keep my hemp gum in that box. This time the promise comes from a more reputable ship captain."

"He'll have a good excuse for not having any dragon bones in stock," Jerreff said. "Chanthor, Morth wasn't revealing secrets; he was speaking common magicians' gossip. Magic fades everywhere, but *here*. . . . Why would anyone send objects of power *here?* What can we pay compared to the Incas? Or Torov? Even Condigeo could pay more than we can!"

"All true," Qirinty said. "Which brings us to the question, why does Morth of Atlantis stay here? We all saw him move a mountain of ice!"

"Forget Morth. He has no power," Samorty said.

"It is a puzzle worth contemplation, even so," Jerreff said. "Here he is weak. He would be more powerful in a land better blessed with magic. An Atlantis wizard could command respect anywhere."

"They're rare, all right," Lady Rawanda said. "And there won't be any more."

A ripple of response ran around the table. Horror brushed its hand along Whandall's hair. Tellers even in Tep's Town spoke of the sinking of Atlantis.

Chanthor said, "Ship captains are still telling stories about the waves. Wiped out whole cities. Do you suppose that's what Morth is talking about? Salt water. Can he raise big waves? That might be useful, if anyone attacked us from the sea."

"Who'd attack us?" Qirinty asked.

"We've been raided a few times," Chanthor said. "The last one was interesting, wasn't it, Samorty?"

Lord Samorty nodded. "Nine dead, though."

"Nine dead, we sold six more to Condigeo, and we got a ship out of it," Chanthor said.

"Oh, what happened?" Rawanda asked.

"Ship's captain ran out of luck," Chanthor said. "Lost his cargo; talked the crew into raiding in our harbor for their pay. Water Devils saw them coming. Happened to be my watch. I took Waterman and his ready squad down. All over in an hour. As Samorty said, nine dead, four of them Water Devils. No Lordsmen hurt, and we made a pretty good profit selling the survivors even after we paid off the Water Devils."

"What about the captain?" Jerreff asked.

"He owes us," Samorty said. "I let him recruit crew from unemployed kinless. Seems to be working well. The kinless bring money back for their relatives to spend here, and we have a merchant ship—not that I've thought of any use for it. It can't bring us rain."

"We're due for rain, though," Chanthor said.

"If Yangin-Atep doesn't chase it away," Qirinty's wife said.

"There's no predicting that," Qirinty said. "But, you know, I think he's less powerful when it rains. Fire god, after all: why not?"

Yangin-Atep. The Lords knew of Yangin-Atep. And they had fires indoors. Yangin-Atep never permitted fires indoors. And they'd hosted

Morth of Atlantis, who had killed Pothefit, but he seemed too frail to defend himself at all.

They talked so fast, and it was all hard to remember, but that was part of a Lordkin's training. Whandall listened.

"We need a small Burning," Jerreff said. "If we stop the Burnings altogether, the lookers won't come here anymore, and we'll all die of boredom. A little Burning, just enough to get it out of their system."

"You're a cynic, Jerreff," Samorty said.

"No, just practical."

"If we don't get some rain soon, there'll be more kinless wanting to move out of the city and into our town," Chanthor said sourly.

"Can't blame them. But we have no place to put them," Qirinty said. "No jobs, either. I've got more servants and gardeners than I need, and without water there won't be enough crops to feed the people we have, Samorty."

"Tell me the last time you didn't see a real problem coming," Rawanda said.

Qirinty shrugged and produced a dagger from thin air. "Someone has to worry about the future."

"And you do it well. Just as Jerreff worries about the past. I'm grateful to you both." Samorty stood. "Now, I'm afraid you'll have to excuse me. I'm on watch tonight." He raised his voice. "Antanio, bring my armor, please."

"Yes, Lord," someone called from the house. A moment later two men came out struggling under a load. They dressed Samorty in a bronze back-and-breastplate. They hung a sword longer than two Lordkin knives on a strap over one shoulder and handed him a helmet.

"Is the watch ready?" Samorty asked.

"Yes, Lord; they're waiting at the gate."

"Armor all polished?"

"Yes, Lord."

"Fine." To his guests, he said, "Enjoy yourselves. If there's anything you need, just ask. Rawanda, I'll be late tonight. I have a double watch."

"Oh, I'm sorry to hear that," the lady said.

"She's not sorry," Shanda whispered. "She doesn't even like him."

"Do you?" Whandall asked.

"Samorty's not so bad," Shanda said. "He was very nice to my mother after my father was killed in the Burning."

There was so much to learn! The Lords who controlled Mother's Day knew supplies were running out. They needed water. Whandall had never thought about water before. There were the wells, and sometimes rivers, and the fountain at Peacegiven Square, and sometimes those were nearly dry. Water was important, but Whandall didn't know anyone who could control water.

But this wizard had brought water once, and he was welcome here now. Because he was a wizard, or because he brought water? And how did you become a Lord in the first place?

"Was your father a Lord, Shanda?"

"Yes. Lord Horthomew. He was a politician and an officer of the watch, like Samorty."

"How was he killed?"

"I don't know," she said.

CHAPTER
5

When it was light, he waited outside Shanda's door. It seemed like a long time until she came out, but the sun was still very low in the east. He fidgeted, and finally said, "I have to piss, and I don't know where, and—"

She giggled. "I told you—the room is at the far end of the hall under the stairs. Didn't I tell you?"

He didn't remember. Certainly he hadn't understood. He thanked her and ran toward the stairs.

"Lock the door when you're inside," she whisper-called.

The room below the stairs had windows too high up to look out, and a door with a latch. Inside a stream washed into a basin at his chest level, then spilled over into a trough on the floor. It was all clean, and nothing smelled. When he came out, there was a man waiting outside the door. He had the round ears of a kinless, and he looked like the man who had brought Samorty's armor. He didn't say anything to Whandall as he went inside.

They ate in the kitchen. Serana fussed over them and didn't seem surprised to find Whandall was still there.

"We're going to play in the big park," Shanda told Serana. "Will you tell Miss Batty for me?"

Serana made disapproving sounds. "I'll tell Miss Bertrana you called her that." She didn't sound like she meant it. "You'll need a lunch. I'll fix up something. You be back by suppertime."

They went to the courtyard where the clothes were drying, and Whan-

38

dall selected a length of rope. He went to the tree branch and threw the rope over it and tied knots in the rope. With the rope there, he felt safer, because he thought that once he was over the wall no one could catch him in the chaparral. Not without magic.

The Lords did magic. Everyone said so. Lord Qirinty made cups dance and pulled a dagger from thin air, but it was Lord Qirinty who had wished they could do real magic. But the *stove* was magic. It all made Whandall's head hurt. Learning things was not the same as understanding them . . .

He started to climb the rope. When he got on the branch, he saw Shanda was climbing up. She wasn't good at climbing.

"Help me up," she said.

He reached down and took her hand and pulled her up to the branch. Then he looked around. One of the men with shovels had seen them climb up, but he only went back to work.

"Can I get back in this way?" she asked.

"You're not going out."

"Yes, I am."

"Shanda, the chaparral is dangerous. You'll get hurt and your stepfather will kill me."

"I won't get hurt if you show me what to do."

"No." He crawled along the tree limb until he was over the wall. She came right behind him. "No," he said again, but he knew it was no use. "Go back and pull the rope to the outside of the wall."

Just near the wall the plants seemed weak and almost lifeless, but farther away they grew thicker. In a mile they'd be luxurious. Two miles farther were the first of the redwoods. "Those are wonderful," he told her. "Wait till you see them close."

But she wasn't avoiding the plants. He stopped her. He showed her lord's-kiss and nettles and thorn bushes, and three kinds of touch-me. "Three leaves," he said. "Three leaves and white berries, and it doesn't just sit there. Watch." He saw a stick on the ground and examined it carefully before he picked it up. Then he rubbed his hands on one end and held it by the other end, moving it closer and closer to a large vine. At a hand's distance, the vine moved just enough to brush the stick.

Whandall showed her an oily smear on the stick. "You wouldn't want to touch that."

"Would it kill you?"

"No, it just makes you swell up in bumps. The vine can kill you. Things it touches only hurt you."

She still wanted to move too fast. He showed her some of the scars the plants had left on him when he was with the foresters. He made her follow just in his footsteps, and whenever she wanted to look at something, he stopped.

There wasn't the ghost of a chance they would reach the redwoods today.

At noon they stopped and ate lunch, then started back. Whandall took his time, pointing out plants even if she'd seen them before. *He'd* forgotten often enough, and Kreeg had had to remind him . . .

She held a branch at the broken end. Glossy red-and-green leaves grew at the tip. "What would happen if I rub that stick on my stepmother's chair?"

"Not the stick, the leaves. Shanda, really?"

She nodded, grinning.

"Well, she won't die. She'll itch and scratch."

"It's magic?" Shanda asked. "If it's magic it won't work at all inside the walls. That's what my stepfather says."

That would explain the cook fires, Whandall thought. But not Qirinty's dancing cups.

"I'm going to try it," she said.

He stood under the rope as she climbed it, in case she fell. She waved from the top and was gone.

It had been a glorious day.

He was out of the chaparral before the light of sunset died, but the night was turning misty. When Whandall reached the hilltops, he could see fog curling in from where the harbor had been. He watched it for a time, humped above the land. Then he heard shouts. Had someone seen him? Water Devils, perhaps someone worse. He couldn't see anyone, but he ran into the fog, running as hard as he could until he was exhausted.

Fog was all around him as he caught the stench of the Black Pit. The Pit itself was not to be seen. What he saw was dark shadows racing toward him.

He ran back the way he had come, but he was too tired to run far. When his breath ran out he trailed to a stop.

He hadn't heard a sound.

He'd seen . . . what had he seen? Dogs or wolves, but *huge*. But nothing chased him now. He had to get past the Pit to get home, and someone had chased him up the hill. A band was more dangerous than shadows.

The shadows came again as he crested the hill. This time he watched. Bent to pick up a sharp-edged rock in each fist, and watched again. He wished with all his heart that he already had his Lordkin knife. He had outrun them before and he could again . . . but they were only shadows. Wolf-shaped shadows, and something much larger, racing silently toward him.

They were less real as they came near. Whandall yelled and swung his rocks to smash skulls, and then he was among them, in them, and breathless with wonder. They were pockets in the fog: half a dozen wolf shapes all merged now into one thrashing bubble of clear air. The larger shape was a cat as big as Placehold's communal bedroom, armed with a pair of fangs very like Lordkin knives. Then that too was part of the bubble, thrashing as it fought the wolves, and Whandall could watch the shadow shapes of huge birds wheeling above the misty slaughter.

They'll never believe me. But what a day!

CHAPTER
6

H e had carried his own clothes in a bundle. Now he put them on over his new ones, so that he could get back to Placehold safely. It took all day. After noon, he ate the roll that Serana had given him. The waning moon was high when he got back home. Hungry, he checked out the tables and cookpot for leftovers. That got him nothing but sticky feet. He crept into the sleeping room and fell asleep at once.

In the morning his toes remembered the clean blond wood that floored Lord Samorty's kitchen as they squished across Placehold's sticky flagstones. In the roar of Placehold's shouts and laughter and curses he remembered the busy quiet around Serana.

He tore a piece of bread off what Wanshig had gathered. Wanshig jumped, then laughed. "Where did you gather the new clothes?"

His sisters and cousins all looked at him. "Pretty," Rutinda said. "Are there more?"

A Lordkin should have guile, even with his own kin. Whandall wanted to think about what he had seen before he talked about it. There was no way to explain that gathering was not a way of life to the Lords and those who worked with them.

So . . . "Clothesline at a house off of Sanvin Street," Whandall said. "Kinless house, nobody looking, but there wasn't anything else worth gathering."

"Too bad," Wanshig said. "Ready for knife lessons?"

"Sure."

They practiced with sticks. Whandall was still clumsy. He'd have been killed a dozen times if they'd used real knives.

"Next year." The uncles who'd been watching the lessons were sure about it. "Next year."

The Lordsmen fought with spears and swords, not with the big Lordkin knives. Whandall thought about the Lordshills, where even the gardeners lived as well as Pelzed and Resalet did. The Lordsmen would live even better than gardeners. Fighters always did. His uncles would never be able to teach him to fight the way Lordsmen did. But someone might. He knew he had to go back.

He washed his new clothes, but he could think of no place to dry them where they would not be stolen. He carried them as a damp bundle when he took to the roads four days later. They smelled of damp.

His path ran through Flower Market. He kept to shadow when he could, and the windowless sides of buildings, and was still surprised to get through untouched.

Beyond Flower Market nobody lived, or so he'd been told. He saw occasional dwellings but was able to avoid them. When he reached the ridge it was nearly dark. He thought of staying in the chaparral, then laughed. He knew a better place.

The Black Pit was stench and mist and darkness, and a misty blur of a full moon overhead. The moon lit shadows that came bounding to greet him. Wolves as big as Whandall himself, all in a leaping pack. Birds big enough to pluck him from the ground. Two cats bigger than Whandall's imagination. Bubbles in the fog, they merged in a frantic seething bubble, and Whandall laughed and tried to play with them, but he touched nothing but fog.

Rumor spoke that the Black Pit had swallowed people. He shied from going too deep into it. He didn't want any more of that alien stench, either. He spread some marsh grass over a flat rock and lay down on that. With two layers of clothes around him, he wasn't even particularly cold.

Half asleep, he watched another shadow edging toward him several feet above the black swamp. It was rounded and almost featureless, and the ghosts already around him made shadows to interfere with what approached. It was even bigger than the cats. Sleepily he watched it come and tried to guess its shape, then fell asleep still wondering.

The gardener's boy's clothes were still damp when he put them on at dawn. His own Serpent's Walk garments were underneath. He wasn't cold, just sodden. He walked his clothes dry before he reached the broad wagon path that must be Sanvin Street.

When he got to the barren lands, a wagon came up behind him. The kinless driver looked at Whandall and stopped. "Need a ride?"

"Yes, thank you." He hesitated only a moment. "Sir."

"Climb on. I'm going to the harbor. Where are you headed?"

"To see . . . friends. At Lord Samorty's house."

"Inside, eh? Well, I'll let you off at the fork. Hup. Gettap." The two ponies drew the cart at a pace faster than Whandall would walk. The kinless driver whistled some nameless tune. He was a young man, not much over twenty.

The cart was filled with baskets with the lids tied on them. "What is that?" Whandall asked.

The driver eyed Whandall carefully. "Who did you say your friend was?"

"Shanda."

"Samorty's daughter?"

"Stepdaughter," Whandall said. "Sir."

"Right. Your father work for Samorty?"

"Yes, sir."

"Explains the shirt," the driver said.

Whandall widened his eyes and looked up at him.

The driver grinned. "If you was to look in one of those baskets you'd see cloth just like what you're wearing. My cousin Hallati has a loom in his basement. Weaves that cloth, he and his wives and daughters. We sold a stack of it to Samorty last month."

Hallati. Whandall had never heard the name, but he would remember it. How many other kinless were hiding valuables?

"Hope we can move Hallati out soon. I don't like this drought much. Gets dry and those Lordkin jackals get ugly. Almost got my cousin's place last time. Almost," the cart driver said, and pulled the animals to a stop. This was the road to the Lordshills. Whandall got out and waved a good-bye.

There were different guards when he got to the gate. They didn't pay much attention to Whandall as he came up the road.

"Don't remember you," one of the guards said. "Where do you live, boy?"

"Lord Samorty's house—"

"Oh. Gardening crew?"

"Yes, sir."

The guard nodded. They didn't bother to raise the barrier, but it was easy to walk around it, and the guards were already talking about the weather by the time Whandall was inside.

There were big houses and wide streets. Palm trees grew at regular intervals, in patterns. The houses were grand. Something more, something weird. Thirty houses shouldn't be quite so similar, though no two were identical; but neither should they remind a boy of a stand of redwoods or a range of hills.

Like a redwood, like a granite hill, each house looked like it had been in place forever. Like . . . Whandall stepped back and looked around him, because he could feel how the shock changed his face. Anyone who saw him would know he was a stranger, staring as if he'd *never* seen a long street lined on both sides with houses, *none* of which had ever been burned and replaced. The flower beds—they were shaped and arranged to fit around the houses! Not one structure showed any sign of haste, of *Get a roof on that before the rain starts!* Or *Use the beams from the Tanner house—they don't quite fit, but the Tanners won't need them anymore.* Or *Just do something to shelter us—don't bother me; can't you see I'm grieving?*

It made him uneasy.

He didn't know what Lord Samorty's house would look like from the front, but it had to be near the wall. He worked his way eastward until he was sure there was only the one layer of houses between him and the wall, then north until he could see the big tree. After that it was no problem finding his way around the back of the house to the fountain. He washed his hands and face and feet without waiting to be told to.

"I didn't really think you would come back," Shanda said.

"I said I would . . ."

"A Lordkin's promise." There was not much warmth in her smile, but then it brightened. "You promised to show me the redwoods."

He thought about that.

"I have leathers. For both of us." She showed him a box hidden under the bed in her room. "I got them from the gardeners. They don't use them anymore."

Whandall examined the gear.

"It's good, isn't it?" Shanda demanded.

"It's good enough," he admitted. "But we'd be out all night."

"That's all right; Miss Batty will think I'm visiting," Shanda said. "I'll tell her I'm staying with Lord Flascatti's daughter. Miss Batty will never check."

"But—"

"And my stepmother wouldn't care if I never came back. We'll take lunch and dinner and—"

Whandall looked up at the sun, low in the west. "It's way too late—"

"Not today, silly. In the morning. Or next day. You don't have to get back today, do you?"

He shook his head. If he never came back, his mother would worry about him a little, but she wouldn't do anything, and no one else would care much. Not unless they thought he'd been killed by kinless.

"Did you try that stick?"

Shanda grinned. "That same night. On Rawanda's chair! Yes! It gave her a little red rash, and it itched her for two days. I think it still does." Her face fell a bit. "Samorty must have got some on his arm, because he got a rash too. I guess he knew what made it, because he yelled at the gardeners about it, and the gardeners yelled back, and they all went out to look for a poison plant, but they didn't find any. I didn't want to hurt Samorty."

Good, Whandall thought. And better that she hadn't been caught, and no one knew where she had been. Or who she had been with . . .

A little red rash. Whandall had given leaves of that same plant to Lord Pelzed, and they'd used them on Bull Pizzle boys. No one died, but a dozen of them were useless for a week, and Pelzed and the Bull Pizzle Lord had made a treaty not to do that again. Pelzed had been pleased. But here it was just a little red rash. Plants lost power here.

"Let's get something to eat," Shanda was saying. "Serana doesn't think I eat enough. She'll be glad to see you."

The kitchen was warm and dry and smelled of foods Whandall could only guess at. Serana filled his bowl with soup and heaped bread on the table, then apologized for not having anything for him. "Will you be staying for dinner?"

"If that's all right," Whandall said. "Ma'am. This sure is good."

Serana smiled happily.

They watched the gardeners, but they avoided everyone else. Shanda showed him the carp pools, with bright colored fish. A pair of servants got too curious, and Whandall was frantically trying to find answers when Shanda laughed and ran away with Whandall following. She led him to another part of the yard.

There was a small, queer house, too small for Shanda and way too small for Whandall. There were rooms no bigger than a big man, and tiny passages they could crawl through, and open walls. The curious servants had followed. Whandall had to wriggle like an earthworm, but he followed Shanda deeper into the maze, into twists and shadows, until no eyes could reach them.

He felt a moment of panic then. If this place should burn! They'd be trapped, wriggling through flaming twists. But the gardeners were all kinless, weren't they? And he wouldn't show the little girl his fear. He followed Shanda deeper yet.

There was a small room at the center, just big enough for both of them to sit up.

"Why is it so small?" Whandall asked.

"It's a playhouse. It was built for my little brother, but he doesn't like it much, so I get to play in it."

A playhouse. Whandall could understand the notion, but he would never have thought of it. An entire extra house, just for fun!

* * *

After dinner they lay on the balcony above the courtyard and listened to the Lords talk.

Four men and three women lolled on couches that would have looked really nice in the Placehold courtyard. No one said anything until an elderly kinless brought out a tray of steaming cups. Lady Rawanda passed them to the others.

Qirinty's wife sipped, then smiled. "Really, Rawanda, you must tell us where you get such excellent tea root."

"Thank you, Cliella. It is good, isn't it?" Rawanda said. There was another silence.

"Quiet lately," Jerreff said. "I don't like it."

"Then you should be pleased," Samorty said. "We caught a sneaker last night."

"Any problems?" Jerreff asked.

"No, there was a Jollmic ship in port. We got a nice burning glass for him. Quintana, isn't it your watch tonight?"

"I traded."

"Traded with who?"

"Well, actually—"

"He paid Peacevoice Waterman extra," Qirinty said. He produced a grapefruit from thin air and inspected it.

Samorty shook his head sadly. "Bad practice," he said.

Quintana laughed. He was round and pudgy and looked very contented on his couch. "What can it hurt? Samorty, you may like parading around all night in armor, but I don't! If there's need, I'll turn out—"

"If there's need, the watchmen will be taking orders from Waterman, not you," Samorty said.

"Not to mention that Waterman will get any loot they find," Jerreff said dryly.

"You worry too much, Samorty," Rawanda said. "You think the city will fall if you don't hold it up—"

Samorty laughed thinly. "It fell once. To us! But peace. It won't fall tonight. More wine?" He poured from a pitcher on the table.

Shanda stirred and whispered, "That's you they're talking about."

"Sneaker?"

"No, the *Lordkin!*"

Whandall nodded. His family, street, city, in the hands of these dithering, bickering Lords. . . . Was he too young to be sold onto some foreign ship? For an instant the idea was indecently attractive . . .

"Yangin-Atep's still asleep," Quintana said. "Watchmen told me there were three fires over in the benighted areas."

"I didn't hear about any fires. Have trouble?"

"Just brush fires. The kinless must have put them out."

"This time," Samorty muttered. "What I worry about is when the Lord-kin won't let the kinless put out the fires."

"Yangin-Atep protects houses," Quintana said.

"But not brush. Suppose all the chaparral burned at once?" Jerreff asked. "Would that wake Yangin-Atep? Half the city could burn if Yangin-Atep wakes while the hills are burning!"

"Now that would be something to worry about," Rowena said.

"Sure would. You're too young to remember the last time," Samorty said. "I was only ten or so myself."

"We don't know what wakes the god," Qirinty's wife said.

"Sure we do. Hot weather. No rain. That hot, dry wind from the east," Qirinty said.

"Sometimes." Samorty sounded doubtful. "I grant you that's usually what things are like when the Burning starts. But not always."

"Get us some rain and things will be all right." Qirinty toyed nervously with a salt shaker, then caused it to whirl about.

"Sure," Rowena said.

"If we can't get rain, maybe we ought to do something else," Qirinty said carefully. He put the salt shaker down.

"What?"

"Finish the aqueduct. Get more water into the benighted areas—"

"Be real," Samorty said. "That's no easier than getting rain!"

"They have a new aqueduct in South Cape," Quintana said. "One of the ship captains told me."

"Sure, and they have wizards in South Cape," Qirinty said. "And dragon bones for manna. We don't. But we could still build the aqueduct—"

"There's no money," Samorty said.

"Raise taxes."

"We just raised taxes," Jerreff said. "You can't squeeze the kinless much more."

"Borrow the money. We have to do something! If there's another Burning it will cost even more to rebuild and we'll *still* have to finish the aqueduct." At the word *still,* Qirinty made a dagger vanish. From his vantage above, Whandall saw how he did it. He might have learned it from a pickpocket. "Doesn't Nico owe us?"

"Sure he does, and maybe he can talk his masons into working with him as a favor, but it would still take two hundred laborers to finish that job. They'd all have to be fed."

"I suppose," Qirinty said sadly.

"Maybe we can talk the Lordkin into finishing the aqueduct." Rowena laughed sourly. "After all, they're the ones who need it."

"Yeah, sure," Quintana said. He poured himself another glass of wine. "But Qirinty's right. We should do something . . ."

Lord Quintana's wife was slim and long, with sculpted hair. She'd arranged herself on the couch so that everyone would see her legs and painted toenails, and she seldom spoke. "I don't see why everyone worries so much about the Lordkin," she said. "We don't need them. What do we care what they do?"

Quintana ignored her.

"No, I mean really," she said. There was a hard edge to her voice. "They need the aqueduct, but they won't work on it. The very idea that they might makes us laugh."

"And when Yangin-Atep wakes and they burn the city?" Samorty said gently. He liked Lady Siresee.

"Kill them."

"Not easy," Qirinty laughed. "There are a lot of them, and after all they won last time."

"Squeeze the kinless much harder and you'll get another war," Jerreff said. "Some of them are getting desperate."

"Yes," Samorty said. "But they'd really be in bad shape after a Burning."

"There are stories," Jerreff said. "Whole city burned down. Even our town."

"Where did you hear that?" Samorty asked.

"At the Memory Guild. Yangin-Atep used to be more powerful," Jerreff said. "He could seize everyone, Lordkin and Lords too. Burnings were really bad in those days. Didn't your father tell you that, Samorty?"

"Yangin-Atep has no power in here." Samorty waved at the sculpted gardens and too-perfect houses. "And damned little in town."

"Sure, and you know why," Qirinty said. "We can fence him out, but we can't control him."

"Gods have gone mythical," Jerreff said.

"Don't be a fool," Samorty said. "You heard what Morth said. And suppose we *could* send Yangin-Atep into myth—what happens then?"

"No more Burnings," Jerreff said.

"At what cost?"

"I don't know," Qirinty said.

"Neither do I, and that's the point," Samorty said. "Right now we've got things under control—"

"Sort of," Jerreff said.

"Enough." Samorty clapped his hands. The kinless servants brought in new trays of mugs. "We have a performance tonight."

"Oh, what?" Qirinty's wife asked.

"*Jispomnos.*"

"No, no, that's long," Quintana said.

"Not all of it—scenes from part one," Rawanda said. "Nobody does the whole thing."

"Even so," Quintana said. "I'll be back . . ." He went off toward the small room under the stairs.

CHAPTER
7

Performance was a way of telling a story. Several people acted out lives that weren't theirs, on a platform with moveable furniture. A man with a booming voice spoke as storyteller. Whandall had never seen anything like it.

The performance was long, and Whandall didn't understand a lot of the words. Jispomnos had beaten his woman, had tracked her down after she fled from him, had killed her and the man he found with her. Whandall understood that well enough. Whandall's uncle Napthefit had killed Aunt Ralloop when he found her with a Water Devil. He'd tried to kill the man too, but the Water Devil had run to his kin.

But Jispomnos's woman was kinless!

The killing wasn't shown.

Guards took Jispomnos away. He walked away when they turned their backs. The guards chased Jispomnos around and around the stage in excruciating slow motion and all sang in a harmony that Whandall found beautiful, but they sang so *slowly!*—in time to somnolent music that ran on forever. . . .

Shanda pulled his ear to wake him. "You were snoring."

"What's going on now?"

"Trial."

He watched for a time. "I don't understand anything at all! What's the trial about?"

She looked at him with wide eyes. "There was a murder," she rebuked him. "It's about whether he did it or not."

"Jispomnos is a Lordkin, isn't he?" Or was the *actor* a Lordkin *playing* Jispomnos?

But Shanda only looked at him strangely.

Whandall swallowed what he was about to say. Shanda wasn't Lordkin. Instead he pointed and said, "The kinless woman and the two men, who are they? They're doing all the talking."

"The men, they speak for Jispomnos. Clarata speaks for the court."

"Jispomnos won't speak for himself?" Cowardice or pride? "Why *two* men?"

"I don't know. I'll be back," she whispered.

Whandall nodded. It had been a long performance.

He watched. It was difficult to untangle. The kinless woman Clarata told of the killing, questioned any who had been nearby, showed bloody clothing. Of the men who spoke for Jispomnos, the little kinless man demanded that Clarata produce Jispomnos's knife. Whandall nodded: no Lordkin would throw away his knife. He argued that the clothing wasn't his, didn't fit. Jispomnos was elsewhere during the killing—in the Eastern Arc, in the woods, in a dockside winery with Water Devils to vouch for him, and on a boat bound for Condigeo—until the audience roared with laughter, covering Whandall's own giggles.

But the Lordkin advocate spoke of Jispomnos's prowess as a fighter, his standing in the bands . . .

Shanda came back. "What did I miss?"

"I think I get it."

"Well?"

"They're not talking to the same people. The little kinless, he's funny, but two of the judges are kinless, so he's talking to them. He tells them Jispomnos didn't do it. But Jispomnos took a kinless as his woman. He lives like a kinless. What the Lordkin judges want to know is, did Jispomnos make himself kinless? The Lordkin advocate, he's telling them that Jispomnos is still a Lordkin. He had the right to track his woman down and kill her."

"The *right?*" Her eyes bugged. *"Why?"*

He had no way to tell her that. It just *was.*

So he lied. "I don't understand that either."

Shanda whispered, "I don't think anyone does. It's based on something that really happened in Maze Walkers. A Condigeo teller wrote this opera. The grownups like it."

The trial was still going on when part one ended and everyone applauded.

The lords and ladies drifted apart. Samorty and Qirinty walked under the balcony. Samorty was saying, "And that's the *best* part. Greatest argument for getting rid of that arts committee I ever saw."

"Let *me* run the arts committee. Or you. Or Chondor. At least we'll have shows that satisfy someone." Qirinty stopped in his tracks. "That's what we need! A show! Not for us. For the Lordkin!"

"Not Jispomnos!" Samorty said. "You'd start the next Burning!"

"No, no, I mean, give them a parade," Qirinty said. "Get their attention and tell them about the aqueduct. Tell them we'll have it done . . . before the rains?" He went back to his couch, looked up at the night sky. "It's the season. Why doesn't it rain?"

"Not a bad idea," Jerreff said. "While all the Lordkin are off at the parade, Samorty here can meet with the kinless association council. Explain what we're really doing with their taxes."

"Find out if they're ready to join the Guard," Siresee said.

Quintana said, "Lordkin hear you're meeting with kinless and not them, there'll be trouble."

Jerreff waved it off. "We'll meet with some Lordkin too."

"Who?" Qirinty asked.

"Who cares? Get the word out, we're meeting their leaders. Somebody will show up."

"Now that's disrespectful," Samorty said. "And the Lordkin want respect."

"No, they don't. They demand it." Siresee's words were meant to cut.

"Well, they say they want it, and they certainly demand it," Samorty said placidly. "I agree, Jerreff, it doesn't matter a lot which Lordkin we talk to. They don't keep their own promises, and none of them can make promises for Yangin-Atep. But we have to talk to them."

"Why?" Siresee asked.

"Time you children went to bed."

Behind him! Whandall jumped, but it was only Serana the cook. "Before Miss Bertrana catches you up so late," she said.

Morning was cloudy, and just after breakfast Miss Bertrana came into the kitchen and took Shanda by the hand. "Your father wants you," she said. "In your pink dress. There are visitors."

Shanda looked pained. She turned to Whandall. "I'm sorry . . ."

"That's all right," Whandall said. "I'd better go home."

"Yes, but have some of my corn cake," Serana said. "I like to see a boy with a good appetite."

"Where did you say you lived?" Miss Bertrana asked.

Whandall pointed vaguely to the west. "Over near the wall, ma'am . . ."

"Well. Miss Shanda will be busy all day. Tomorrow too."

"Yes, ma'am. Too bad, Shanda."

"Are they showing me off?" the little girl asked.

"I wouldn't put it that way, but it's Lord Wyona's family." Miss Bertrana said the name reverently. "Come on; you'll have to change."

Shanda hesitated a moment. "You'll come back?"

Serana was at the stove rattling pans. "It takes two days each way," Whandall whispered.

"Please?"

"I'll be back," he said. "Really. I just don't know when."

"Next time we'll get to the forest." Shanda lowered her voice. "I'll leave some things for you in my room, in the chest. You can have all the boys' clothes there."

The chest was nearly full, and Whandall couldn't tell the boys' clothes from the girls. Most of the things were too small anyway. Shoes: fancy, not sturdy. They wouldn't last a week in Serpent's Walk. There was far more stuff here than he could carry, and even if he could carry it, what then? He'd look like a gatherer. If the Lordsmen didn't catch him, his own people would.

There were boys in the yard playing a complicated game. Hide and run, track and pounce. Imitation Lordkin. Pitiful. Whandall watched them while he thought.

He'd need an outfit, a way to blend in here when he returned. But anything that would blend in here would stand out in Serpent's Walk.

A Lordkin had to be crafty.

It came to him that he could wear his own clothes underneath, then two more layers of Lord's clothing topped by the loose jacket, and still not look too odd. Those boys were all bulkier than he was. They ate better—and more often.

When he was dressed, he felt bulky. He left Shanda's room carefully, with a twinge of regret for all the stuff he was leaving behind, too much to gather. He left by going over the wall. Guards might notice how much he was wearing.

No one paid any attention to him while he was in the area near the Lordshills. There were people and carts on the road. No one offered him a ride, but no one stopped him either. At the top of the ridge he stopped and looked back at the Lordshills and their wall. Then went on. He knew where he could sleep safely.

The Pit was beginning to seem a friendly place. The moon was still near full. The light picked up the shadows of predators coming to greet him while he made himself comfortable. Through the ghosts' restless pockets in the fog he watched some larger shadow. He couldn't see it move, but every time he dozed and woke, it was nearer yet.

Then he saw something swing above it—a limb—and he knew its shape.

It was twice the size of one of the giant cats, with a rounded body, and it was upside down. It was hanging from an imaginary cylinder, perhaps the branch of a tree eons dead, by its four inward-curving hands. Its head hung, possibly watching Whandall himself. One of the tremendous cats suddenly discovered it, turned, and sprang, and then the horde of beasts was tearing it into wisps. The creature fought back, and birds and giant wolves too became drifting shreds of fog.

In the morning he put on everything he had, with his old clothes on top of it all. He looked bulky and he couldn't run, but he might get through . . .

CHAPTER
8

He had reached Bull Pizzle territory when he heard shouts. Sanvin Street was supposed to be safe, outside the jurisdiction of any band, but five older boys were coming toward him. Whandall began to run. They chased him down and tackled him.

"Hoo!" one of them shouted. "Look what all he's got!"

"Where?" another demanded. "Where'd you gather stuff like this?" When Whandall didn't answer, he hit him on the head with his fist. "Where?"

"Lordshills," Whandall said.

"Yeah, sure. Now where?" They hit him some more and sat on his head.

"Leave me alone!" Whandall shouted. He wanted to scream for help, but it wouldn't do any good. They'd just call him a coward and crybaby. But he could shout defiance . . .

"Serpents!" He heard the cry from down the street. "Serpent's Walk!" A dozen older boys, led by his brother Wanshig, were coming.

"Bull Pizzle!" his tormentor shouted. Then the others were there. Whandall felt the weight lift from his head. There were the sounds of blows.

"You all right?" Wanshig asked. "Come on, let's get out of here."

When they were back at Placehold, Wanshig thanked the others. "Somebody'd better tell Lord Pelzed," Wanshig said. "We may have trouble with Bull Pizzle."

"I never left Sanvin Street," Whandall protested.

Wanshig shrugged. "So what happened? Get anything good?"

"Just some clothes, and look, they tore them, and they gathered my jacket and shoes." Whandall felt bitter disappointment. Nothing had gone right this time. "This stuff is too small for them anyway—"

"Nice, though." Wanshig fingered the shirt Whandall was inspecting. "Nice. You just need a way to get stuff back to Placehold. Take one of us next time."

Even his own family lusted for what the Lords threw away!

"It wouldn't work," Whandall said. "It was . . . sort of an accident that I got in and made friends inside." They'd never believe him if he said that Shanda had given him all those things. Or they'd want to know why. "Nobody notices me. But the Lordsmen wouldn't let a bunch of us in."

"How many Lordsmen?"

"Lots," Whandall said. "Two at the gate, but there are others just inside."

"Yeah, we heard that," Wanshig said. "And they have magic too. Did you see any magic?"

"Maybe a little."

"Ten, twenty years ago, before I was born, three bands got together and went to the Lordshills to gather. None of them ever came back," Wanshig said. "None."

Maybe magic, Whandall thought. *And maybe it was only guards with armor and spears fighting together with the Lords to tell them what to do, and a ship to carry the losers away.* But he could never explain that to Wanshig.

He said, "Wan, there's going to be a big show. The Lords will have a show in the park, and give away some presents, maybe do some magic."

"When?"

"Five days, I think," Whandall said. He counted on his fingers. "Five days counting today."

Wanshig smiled. "Good. Don't tell anyone. *Anyone.* We'll keep this for the family."

"What will you do?"

"I'll have every Placeholder who can pick a pocket ready for them. We'll have first pick of the crowd." Wanshig nibbled his lip, considering. "We can't keep Bull Pizzle out of the park. Can we make them go somewhere else? Something to get them to the other side of town . . ."

Whandall watched his brother think.

Wanshig grinned. "Did they go through your pockets?"

"You got there first."

Wanshig's grin got bigger. "So they don't know you weren't carrying gold. Whandall, Iscunie has been seeing a Bull Pizzle boy. She can tell him you gathered some gold in the harbor town and ten of us are going back for more. We'll be coming back the morning of the parade, on the south side. That'll get every Bull Pizzle down there, and we'll have the park to ourselves."

* * *

There were drums and flutes, and five wagons. Thirty Lordsmen in shiny bronze armor marched with spears and shields, and when they got to the park they did a complicated thing of marching in a circle. Then more Lordsmen came and filled in between them so that the circle was protected, and the wagons came in.

A family of kinless strung a rope between two thick trees, as high as a man could reach and so taut that it hung almost straight. A kinless boy younger than Whandall walked from one tree to the other along the rope, turned and walked back, perfectly balanced, while kinless and a few Lordkin whistled and applauded. Whandall realized that these must be the Ropewalker family, who sold rope near the Black Pit.

The Lordsmen were still at work. A portable stage unfolded out of one of the wagons. Another wagon was covered by a tent. When the stage was up a man came out costumed in feathers like an eagle.

The kinless gathered around the wagons. More Lordsmen walked through the crowds. Flutes played, and drums, and someone passed out little cookies to the children. There was a little round platform that turned, with wooden dragons on it for children to ride.

At first it was turned by kinless running around it. When the Lordkin pushed all the kinless children off and took their places, the kinless drifted away into the crowd. A couple of Lordkin fathers tried to get older boys to push it, but nobody would, so after a while it sat there unused while people watched the show.

Most Lordkin kept to themselves in one corner of the park, but Placehold pickpockets moved among kinless and Lordkin alike. One was caught. The kinless man shouted curses at him, but when Lordkin men moved toward him, he let him go with more curses.

A troupe of acrobats came out onto the stage. They flew for short distances with the aid of a seesaw. Another climbed a long pole and hung by his teeth. A man and a woman, both Lordkin, ate fire, and a burly kinless man swallowed a long thin sword. The Ropewalkers danced on their tightrope, this time the boy and a younger girl, who did a backward somersault while an older man stood under her as if to catch her if she fell. She was very steady and he wasn't needed.

Whandall moved closer to where they were passing out cookies. One of the girls . . .

"Shanda," he said.

She looked startled. "Oh. I didn't recognize you."

Whandall saw her look nervously up at her stepfather on the platform, where he was about to make a speech. Whandall took a cookie. "Are they still looking for Lordkin to talk to?"

"I think so, but they haven't," she said.

Lord Samorty began his speech about the new aqueduct and how it would bring fresh water from the mountains. The kinless cheered in places.

"Will you take me to the redwoods?" Shanda asked. "Not for a while. We'll be doing this show in other parts of town."

"I'll try. Before the rain if I can. Rain makes everything grow and it's harder."

Something bright appeared on the stage, then vanished. "An evil wizard is keeping the rain for himself," Samorty was saying. "We'll beat him. There'll be rain!"

Kinless and Lordkin alike cheered.

"But now there's a water shortage, and it's very hard on the horses and oxen," Samorty was saying. "Delivery is difficult. So next Mother's Day will be special. There'll be nine weeks' rations and some other extras."

The Lordkin cheered.

"And that will have to last for two Mother's Days," Samorty was saying. "And you'll all have to come to Peacegiven Square to get it, because we won't be able to bring everything to the usual distribution places."

Crowd noises were drowning out Samorty. He waved, and three magicians came on the stage. They made things appear and disappear. One called Shanda up on the stage and put her in a box, and when it was opened, she was gone. Whandall looked for her, but he couldn't see her.

Wanshig came up behind him. "Lord Pelzed isn't happy," he said, but there was a laugh in his voice. "He's got all of Serpent's Walk out picking pockets now, but we got the best. Good work."

The magicians made a vine grow.

"I know how to make Pelzed happy," Whandall said.

"How?"

"He can meet the Lords."

"You don't know any Lords."

"I know who they are," Whandall said. "That was Lord Samorty who made the speech—"

"Everybody knows that."

"And the man over there talking to the magicians is Lord Qirinty. He's a magician himself, or at least a pickpocket, and the fat one in armor with the Lordsmen, that's Lord Quintana. The pretty lady serving soup is his wife."

"So you know who they are."

Whandall hadn't heard Pelzed come up behind them. "What else do you know?" Pelzed demanded. "Wanshig, you didn't share. We'll have to talk about that."

Wanshig looked worried.

"Lord Pelzed, I heard the Lords wanted a Lordkin leader to talk to," Whandall said.

Pelzed looked crafty. "Say more."

"They want the most powerful leader in this part of the city," Whandall said. "But I don't know what they want from him."

"That's me," Pelzed said. "Go tell them."

Whandall hadn't thought this out far enough. "Uh . . ."

"Do this for me and we'll forget what happened this morning," Pelzed said. He pointed up on the stage. "See that guy?"

"Foreigner," Wanshig said. "I've seen him before—"

"He's a teller," Pelzed said. "If I meet the Lords he'll tell everyone else. Whandall, how sure are you about their wanting to talk to us?"

Whandall thought about it. They hadn't wanted to talk to the Lordkin, but they thought they'd have to, only Whandall didn't dare tell Pelzed that. "I heard them plan it out over dinner," Whandall said.

"Whandall's a great sneak," Wanshig said.

"I remember," Pelzed said. "Well, go tell them I'm here."

"No, you come with me, Lord Pelzed," Whandall said. "Shig, you come too." He led them back behind the tent. As he'd hoped, Shanda was there. Whandall bowed as he'd seen kinless do. "Lady, this is Pelzed, the leader of Serpent's Walk."

The little girl looked surprised, then smiled. For a moment Whandall was afraid she'd wink or grin, but she just said, "Pleased to meet you. I'll go tell my father you're here."

She came back with Samorty, who invited Pelzed past the guards. No one invited Whandall and Wanshig, so they went back to watch the show. When Pelzed came out, he had a new burning glass and was very proud. He showed it to everyone. Then he found Whandall.

"You called me Pelzed. Not Lord Pelzed," he said.

Whandall had thought that through. "I thought the Lords might not like hearing you called Lord. They can make you disappear, Lord Pelzed," he said.

"You really have been in Lords' houses."

Whandall nodded. He already regretted letting them know.

"What did they want?" Wanshig asked.

Pelzed waved his hands. "It was important. Labor peace. How to organize for the new distribution on Mother's Day. They're going to let more female hemp plants grow in some of the fields. Important stuff I can't talk about. There'll be a meeting tonight. Be there, Wanshig . . . Whandall. Be there."

The meetinghouse had stone walls but no roof. There had been a roof, but it hadn't been strong enough. One night the men of Serpent's Walk had climbed onto the roof; no one remembered why. The beams broke. The kinless family who had once lived in the house couldn't be found, so Serpent's Walk couldn't meet there when it rained. It didn't rain much anyway.

Whandall and Wanshig had to tell everyone how Lord Pelzed was summoned to meet with the Lords, while no one from Bull Pizzle or any other band had been called. Only Pelzed.

They spoke of the new Mother's Day. Everyone would be in one place. They'd need all the women to collect and carry, and all the men to protect the women and their gifts.

"It'll be safe in the square," Pelzed's advisors said. "Lordsmen will see to that. But outside—"

"We need two bands," Pelzed said. "One to protect our stuff. Another to see what we can gather from Bull Pizzle."

Bull Pizzle will be doing the same thing, Whandall thought.

Pelzed appointed leaders. Wanshig would be one of them. Whandall thought he'd be in Wanshig's band, but he wasn't. He couldn't fight yet, so he was afraid he'd be assigned to help the women carry. That would be shameful. But the meeting was over before anyone told him what to do.

When everyone else was leaving, Pelzed made Whandall and Wanshig stay behind. Pelzed sat at the head of the table, with guards standing behind him. "Sit down," he invited. "We'll have some tea."

Everyone knew about Pelzed's tea. It was made with hemp leaves, and enough of it left you babbling. Pelzed sipped at the hot brew. Wanshig gulped his. Whandall sipped, just keeping up with Pelzed. It made his head spin, just a little.

"So. You have been to Lord's Town."

"Yes, Lord," Whandall admitted.

"And you brought back fine clothes. What else is there that we can gather?"

"Everything," Whandall said. "But you'll die of it. They have magic. Lord Pelzed, they have stoves inside their houses! The fires don't go out. Yangin-Atep . . ." He didn't want to say it, not here where Yangin-Atep ruled.

"I saw the Lordsmen in their armor," Whandall said. "And big swords, and spears. Every night a Lord puts on armor like that, and so do the Lordsmen, and they go on watch."

"Where do they go?" Pelzed demanded.

"Everywhere. They call it the watch, because they watch for gatherers. Not just in the Lordshills. There's a village outside the walls, and they watch there too. And they have magicians." How much could he tell Pelzed? Whandall was trapped between loyalties. He owed Pelzed, he *belonged* to the Placehold, but the future he longed for might be with the Lords.

"We saw the magic," Miracos said. He was the advisor who stood at

Pelzed's right. Sometimes he spoke aloud and sometimes he whispered in Pelzed's ear. "Vines growing. Fireballs."

"And I saw the Black Pit," Whandall said.

Everyone wanted to know about the Pit. Whandall told them as much as he dared. No one believed him.

"There's a wall around Lordshills," Miracos said. "But there's no wall around those big kinless houses? Lord's Town?"

"There is in back." Whandall tried to explain about the little squares, tables and plants in the middle, houses around them, walls behind the houses. "And the watch is there."

"This watch," Pelzed asked. "Swords. Armor. *Kinless?*"

"I think so. It's hard to tell with those helmets."

"Kinless with armor. Weapons," Miracos said. "Bad."

"They never come here," Pelzed said. "Lords do what Lords do." He made it sound profound. "But tell us more about those kinless homes. What's there? What can we gather?"

Whandall described some of what he had seen, shops with pots and beads and cloth, clothing hung on lines, people sitting in the squares drinking from cups and talking.

"No Lordkin there," Miracos said. "Maybe we could go live there."

"Lords won't let us," Pelzed said.

"Lords always telling us what to do," one of the guards said. "Like to show them my knife. Right up them."

"Lords make the kinless work," Pelzed said. "If you could do that, if *I* could, we'd have a roof! Whandall, go back. Take someone with you. Wanshig. Take Wanshig; bring me back something. Go learn the way."

"I heard three bands went to the Lordshills together to gather," Wanshig said. "Three together, and none of them ever came back. Dirty Bird was powerful before that happened."

"You scared to go with Whandall?" Pelzed demanded.

"Yes, Lord. Anybody would be scared. Whandall's the only one I ever met who went into Lord's Town and came out. Only one I ever *heard of* doing it."

"Not talking about inside the walls," Pelzed said. "Lords are Lords. Leave Lords alone. But those kinless houses out there, that's different. Go look, Whandall. When everyone's carrying stuff, the way will be clear; you can bring things back. Go see what you can find. I'd like me a shirt like yours . . ."

Whandall was glad of being small. His shirt wouldn't fit Pelzed. But if a little Lord's girl could keep what was hers, maybe a Lordsman could too.

CHAPTER
9

Serpent's Walk was coming to know a certain visiting looker. After the carnival, everyone knew his face.

The boys knew his names: he was Tras Preetror of Condigeo. Tras fascinated them. He spent the whole day in idleness, like a Lordkin. The kinless liked him even when he was with Lordkin, because Tras paid for what he took.

Not always, though. Sometimes he told stories instead.

He would walk away from a fight, or run, but sometimes he *talked* his way out. Wanshig got close enough to see Zatch the Knife accost Tras. He reported that they were presently talking like brothers long separated; that Tras Preetror shared a flask with Zatch. Zatch took nothing else.

Everything about Tras Preetror was exotic, peculiar. Whandall knew he had to see more.

The boys of Serpent's Walk kept getting caught because they went in bands. Bands could hide in the forest, because the forest was roomy. In the city people occupied what space there was. Getting caught got you laughed at. Whandall preferred to lurk alone.

Others learned that Tras Preetror was staying with a kinless family in the Eastern Arc. The kinless had bought protection from the Bonechewers who owned that area, so the house was nicer than most. It also meant that Whandall risked more than being laughed at if he got caught.

Three days after the carnival, the morning's light found eleven-year-old

Whandall on the roof, just above Tras's curtained window. He'd slept there, flattened on the slope of the roof.

He heard Tras wake, piss, and dress himself, all while singing in the rolling Condigeano tongue. Tras's footsteps went straight to the curtained window. His arm reached through with something in his hand.

"Come down, boy," he said, tormenting the syllables of normal speech. "I've got something for you. Talk to me."

Whandall flattened against the roof while he thought it over. He hadn't gathered anything from the room. The teller couldn't be angry about *that*. He was singing again . . .

Whandall joined in the chorus and swung on in.

"You sing pretty," Tras said. "Who are you?" He held out his gift. Whandall tasted orange wedges in honey for the first time.

"Name Whandall of Serpent's Walk. Happy meet you, Tras," he said in Condigeano. He'd practiced the words while he and others eavesdropped on the lookers.

"Happy meet you, Whandall," Tras said in bad talk-to-strangers speech. "I talk to other . . . you call *Lordkin?*"

"Lordkin, yes, of Serpent's Walk."

"Tell me how you live."

He understood the words *how you live,* but Whandall couldn't make sense of them. "How I guard my self? My brothers teach—*will* teach me how to use a knife. I walk without one until I know."

"What you do yesterday?"

"Hid in the . . . hid. Watched this house. Can't see roof. No Lordkin around. Climb house next door, look at roof. Go for blanket, come back, sleep on roof. Wait for you. Tras, speak Condigeo."

Tras said in his own speech, "Are a lot of your days like that?"

"Some."

"Maybe. . . . Tell me how the *kinless* live."

"I don't know."

"Mmm." Disappointed.

Whandall said, "I know how woodsmen live. Woodsmen are kinless."

"Tell me."

Whandall began to speak of what he'd learned. The dangerous plants, their names, how to recognize and avoid them. The rite that woodsmen performed before they felled a redwood and cut it up. What they ate. How they talked. Why none but Kreeg Miller would help injured Lordkin children. How they came to accept Whandall.

Tras listened intently, nodding, smiling. When Whandall ran down he said, "There, now, you've told me a lot about yourself. You rescued your brother. Lordkin don't work, but you carried water when you saw there was need. Lordkin don't learn about the forest, even the ones who go in as children. Lordkin like to watch without being seen. You gather, but the kinless try to stop you, because what you gather is what they make or sell or use. You don't worship trees, but you worship Yangin-Atep. You see?"

"Tras? Show me what you say. Tell me how you live."

Tras Preetror talked.

He had come to watch the Burning, to travel afterward and tell what he'd seen. "If you want to see the world, a teller is what you want to be. Wherever you go, they want to know what it's like where you came from. Of course you should know the speech. My family could afford a woman of the Incas to teach me and my brothers and sisters and cousins. We learned geometry and numbers and incantations, but I learned Inca speech too. . . ."

Tras mangled the words and rhythms of normal speech until Whandall's head hurt. Sometimes he didn't have the words. Finding them turned into lessons in Condigeano speech.

". . . *Rich*. If I was rich, I could get my own ship and take it where I wanted."

"Tras, someone could take it away and go where *he* wants."

"Pirates? Sure. You have to be better armed than they are or carry a better wizard or somehow persuade a pirate that you do.

"Once upon a time, two Torovan privateers had us bracketed far from shore. Privateers are pirates, but a government gives them a license to steal—I mean gather. Who has a better right?" Tras laughed and said, "But *Wave Walker* carried a wizard that trip.

"We watched. Acrimegus—he was *our* wizard—sent a beam of orange light from his hand down into the water near one of the other ships. It was just bright enough to see in twilight. He held it there, on and on, while we maneuvered and the two ships countermaneuvered and came closer and closer. Then the water boiled at that one spot. When Acrimegus gave us the signal, we all pulled the sails down and then crowded along the rail. The privateers must have thought we were crazy.

"A head broke the surface. It was almost the same size as the nearest ship. All of us shrieked and went running below, all but Acrimegus. I stuck my head back out to see the rest. The head was rising and rising on what looked like leagues of neck. It turned toward *us*. Acrimegus waved and danced and shouted, 'No, no, you massive great fool,' until it turned toward the privateer and started to dip—"

"What *was* it?"

"Well, an illusion, of course, but the privateers turned about and ran. What made it work wasn't just Acrimegus's light effects, but the details, the way he acted, the way *we* were acting."

"Were you frightened?"

"I pissed in my kilt. But what a story! I'd travel again with Acrimegus any day. Now you tell me something."

"I've seen a Lord."

"So have I. Where was your Lord?"

"At home, in Lordshills. He had a fountain. And a room inside where they can cook. A room to piss in, with running water. And a room where kinless wrote things on paper and put them in jars, but I couldn't go in there." Whandall decided not to speak Samorty's name. He would hold that in reserve.

"Can you read?"

"No. I don't know anyone who can read." Except the Lords could read. And Shanda.

"You do now. What did your Lord do?"

Whandall was still trying to understand what he'd seen on two visits. "He had other Lords to dinner, and a magician. People who weren't Lords brought the food and took it away, and all the Lords did was talk and ask each other questions. At the end they acted like they'd fixed something broken, only . . . only it was the next Burning. They think if they can make people talk to each other, they can miss the next Burning. And at the end he put on armor and went out with some other armed men."

"Did they . . . do *you* think they put off the next Burning?"

No grown man or woman could answer that question. Whandall didn't think even Lord Samorty knew that. Whandall said, "No."

"Then when will it happen?"

"Nobody knows," Whandall said. "There was another Lord who made cups move in a circle. Like this—"

"Yes, that's called juggling."

"How do you do it?"

"Years of practice. It isn't magic, Whandall."

"It isn't?"

"No."

"There was a . . ." Whandall couldn't remember the word. "People pretending to be other people. Telling each other a story like they don't know they're being watched. *Jispomnos,* they called it."

"I've seen *Jispomnos.* It's too long for after dinner. It runs on forever! You saw just pieces, I bet. Was there a part where the wife's parents want blood money?"

They talked through the morning and deep into afternoon. Whandall practiced his scanty Condigeano from time to time, but usually they were each speaking their own language.

Tras spoke of his own affairs without hesitation. Still, it was hard for even a teller to tell how he lived . . . to see it from inside . . . to see what a stranger must miss. They had to walk circles around their lives, to sneak up on the truth.

"Do you know who your father was?"

Whandall said, "Yes. Do you?"

"Yes, of course," Tras said.

"What you did with your face. It looked like you wanted to fight."

Tras shrugged uncomfortably. "Maybe for just a moment. Sorry. Whandall, it's an insult to ask if anyone but my father is my father." Tras changed to local speech. "This not Condigeo. *You* feel I still respect you?"

"Yes, but we don't say *father.* Resalet—" Tras lofted one eyebrow. Whandall explained, "Resalet is father to my brothers Wanshig and Shastern and two of my sisters. He tells us, *'I* know who *my* father is. So do you. But maybe I'm talking to one who isn't so lucky. I don't throw it in his teeth. You don't either. You say *Pothefit.* You and I and he know who I mean. Even if we're wrong.' "

"Pothefit. Your father. Have other name?"

"Not to tell."

"Live with you?"

"Pothefit was killed by a wizard."

Tras's face twisted. The man's face was so alien, it was hard to tell just what he was showing. He said, "When was that?"

"My second Burning. I was seven. Five years ago." *Almost five,* Whandall thought.

"I missed it. My ship left late. Now nobody seems to know when the next Burning will start," Tras said.

"Nobody knows," Whandall agreed.

Tras Preetror sighed. "But someone has to know. Someone has to set a fire."

An odd viewpoint, Whandall thought. "Yangin-Atep sets fire."

"They used to know, here in Tep's Town. In late spring, every spring, you'd burn the city. Now it's been . . . three years? What do you remember of the Burning?"

Whandall tried to tell him. Tras listened for a bit, then asked in Condigeano, "A wizard killed this Pothefit?"

"It was said."

"Odd. *I'd* know if there was a powerful wizard in Tep's Town."

"He's here. I've seen him. Someday I'll see him again. I don't know enough about magic yet. I don't even have my knife."

Tras said, "I've seen those knives. Half a pace long, plain handles, maybe a little crude?"

"Crude?"

"A Condigeano merchant would spend more effort. Inca smiths get *very* fancy. Here, someone would just take it away from him."

Whandall frowned, remembering something. "Why did you laugh?"

Tras looked guilty. "You caught that? I'm sorry."

"Yes, but why?"

"Magic wears out. It wears out faster in cities because there are more people. Everybody knows a *little* magic. You ever try to work a spell near a courthouse? It's bad enough in Condigeo.

"But here! There's something about Tep's Town that eats the magic right out of spells and potions and prayers. Here, it's hard to imagine what a wizard could do that would hurt a careful man. He must have taken your f—taken Pothefit by surprise."

How? A man so old that he might die before Whandall had his knife! A gatherer must be wary, ready to run or fight. What could Morth of Atlantis have done to surprise Pothefit?

But Whandall only asked, "Have you been where magic is strong?"

"They're dangerous places. Deserts, the ocean, mountain peaks. Anywhere magicians have a hard time getting to, that's where magic can still leap out and bite you. But I like to go look," Tras said. "I'm a teller. I have to go to where I can find stories to tell."

"What will happen when all the magic is gone?"

Tras looked grave. "I don't know. I don't think anyone knows, but some magicians say they have visions of a time when there is no magic, and everyone lives like animals. Others say that after a long time there'll be a new age that doesn't need magic."

Whandall's mind's eye showed him Tep's Town spreading to cover the world . . . just for a moment, before he blinked the image away.

What Whandall remembered best of that afternoon was how little he understood of what he'd seen of his world. But he'd learned just by talking, and the teller didn't seem disappointed.

CHAPTER
10

Of course Whandall asked Tras Preetror about Lords.

Strangely, Tras wanted *him* to find out more.

"Tras, we saw you with them on the wagon. You spoke to them," Whandall said.

"We see them when they want to be seen," Tras said. "A show for tellers. But you've seen Lords when they didn't know. Whandall, everyone is curious about your Lords. Who are they? Where do they come from? How do they get their power?"

"Don't other people have Lords?"

"Lords, Kings, and a hundred other ways to keep chaos imprisoned," Tras said. "But Tep's Town is different. You burn down your city, the kinless rebuild, and everyone thinks it won't happen without the Lords. Maybe everyone's right. I want to *know*. Whandall, don't you want to go back?"

Whandall was learning how to survive in the streets of Serpent's Walk. In the "benighted sections" he had enemies but also friends and guides. He was actually getting good at it. In the Lordshills were dangers he didn't understand. No, he didn't really want to go back; not now. Not until he understood better what he might do there.

He had no place in Lordshills. Or in Lord's Town nearby, where kinless and Lordkin lived together and hung clothes out to dry. But he might learn, in time. The kinless in the pony cart had spoken of moving his relatives to Lord's Town. And there were gardeners, and Lordsmen living inside the walls of Lordshills. They had to come from somewhere. He had to learn these things. But where? Going to Lordshills without knowing more could be dangerous.

There was his promise to Shanda. But he'd *told* her it might take time.

He tried avoiding the teller. It made life less interesting, and Tras sought him out anyway. Whandall began to wonder: what would the teller *do* to persuade him?

Whandall hadn't looked at the clothes Shanda had given him in a third of a year. When he saw their condition, he put a kilt and shirt on under his Serpent's Walk gear and took them to show the teller.

They were torn. They stank. "It's all like this," he told Tras.

"Dry rot. And how did they get ripped?"

"Bull Pizzles caught me. And afterward I couldn't hang them up to dry without somebody gathering them."

Tras offered to get him some soap.

Whandall explained that soap was unheard-of treasure. His family would gather it from him, if he could get it *that* far. Unless . . .

Tras grumbled at the price, but he paid.

Whandall went home by hidden ways, concealing a whole bag of soap. Guile and a brisk breeze hid him through Dirty Bird to Serpent's Walk, and from there a cake of soap bought him an escort back to the Placehold.

He could think of only one way to hide so much soap. He started giving it away.

His mother praised him extravagantly. Brothers took a few cakes to give to their women. He spoke to Wess, a girl two years older than Whandall, the daughter of his aunt's new lover. For the luck that was in his words or because she liked him or for the soap she knew he had, she lay with him and took his virginity.

Now Placehold reeked of soap, and Whandall could safely use the rest. He cleaned the clothes Shanda had given him. Pants and two shirts had rotted too badly; they came apart. He found he could still assemble a full outfit.

He went back to Wess and begged her to sew up the rips. They didn't have to hold long, or to stand up to more than a second glance. When Wess agreed, he gave her another cake of soap.

It would not do to trade with a Lordkin, man or woman. But a gift would persuade Wess not to forget her promise or keep it badly. He could see himself in the Lordshills, trying to get into pants that had been sewn shut at the cuffs!

His clothes must have been good enough, because the guards paid no attention to him at all. This time he knew the way to Samorty's house.

Dinner in Serana's kitchen was as good as he remembered. There was always more than enough food in a Lord's house. Whandall thought that must be the best thing about living here. You could never be hungry.

Shanda had new clothes for him.

"When did you get these?" Whandall asked.

"Just after the carnival," she said. "When you didn't come back, I thought about giving them to the gardeners, but you said it might be a long time."

Whandall was impressed: not that she had saved them for him, though that was nice, but that she could keep things a long time. No one gathered from her room. He'd seen clothes hung to dry, unguarded.

The Lords had gone to someone else's house, so there was nothing to do. Whandall slept in the empty room next to Shanda's.

In the morning they went over the wall with a lunch Serana had packed. Whandall inspected Shanda in her leathers before he let her go further. He was no less careful with his own.

The hills near the Lords' wall were ablaze with flowers. It was glorious, but Whandall had never seen the chaparral like this. All the patterns and paths he remembered were gone.

The chaparral seemed well behaved this near the Lords' wall. Whandall tried to urge caution, but Shanda was entranced by the beauty. The farther they went, the more vicious it all became. Yet the hills still flared in every conceivable color! Every bouquet of swords had a great scarlet flower at the tip. Touch-me displayed tiny white berries and pale green flowers with red streaks. Hemp plants grew taller than Whandall. They looked inviting, but Whandall wouldn't touch them.

"I've never seen the woods like this," he confessed. "Don't pick anything, okay? Please?"

There were few paths, and animals had made those. At least Shanda seemed to be taking the plants seriously. The whips and morningstars were visibly dangerous, and she'd seen what touch-me did to her stepmother. He watched her weave her way through a patch of creepy-julia, very cautious, very graceful, very pretty among the black-edged lavender flowers. But she kept stopping to look.

He wove a path through touch-me and bouquets of swords to an apple tree. She followed carefully in his footsteps. They ate a dozen tiny apples and, in a field of high yellow grass, threw the cores at each other.

It was well past noon and they were ravenous again before they reached the redwoods. They were a thousand paces outside Lord's Town.

These trees seemed different. They were not taller or larger, but none of them had ever been cut. Perhaps the Lords protected their view of the forest from the woodsmen.

At Shanda's urging he kept moving until the city couldn't be seen at all. All was shadows and wilderness and the huge and ancient pillars.

"This won't hurt you," he said. "Watch your feet!" He walked a crooked path to a twisted trunk that was half bark, half glossy red wood.

"Freaky."

"Yeah. Firewand. This's all right too." A pine tree loomed huge next to children, but tiny beneath the redwoods. Whandall plucked a pine cone and gave it to her. "You can eat parts of this." And he showed her.

Pelzed had been impressed with his knowledge of the forest. Would Shanda's father?

Serana's packed lunch was clearly superior, but Shanda picked another pine cone to keep.

They were late starting home. Whandall didn't worry at first. He only gradually saw that as shadows grew long, the world lost detail. The sun was still up there somewhere, but not for them. You couldn't quite tell where anything was: paths, morningstars, touch-me, a sudden drop.

He found them a patch of clear ground while he still could.

There was a bit of lunch left over. No water. The leathers had been too hot during the day, but they were glad of them now. He and Shanda still had to curl up together for warmth.

He felt stirrings, remembering the clumsy coupling with Wess. Wess was older. He'd thought she would know more than he did. He might have been her first—she wouldn't say—and he still didn't really know how.

The plants were very close—the thought of getting touch-me between his legs made him shudder—and Shanda wasn't at all interested. Instead they lay looking at stars. A meteor flashed overhead.

"Lord Qirinty keeps hoping one of those will fall where he can find it," Shanda said. "But they never do."

Deep into the black night, when he felt her uncoiling from him, he made her piss right next to him where he knew it was safe. He held his own water until the first moments of daylight.

They could take off the masks when they got closer to the wall, but it wasn't safe to remove the leathers.

When they came in over the wall, Miss Bertrana was waiting by the rope. She took Shanda's hand. Whandall tried to run away, but two gardeners grabbed him. They didn't hurt him, but he couldn't get away. They followed Miss Bertrana and Shanda into the house.

Lord Samorty was sitting at a table talking to two guardsmen. Miss Bertrana brought Shanda to the table. Samorty eyed Shanda's leather leggings. "Where did you sleep?" he asked.

"In a clearing."

"Do you itch?"

"No, sir."

He turned to Whandall. "So you know the chaparral." He got up to inspect Whandall's earlobes. "Interesting. Who did you learn from?"

"Woodsmen."

"They taught you?" Disbelieving.

"No, Lord; we lurked."

Samorty nodded. "I've seen you before. Sit down. Miss Bertrana, I'll thank you to take Miss Shanda to your rooms and discover her condition."

"Sir?"

"You know very well what I mean."

"Oh. Yes sir," Miss Bertrana said.

Shanda started to protest. "Father—"

"Just go," Samorty said. He sounded weary and resigned to problems, and his voice was enough to cut Shanda's next protest off before it began. She followed Miss Bertrana out.

"Where have I seen you, boy?" Samorty demanded. He didn't seem angry, just annoyed by the distractions, and very weary.

Whandall didn't know what to say, so he stared at the table and said nothing. There was something carved into the table, lines, some curved, a big square shape with smaller square shapes in it . . .

"You like maps?" Samorty asked.

"I don't know," Whandall said.

"No, I guess you wouldn't," Samorty said. "Look. Think of this as a picture of the way the city would look if you were high above it. This is the Lord's Town wall." He indicated the square. "This is this house, and right here is where you two went over the wall."

Whandall's terror warred with curiosity. He bent over the carving to study it. "Is it magic, Lord?"

"Not now."

Whandall stared again. "Then—that's the sea?" he asked.

"Right. Now, how far from the wall before the chaparral gets really nasty?"

"Two hundred paces?" Whandall said. "Two hundred and it will hurt you. Five hundred and it kills."

"How far did you take my daughter?"

Whandall's voice caught in his throat.

"We know it was a long way because we saw you coming back," Samorty said. "And you were a lot more than five hundred paces out, far enough that nobody would go out after you. Where did you take her? Show me on this map."

"We had to go around a lot of . . . bad places," Whandall said. "So I'm not sure. Are these the trees?"

"Yes."

He put his finger into the forest. "About that far."

Samorty looked at him with new respect. "Is there hemp out there?"

"Yes, Lord, but it's dangerous."

"How?"

Kreeg Miller had told him a tale. "We heard the woodsmen say that once they found four men dead with smiles on their faces. They'd let one of the hemp plants catch them. They went to sleep and it strangled them."

Miss Bertrana came in without Shanda. "She's fine," she said.

"You're certain."

"Oh, yes sir, intact—no question about it. And there's no rash either."

"Good. Thank you. You may go."

"Yes, sir." Miss Bertrana escaped happily.

"Let me see your hands," Samorty said. He recoiled from the dirt and clapped his hands. "Washbasin," he said to the kinless who came in answer. "Now. Wash up," he told Whandall. His voice was almost friendly now.

Whandall washed his hands carefully. Whatever Miss Bertrana had said seemed to have calmed Samorty and given him some new energy, as if one of his problems didn't matter anymore. When Whandall was done washing, Samorty inspected his tattoo.

"Serpent's Walk," he said almost to himself. "I remember you. You brought Pelzed to see me."

"Yes, sir—"

"For which I thank you. What's your name?"

Whandall was too afraid to lie. "Whandall Placehold."

"Well, Whandall Placehold, there's no harm done here. You want those leathers? Keep them. And here." He went to a box on a table in the corner, and came back with a dozen shells. "Take these."

"Thank you, sir—"

"Now don't come back," Samorty said.

Whandall had never had a dream ripped out of him. It hurt more than he thought anything could.

Samorty clapped his hands and told the kinless servant, "Bring me Peacevoice Waterman. He should be just outside."

Peacevoice Waterman was big and almost certainly Lordkin.

"Peacevoice, this is Whandall Placehold. Take Whandall Placehold to the gate. Show him to the watch, and tell them he's not welcome here any longer."

"Sir."

"Tell him too," Samorty said.

When they reached the gate, Waterman took out his sword. "Easy or hard way, boy?" he demanded.

"I don't know what you mean—"

"Don't you? It's simple. Bend over, or I'll bend you over."

Whandall bent. Waterman raised the sword . . .

The flat of the sword made a loud whack as it hit Whandall's buttocks, but he was still wearing the leathers and it didn't really hurt at all. Not compared to the loss he felt. Waterman hit him five times more.

"All right. Get," Waterman said. "Go gather somewhere else."

"This was all given to me!"

"Good thing too," Waterman said. "Boy, you don't know how lucky you are. Now get out of here. Don't come back."

CHAPTER
11

Tras Preetror was both disappointed and intrigued. "For what that soap cost me," he said, "I could have got a dozen stories from that wizard. From you it's all hints at something bigger."

Whandall had not spoken of the map. He had to keep *something* back. He asked, "Wizard, Tras?"

"Morth of Atlantis. You must know him."

"Yes." Whandall didn't say that it was Morth of Atlantis he had seen at Lord Samorty's dinner.

"You have to go back, you know," Tras said.

Whandall felt his buttocks. He wasn't hurt this time. The leathers hadn't been interesting enough to attract attention from the Bull Pizzles, so he'd gotten home safely with the shells Lord Samorty had given him. Would woodsman's leathers help him win a fight or only hamper his swordplay?

But he remembered the sound of that sword hitting him. It was sharp, and if it hadn't been turned to hit him flat, he'd have lost a leg. Whandall was sure that even the flat would hurt dreadfully without the leathers. "No."

"Think of the stories," Tras said.

"They know me. They won't let me in."

"The tree—"

"They *know* about the *tree,* Tras," Whandall said.

"There has to be a way," Tras said. "Nobody talks about the Lordshills. Not the Lords, not the people who live there. There have to be stories."

"Morth has been to Lordshills, and he knows things he's never told the Lords. He brought water to Tep's Town," Whandall said. Maybe he could interest Tras in Morth and then he'd leave Whandall alone.

Whandall had forgotten Pelzed.

Ten days later he was summoned to the Serpent's Walk meetinghouse.

Pelzed was all smiles. He poured from a teapot and slid hot hemp tea over to Whandall. His eyes commanded. Whandall drank.

They drank hemp tea at Serpent's Walk meetings, but it was never as strong as this. Whandall was sweating and hungry before he drank half of it. His head—he heard things, pleasant sounds.

"The teller says you won't go back to Lord's Town," Pelzed said.

"Lord? You talk to Tras Preetror?"

"That's not your business."

"Did he tell you I got caught?" Whandall demanded.

"No. You look all right. Any broken bones?"

"No, Lord, b—"

Pelzed waved it away. "What did you see?"

"Redwoods," Whandall said. "The inside of a Lord's house, a big room where he calls people and gives orders." And a map. If he told Pelzed about maps he'd have to draw them for him. "A big Lordsman with a sword beat me and told me never to come back. So I won't, Lord." They would beat him, but worse, they would send him away again. Whandall had tried to forget Lordshills and the Gift of the King.

"Tras says he will pay for a new roof on the meetinghouse," Pelzed said.

"Tras is generous."

"If you take him to Lord's Town. Have some more tea."

"I can't go there!"

"Sure you can. Tell them I sent you," Pelzed said. "Tell them you have a message from Lord Pelzed of Serpent's Walk. They know me!" he said proudly.

A Lordkin should have guile. "They won't believe me," Whandall said. "You're important, but I'm just a boy they already threw out." Inspiration. "Why don't you go instead, Lord?"

Pelzed grinned. "No. But they'll believe Tras Preetror," he said. "He'll tell them. Have some more tea."

They'd told him never to come back. Maybe this way would work,

Whandall thought. His head buzzed pleasantly. This time he would watch, do nothing, learn the rules and customs.

The gardener's clothing wasn't fine enough for an emissary of Lord Pelzed. Pelzed sent gatherers to inspect the kinless shops. When they found something Tras Preetror thought might do, Serpent's Walk built a bonfire at the street corner nearest the shop. Others began making torches. Then Pelzed offered a trade: new clothes, and there wouldn't be a burning. The kinless were happy to accept.

Tras hired a wagon to take them to the Lord's Town gate. The kinless driver was astonished but willing so long as he didn't have to go further into Tep's Town than Ominous Hill.

Whandall took the opportunity to examine the ponies that pulled the wagon. The beasts tolerated Whandall's gaze but shied from his touch. Bony points protruded from the centers of their foreheads.

They passed the Black Pit. "You want to be a teller, you have to look for stories," Tras said. "There must be stories about the Black Pit."

Whandall gaped as if he'd never noticed the place before.

"Fire," the kinless wagoneer said. "Used to be fire pits, my grandfather said." His voice took on the disbelieving tone kinless used. "Fires and ghost monsters, until Yangin-Atep took the fires away. Now the Lords've put up a fence."

The guards watched with interest as they came up the hill. A quarter of the way up, the ponies slowed. The driver let them go on a few more paces, then stopped. "Far as I go."

"Why?" Tras Preetror asked.

"Bad on the ponies. Can't you see? Look at their foreheads."

Horns as long as a finger joint had shrunk to mere thorns. The beasts actually seemed to have *shrunk*.

Tras said, "But the hill's not that steep."

"Just the way it is here," the driver said.

"I saw horses go in the gate!" Whandall said. But they hadn't borne these bony nubs.

"Lord's horses. Bigger than my ponies." The driver shrugged. "Lord's horses can go up that hill. Mine can't."

"You were paid to take us to the gate!" Tras said.

The driver shrugged again.

"We'll have to walk, then," Tras said. "Not so dignified. Here, Whandall, stand straight. Look proud."

They walked the rest of the way up. "Let me do the talking," Tras said. He walked up to the guard. "We're emissaries from Serpent's Walk. That's

Whandall, nephew to Lord Pelzed of Serpent's Walk. We'd like to speak to Lord Samorty."

"Would you now?" the guard asked. "Daggett, I think you'd better go get the officer."

Tras began another speech. "Don't do you no good to talk to me," the guard said. "I sent for the officer. Save it for him. But you do talk pretty."

Whandall recognized the officer as Lord Qirinty. Peacevoice Waterman was with him.

"You, lad," Waterman said. "Didn't we tell you to stay away from here?" He turned to Qirinty and spoke rapidly, too low for Whandall to hear. Qirinty's eyes narrowed.

"We are emissaries from Lord Pelzed of Serpent's Walk, to talk about the new aqueduct," Tras said.

"And what would Lord Pelzed of Serpent's Walk have to do with the new aqueduct?" Qirinty asked. His voice was pleasant enough, but there was more curiosity than friendliness in it.

"He can get you some workers—"

Qirinty laughed. "Sure he can. Peacevoice, I don't think we need any more of this."

Waterman's badge of office was a large stick. He smiled pleasantly as he walked over to Tras Preetror and eyed his head expertly.

"Your superiors won't like—"

Waterman whacked Tras just over the right ear, and Tras dropped like a stone. Waterman nodded in satisfaction. "Mister Daggett, this one's for you," he said. "Sort of a bonus, like." He turned to Qirinty. "Now, about this lad—"

"Well, he doesn't learn very well, does he?" Qirinty asked. "He's done us no harm, and I believe you said Samorty's daughter likes him?"

"Yes, sir, I expect Miss Shanda won't like it a bit when we feed him to the crabs."

"That may be a bit drastic," Qirinty said. "But do see that he understands this time."

"Yes, sir."

This time Whandall wasn't offered a choice of hard or easy. Waterman swung the stick. When Whandall put his hands up to protect his head, the stick swung in an arc to his legs, hitting him just behind the knee. Whandall yelled in pain as he fell to the ground. He doubled over to protect himself.

The other guard kicked him in the back, just above the waist. Nothing that had ever happened to him hurt that bad.

"Now, now, Wergy," Waterman said to the guard. "He's going to need them kidneys to pee with."

"They didn't give me a choice!" Most of that came out as a scream as the stick descended, this time on Whandall's upper left arm, then swung instantly to hit his buttocks from behind. "They didn't. I had to come!" Another blow to his left arm. After that Whandall didn't notice who hit him or where. He just knew it went on for a long time.

CHAPTER
12

When he woke, it was dark. He felt a jolt and closed his eyes tightly, afraid he was being beaten again, but finally he opened them to see that he was in the back of the cart. They were just passing the Black Pit.

The kinless driver turned when he stirred. "You going to live?" he asked without much interest.

"Yes . . . thank you—"

"Had to come this way anyway," the driver said. "Here, have some water." He passed back a flask. Whandall's left arm wasn't working at all. He was surprised to find that his right would lift the flask to his lips. Every muscle of his body seemed to be throbbing in unison.

It was nearly dawn when they reached Peacegiven Square. The driver lifted him down from the wagon and left him lying by the fountain. His brothers found him just before noon.

It was late afternoon before Whandall remembered that Tras Preetror wasn't with him. He spent some hours wondering what might have happened to him. Maimed, flayed, impaled . . . were there cannibals among the ships of the harbor, to whom Tras Preetror might have been sold? Such thoughts gave him some comfort.

His left arm was broken. Other agonies masked the pain, and nobody ever set it. He cradled it, held it straight as best he could, and finally Mother's Mother used a strip of cloth to bind it rigidly against his chest. It healed a little crooked.

While Whandall lay healing in his room, his mind roamed free of probability and logic. Mad dreams, mad schemes chased each other through his head. Rescue Shanda from her unparents. Kill Pelzed, take his place, increase his power until he was the equal of a Lord. Become a teller, roam the world . . . which in his mind was a great foggy swirling wall of rainbow colors.

His mother had him moved to a room closer to hers, shared with her latest infant and three others. Mother's Mother brought him soup. It was all he was able to eat. Two days passed before he could get to a window to piss. A week before he could walk around Placehold.

A cousin and her man had gathered his room while he healed in the nursery.

He couldn't lift or gather. They set him to cleaning the kitchen and the public areas alongside much younger girls and boys.

Wess was with Vinspel, a dark man of Serpent's Walk who had been visiting Whandall's sister Ilyessa but found Wess more attractive. She avoided being caught talking to Whandall alone. When he ran her down, he saw a look in her eyes that made him wonder what he looked like. Crippled. Marred. He took to avoiding Wess. She didn't need more soap.

It was bad to be a weakling in Placehold, but the street would have killed him. When he could climb to the roof, they set him to working on the rooftop garden. It was less shameful than cleaning, and he couldn't be seen by anyone outside Placehold.

The Placehold had a large flat roof strong enough to support a foot of dirt and buckets of water. Rabbits couldn't get up there, and most insects didn't. Picking bugs off carrots was work for girls and young boys. Whandall resented having to do it, but there wasn't anything else for a one-armed boy who couldn't use a knife.

Like the plants of the forest, the crops fought back.

If they were attacked by rabbits or insects or pulled up when young, they developed poisons. You could pluck a young carrot or an ear of corn and cook it quickly and it wouldn't be deadly, but leave it a day and it would bring tumors and painful death. Traders sometimes bought Tep's Town root vegetables, and Whandall had once asked Tras Preetror what they did with them.

"Sell them to wizards," Tras had told him. "Most places, they'll kill even a wizard, but Tep's Town doesn't have so much magic. The plants still fight back, but not so hard. Wizards eat Tep's Town carrots to gain strength."

"Tras?"

"Anything that doesn't kill you makes you stronger," Tras had said in the voice he used when quoting somebody dead. Now Whandall remembered and hoped it was true.

Mostly, garden workers protected crops from rabbits and insects until they were big and old and tough. Plants gone to seed didn't care whether they were eaten. These they pulled up for food. Old carrots, onions, and potatoes would keep a long time.

It was work for kinless, but no kinless could be allowed up on the Placehold roof. Whandall found it a pleasant way to pass time. The work wasn't hard, except for carrying buckets of water up the stairs, and that was done in an hour each day. The rest was only tedious. He had to crawl along the vegetable rows looking for insects to kill. The view from the roof was wonderful.

Whandall remembered the carving on Lord Samorty's table. A "map." From the roof Whandall could see all of Serpent's Walk and some of the other band territories and could see where people went on Mother's Day and afterward. He tried to draw the patterns.

A room opened up for him just when living with crying and crawling infants was about to drive him crazy. Shastern led him to a tiny room just below the roof. He'd have to do something about the unwashed smell . . . which suddenly struck him as familiar.

"Lenorba's room," he said.

"Was."

"Where is she?"

"Nobody knows. We needed an extra woman at the last Mother's Day. We took Lenorba. Of course we stopped at the border of Peacegiven Square and the women went on. Lenorba never came back. They got her."

Whandall nodded. It was thirteen years ago, and most people must have forgotten what Lenorba had done . . . yet he could feel no surprise.

His arm stopped hurting, and eventually he took off the swaddling strip Mother's Mother had used to bind it up. The arm was crooked, but he could use it. Hauling water up the stairs helped strengthen it. Picking insects off carrots gave him skill in small movements.

After Whandall's arm healed, he took his knife lessons seriously, although the instruction was haphazard. Whandall thought about each lesson and practiced on the roof. He wondered why you did things a certain way. Then he discovered that if he practiced foot movements with no knife, his arms just held out defensively, he could concentrate on getting the steps exactly right. Then he thought about the cloak over his left arm, moving that as a shield, and learned precisely where his arm should be to protect against a thrust or a slash. Then he learned knife movements, standing still and concentrating on his hand and arm. Each time he thought about getting one thing right.

His uncles and cousins had nearly given up in disgust, thinking Whandall slow and simple. "Must have got hit in the head," one of his uncles said, not bothering to lower his voice so Whandall wouldn't hear. Whandall went on practicing, one move at a time, concentrating on getting each one just right.

When Whandall thought he had learned all the moves they would teach him, he put them all together.

His uncles were astonished at the result. Suddenly he could best his cousins, younger and older, in mock duels with wooden knives. He was growing stronger, and now he was quick and deceptively fast, and he used his limbs effectively. One day he bested Resalet. The next, Resalet and his grandson working together. That was the day they pronounced him ready to go to the streets again and gave him a knife of his own. They said it had belonged to Pothefit. Whandall knew better, but the lie pleased him.

Even so, he was wary on the streets. Rumor said that Pelzed was most unhappy with him. His first foray was a walk with his brothers, a seeking for conversation . . . and he found he was treated with respect. He was Whandall of Serpent's Walk, and so long as he stayed in the Walk or allied territory, he was safe. He thought of asking for a face tattoo, but he put that off. He still had sores on his head, and a scar at his left eye. It was an angry red ring with a white center, painful to touch. His left arm was shorter than his right. In time the pain faded, but he grew slowly.

PART TWO

Adolescent

CHAPTER
13

Girls. Suddenly they snagged at Whandall's eyes. The sight of a pretty girl held all of his attention. If he was talking to Lordkin or gathering from a kinless, a clout across the head might be his first return to sanity.

What had changed? Whandall's loins worried at him like a bad tooth.

Girls weren't eager to go with a scarred thirteen-year-old with no tattoo.

He'd avoided Wess while he was healing. He didn't want her to see him that way. Now Wess was avoiding *him*, and Vinspel wouldn't let a man near her anyway. The other boys found ribald amusement in the ring-shaped scar at his eye. Maybe it was even worse than he'd guessed.

Other boys talked about girls they'd had, and Whandall joined in, telling stories as Tras Preetror had taught him. You didn't doubt another boy's story. If he needed to prove himself a man, he might do it with a knife.

Whandall could do that. The first time a Bull Pizzle challenged him, Whandall had startled him and everyone else. The fight was over before it started, the Pizzle disarmed with a cut across the back of his hand. Whandall could have killed him easily, but that would start a blood feud. Instead he took his knife. The next day two more Bull Pizzles challenged him. They were both young, with knives but no face tattoos. In minutes Whandall had two more knives. Then Lord Pelzed and the Bull Pizzles met, and Whandall was told to stay out of Pizzle territory, and everyone left him alone.

His skill impressed his uncles but not the girls. What did impress them? No man knew.

Girls were never found alone. They were with older, tougher boys, or even men; a few had brothers who guarded them fiercely. Whandall spoke of trying his new skill with a knife. The next night he was summoned to speak with Resalet.

"So you're able to fight all of Bull Pizzle, and possibly Owl Beak as well," Resalet said. "Alone, without help. It seems we taught you well."

Whandall at thirteen thought he was immortal, but part of him knew better. There was a black pit in his stomach when he said, "Only kinless are abandoned by their kin."

Resalet said, "Now think on this. You will fight for a woman. You will win, and her man, or his brothers, or *her* brothers, or all of those, will fight you. You are skilled, but you're small. Blood will flow. Someone will die. When you are killed, the Placehold will demand blood money from those who killed you." He eyed Whandall carefully. "For fools we don't need *much* blood money."

Whandall shuffled his feet, unable to reply.

"You're too young to fight for a woman," Resalet told him.

"I feel like I could," Whandall said.

Resalet grinned, showing wide gaps in his teeth. "Know what you mean. But the Placehold can't start a war over getting you a woman. Shall we buy you a woman for a night?"

Whandall understood that the word *buy* was an insult. Still, he considered the offer. . . .

There were women who lived with their children but no men. Some were always popular. Others might have a suitor for a few days after Mother's Day; then they were around for a jewel or a shell or a skirt, or a shared meal and a place to sleep, or for nothing. What would any of them do for soap? But Tras's soap had near killed Whandall, and Tras was dead or gone, and what kind of woman would look at a strange, scarred boy this soon after Mother's Day?

"Not just yet," he said, "but thanks."

Resalet nodded sagely. "You'll be a good Lordkin, someday. But you're not one yet. Grow more before you take a tattoo."

"You won't take my knife!"

"No. But carry it softly while you grow."

Ask! But who could he talk to? Boys his age were afraid of him, and older boys laughed because he knew so little. His mother had no time for him.

He used a shell Samorty had given him to buy a melon—fruit soft enough to eat without teeth—and brought it to Mother's Mother. Dargramnet hacked it with her sleeve knife and ate it noisily.

"Girls," Whandall prompted, and waited.

The thin lips parted in a smile. "Yes, yes, I see them now. Not like they were when I was a girl. Go with anyone now. They'll learn. Too late, they'll learn too late. I warned them, I warned them all. It's very hot today, isn't it?"

She didn't always hear or remember what Whandall said. Whandall wasn't sure she knew who he was. Still, the stretch of years within her mind must be worth exploring. What had the girl Dargramnet wanted in a man?

He asked, "What were the men like?"

Mother's Mother spoke of the men she'd known. Strif, Bloude, Gliraten—old lovers came and went in Dargramnet's mind as they must have in life, interchangeable inside broken stories, until Whandall couldn't tell one from another. Her second son Pothefit, strong enough to lift a wagon, stubborn as a Lord. Wanshig and Whandall, her first grandsons, Thomer's sons by Pothefit and Resalet, cousins who shared everything. "Most of them dead, now. Killed in knife fights. Burnings. Just gone."

Whandall nodded. Many of the boys he'd grown up with were dead. They'd survived the forest, but not the city. Tep's Town killed boys. Did other cities? Did boys die so young in Lord's Town or in the Lordshills or Condigeo?

One could watch and try to learn.

Unattached women without kin to protect them were hard to find, and they wanted big men to be with . . . except on Mother's Day. The Lords didn't give their gifts to women who had men. Women went to Peacegiven Square alone, and one need only listen to learn who had a man waiting.

Most girls wanted to marry. Most men didn't, but they wanted their sisters married. One or two of Whandall's sisters' friends might be ready to marry, but that was too big a bite for Whandall at thirteen.

Not that he'd reasoned any of this out, exactly. But every Lordkin knew that there was a time when a man need not ask. Whandall remembered a high optimism, a firelight feast for eyes grown bored with daylight, frenzy and excitement, couples pairing off, when he was seven years old. . . .

"Shig, when will the Burning come?"

Wanshig laughed. "You're a looker now?"

They were at dinner in the Placehold courtyard. The sky was red with sunset. Speech ran softly round the circle of adults and the smaller circle of children.

Wanshig was eighteen now. He'd watched Whandall practicing with his knife and twice had joined him on the roof, not ashamed to learn from his younger brother. Whandall liked him best of all his kin.

Now Wanshig set his spoon down and said, "Nobody knows. Long ago it was once a year. Now, every four or five. Even when Mother was a little girl, they couldn't tell anymore. Maybe gods sleep, like your Uncle Cartry after a Lordsman whacked his head. Maybe Yangin-Atep isn't dead—he just never wakes up."

"Did Yangin-Atep take you?"

Wanshig laughed again. "No! I was only . . . twelve, I think."

"*Someone*, then."

"They say Yangin-Atep possessed Alferth and Tarnisos. You don't know them, Whandall. They're crazy enough without help. All I know is, we see fires south of us, smoke blowing our way. Resalet whoops and dives into Carraland's Fine Clothes, and we all follow. Carraland runs away shouting out looker gibberish—"

"What happened to Pothefit?"

That snapped Wanshig out of his wistful nostalgia. "Whandall, do you remember when they came in with the cook pot?"

"Yes, Shig."

Pothefit and Resalet were shadows against the dancing blaze from the granary, carrying the cauldron through Placehold's main door while Wanshig and another brother pretended to help.

"We gathered it out of a wizard's shop on Market Round. We piled stuff in the cook pot too, but we went back for more, and to burn the place. An Atlantis wizard, a stranger, he didn't know any better than to come back to his shop during the Burning. He found us. Pothefit was trying to set the shelves alight. The wizard waved his hand and said something, and Pothefit just fell over. Rest of us got away."

Lord Samorty's courtyard . . . "I saw him. Morth of Atlantis."

"Me too. That shop on Market Round, he built it again after the Burning."

"No, Shig, Morth of Atlantis was too old for that. He was almost dead."

"Right, and cook fires burn inside. Whandall, that is Morth of Atlantis, the shop on Market Round."

"Where does he go at night?"

Wanshig cuffed him hard enough to make the point. "Don't even think it. Never remember a killing after the Burning."

Whandall rubbed his ear. "Shig, you've killed."

"Barbarians, lookers, kinless, uglies, anyone who's insulted you . . . you can kill. But that's only during the Burning, Whandall, and it's not a big part of it. It's only . . . it's bad to hold your anger locked in your belly for too long. You have to let it go."

Something in the conversation had attracted Resalet's attention. "Whandall, how do you reckon we keep the Placehold when everybody wants it?"

"We watch. We can fight—"

"We can fight," Resalet said. "But we couldn't fight everyone."

"Serpent's Walk," Whandall said.

Resalet nodded gravely. "But Serpent's Walk can't fight Bull Pizzle and Owl Beak and Maze Walkers all together. And what happens if Lord Pelzed wants to live *here?*"

Whandall had never thought of *that.*

Resalet grinned, showing as many black spaces as teeth. "We're smarter than they are. We have rules," he said. "And the first one is, don't start fights you can't win. Don't even start fights that will cost you strength. But once you do get in a fight, win it no matter what happens, no matter what it costs. Always win! Always win big. Make an example of your enemies, every time."

"Lords do that too." They'd done it to Whandall. "What if you can't win?"

Resalet's grin widened. "You never think about that once it's started." He went back to his soup.

Whandall was about to say something, but Wanshig put his bowl aside and stood up. "Show you something."

"What?"

"Come on." Wanshig pulled a burning stick from the cook fire and ran, whirling it round his head.

He was through the courtyard's narrow entrance with Whandall just behind him. The flame gleamed pale in the dusk. Wanshig skidded around another corner, crossed the street diagonally, and . . .

Whandall, running behind him, saw Wanshig hurl the torch through the window of Goldsmith's wire jewelry shop. The owner was just about to pull the shutter down for the night. He screeched as the torch went past his ear—

And the flame snuffed out.

Wanshig kept running past the store, whooping. Whandall followed. In the shadow of an alley they stopped to breathe, then to laugh.

"See? If the Burning isn't on us, indoor fires just go out. Then maybe you get laughed at and maybe you get beat up, depending. *So don't be the one to start the Burning.* Let someone else do it." Wanshig grinned. "You were about to get a beating," he said.

"I just wanted to know—"

"You wanted to know what happens if so many come after us that we can't win," Wanshig said. "Whandall, you know what would happen. We'd run away. But Resalet can't say that! Not even inside the Placehold. If the story got out that you could take the Placehold without killing every one of us, that any of us even thinks that way—we're gone."

CHAPTER
14

One day a fire began in the brush behind a kinless house just outside Serpent's Walk territory. All the kinless in that area turned out. They brought a big wagon pulled by the small kinless ponies. It had a tank on it, and kinless men dipped water from it and threw it on the fire until it was out.

Whandall watched from behind a flowering hedge. On the way home he gathered an apple to give Resalet.

"Why do they bother? The fire would go out. Wouldn't it?" Whandall asked.

Resalet was in a mellow mood. "Kinless don't believe in Yangin-Atep," he said. "So Yangin-Atep doesn't always protect them. Against *us*, yes, unless there's a Burning. Sometimes against accidents. Not always, and the kinless don't wait to find out."

"Those wagons—"

"They keep them in the stable area," Resalet said.

"What if the fire is too far away?"

Resalet shrugged. "I've seen them turn out with buckets when there's water in the River of Spirits."

The River of Spirits flowed out of the forest and down through Lordkin territory before it reached the kinless area. It stank. Whandall thought he'd rather see Placehold burn than have a fire put out with what was in that river.

There was much to learn about Yangin-Atep, and one could ask. Mother's Mother told him some. When she was a girl she had heard a tale that the kinless had once been warriors with a god of their own, before Yangin-Atep and the Lords brought the Lordkin to Tep's Town. She couldn't remember who had told her the story, and she thought the days were hotter than they used to be.

Days were long for Whandall. He was smaller than other boys his age, and the months spent healing, and afterward doing children's work, had lost him what friends he might have had. His best friend was his older brother Wanshig, and Shig didn't always want a smaller boy hanging around with him.

There was little to do. His uncles were content to have him hang around Placehold in case of need, but that was no life.

His younger brother Shastern had grown while Whandall was recovering. Now anyone seeing them together took Shastern for the elder. Shastern was deeply involved in Serpent's Walk activities. He was leader of a band that gathered from the kinless in Owl Beak.

"Come with us, Whandall," Shastern urged. "Lord Pelzed wants us to look at a street in Bull Pizzle territory."

"Why? I can't run fast."

"No, but you can lurk. If you don't do it, I'll have to."

Whandall thought about that. "You didn't used to be very good at lurking."

"I'm learning. But you're better."

"What are we looking for?" Whandall asked.

"Dark Man's Cup Street. It's right at the border—"

"I know where it is," Whandall said. "There's nothing there! Shaz, there's nothing to gather. What would Lord Pelzed want with that place?"

Shastern shook his head. "He didn't tell me. He said to find who's living there now. When was the last time you were there?"

Whandall thought back. "Six weeks? I was following a kinless, but maybe he knew I was behind him." Whandall shrugged. "I lost him in the trash on that street. It's that bad."

"Come tell Lord Pelzed."

"I think he's mad at me—"

Shastern shook his head. "Not that I know of. Whandall, you have to see him sometime. This way you can do him a favor."

"All right." Whandall felt his heart beat faster. Suppose Pelzed—Lord Pelzed!—wanted him to pay for the cart and clothes? Or the roof Tras Preetror had promised? But Shastern was right—he had to know sometime.

Pelzed found time for the boys that afternoon. "Shastern says you followed a kinless to Dark Man's Cup," he said. "Have some tea."

The tea was weak and didn't do anything to Whandall's head. He sipped and found it good. "He was kinless," Whandall said, "but he didn't live there."

"Who does?"

"I only saw some women."

"Lordkin?"

"Yes. I think so," Whandall said. "Lord Pelzed, Dark Man's Cup looks like there hasn't been a kinless there for years! It's all trash and weeds in the street, and it stinks."

"Children?"

"Two babies," Whandall said. "Dirty, like their mothers."

"No men?"

"I didn't see any."

"Go find out," Pelzed said.

"Lord—"

"Go find out. There'll be men. Find out who they are."

"Lord, why? There's nothing there!"

"But there could be," Pelzed said. "And I'll send Tumbanton with you. Have some more tea."

Dark Man's Cup lay on the other side of a small gully that had running water during the rainy season but was usually dry. The creek bed was filled with trash and sewage, and there was no bridge. Three boys and an older man picked their way through the trash, with Whandall in the lead.

Tumbanton was usually seen at Pelzed's right hand. He was the whip hand, the trainer, when a boy joined Serpent's Walk. He'd saved Pelzed's life twenty-six years ago, when they were both no more than gatherers. He'd defended their retreat when a raid on Maze Walkers went disastrously wrong. Six had died. Tumbanton and Pelzed had escaped. Tumbanton usually went without a shirt to show the maze of scars from that event. He loved to tell the story.

But he'd picked up a trace of a limp too, and a noisy, wobbly walk. His son Geravim, with no scars to speak of, seemed as clumsy as his father.

"What's Pelzed want with this place anyway?" Geravim asked as he shook filth off his sandals.

Tumbanton must know that, but he didn't speak.

"Maybe he thinks he can get the kinless to build a bridge," Shastern said.

"Wish they'd done it already," Geravim muttered.

And why would they, when the Lords and Lordkin would only gather what they built? But they did. Kinless did work, sometimes, and only men like Pelzed knew why.

Pelzed's family had never been important. How *had* he become Lord Pelzed?

Whandall caught a whiff of cooking meat. It was faint, nearly masked by the smells of sewage and decay, but it was there.

"Something?" Shastern asked.

"Probably not," Whandall said. "Wait here, I'll be right back."

There was no wind, but when he'd smelled the cook fire there had been a puff of air from the south. Whandall went that way, downstream if there had been any water in the gully. There were thickets of greasewood and sharp plants like lordswords except these were smaller and didn't move to strike at him. Another patch looked like a variety of lordkiss, three leaves and white berries, but the leaves were sickly red. Ahead was a patch of holly, thorns, and berries. There was a tunnel in the thorns and rabbit droppings on the path. He sniffed. Fresh.

The way led steeply down. The center of the gully was deep, a dry streambed, but on the sides there were shelves of flat land fifty feet wide and nearly that far above the streambed. Above them were thickets all the way to the top of the gully and beyond, but the shelves themselves had clear patches among the weeds and chaparral. The smell of cooking meat got stronger as he went south. When he reached the end of the narrow twisting passage through the holly bushes he stayed prone and used his knife to part the weeds ahead of him so he could look without being seen.

He saw a cook fire. A slab of meat roasted on a spit above it. Behind the fire was a cave into the gully bank. The entrance was hidden from above and most other directions by holly bushes and scrub oak.

Three kinless men sat by the fire. They were sharpening axes. A kinless girl came out of the cave and put sticks on the fire.

A patch of hemp grew just beyond the camp area. These plants seemed different from the hemp that grew in the fields between Tep's Town and the Lordshills, taller and more lushly green. As the girl passed, Whandall saw the plants stir in a breeze he couldn't feel. Wild plants would have done that too.

Whandall couldn't make out what the kinless men were saying. He wriggled backward until he could turn around, then went back to Shastern and the others.

"Find something?" Shastern asked.

Whandall shook his head. He might have spoken, but Geravim and Tumbanton weren't relatives. The rogue kinless wouldn't have much worth gathering, but he'd keep this a secret for the family.

The gully had always been a no-man's-land, used as a garbage dump by Serpent's Walk and Bull Pizzle alike and serving as an easily recognized boundary. Dark Man's Cup was the first street on the other side, about a hundred feet from the gully. Beyond it was a tangle of streets and thistle fields mixed together before the town proper started again.

There were nine houses on Dark Man's Cup. Five had roofs. One of the roofless houses was stone and would be a good house if someone could make the kinless build a roof. Two of the roofless structures had been used as garbage dumps and outhouses, and only three of the houses with roofs seemed to be inhabited. Those stood apart, three houses together along a field partially cleared of weeds.

Every wall of every house, inhabited or not, had a Bull Pizzle mark. They watched a boy about Shastern's age repainting the Bull Pizzle mark on his front wall.

Whandall left Shastern and the others at the edge of the gully and crept through the trash piles in the yards behind the houses. Each household had a small cleared patch in back where they built the cook fires and another small area where children played. Weeds grew everywhere, even in the cleared patches. Everything stank. One house had a dog, but it didn't seem interested in anything outside its own yard.

There were snares in the animal paths behind the houses. Whandall automatically avoided them as he crept toward the inhabited area. He moved quickly but silently, and no one noticed him. Whandall grinned to himself. Watching the kinless woodsmen had been good practice.

Whandall saw only four men. Two were ancient and sat in toothless conversation near a cook fire in one of the yards. One was about twenty. The other was the boy who had repainted the Bull Pizzle sign.

Whandall watched to see if anyone else would come. Then he heard a rustling behind him.

He turned see Shastern coming. Shaz walked carelessly along a game path—

"Watch out! Traps," Whandall said. He tried to keep his voice low, but one of the old men must have kept his hearing.

"Spies!" the old man shouted. "Spies! Bull Pizzle! Spies!"

And the warning had done no good. Shastern was entangled in a snare. When it tripped him another snare caught his arm.

There were shouts from somewhere to the east.

Whandall ran back to Shastern. When he reached him, there were more shouts, louder.

"Bull Pizzles coming," Shastern said. "Cut me loose!"

It was hard to cut the leather thongs without hurting Shastern. Finally Whandall had his brother's arm free. Together they freed his legs. Shastern stood and grinned feebly.

"Now what?" Whandall asked.

"Now we run like hell, big brother!" Shastern said. He ran for a few yards, then went down as another snare caught him. By the time Whandall had helped cut him free, the shouts of the Bull Pizzle warriors were much closer. They couldn't see anyone, but it sounded like the warriors were just behind them. Shastern ran in bounding leaps, hoping to avoid the snares.

Whandall ran behind him, watching for traps, as Shastern got farther and farther ahead.

Geravim and Tumbanton were gone. Shastern was far ahead, and Whandall heard shouts behind him. He was nearly winded. They would catch him soon. Better to stop while he could still fight.

He looked for a place to stop. A corner would be best, but there weren't any. There weren't even walls here. The best refuge he could see was a holly bush. It would be useless against a spear but it would protect his back from knives. He ran to the holly bush, scooped a handful of dirt, jacket over his left arm, turned. The big Lordkin knife felt good in his hand and he tried to grin as he'd seen big Lordkin men do when they were menacing kinless.

There were only three of the Bull Pizzles. All were bigger than Whandall, the oldest probably twenty. He had seen none of them before. Whoever lived on Dark Man's Cup was content to let others defend it for them.

One had a knife. That didn't worry Whandall, but another had a big club studded with obsidian blades. The third boy had a rock tied onto a long rawhide thong. He swung it around his head in a lazy circle, the rock still moving fast enough that if it hit Whandall it would brain him.

As the first Bull Pizzle came toward him Whandall threw dirt into his face, then lunged forward, slashing, before retreating to his bush. Blood flowed from the Bull Pizzle's chest and the knifeman howled in pain.

The older boy had the club. He gestured to his companions to spread out. "He's fast, but he can't get us all." The Bull Pizzle leader grinned. A tattoo marked his left eye. "What you doing here, boy? Looking to get killed? What band marks itself with a *target?*"

Target? Oh, he meant the scar around Whandall's eye.

Whandall looked for a way out. There didn't seem to be one. "We were following a kinless for shells," Whandall said. "But we lost him, then my . . . friend was caught in a snare. We did you no harm."

"You're in Pizzle territory," the older boy said, then glanced expertly at Whandall's hand. "We don't want Snakes here!" He gestured again, to spread the other two out farther. The boy with a knife had stopped snuffling when he found that his cut wasn't serious. Now he tried to rub the dirt from his eyes. He moved over to Whandall's left side, away from Whandall's knife. His knife was held clumsily. A beginner, Whandall thought. He'd be no problem at all.

The club worried him. It was long enough to reach him before he could strike. Whandall had never faced a club before. "You scared to use a knife?" Whandall taunted.

"No, just careful," the older boy said. "You want to give up?"

"What happens if I do?"

The club man shrugged. "Up to our chief," he said. "Don't know what

Wulltid will want to do with you. Can't be worse than what we'll do if you don't give up!"

The problem was, it could be. On the other hand, Pelzed might ransom him, since he'd been sent by Pelzed. There wasn't an active war with Bull Pizzle. But Pelzed wouldn't be happy . . .

"You going to give up?" the club wielder asked. "Running out of time—"

"I have lots of time," Whandall said. He'd caught his breath now. The situation was bad. The boy with the bola had moved well off to Whandall's right and was swinging it faster now.

The club man raised his weapon. "Last chance."

"Yangin-Atep!" Whandall shouted. "Yangin-Atep!"

The Bull Pizzle leader was startled for a moment. He looked around as if expecting the fire god to appear. Then he laughed. "Yangin-Atep loves Bull Pizzle as much as Snake Shit!" he roared.

"Which is not at all," the knifeman said. "Maddog, I don't care if he gives up—I get to cut him!"

"Yeah, I think so. Yangin-Atep! Yangin-Atep isn't going to wake for you."

Whandall didn't think so either, but it had been worth trying.

"Serpent's Walk!" The shout came from the gully.

"Snake Feet!" Whandall answered.

"Coming!" It was Shastern's voice. There was wild thrashing in the gully. "We're coming!"

Maddog listened. It sounded like half a dozen Serpent's Walk warriors, and he didn't like the odds. "Stay out of Pizzle territory!" he shouted. He gestured to the others, and they withdrew toward the east.

As soon as they were away, Whandall ran toward the gully and over the lip. Shastern was there alone. He had a tree branch and was bashing at the chaparral. "We're coming!"

"Good to see you, Shaz," Whandall said.

Shastern grinned. "Good to see you, big brother. Now let's run before they find out it's just me!"

"Geravim and Tumbanton?"

"Ran."

CHAPTER
15

Pelzed listened carefully to Whandall's account. "No one important living there," he said. "None of the people who chased you live there. You're sure?"

"Yes, Lord." Whandall hesitated. "Lord, may I ask—"

Pelzed's eyes narrowed. "Thinking of taking my place?"

"No, Lord. I couldn't do it," Whandall said.

Pelzed considered that. "I think you're smart enough to believe that," he said. "Whandall, what I'm looking for is territory we can claim."

"But it's not worth claiming!" Whandall exclaimed.

Pelzed smiled. "Glad you think so. If you think it's worthless, Wulltid of Bull Pizzle will be sure of it."

Pelzed and Wulltid met in Peacegiven Square under the watchful eye of the patrolling Lordsmen. They had agreed to bring only four men each. Wulltid brought four great hulking bodyguards. Pelzed had two of his regular guards, but he also brought Whandall and Shastern.

"You raided my territory," Wulltid began abruptly.

"Calm," Pelzed said. "Have some tea." He poured from a stone jug wrapped in straw to keep it hot. The cups had been kept warm the same way. Pelzed lifted his cup, sipped, and nodded. "So. Greetings, Chief Wulltid."

Wulltid stared sourly at Pelzed, lifted his cup, and drank. "That's pretty good," he admitted. "Greetings, Lord Pelzed. But you still raided my territory."

Pelzed swept his hand to indicate Whandall and Shastern. "I sent these two boys to see what you've made of Dark Man's Cup," Pelzed said. "Which is nothing at all. Two boys, to a street you don't care about. Now how's that a raid?"

"Still my territory," Wulltid said.

"Let's talk about that. What will you take for it? Hemp? How much hemp? Maybe some tar?"

"Hemp? Tar?" Wulltid glared at Whandall. "Boy, what did you find there? Gold?"

"Trash. It's a trash heap, Chief Wulltid," Whandall said. He turned to Pelzed and repeated, "A trash heap, Lord!"

"So why does your boss want that place?" Wulltid demanded.

Whandall's perplexity was genuine.

"It's simple enough," Pelzed said. "I've got some relatives who need homes, and some kinless who'll build for them. Need a place. Dark Man's Cup won't be too bad once all the trash is thrown in the gully."

"That's what I thought," Wulltid said. "But the kinless I put in there wouldn't stay. Yours won't either."

"That's my problem," Pelzed said. "Now just what do you want for the Cup? It's not like it's worth much."

"What if I said I don't believe you?" Wulltid said pleasantly. "There's more to this."

"They're not close kin. . . ." Pelzed smiled. "Lord Samorty asked me. The Lords want that area cleaned up."

"Why?"

"Who knows why Lords want things? But they asked me."

"What did they offer?"

Pelzed sighed. "Five bales of hemp."

"Five! They only gave me three!"

"You took it? But you didn't get it clean," Pelzed said.

Wulltid scratched his head. "I tried. I could have kept that place clear for two years. Three, even. But that Gemwright wanted five years! I had to promise five! Gemwright—he's one crazy kinless."

"You didn't even give him two years," Pelzed said cheerfully. "Bull Pizzles were gathering in the Cup a year after the kinless moved in."

Wulltid sipped tea without comment.

"So the work stopped. You couldn't keep your people from gathering, the kinless moved out, and now you're stuck protecting a place that nobody worth anything will live in! Chief, I'm doing you a favor taking that slum off your hands. But I'll give you half a bale."

"You're getting five bales," Wulltid said. "I want two for Dark Man's Cup."

"One," Pelzed said. "You have three already."

"Two."

"All right. Two," Pelzed said. "But we get a Lord's Witness to this deal."

Wulltid shrugged. "You'll pay him, then. I won't."

The Lord's Witness was accompanied by two Lordsmen guards and a kinless clerk no more than Whandall's age. The clerk dressed like servants Whandall had seen in Lordshills. The Witness wore a tight-fitting cap that completely covered his ears, and dark robes of office.

The clerk spoke in a high-pitched voice. "You wish the attention of a Lord's Witness? That will be ten shells in advance."

Pelzed laid them in a row, one smooth motion, ten shells marked by a Lord's Clerk. The clerk swept them into a leather pouch. He turned to the Witness. "They have paid, Honorable."

The Witness sat down to listen.

"An agreement between Lord Pelzed of Serpent's Walk and Chief Wulltid of Bull Pizzle," the clerk said. "Speak, Wulltid of Bull Pizzle."

"We give the street known as Dark Man's Cup to Serpent's Walk," Wulltid said. "Serpent's Walk will complete what's left of the work Bull Pizzle was paid to do. We will remove all Bull Pizzle people within two days and never return. Serpent's Walk has to repaint all the signs; we won't do that."

The clerk wrote on what looked like a sheet of thin white leather. When Pelzed tried to speak, the clerk held up a hand until he had finished writing. "Now. Speak, Pelzed of Serpent's Walk."

"We will complete the work offered by Lord Samorty's clerk. The Lords will pay us five bales of hemp and two buckets of tar. We will pay two bales of hemp to Bull Pizzle.

"In return, all trash will be removed from the street and yards, five houses of kinless will be established, and no one will gather in Dark Man's Cup for five years."

The clerk wrote again. "Do both of you accept this?" he demanded. "Then mark this vellum. Thank you. That will be twenty more shells."

Afterward, Pelzed was talkative and amused. "It was easy!" he crowed. "Wulltid never suspected a thing!"

Whandall didn't ask, but he *looked.* Pelzed laughed. "We had no way to expand in that area because of the gully," he said. "I've always wanted something on the other side. The gully may be worth something. Clean it up and a kinless could grow hemp there, I think."

Whandall remembered the hidden kinless camp.

"So I wanted it," Pelzed said. "I could have bought it, maybe, but this way is better. Look, Whandall—now the Lords know Bull Pizzle took their three bales, and two more of mine, and did nothing for it. Five bales for nothing. I'm getting the three Bull Pizzle got, and I'll get it cleaned up."

Whandall waited a respectful moment. "How, Lord?"

"My kinless believe me when I tell them they'll have five years with no gathering," Pelzed said. "Do you believe me, Whandall?"

Whandall didn't answer instantly. Pelzed asked, "You know Fawlith?"

"The beggar who babbles all the time?"

"That's him. We caught him and his brother gathering on a street where I promised the kinless we'd leave them alone."

"I didn't know he had a brother."

Pelzed just grinned. "Want to live in a house of your own?" he asked. "I'll need two Lordkin families in the Cup. To watch over the kinless there. Ready to start a family?"

Whandall thought about it for a moment. "Thank you, no, Lord, I have a home." He shrugged. "I don't have a woman."

"Fine house will get you a woman," Pelzed said. "Even with that eye. But you're young. Ask me when you're ready. I owe you for this."

"Three of them," Shastern said, much later. "And you held them off until I scared them away. Tell me how to do that."

Whandall tried to explain. He told Shastern how he'd practiced each move, thinking about that and nothing else, and how it had taken months.

Shastern didn't believe him. There had to be a secret that Whandall wasn't telling him. Shastern left in disgust, leaving Whandall more alone than ever.

CHAPTER
16

As the scars of Burning faded, the lookers dwindled. They never went away entirely. Though Tras Preetror was gone, other tellers remained.

A teller gave Shastern a handful of fruit to torch Carver's lumberyard. At a dead run and with a blood-curdling whoop, Shastern hurled paired torches past a heap of beam ends and into the work shed. The fires went out, of course. Shastern shared the fruit around afterward.

They never told the lookers what happened to fires outside the shed.

Whandall liked lookers. Like most kinless, they made little trouble when their things disappeared. A looker who made a fuss would be returned to the docks in bruised condition, and who would complain? Many—not just tellers—carried little flasks of wine as gifts in return for stories or guidance. Some carried preserved fruit for children. And, of course, they told stories.

In spring again, three years after the beating, Pelzed summoned Whandall to his roofless hall.

Tumbanton wasn't about. It came to Whandall that he hadn't seen Tumbanton or Geravim the last few times Pelzed summoned him. Tumbanton and his son might be avoiding Whandall, after leaving Whandall and Wanshig to the mercy of the Bull Pizzles.

These days Whandall had the status of a man, even though he had not selected his tattoo. Tentatively he opened conversation with some of Pelzed's men and found them speaking openly, treating him as an equal.

But when he asked after Tumbanton, nobody wanted to hear that question. Whandall hid his amusement and, naively, asked after Geravim too.

Talk died. Whandall meandered casually toward Pelzed's rooms. He'd best not name those names again until he knew more.

The Serpent's Walk Lord offered hemp tea, and waited until Whandall had sipped before he spoke. "Tras Preetror is back."

Whandall stared. "I thought they'd fed him to the crabs!"

"Seems not. He owes me a new roof. Anyway, I'd like to hear his story. Wouldn't you?"

Whandall had learned caution. He only nodded, *Go on.*

"I want to meet him, but I hadn't decided who to send. Anyone else, he might not pay attention. If I send you, he'll try to explain what went wrong. Bring him here, right?"

"Lord, I am your messenger and no more. He comes or he doesn't. Where would I find him?"

"Nobody knows." Pelzed smiled; the tea was making him mellow. "Not in the Lordshills, I think."

Tumbanton thought Pelzed owed him. Pelzed might be tired of hearing it.

Tumbanton had heard Pelzed's prohibitions but might think himself an exception.

Tumbanton and his son had explored Dark Man's Cup. It gave them a proprietary interest. . . .

Whandall couldn't ask around Pelzed. He couldn't ask in Dark Man's Cup: stray Lordkin dared not be seen there. But Pelzed had set two Lordkin families, Corles and Trazalac, to guard the Cup. When Stant Corles came to the Long Mile Market to shop, Whandall was there with a cold baked potato.

Stant only knew that four Lordkin had tried to gather from the kinless in the Corles family's charge. They'd moved into the house under cover of night and held the family as terrorized prisoners. When it was over, the kinless were freed and three Lordkin had been given to the Lords. No telling what would happen to them. But the fourth, the older man with all the scars . . .

"We strung him up and played with him. He lasted two days. Not my idea. Long as he could talk at all, he kept trying to tell us he was friends with Lord Pelzed. Old man Trazalac, he thought that was *way* too funny. He never said why, and you know, I'm not inclined to ask twice."

Tras Preetror was in the village near the harbor. That was already too close to the Lordshills for Whandall.

Peacegiven Square was neutral territory and was the closest place to the hills and hemp fields separating the "benighted area"—most of Tep's Town—from Lord's Town, the harbor, and Lordshills. The Lords had changed the way things were done. Before the carnival, carts and guards came to local parks once each month. This year they gave out more, but the women had to go farther to get it.

All the women had to travel to Peacegiven Square each eight weeks. Thence the Lordsmen guards and kinless wagoneers brought baskets of grain and jars of oil. Sometimes there were fruits, and twice a year there might be cheese. The kinless clerks were protected by big Lordsmen with helmets and spears.

There were things the women had to say. "I am a widow." "I have no home." "My children are hungry!" "No man protects me."

Any men must hang back at the edges of the square. The clerks would give only to single mothers and to women too old to have children. Many a woman must borrow a child.

The Lordsmen and their kinless clerks passed out the goods and the women carried them out of the square. Then the fights started.

Men gathered from unprotected women. All the Placehold men would make a circle around Mother and Mother's Mother and the aunts and sisters and cousins. Placehold had a cart pulled by the younger boys. Some goods went into the cart, but not all, because another band might gather the cart.

Placehold was large enough, with enough women, that it was better to protect what they had than to try to gather more. They'd learned that the first Mother's Day after the carnival. Others were learning too.

They had finished packing everything in carts or hanging it on poles for the women to carry when Whandall saw Tras Preetror.

He told Resalet, "Pelzed wants me to talk to him."

Resalet eyed the crowd, then nodded. "We can spare you this time. It's well to keep peace with Pelzed. Come home when you can."

Tras looked older, thinner, more wiry. The sight of Tras made Whandall's bones ache with memories. "They told me they'd fed you to the crabs," he said.

"They told me they'd done that with you," Tras said.

Peacegiven Square was clearing fast, with households and families and bands moving rapidly away, trying to get home safely before someone gathered everything from them. Tras selected an outdoor table at the street corner and ordered honey tea for both of them. He inspected Whandall as they sat.

"Clearly they didn't. You've grown. Got your knife too."

"I thought I was crippled for life," Whandall said. "Tras, you said you could persuade them, but you can't persuade people who don't listen! What did they do to you?"

"Sold me as a deckhand," Tras said. "I was two years working off the price they got for me." He looked down at his callused hands. "Sea life is hard, but I'm in better shape than I've ever been. Got some good stories too."

"Lord Pelzed wants to hear them. He says you owe him a roof."

Tras Preetror laughed like a maniac.

Whandall found that irritating. He asked, "Been back to the Lordshills?"

The laugh caught in his throat. "You were right, of course. But they don't care what I do now. I saw that Peacevoice Waterman at the docks when my ship came in. He was surprised I was a passenger and not crew, but all he did was warn me to stay away from Lordshills. I didn't need that warning this time." Tras looked up at the olive tree sheltering them. "But, you know, maybe there's a way . . ."

"Not with me, Tras," Whandall said.

"Next Burning?" Tras asked. "Get your friends, relatives, everyone you know, and take Yangin-Atep to the Lords. That'll teach them—"

"Teach somebody, maybe," Whandall said. "But it won't be me." For a moment Whandall thought of life without the Lords. It would be vastly different. Better? He couldn't know.

The tea was pleasant, different from the hemp tea that Pelzed served. Tras must have seen that Whandall liked it, because he ordered more. He sipped carefully. "Touch of hemp and sage," he pronounced. "The bees must go to the hemp fields."

Whandall looked puzzled.

Tras asked, "Don't you know where honey comes from?"

Whandall shook his head.

"I guess loggers don't have honey," Tras mused. "Bees make honey. Then beekeepers collect it."

Worlds opened when Tras spoke. Beekeepers would be kinless, wouldn't they? Where did they keep the honey they had gathered? Did the bees protect them? Whandall asked, and Tras Preetror knew. . . .

"Other places, a beekeeper negotiates with the queen. He agrees to guard the hive, or maybe he grows them a garden. They like gold. Here the queen's magic won't protect the hive from animals and gatherers. I guess you can just take the honey, but so can anyone else. I'd guess some kinless has to guard the hives, drive off bears, hide the location from Lordkin. . . . Only . . . I heard something. What was it?"

Whandall was thirsty for knowledge. He had not guessed how much he missed Tras Preetror. He watched Tras wrestle with his memory. . . .

"D-daggers. The Tep's Town gatherer bees have started growing poisoned daggers like little teeny black-and-yellow Lordkin," Tras said gleefully. "Right. Your turn."

Whandall had missed that too. He told how he had been returned to the

Placehold and tended in the Placehold nursery. How he had moved into the tiny room upstairs. "Lenorba's room. They finally got her, thirteen years late."

"Who?"

"I heard the tale when I was a little boy. You've seen *Jispomnos* played, Tras. You know that what a man does with his woman is nobody's business but theirs—"

"Even murder."

"Right. A woman who kills her man doesn't see much hassle either. Maybe he's slapped her around and everyone knows it, everyone sees the bruises. But it wasn't like that with Lenorba and Johon.

"Johon of Flower Market moved in with her because she was a little crazy, 'specially for sex. Then when he got tired of that, she didn't. She was with a lot of men. One of 'em beat Johon up. Johon went home and beat up Lenorba. Then they talked, and both said they were sorry, and they went to bed. She wore him out. He went to sleep beside her and she killed him in his sleep. Then she ran home to the Placehold.

"She really seemed to think that all she needed was a bruise to show. It's not like that. Flower Market let it be known that if they found Lenorba outside the walls they'd kill her. So she never left again.

"Wanshig told me the rest. There weren't enough women in the Placehold to get us what we needed on Mother's Day, unless they took Lenorba. They gave her a baby to hold . . . gave her my little brother Trig. The men escorted the women to Peacegiven Square, but they had to stop at the border, and all the women went on. Afterward they found Trig sitting on the dais, right on stage, sucking on a plum. They never found Lenorba."

The square was nearly deserted now.

Wanshig came across the square to stand beside Whandall. He eyed Tras Preetror suspiciously. "We got the cart home safe," Wanshig said. "So I came back to look out for you. Last time you went with him, you were a year healing. More," he added, looking at the bright red circle of inflammation by Whandall's left eye.

Tras looked pained. "They let him come home," he said. "I was two years buying my way off that ship!"

Wanshig sat without being invited. "You were on a ship?"

"Yes."

"Where did you go? Condigeo?"

Tras laughed. "The long bloody way! When we got back to Condigeo I bought my way free. But first we went north."

"Where?" Wanshig asked

"Lordship Bay, first. They call it that because your Lords have kin there, or say they do. Then Woodworker Bay, then around the cape to

Sugar Rock. North of that is Great Hawk Bay. One day I may go back there. Best fish restaurant anywhere, run by a burly merman called the Lion. Then we went south, but our wizard wasn't good enough; a storm drove us past Condigeo to Black Warrior Bay."

Whandall was surprised to see that Wanshig was listening in fascination. "I've never even seen the harbor up close," Wanshig said. "So you went to sea, and Whandall got his arm broken. I think you owe my brother."

"Pelzed says I owe him a roof."

"Pelzed knows you'll never pay," Wanshig said. "This is different. You owe Whandall."

Tras shrugged. "It may be, but how do I pay? It took nearly everything I had to buy myself away from the captain!"

"Why did you come here?" Whandall asked.

"Stories. It's a risk. If I stay away too long, I'll forget the Condigeano speech. You know how languages change. There'll be slang I don't know. What kind of teller would I be then? So I stayed in Condigeo long enough to learn, but I had to come back. It's time for a Burning, and I can't miss the next one. How long has it been, six years? Do you feel the Burning near?"

Wanshig said, "The next teller who asks that question dies."

Whandall asked, "Why is it so important?"

They were mixing Condigeano and common speech. Whandall was still the only Lordkin who could do that. Wanshig wasn't able to follow much of what they were saying. Tras said, "The fewer tellers watch the Burning, the better a story it makes. When the others go home, that's when it pays me to be here. But I wish your Yangin-Atep would stir himself."

"Alferth and Tarnisos started the last Burning," Whandall told him. "Shall I show them to you?"

"Man, those guys are weird," Wanshig said. He shifted to an accent used mostly inside Placehold and spoke too rapidly for Tras to understand. "And you don't know where they are."

"I can find them," Whandall said.

"Sure." He looked at Tras, who was trying to understand what they were saying. "You're really not mad at him, are you?"

Whandall shook his head. "Not anymore."

"Well, they're over in Flower Market Square."

"How do you know that?"

"It's where they hang out now. There's a truce between Flower Market and Serpent's Walk." Wanshig changed to common speech. "You want to talk to the Lordkin who started the last Burning, give my brother five shells. You can afford that. Some other time we'll talk about more."

* * *

Alferth was a surly, burly man near thirty. There was a distorted look to his nose and ears. Whandall wasn't old enough to work out what had him so angry all the time, but he could imagine what Alferth's meaty hand would feel like, swung with that much weight behind it. He had no urge to talk to Alferth himself. But he stayed close after pointing Alferth out to Tras Preetror.

Tras sat down at Alferth's table at the end of a meal, set a flask between them, and asked, "What was it like to be possessed by Yangin-Atep?"

Alferth expanded under the looker's interest. "I felt an anger too big to hold back. Tarnisos screamed like a wyvern and charged into old Weaver's place, and I charged after him. We kicked him and his wife—I never saw his kids—we took everything we could, and then Tarnisos set the place afire. By then there were too many of us to count. I had an armful of skirts. For half a year I had a skirt for every woman who—"

"Why Weaver?"

"I think the old kinless refused Tarnisos credit once."

Tras asked, "Why would *Yangin-Atep* start with Weaver?"

Alferth's laughter was a bellow, a roar. Whandall left with a gaping sense of loss, a pain in the pit of his belly.

CHAPTER 17

When Whandall was an infant, Morth of Atlantis had brought water to the Lords. He must have been paid well. Now he kept a shop in what the Lords called the benighted section, far from the docks and the Lordshills.

It was not right to be stalking the man who had killed Pothefit during a gathering. *Never remember a killing after the Burning.* But Morth was a knot of enigmas. . . .

Why would a wizard of power live in the benighted areas?

Why would a Lordkin of fourteen years' age visit a magic shop? Whandall had better have an answer ready for *that*.

He blocked the path of a dumpy woman in Straight Street. The kinless looked at him differently now he was near grown—no longer cute, not yet menacing while his knife was hidden—but still she fished in her purse and gave him money. Probably not enough. It didn't have to be.

He watched until the shop was empty of customers before he went in.

Morth of Atlantis was younger than he remembered from that night in Lordshills. Against all reason, Whandall had somehow expected that. It didn't even startle him that sparse hair white as salt was now sandy red. But he was still an old man of dubious humanity, tall and straight, with dry brown skin and a flat belly and an open, innocent face with a million wrinkles. A little silly, a little scary.

Whandall asked, "Can you cure pimples?"

The magician peered close. One quick straight thrust could have cut his throat, but what spells protected him? "You've got worse than pimples." He touched the inflammation by Whandall's eye. His hands were surprising: fingers widest at the tips! "That's ringworm. It'll never go away by itself. Thirty shells."

Whandall cursed mildly and showed the five the woman had given him. "Maybe later."

"As you wish."

A kinless would have bargained. Lordkin didn't, and maybe magicians didn't. Whandall asked, "You're from Atlantis?"

The man's face closed down.

"I'm Seshmarl of Serpent's Walk." Whandall knew better than to give his true name to a magician. "Savant, our younger street-brothers wonder about you. If you don't want to be asked over and over how you escaped Atlantis, tell it only once. I'm a good teller. I'll tell them."

"Are you?" Morth smiled at him. How could an old man have so many teeth? "Tell me a story."

Whandall hadn't expected this, but without a stammer he said, "Yangin-Atep was the god who brought the knowledge of fire to the world. But Zoosh beat him in a knife fight, so men began to serve Zoosh instead of tending fires for Yangin-Atep. Lifetimes later, only the Lordkin still serve Yangin-Atep. When we came south from the ice, Yangin-Atep traveled with us. Have you heard the tale?"

"Not from your view."

"We weren't finding enough wood until the Lords showed us the way to the forest. There we hunted during the day and built big fires at night. In the forest Yangin-Atep grew strong. We cut and burned our way through, and that was how we found Tep's Town. The kinless called it something else, of course."

"Valley of Smokes," the magician said.

Whandall was taken aback. *"Kinless* called it that?"

"Have you seen how red the sunsets are here? Or how hard it is to breathe after the Burning? Something about the shape of the land or the pattern of winds keeps fog and smoke from blowing away. It isn't your fire god. Something older. A kinless god, maybe."

During the Burning and after, Mother's Mother's breath rasped as if she were dying. Whandall nodded.

"But the harbor is Good Hand, for the look of curled fingers." Morth saw Whandall's unspoken *Huh?* and added, "You have to see it from the air."

Oh, right, from the air. The magician had him totally off balance. *Story,* he was in the middle of a story—

"The kinless couldn't fight us, because Yangin-Atep was strong again. So the kinless came to serve us. They still wear the noose, as we still hold their lives." Just as Mother's Mother had told the tale to her grandchildren, with no mention of alliance with the Lords.

"I never would have taken that for a noose," Morth said. "A strip of colored cloth around the neck? Hangs down the chest?"

"That's it."

"I've walked along the woods many times. Where is this wide path your folk burned their way through?"

"North from here, but it's been lifetimes . . . six lifetimes, anyway. Maybe the trees grew back?"

The magician nodded. "That's Lordkin and kinless. What of the Lords?"

"We met them before we found the forest. They showed us how to gather wood, taught us about Yangin-Atep and Zoosh—"

"Why would they know about Yangin-Atep and Zoosh?"

"I don't know. The Lords have not always been with us, but they were with us when we took this land. They spoke to the kinless. They keep the kinless working."

"But you are Lordkin. Are you kin to the Lords?"

Whandall shook his head. "I've asked that. No one says different, but no one says so either."

The magician smiled thinly. "I see. So now you take what you want from the kinless, and the Lords gather from you."

"No, the Lords gather from the kinless, seldom from us. They have their own lands, and the harbor. And . . . ?"

The magician nodded. "All right. You know the story of Atlantis?"

"The land that sank. A long way from here."

"Right on both. A very large land mass a very long way from here, and it sank because the swordsmen came."

Whandall just looked at him.

"I was wizard to the fishing folk, human and mer. I was blessing a new ship at the docks. Attic warships came into sight, east of us. Hundreds. The captain decided I could finish my spells while we sailed for safety. I could have stayed and fought alongside the priests, but . . . it was too late."

"Did you know Atlantis was going to sink?"

"Yes and no. Something was coming sometime; everyone knew that. A thousand years ago, priests of Atlantis were already making spells to keep the land quiet. The quakes were long postponed. We didn't know they would come that *day.* The Attic soldiers must have reached the priests during the Lifting of Stone ceremony.

"After sunset we saw waves like black mountains marching toward us. Our ship floated above the water, but the waves below and the wind they took with them tossed our ship like a child's toy."

"And you brought water to Tep's Town?"

"Wh—? Yes. Yes, that was me. It's a good story. I'll tell you another time."

Nobody but Tras Preetror did that: traded information for information.

Whandall smiled. *A mountain of ice had come from the end of the Earth at Morth's bidding, scouring across lands belonging to the Lords.* Whandall would know if Morth told the story right, and Morth had no way to know that Whandall knew.

A long city block away, Tras Preetror stepped out of a shadow to intercept him. He wanted to talk about Morth of Atlantis. Did Lordkin deal much with magicians? with barbarians? with magic, other than their own peculiar fire magic? What was Whandall doing in Morth's shop, anyway?

What was Tras doing waiting for him here? Whandall didn't ask that. He said, "Morth is funny. He trades what he knows for what you know, like kinless trade shells for goods. Tras, what's it like to sail on a trader?"

Tras offered strips of jerked meat. "I expect all magicians do that. Information is what they sell, in a way. What did you trade with him?"

Whandall ate. "Yes, Tras, but what's it like to sail on a trader?"

"I prefer not to be reminded of my experience . . ."

Whandall waved and turned away.

"All right." Tras Preetror looked at him hard. "It's no fun as a deckhand. It's different as a passenger, as a teller. Tellers do a lot of traveling. We get over being seasick quick, or we quit, or travel on land instead."

"What's seasick?"

How to survive seasickness, and how to survive a storm, and what you ate at sea—it was different for passengers and crew—and what you'd better eat on land to get healthy again. Weather magic and how it could kill you. Tras was skilled at telling. "You never know how strong the magic is when you're on the ocean. The manna—you understand manna?"

Whandall shook his head. He'd heard that word. Where? On Shanda's balcony!

"Boy, you're going to owe me. Manna is the power behind magic. Manna can be used up. The man who learned *that* ranks with the woman who learned what makes babies. At sea there are currents, and manna moves with those. A spell to summon wind might do nothing at all, or raise a tempest to tear your ship apart. There are water elementals and merfolk."

"Does Morth know about this?"

"Have you ever seen an *old* Atlantis ship?" Whandall shook his head, and Tras said, "The bottom has windows and hatches. It floats above the water."

"Above the water. Above land too?"

"The most powerful did. No longer, I think. And the ships they built in this last hundred years, before Atlantis sank, they're ship shaped. If some ocean current swirls away the manna, down comes the ship, *splash,* and then you don't want windows breaking below the water.

"*Sure,* Morth knows about manna. Likely he thinks it's his most secret secret. So, Whandall, are you thinking of taking up sailing?"

"Tras, we never see the docks. The Water Devils don't want anyone else there."

"That's all that's stopping you?"

Whandall had seen ships, but only from the top of Wheezing Hill. He'd be guessing. Well . . . "I can't see why a ship's captain would let a Lordkin on. Wouldn't it be dangerous? What if a sail disappeared, or that tube they look through, or that big board at the back—"

Tras was laughing. "Rudder. Damn right it would. Whandall, you couldn't buy or beg your way aboard a boat, and kinless can't either, because most barbarians can't tell kinless from Lordkin. You'll never learn enough to *steal* a ship, and the dockside Lordkin won't help you do that because they'd lose the trade, such as it is."

"Do you think I could become a teller?"

Again Whandall was subjected to intense scrutiny. "Whandall, I think you could. You've got the knack already, trading information with me like a kinless sweets merchant. But anyplace these boats go, they know about Lordkin, and you have the look. You'd never be welcome—anywhere."

Whandall nodded, trying to swallow his disappointment. He said, "Morth was blessing a new ship at the Atlantis docks when . . ."

CHAPTER
18

On a later day Whandall returned to Morth of Atlantis.

He lurked a bit before he went in. Tras Preetror seemed to be following him around, and he didn't like that. How could anyone lurk, hide, spy, gather, with a *teller* hovering at his elbow? But Tras wasn't about, and Whandall—*Seshmarl* went in and bought an acne cure for fourteen (not thirty) shells. It was an evil-smelling cream altered by gestures. It hurt when he rubbed it in, but three days later the ring-shaped inflammation was fading from his eye, and his pimples were smaller too. In a week his skin was clear except for the ringworm, and that was smaller. Morth gave value for money.

He came again and asked about love potions. Morth wouldn't sell those. He considered it wrong to tamper with another's mind. Whandall nodded and pretended to find that sensible, and wondered who the man thought he was befooling.

"I could have used a love potion a time or two," the wizard said. "Can you guess how lonely it's been for the last Atlantis wizard in a town of no magic?"

"You're talking to a Lordkin. That's lonely."

"Yes. Come any time, Seshmarl, even if you can't afford to buy. Wait now, I can do tattoos," Morth said suddenly. "You're Serpent's Walk? Would you like a serpent tattoo?" He waved at an elaborate golden-feathered serpent, somewhat faded, displayed on one wall.

"Beautiful." He'd never find money for that! "I have a tattoo," Whandall said, and gave Morth a glimpse of the tiny serpent in the web of his thumb. "I haven't asked for another yet."

Morth looked down at Whandall's hand. His brows furrowed . . . but he only looked up after a moment and leaned close into Whandall's face. "A tattoo would be painful over ringworm and look odd too. But I see my cure is working."

"Yes." Whandall pointed at the feathered serpent and asked anyway. "How much for that? Where the ringworm was?"

Morth laughed. "I'd ask enough to put a new room on my house, normally. Here . . . where would I find a client? Seshmarl—no, wait." Morth took Whandall's right hand, the knife hand, in both his hands. Bad manners. He spread the fingers wide. Morth wasn't just staring at Whandall's hand now; he was pulling it toward the oil lamp above them. Astonished, Whandall let him do that.

Light fell on his hand. Morth had an open face, not used to hiding things, but now Whandall couldn't tell what he was thinking. He said, "You're going to leave Tep's Town."

"Why would I want to do that?"

"Can't tell. Maybe you *don't* want to. Will you take a word from me?" Morth was still studying . . . *reading* Whandall's hand. "Never go near rivers or the ocean. If you depart by land, it's likely your own idea. But you might visit the docks and travel the rest of the world as an oarsman with a bump on his head or be carried in the bellies of a school of fish."

Whandall had to clear his throat to speak. "We can't go to the docks anyway. Water Devils don't like people from outside. Morth, do you know your future?"

"No."

"What can I give you to put that tattoo on my face?"

". . . Yes. Seshmarl, I have some errands for you. And one day, when you are fully healed and your, um, bandlord has given permission, come to me. The tattoo will be my gift."

There were days he came with no excuse but the whim to talk. He would watch Morth and his customers discuss their needs. Then Morth would hand them something from under the counter; or step to a shelf and mumble and wave, or only stand watching for several seconds before snatching up some box or tiny flask, as if avoiding invisible teeth, and give it to the customer with elaborate instructions.

One could ask.

Medicines for pain? Yes, Morth had those (but his hands stayed still and his eyes didn't move from Seshmarl's). For wheezing, shortness of breath? Morth sold a lot of that, especially after the Burning. He bought herbs from loggers.

Philosopher's stone? Unicorn's horn? Boy, you've got to be joking! Magical cold torch? Spell of glamour? Invisibility? Levitation? Those didn't work here either. "I had a cook pot once that would cook without fire. Never knew what to do with it. Didn't use it because I would wear it out. I couldn't sell it because it wouldn't work very long. Finally it was stolen, not that it will have done the thieves any good. Magic is weak in the Valley of Smokes."

"Well, it would still be a pot," Seshmarl said.

"True."

"Is it that way everywhere?"

"Less so some places." Morth's eyes went dreamy.

"Why here?"

Morth shrugged. "Yangin-Atep. Magic is the life of a god. It's like you can't keep honey where there are ants. Atlantis had no god."

"Can you do prophecy?"

"Seshmarl, to know the future is to change it, so that time wriggles like a many-headed snake. What you see is false because you've seen it. Even if there were magic enough, how could I read the lines in my own hand? We student wizards couldn't even read each other's lines; our fates were bound up together, tangled." Morth shrugged as if great weight sat on his shoulders. "I read part of your fate because you might leave. See, time spreads ahead of us like this . . ." He reached above his head. "This fan. Your most likely future leads to places where magic still holds power. Traces of manna flow back through time to weave meaning into the lines on your hand."

"I'm going to leave?"

Morth took his hand again and spread it in the lamp glow. "Do you see? It's the pattern the lines make with the ambient magic, anywhere in the world but here. Yes, you still have the chance to leave, and you should still stay clear of water, except for bathing."

Bathing? Whandall saw only his hand. He asked, "Morth, why would a magician live where there's no magic?"

Morth smiled. "Seshmarl, that's not something I'd tell anyone."

Morth had said that Whandall would leave Tep's Town. In his present state that seemed desirable. Had he healed enough? Did he know enough?

He tried to beg money from Resalet. "Just suppose, now, suppose Morth sells me a potion of easy breathing for Mother's Mother. I might see where he takes it from. If it's where the pimple salve came from, then that's the medicines, and if he's lying about unicorn's horn, which is supposed to be *priceless*—"

"Stay out of that magician's shop." Resalet's finger stabbed Whandall's chest. "You don't know what he can do. Read minds? Make you die in a month? He's the man who killed your father."

"I know that."

"But does *he?* Stay away from Morth of Atlantis!"

If he couldn't *buy* from Morth, was there anything Morth might want from Seshmarl?

He asked. Morth said, "I want to know more about the forest."

"You buy your herbs from loggers. Ask them."

"That is a very strange situation," Morth said. "Lords tell the loggers where they can cut down trees. I mean, *exactly* where and which. They don't log themselves—"

Whandall suggested, "Maybe they're hiding something in the forest."

"Yes, and maybe they just like telling people how to live their lives!" Morth took dried leaves from a jar. "Here, smell this. Do you know it? Does it grow there?"

"Wait . . . yes. Sage. Grows where the trees open out. It doesn't kill, and it smells great when you walk through it. Hey, they use this for cooking at Samorty's house!"

"Yes, it's good for that and other things. What about this one?"

Whandall took the sheet of pale bark—rubbed it, sniffed it, held it to daylight in the doorway. "I don't think so."

Morth smiled. "Willow bark. I didn't think it grew around here. What about this?"

Long leaves. "Yes. Foxglove," Whandall said.

"It can be valuable. Do you know of poppies?" He showed a faded flower.

"I know where there are whole fields of them," Whandall said. "The loggers say they are dangerous." He didn't add that he had been to the poppy fields and nothing happened.

They whiled away an afternoon. Morth was dubious: he didn't want Whandall—*Seshmarl*—picking plants that were *not quite* what he wanted. That was dangerous. "Bring me the whole plant or a whole branch when you can, so I'll know what I have."

Morth sent him to where there were no loggers. Whandall didn't want to meet loggers anyway: he was no child, and he'd be on their turf. Kinless or not, they had axes and severs. He sought Morth's plants in the old growth and found them rarely.

On his second foray he approached the Lordshills from the forest side.

There was the blank wall back of Lord Samorty's house. The tree had been cut back, and there were marks on the top of the wall where it had been repaired. Whandall watched the hill for a time. No guards . . . and if they chased him into the wood he would outrun them or lead them into lordkiss. He half ran, half crawled within range of the wall, then hurled what he was carrying. He was in shadow when he heard the splash. He didn't wait for more.

But a pine cone had splashed into the laundry pond, and Shanda would know of it. She would know he was alive.

CHAPTER
19

orth's plants were rare, but they both understood that Morth
sought knowledge too. He was using Whandall's explorations to
map the forest.

Morth wasn't stingy with his rewards. Whandall collected medicines to
ease pain and reduce a swelling and bring sleep. Foxglove leaves made a
powder that would send a man into jittery mania just before a fight. Poppies yielded a brown gum that gave good dreams. All of these lost their
power if not used, and often Whandall had more than Morth and Placehold
combined would need.

He began trading them for favors on the street.

Morth always told how to use the powdered leaves. Sniff carefully.
Never more than once a week, and don't ever heat them first. Whandall
was careful to do the same.

Then one day he was summoned to Pelzed.

Pelzed was angry. "Did you give Duddigract some of your foxglove?"
he demanded.

Duddigract was one of Pelzed's advisors, a big man with a bad attitude,
always muttering about what he'd like to do to the Lords. He was usually
behind Pelzed. Today he wasn't anywhere to be seen.

"No, Lord. We don't get along."

"He's dead," Pelzed said. "Some Maze Runners raiders came into the
Walk. I sent Duddigract to deal with them." He turned to one of the men
behind him. "Renwilds, tell it again."

"Yes, Lord. Duddigract saw the Maze Runners. Five of them. There were only six of us, but Duddigract looked mean. The Maze Runners looked scared, and I was sure they'd run if we gave them a chance. We could chase them out. They'd run, they'd be gone with no blood shed, and they'd drop anything they gathered. I started to say that to Duddigract, and I saw he had a leaf full of white stuff. He took a big sniff of that, then he stuffed a wad of brown gum in his mouth and chewed, then he took another big sniff from the leaf. We tried to say something but he just grinned, said it would be a shame to waste it, now he was ready to fight."

Pelzed looked to Whandall. "You know what he's talking about," Pelzed said.

"Yes, Lord. I always tell people how dangerous the white foxglove powder is. The brown gum is safe enough, that just puts you to sleep, but the white is dangerous."

"What does the white do?" Pelzed demanded.

"Lord, I don't know. I just know that's what Morth of Atlantis tells his customers. He never sells them more than a pinch or two of white, and he makes them sniff it there in the shop. He won't sell them any more until it's been a week or more. Brown he'll sell any time, but not white."

"Say more, Renwilds," Pelzed ordered.

"I'd say that magician knows what he's talking about," Renwilds said. "Duddigract sniffed that stuff and got a big grin, and all of a sudden he was a wild man. He took out his knife and before any of us could say anything he was all over the Maze Runners. They were ready to talk, you know, brag a little before they ran, and we were all set to brag back, and there's Duddigract with his knife out. He cut down two with no warning; they didn't even get to draw. By then the others had their knives out and one of them cut Duddigract, and Lord, it was like he didn't even feel it. Duddigract yelled, but it wasn't like he was hurt, it was like the Burning had come. We were sure Yangin-Atep had him, but Duddigract didn't want to burn anything. He just wanted to kill! He killed another Maze Runner, and the others dropped everything and ran. They were really scared, but so were we, Lord. When the Maze Runners ran, Duddigract looked at us like he didn't know us!"

Pelzed nodded grimly. "Go on."

Renwilds shrugged. "It was that powder, Lord. It summons invisible monsters."

"Uh huh. Why didn't you chase the Maze Runners?"

"Too fast, Lord, and we'd have had to get around Duddigract! So we were trying to figure what to do when Duddigract screamed again and fell down, babbling about how monsters were after him, and he curled up like he was going to sleep, only he never woke up."

"Where did he get it?" Pelzed demanded.

"He wouldn't tell us, Lord. Said he'd gathered it, but he wouldn't say where."

Pelzed turned to Whandall. "Well?"

Whandall told what he knew. "Lord, about a week ago some Black Lotus warriors caught me near the east border. There were too many to fight, so I let them gather a bag of powders I was taking to Morth. Maybe there was enough in there to do that to Duddigract. Or maybe they mixed the powders. But I don't know how they got from Black Lotus to Duddigract!"

"You didn't tell me they gathered anything, Whandall. Just that they'd chased you."

"I was embarrassed, Lord."

Pelzed nodded thoughtfully. "I sent Duddigract to look into it," he said. "He must have caught up with the Lotus warriors. And he never told me! Never told me!" Pelzed grew visibly angry, but not with Whandall. "It's his own fault, then," Pelzed said. "But Whandall, be careful with those powders."

"I will, Lord."

But there were always more powders, and friends were always ready to accept them. There was so much he could buy with foxglove.

But some liked the stuff too much.

One day three followed him home. Resalet came out with two uncles and chased them away.

That evening Whandall was summoned to Resalet's big northeast room on the second floor. Resalet eyed him critically. "Dargramnet says you're smart," Resalet said. "Or used to say it."

Whandall nodded. It had been a year since Mother's Mother had recognized Whandall when she saw him. Now she sat by the window and talked of old days and old times to anyone who would listen. The stories were interesting, but she told the same ones over and over.

"So if you're smart, why are you acting like a fool?"

Whandall thought for a moment, then took a handful of shells from his pouch and laid them on Resalet's table.

"Yes, bigger fools than you will pay," Resalet said. "And if they think you keep that stuff here? They'll come to take it. We'll have to fight. We'll lose people; there'll be blood money. The Lords may get involved. We can't fight Lordsmen!"

"Lords don't care about hemp," Whandall said. "They keep hemp gum! In ebony boxes."

"Don't show off for me, boy," Resalet said. "I know you've been to

Lordshills, and look what it got you! You came in beat up and useless, a lot more trouble than you were worth. Hadn't been that Dargramnet likes you, we'd have thrown you out to the coyotes. I don't know what the Lords do at home, but down here hemp trouble gets you Lordsmen. Enough Lordsmen and they tear your house down. This is Placehold! We've had Placehold longer than I've been alive, and we're not going to lose it because of you."

Whandall tried to change the subject. "The Bull Pizzles sell hemp. Pelzed serves hemp tea."

"Pelzed is damn careful with his tea," Resalet said. "And since when did Serpent's Walk learn from Bull Pizzle?" He shook his fists violently. "And I don't care if Serpent's Walk sells hemp; we're Placehold. Whandall, if you want to trade powders, do it somewhere else. Get your own house. Placehold doesn't want the trouble. Do you understand me?"

"Pelzed offered me a house in Dark Man's Cup," Whandall said. "Should I take it?"

"If you like."

Whandall was startled to realize that Resalet meant it. Up to then it was just a boy talking to adults, but Resalet meant it. He really could be thrown out of Placehold.

He thought about living alone. It might be fun. But the other boys his age who moved out of their households to live alone were mostly dead.

Coscartin wasn't dead. Coscartin had half a dozen other young men living with him, and that many women, and some kind of arrangement with Pelzed. The stuff he dealt in was supposed to come from the Water Devils.

"I'd rather stay here."

"Then give up the powder," Resalet said. "Give it up right out loud. Give away all your stock. Make sure everyone knows you won't have more."

"But why?"

"Because I tell you—"

"Yes, I understood that," Whandall said. "I mean—what do I tell them?"

Resalet chuckled with the first sign of amusement since Whandall had come into his room. "Tell them you had a vision from Yangin-Atep."

"No one will believe that!"

"Then tell them anything you want, but you bring more of that stuff here, you're going out."

They told stories about Whandall's party for years. He brought out everything, white powders and yellow foxglove leaves and brown gum. He parceled it out with care. Wanshig found some hemp. Tras Preetror wrote two songs and told stories, but as the night went on his speech became an endless stream of babbling.

Shealos managed to finesse three times his share of the brown poppy gum. Whandall let him do it: he was a noisy whiner when thwarted. Shealos went to sleep in a corner, where the Forigaft brothers must have found him.

No one was seriously hurt.

There would never be another party like it. But it left ripples. . . .

Two young Lordkin ended up in the river, unhurt but stinking.

Three girls became pregnant.

Shealos didn't wake until sunset the next day, in the middle of an intersection, stripped naked and painted with the wrong band signs and a short written message.

A blank wall in the kinless house Whandall had taken over for the party bore more words, written inside a pattern made from ten local band signs . . . kind of pretty, really, but any band would take it as a killing insult.

More messages were found scrawled in bright red paint on the long wall around Dead Town on the day after Whandall's party. Dead Town was where folk were buried if no family claimed them. Nobody painted band signs in Dead Town: all factions were welcome there.

Pelzed was asked to summon the Forigaft brothers.

These four brothers had somehow learned to read. It made them arrogant. The brothers painted messages on any clean surface. You couldn't tell what they said, not even by asking one of them, because they would lie. The night of Whandall's party they must have gone crazy on the powders. Whandall remembered their antics, howling and gymnastics and . . . wait now, he'd *seen* them doing that to his wall, and he'd laughed like a loon. He didn't remember seeing them leave.

The brothers were scattered about Serpent's Walk and Peacegiven Square. They were easy to spot. They mumbled to themselves. They shouted foul and cryptic threats and accusations into the faces of passersby. Two brothers tried to write something on Renwilds's burly belly, using yellow paint and their fingers. Renwilds let them finish, then knocked them both senseless.

They were all crazy as loons. Pelzed fed them for two weeks, then somehow traded them to the Wolverines, who lived below Granite Knob, for a wagonload of oranges.

Whandall copied some of their marks off a wall and brought them to Morth.

" 'I was not Lordkin! Zincfinder tattooed my corpse!' " Morth read. " 'Search the sand at Sea Cliffs for the treasure I died for.' 'She hid my knife!' " He looked up. "Your Dead Town must have its share of murder victims. When your mad readers were spraying the graveyard, the ghosts wrote messages on their minds. Justice carries its own manna."

Sometimes Whandall regretted his decision. He could have been living in a household of sycophants and women, like Coscartin. . . .

Coscartin and all his household were killed by rivals unknown, half a year after Whandall's party.

CHAPTER 20

When Wanshig reached fifteen he began working with Alferth. Alferth was a tax taker, which gave him avenues into kinless commerce. One afternoon Wanshig pulled Whandall away from his friends, back to the courtyard of the Placehold house.

"Taste this," Wanshig said. "Just a sip."

It was a small clay flask. The fluid inside had a fire in it. Whandall almost choked. "What—"

"Wine."

"Oh. I know about wine."

That made Wanshig laugh. "Well, you're clever in spots, little brother, and you know how to keep your mouth shut. Can you think of a way to make the kinless bring this stuff in to sell?"

They shared the bottle unequally. "Outside Tep's Town there are taverns," Wanshig said.

"How do you know this?"

"Tellers," Wanshig said. "And do you remember Marila? She was a Water Devil, and she listened at home. Stories of other lands. And of the docks."

"And what are these taverns?" Whandall asked.

Wanshig smiled dreamily. "Gathering places. For men, or even men and women together, to drink wine, be together with friends, celebrate. There are wine shops everywhere but here. Why not Tep's Town?"

But wine was doing a slow burn inside Whandall. "Yangin-Atep's fire," he pronounced. "Magic?"

"Yeah."

Wine felt good. *Whee,* Whandall thought, and he felt words bubbling to his partly numb lips. *Resalet ran away,* he thought. *He left my father to die.* Things he didn't want to say to any Placeholder, ever. *Lordkin don't work for anyone.*

Shig said, "I don't work *for* Alferth. I work *with* him."

He'd said it out loud! Whandall slapped his hand across his mouth. He tried to say—

"No, little brother. You have to work *with.* Otherwise you're all alone," Wanshig said. "Sometimes it's hard to tell which is which. It runs the other way too. Some Lordkin work. Some kinless take things."

"—said what?"

"Kinless loses his work, what can he do? Got to have food. Blanket. Shoes. He gathers them. We'd kill him, sure—he doesn't have the *right*—but why would anyone catch him? Something's missing, nobody asks who gathered it. Never mind that, little brother. Why don't the kinless keep wine shops?"

"Wine *shops?* If it feels this good?" Whandall gestured widely; Wanshig ducked. "Someone wants wine, just smash in the door! If it's too strong, go for help. If the winetender tries . . . we beat on him, kill him, maybe. Kinless would be crazy to keep this stuff around."

"Taverns, then. Make them sell drinks one at a time."

Whandall, with wine buzzing in his ears and his blood, could feel what was wrong with *that.* Kinless and barbarians might drink wine and keep their self-control. In the Burning City men would drink; then unguarded words would bubble through their lips and they would fight. No tavern would survive.

Shig said, "The most we ever get *here,* someone pops up on a street corner with maybe eight of these little flasks. When they're gone, he's gone. He's not there long enough to be robbed."

"Where's he get it?"

"The flasker? Lords and kinless get some wine through the docks, from Torov and Condigeo. If the rest of us find out, we take it, of course, so they give some to the Water Devils. And there's another place."

They wobbled as they stood, and Wanshig led him north. Whandall's head cleared quickly. The wine was gone. There hadn't been much, just enough for two.

The houses north of Tep's Town ended at the forest. Wanshig led off northwestward. Whandall was sober now and full of questions, but Wanshig only smiled.

Here the forest withdrew from the city, leaving a delta of meadow, the Wedge, with a slow stream, the Deerpiss, meandering down its center. Whandall had known of the Wedge all his life, and only began to wonder as Wanshig led him up the stream. Why hadn't the meadow filled with houses?

Where the Wedge converged to a point, a two-story stone house strad-dled the stream like a blockage in a funnel. On either side the road would be wide enough for wagons, but gates blocked both sides.

Two men emerged from a second-story door. One started down the ladder.

Whandall had seen Lordsmen's armor and lumbermen's leathers. Both men wore what lumbermen would wear, like what the boy Whandall him-self had worn. Both men were masked in what might have been lumber-men's leathers, but were not.

Wanshig ran at the rightward gate. Whandall followed at speed. Wan-shig climbed the gate like a monkey, with Whandall right behind him. Lordkin didn't ask permission; they went where they would.

The two armored men scrambled to the ground and lifted weapons. They carried . . . not quite severs. Hafts ended in straight blades sharpened on both sides.

Whandall didn't hear what words Wanshig spoke, but the men stepped aside, glancing incuriously at Whandall as he dropped to the ground. They were climbing back up as Wanshig led off along the stream. The forest had closed in at the banks.

Now out of earshot, Whandall asked, "What was that place?"

"Guardhouse," Wanshig said. "After our fathers took Tep's Town, we made the kinless build that across our path. The path is gone, but the Toronexti are still here. They let anyone through, but they take part of what they're carrying. It's custom. These days they guard something else too."

"The path. I could tell Morth—" He bit it off, eons late. Was it the wine, this long after? "I have to *see* him, Shig. Don't worry, I won't do anything stupid."

Wanshig seemed unsurprised. "How did he kill Pothefit?"

"I haven't asked yet."

"Don't ask. But find out."

Where the stream bent to the right, Wanshig walked straight into the forest.

The tall straight spikes must be young redwoods. Mature redwoods had been felled here; huge stumps remained. Wanshig led them a careful crooked path around morningstar plants, nettles, spear grass, red-and-green clumps of touch-me. Whandall was ready to snatch him to safety, but his older brother *had* learned.

They'd traveled a couple of hundred paces before the trees opened out. Here were croplands, a wide expanse of vines planted in straight rows. Kinless men and women were at work. There were Lordkin about too.

Wanshig and Whandall watched from their bellies. Wanshig said, "The Lords get some of their wine here, but of course they need somebody to protect it. That's where Alferth comes in. He got the Toronexti to do it. He leaves them half."

"What kind of half?"

"He cheats a little. They cheat a little." Wanshig began creeping backward. "I wanted you to know. If you've got any ideas—"

"Do we really want more wine in Tep's Town?"

"We do if it's *ours*."

But wine makes us kill, Whandall thought, *and mostly we kill each other. Lords drink wine without problems. Kinless can handle it. We teach kinless to control themselves. Barbarians learn or die. With us, though . . .*

He said, "What we were drinking, did it come from here?"

"Right," said Wanshig.

"What the lookers give us, is it—"

"Better. Smoother."

"It's not the best, I bet." Wanshig glared, and Whandall said, "Lookers know we don't know the difference, so they buy cheap. Some barbarian somewhere *knows* how to make better than we've got. We should find him and talk him into working for us."

Wanshig shrugged his eyebrows. *Talk?* Barbarians brought in wealth. The Lords would spit fire if a barbarian was kidnapped. Alferth wouldn't dare.

But better wine would be better for the city than more wine, Whandall thought.

CHAPTER
21

R esalet had told him to avoid the magician and give up all his plants and powders. Whandall hadn't seen Morth in just under a year. The boy Seshmarl had grown older. Had he come to look too dangerous?

Two kinless customers looked at him nervously. The magician flickered a smile at him, then finished serving them. When they had left, the magician said, "Seshmarl! Tell me a story!"

Information for information. "If you follow the Deerpiss north out of the city, you get to a meadow, then a guardhouse with masked and armored men. They'll take some of what you're carrying. What they're guarding is the old path where my people cut their way through the forest to the Valley of Smokes. But don't go there, right? Just look."

"You *have* been busy," Morth said.

Whandall smiled.

"Is the path still open?"

"I don't think so."

"What if I want to *leave* Tep's Town?"

"The docks—"

"I can't go near the sea. I tried going south once, but it's all marshes."

"I don't know anything about that. Nobody goes that way."

"Seshmarl, the forest—"

"Not through the forest. Been two hundred years. The woods grow back. There's poison plants and lordkiss and morningstars and hemp and foxglove." He didn't intend to speak of the vineyard.

"Curse! And a guardhouse too?"

"You face *them*, you'd better have a story. But don't you have some spell for finding paths?"

The magician didn't answer. He told a story instead. "The fire god lost many battles. Sydon drowned his worshippers in Atlantis. Zoosh used the lightning against him in Attica, and is said to hold him in torment. Wotan and the ice giants battled him in the north, and again they torment him still. In many places the Firebringer bears a great wound in his side. Here too, I think. Your people must have fled Zoosh's people. You Lordkin may well be the last worshippers of Yangin-Atep."

"Yangin-Atep gave us everything. Heat, cooking—"

"Burning cities?"

"We don't burn the whole city, Morth. Only tellers say that. At any Burning we lose . . . Resalet says three or four hands of buildings."

"It's still crazy."

Whandall said, "Even a wizard might want to avoid Yangin-Atep's anger."

Morth smiled indulgently. "Yangin-Atep is near myth. His life uses the magical strength that would give my spells force, but there's little of that to start with. In these days magic works poorly everywhere. Yangin-Atep does not stir. I would sense him."

"Can you predict the Burnings?" Tras Preetror would pay well for that information.

"Sometimes," Morth said mysteriously.

He couldn't. But he knew when Yangin-Atep would wake. He had to. "Why did you want to know about the forest?"

"I want to get out," Morth said.

I can't go near the sea, he'd said. Whandall took a wild guess. "Will the ice chase you?"

Morth swallowed a laugh; it looked like a hiccup. "What do you know of that?"

"You brought a mountain of ice once. I wondered how. But if ice would chase you, the Lords would pay well, so it's not ice. Waves? Salt-water?"

"You know a lot," Morth said, no longer amused. The wizard took Whandall's hand again, stared, and nodded. "You have destinies. Most have only one, but you have choices. One choice may lead to glory. Be ready. Now tell me about the path through the forest."

Whandall persisted. "Why do you want to leave? Is it the elemental?" He still didn't know what the word meant.

"Last month I hired a wagon to take me to the harbor. I'd heard noth-ing of a water sprite in many years. As I crossed the last hill, a single wave rose and came toward me. The sprite is still out there in the harbor."

"Does Yangin-Atep protect you, then?"

"In a manner of speaking, yes, Seshmarl. The fire god won't permit a water sprite here. I'd heard about the Burning City all my life, but I never wanted to live here. Few do. Seshmarl, I came to *hide!*"

"The lookers come."

"Oh yes, tellers have made this city famous. Fools used to visit every spring to see the Burning. I suppose the lookers bring money that helps pay the cost of rebuilding. To me it all seems quite crazy. But it does make your city safer."

Whandall swallowed his anger. A Lordkin should have guile . . . never remember a killing after the Burning. . . . "Yangin-Atep protects us most of the time. Fires *don't* burn indoors." *Not here.* "Are there other cities where fires *can't* start by accident?"

"Oh, magic can protect a building," Morth said, "and I know a spell to douse a fire that works even in Tep's Town."

"The Lords cook indoors," Whandall said. "And they lit torches in the big room after dark. Not just candles, torches."

Morth said nothing.

It had been dry in Tep's Town for two years. "You brought water once."

"A water elemental chased me, embodied in an iceberg from the south-ernmost end of the earth. It hunted me, to kill me. Seshmarl, when things move, they want to keep on moving," Morth said. "The bigger and heavier it is, the harder it is to stop. The iceberg was the biggest and heaviest thing that ever came here."

"What stopped it? Yangin-Atep!" Whandall realized suddenly. "You used Yangin-Atep to turn that curse to an advantage."

"Destinies," Morth muttered to himself. "Yes, Seshmarl. That's a lot of what magic is, understanding how things work and turning them to your advantage. I let it chase me until there was no manna to move the iceberg farther."

"But you can't do it again."

"The elemental won't do it again," Morth said. "It would have to go far away to find ice. It won't go that far from me." The magician looked out the window, but he wasn't seeing the street outside. "This tale is not one to be told, Seshmarl. It might reach the Lords."

And that was valuable information, Whandall thought, though he didn't know how to use it. "My teacher says I can have a tattoo now," he said diffidently. "My brother wanted to do it, but I said I knew an artist."

For a breath he wasn't sure Morth had heard. Then the magician said, "Wonderful!" and wheeled around. "The same? The winged serpent of Atlantis? Let me show you."

He took a box from a shelf and reached inside. He unwrapped a fine cloth and let it hang from his fingers. It was a scarf in gold and scarlet and blue. "Here, do you like it?"

"Oh, yes." The scarf was *new*. It was far finer than the faded painting he'd once seen on Morth's wall . . . which had disappeared sometime in the past year.

Whandall couldn't take his eyes off the serpent in flight. It sported a crest of feathers, and little feathered wings on either side of its neck, like no serpent he'd ever heard of. The colors blazed.

But it was *big*. It would cover his face and shoulder and half his arm! Whandall remembered getting his thumb tattooed. "If it won't . . . how much does it hurt?"

"Hurt? No. Here, sit." He settled Whandall cross-legged on a rug.

Morth spread the scarf over the box and moved Whandall's arm until the scarf was under his upper arm and shoulder. The lines and colors of the scarf lifted and crawled along his skin. Whandall's eyes tried to cross. He felt a stirring as if a snake were settling on his arm, squeezing, sliding up his shoulder, his neck, his face. There was no pain, no swelling, no blood.

He hid out for a night and a morning. "I stayed the night. I didn't want to face anyone. It just hurt too much," he told Resalet.

Resalet's eyes were popping. He stripped off his tunic in one angry maneuver and moved against Whandall, arm to arm, to compare his own faded blue snake, fifteen years old, to Whandall's four-color god-thing. He cursed. "It's wonderful! How can I get one?"

"I'll ask."

"Ask who? Is it Morth again?"

Whandall admitted it. Resalet said, "Tell me all about it."

Whandall thought it prudent to describe near-unbearable pain, as if a snake's fangs had sunk into him.

"I don't care if it hurts. It just floated off the scarf and crawled up your shoulder? Did he say anything? Gesture?"

"Picked it up, put it down. Shall I ask if I can bring a . . . mmm . . . an uncle? It might cost a lot."

"No, don't bother. Does he know who you are?"

"Seshmarl. Of·Serpent's Walk. He had to know that much."

"You be careful with Morth of Atlantis, Whandall. No more powders! No more hemp!"

Whandall went back on another day and waited until the shop was empty before he entered. He'd gathered a wine flask, and he set it on the counter. They sipped it together.

Then Whandall asked, "Is this magical?"

Morth laughed. "No. It's not very good either, but there's not enough here to hurt us. Can you tell me any more about how a man might leave Tep's Town?"

Whandall shook his head. "But I know of a safe place. Most of the city is afraid of the Black Pit."

Morth was astonished. "How did you come to know that?"

"I've slept near the Black Pit. Nobody bothers you there, and the monsters can't touch you."

Morth nodded. "If there was manna about they'd be dangerous enough. The cats of Isis, the hounds of Hel, the birds of Wotan, some tre*men*dous war beasts, they all died by thousands of thousands in a war of gods. Only a tiny fraction wound up in the tar. Gods themselves went myth in that last battle," he said.

"Morth, tell me again about the iceberg."

Morth looked thoughtful. "You know the story."

"Yes, but I don't understand it all. Magic doesn't work here, but you make it work."

"And should I tell you?" Morth said, half to himself. "Let me see your hand again." He studied Whandall's palm. Then the magician sipped wine, and settled himself to tell the story.

"The wells of Atlantis dried up ages ago. We were too many for the rivers to support, and nobody *likes* rain. For a thousand years the people of Atlantis drew their water from the end of the world. Atlantis magic has ruled water for as long as we can remember. We send—sent—water sprites south to fetch icebergs and bring them to be melted for our water. When . . ." Morth considered, then went on. "When I left Atlantis instead of staying to fight, an iceberg was in sight of the harbor. The priests commanded the water sprite to hunt me down and kill me. I crossed an ocean and a continent and I reached the coast with a mountain of ice chasing me.

"At Great Hawk Bay the mers at Lion's Attic told me about Tep's Town. I was almost here before my ship sank down in the desert.

"I *knew* the elemental could get this far. I could hope it couldn't get any farther, not in the fire god's domain. To the Lords I swore I could bring an iceberg to that dry lake they call the Reservoir now, in the Lordhills. Yangin-Atep had power there in those days. I told the Lords to pay me on delivery, and I hoped that Yangin-Atep had the power to stop the ice."

Whandall nodded, then sipped the last half-swallow of wine.

That amused Morth. "Don't you wonder how I knew they'd pay? Never occurred to you? Lordkin! Two or three Lords were *very* irritated. That cursed sprite took a mountain of ice across land they owned."

Whandall nodded. "Samorty's turf. Chanthor's."

Now Morth looked surprised. "You knew?"

"That much. How did you make them pay?"

"I led them to wonder what their houses would look like if another iceberg crossed Blawind Hills."

"What about the water thing? Melted?"

"No. The damned elemental is waiting offshore. I can't ever go near water. But I spent the Lords' money long ago, and I can't pull that stunt again."

"Are you afraid of the Burning?"

"Oh, no. I'll sense when Yangin-Atep rises. I can see that much. There will be one, maybe two small Burnings, then a big one," Morth said. "Then I'll get out. I never want to see *that* again."

Whandall wondered if Morth wasn't whistling through Dead Town. Not Seshmarl's problem. He said, "The Toronexti—the tax guards—will take almost everything you own."

"Perhaps they won't see it all," Morth said.

"Were you here last time?" *When my father died!*

"Yes." The alien face turned haggard. "I could have been killed. There was nothing, *nothing* to tell me that Yangin-Atep was awake, not even after I saw smoke and fire pluming up. I went home to keep my house from burning. That night I went back to the shop. Stupid. Thieves—*gatherers*—had already stripped it bare. I was looking around and planning how to rebuild when more gatherers came in and saw me."

His mouth was very dry. Whandall asked, "What happened?"

"I used a calming spell."

"What?"

Belligerent and guilty, Morth said, "It's simple magic, so simple it even works here. It takes the anger out of a man, and puts out fires too. I've used it before. It isn't as if I wanted to hurt them. I threw a calming spell at the big one when he came at me with that knife. He went down like a handful of sticks. The others screamed and ran away."

"Dead?"

"Dead and *cold!* I pulled him outside and left him. A barbarian pulling a dead man by the ankles and nobody paid any attention! Seshmarl, does Yangin-Atep really possess people?"

"I think so." Shouldn't a wizard know?

"That thug was all anger, all fire. Yangin-Atep must have had him, and when I sucked the anger out of him, I think his life came with it." Morth looked up. "The Burning. What did you see?"

"I was only seven."

"Did you feel Yangin-Atep? I've sometimes wondered what that's like."

"No. Maybe next time."

Four kinless came in then. Whandall sensed their unease and left.

And maybe Yangin-Atep heard Morth's insults, sluggishly, in his coma.

PART THREE

The Burnings

CHAPTER
22

For three years rain had been sparse. Even the trees with their deep roots showed the dryness. The reservoirs went dry. Some said that the fountains in the Lordshills were still running, others said they weren't, and no one really knew.

A few kinless purchased rain. Weather wizards were rarely successful, but some sold the names of their clients: kinless who had money to throw away. There were beatings and robberies, leaving less to be spent on weather wizards.

The Deerpiss became a trickle, then dried up. Wells went dry. The Lords sent out a decree that water must be used only for drinking and washing. The kinless agreed, and demanded even stricter rationing. Lordkin didn't listen to such stuff. They used water to cool themselves and their homes, until even drinking water was a trickle, and there would be none to douse fires. It was a dry season, without water, and *that* might have been what wakened the fire god, twelve days after Morth belittled him.

Whandall alone wasn't big enough to get water when bigger men were thirsty. That morning Wanshig and Whandall escorted the women and younger children across the central city to a working well. Resalet stayed in with a hangover. The other Placehold men were not to be found.

Elriss was new. She stayed at the periphery, helping to keep the older women in place and moving. Wanshig hovered close to her. He'd brought Elriss home twenty days past, and she had his heart and mind.

Mother's Mother hadn't been outside the walls in many years. Whandall heard her muttering at everything she saw. The dirt. Bad manners among the Lordkin. Sullen faces among the kinless.

At least thirty kinless were using the well. At the sight of the approaching Lordkin family, they drifted away in little clumps.

The bucket brought up a scant mouthful.

The kinless had taken it all! And that alone might have started the Burning. But Whandall, waiting for his turn to scoop up a handful of water for Mother's Mother, smelled smoke on the windless air. Too early for a cook fire . . .

"Stay together," Wanshig snapped. "Get the women and children home."

The Burning had begun.

They had to go out of their way several times.

Fire was just catching in the message-service offices. Kinless were trying to get the horses out. Others were fighting the fire with wet blankets. The kinless fire wagon had just come when half a dozen Lordkin waded into the kinless with curses and long knives. Firefighters fell bleeding. Others ran. One Lordkin sat on a kinless man's head and beat on his chest with a rock. Another came over and kicked the kinless man and laughed.

Mother's Mother was leaning on Mother, gasping. "Monsters! We never killed! We only burned; we never killed!" Mother and Whandall led her rapidly away from the scene.

Whandall looked at Wanshig and didn't ask, *Is it true or is she crazy?*

"Maybe men didn't tell women everything. Even then," Wanshig said quietly.

It was peaceful on Angle Street, where the land humped a bit to hide the smoke southward. Faces turned curiously toward a crowd of women with only two men for escort, and Wanshig whispered, "Relax. Stroll. Just another dull morning, okay?"

And Whandall tried to feel that. Take it easy, nod at Mother's Mother's ranting and hope nobody hears. Elriss looks like she needs any strong man's help, but Mother's taking care of that, easing her back where she doesn't show.

Tras Preetror the teller hailed him. "Whandall! What are you doing? Don't you know what's happening?"

Wave at Tras Preetror, smile, walk toward him. "Hello, Tras." Breezy, a little bewildered: "What are you talking about?"

Tras made no effort to hide his delight. "Oh. Guarding the women, good idea. But why aren't"—he waved about him, voice rising—"*they* doing something? Isn't the Bur—"

Whandall slammed a quick punch at Preetror's heart. Shut off his breath! Tras was expecting it; he dodged and turned, sloughed the blow, backed out of reach. "Isn't the Burning supposed to happen all at once? Do you *feel* Yangin-Atep? Do you feel the rage?"

A teller's task isn't to keep the peace. All these years Whandall had known Tras Preetror without ever quite grasping that truth.

Too late now. Angle Street had heard his message. Lordkin were disappearing into shops. Kinless were fleeing, converging into a pack. Tras joined them, bubbling with news.

Wanshig had Whandall's arm. "Move *out,* Whandall. Through there. You lead; I'll trail. Elriss, follow Whandall."

Another street. Pelzed passed with nine Serpent's Walk men. "Whandall! Wanshig!" Pelzed shouted. "We're going to Lord's Town! Come with us."

Whandall waved to indicate the women.

Astonishingly, Pelzed nodded calmly, as if he understood the need. "We can't wait," he said, and gestured his Serpent's Walk warriors toward Sanvin Street. "You'll miss the best." Then they were gone, and the smell of smoke was thicker yet.

Three cross-streets later: the Burning had arrived before them. A handful of lookers confronted a pudgy Lordkin in his forties. Did he need help?

No, the barbarians were merely bewildered, and the Dirty Bird was shouting into their faces while his arms described expansive circles. "It's free! Take it—it's all ours!" Joyfully he tried to lead them into a shoemaker's shop, where a score of gatherers were already seated on the dirt floor, passing shoes back and forth, trying to find something to fit.

The party atmosphere called to Whandall, but Wanshig steered the Placehold women around that scene too.

And finally home, and upstairs to the more defensible second floor. Placehold had stone walls. The floors would burn, but they were thick wood, and it would take determined effort to get them blazing. No one in the past had ever taken the time. The women were as safe as they would ever be.

And Whandall asked, "Now?"

"Yes, O eager one—" Whandall was halfway down the stairs. All the fine loot would be gone! Wanshig shouted down at him. "Wait! Where are the rest of us?"

Whandall stopped himself with an effort. There was a surging in his blood and a heat in his loins. Both were familiar, but they had never been this strong. The Whandall who once sat on Mother's Mother's lap and listened to stories of a better time watched the rest of himself losing control and whispered its disapproval.

"Where are they?" Wanshig demanded. "Resalet, Shastern, the other men? The boys?"

"Gathering!"

"Whandall, I thought Resalet would wait!" Wanshig clambered down after him. "He's gone. All the men are gone."

"Shig, they're just out gathering and partying with everyone else."

"Resalet has been talking about Morth of Atlantis," Wanshig said. He looked up the stairs to see Elriss staring down at him.

"Come back," Elriss said.

"I think they went to Morth's shop," Wanshig said. With an effort he turned away from Elriss and followed Whandall outside. "I think they went as soon as the fires started."

"What would he want there?" Whandall demanded.

"Powders. Hemp," Wanshig said.

"Resalet hates that stuff!"

Wanshig laughed.

"Resalet's afraid of Morth," Whandall said. "What about 'Never remember a killing after the Burning?' "

They were back in the street. Where the granary had been, the new restaurant was burning: a hard-luck site. Eastward, a shouting match over who had first claim to an ornate desk was about to turn violent, while someone disappeared with the matching chair.

Wanshig looked back to the Placehold. "Who'll watch the women?" he demanded. "Someone has to stay." He looked at Whandall and saw almost uncontrolled eagerness. "And I know, I know, it won't be you, little brother."

A kinless hurried past pulling a cart. "Help me!" the kinless shouted. A dozen youths, Serpent's Walk, Flower Market, Bull Pizzle all mixed together, ran after him, shouting and laughing. The cart overturned almost at Wanshig's feet, and the kinless merchant ran on unencumbered. Rings with red stones spilled out of the wreckage and Wanshig scooped up several. He handed one to Whandall.

"Ours!" a Bull Pizzle shouted, but he was laughing. He saw Whandall's elaborate tattoo, looked up to the walls to see the Serpent's Walk signs, and eyed Whandall nervously. No one moved for a moment. Then the Bull Pizzle laughed again and dove into the mob at the cart. They tore the cart apart and left in a bunch, carrying dresses and trousers and a coil of rope.

There was smoke to the west. Wanshig turned that way, hurrying. "Whandall, you've been spying on Morth. Is there anything our fathers should know about him? Anything that might hurt them?"

That *was* why he'd gone to Morth, wasn't it? Months ago. Whandall thought he remembered other reasons. Morth was nearly a friend. But those memories conflicted with the fire in his veins. Whandall said, "He told me about the spell that killed Pothefit. He won't use that again. But you don't exactly ask a magician, 'Please tell me what you use to stop Lordkin from taking things.' "

"Then what exactly do you ask him?"

"I watch. I listen. Shig, some things he just picks up and sells. Other things he waves his hands or mutters under his breath. Some of those, it's never the same twice, so maybe he's bluffing. I can't tell you what to take." He stopped, remembering. "Shig, I don't think Morth will be there at all."

"He lives at the shop."

"He'll be afraid. He didn't mean to hurt Pothefit!"

They were jogging now, moving wide around gatherers staggering under loads of valuables or trash. Whandall stopped suddenly.

Men his own age were gathering a kinless woman. It looked like fun. More: he knew her, Dream-Lotus Innkeep of the western edge, four years his elder and very lovely. He'd never quite worked up the nerve to approach her, to learn if she would have the love of a young Lordkin, and now he need not ask.

Wanshig tried to pull him away. Whandall resisted. "Come *on*, Shig—"

"No. Elriss would kill me." He looked into Whandall's face and gave up. "I'll go on ahead. Maybe I can get them to hold up." His grip closed like a vise on Whandall's arm. "You *follow* me, yes? You don't stop again."

"Yes, Shig, yes."

CHAPTER
23

He was ready to follow Shig. Pulling his clothing on, checking his own belongings, trading jokes with the others, happy—when he saw that the man now on top of Dream-Lotus was strangling her!

Before the sight had quite registered, Whandall's knife was out and moving in a downward arc. Neatly, precisely, he sliced the man's left ear off.

The man bellowed. His rutting urge had his lower body in thrall, but his head and shoulders tried to turn, tried to reach his belt and knife.

The man who held Dream-Lotus's wrists had only begun to react. Horrified at the strangling, or horrified at Whandall's meddling: no way to tell. Someone else bellowed and snatched at him. Whandall rolled across the strangler's back, notched his other ear, then ran, slashing backhand at his nose and unexpectedly nicking the tip and upper lip. The strangler let go of Dream-Lotus's throat and stood up. Dream-Lotus sucked air in a whistling shriek while Whandall ran.

He'd once heard a man say that strangling a woman would make her react, that it was a greater kick. He'd thought that was disgusting; he thought so now.

There were too many following him to stop and make a stand. Skill was no use here. Run! The strangler himself was in the lead, legs pumping hard, barefoot to the hips. Big guy, and scarred, under a tattooed orchid.

But the knife, so quick! Maybe he could have talked? Persuaded the man to . . . what? Nobody plays at sweet reason during a Burning.

Through here! Rigmaster's ropewalk was a long building with no windows but plenty of hemp in storage. It had started to burn. Maybe the strangler would step on a live coal. Whandall caught a lungful of smoke, realized his mistake, and swerved away, rightward around the pall of pale smoke, then hard left. Someone ran out of the building, a kinless carrying a bundle. He saw Whandall, screamed, and ran hard, still carrying what looked like carved wooden blocks. They'd have burned, but what were they? If Whandall weren't running for his life he'd have found out—

When Yangin-Atep possessed a man, was this what he felt? It didn't feel divine. For that moment he'd felt so wonderful, he'd been so *grateful* to Dream-Lotus. Then someone was hurting her, and the chance to rescue her was all he could have desired. It felt very natural to cut the strangler, and not at all divine.

Feet pounding hard, Whandall completed his arc around the cloud of hemp smoke. The strangler was a trace of shadow, and yes! he was cutting across, through the rope factory itself! There were other shadows in there: the strangler's friends.

Maybe they'd all chase Whandall and let Dream-Lotus go. Maybe the strangler would outrun the rest, use all his strength catching up, to die under Whandall's knife. Would Dream-Lotus be pleased, grateful for such a gift?

Maybe not. They were squeamish, the kinless, and after all, Whandall too had raped her.

Behind Whandall the strangler ran out of the burning structure, choking and half blinded and reeling with the effects of hemp smoke. He slowed, hearing the laughter that followed him. He looked down, realized his nakedness, and began to laugh despite the blood that flowed from nose and ears. Those behind him staggered about in a giggling fit. They collapsed in laughter as more of the hemp smoke blew past them.

Whandall slowed too, to laugh and gesture, then ran on. Which way was Morth of Atlantis?

As the danger faded, Whandall remembered his thirst. Water was what he would be gathering if he dared stop. What would Resalet expect to find in Morth's shop, of all places? Wanshig must be wrong!

But Whandall kept running, because he knew in his gut that Wanshig was right.

As he ran, his mind caught up.

The scarf! Resalet thought he could gather a tattoo from Morth of Atlantis!

Tras Preetror was interviewing a handful of gatherers in Silda's Handmeals. The gatherers were preening, proud that their lives would be made legend in lands they'd never see. That son of a dog had helped to spread the Burning beyond its reasonable bounds. If Whandall could catch Tras alone—

You don't stop again. Whandall didn't stop. His head was clearing.

He should be nearing Morth's shop.

Morth's defenses might have preserved him—but might also be used up by now. Random looters wouldn't know what was safe to take. He hoped his brothers and uncles had waited. He should have come sooner.

Some landmarks were missing: the belfry, the Houses of Teaching. The tallest structures must have made the best torches.

That glare of light and heat to his left: Wood's lumberyard? Lordkin had piled beams into a tent shape to burn better. Just beyond it—

Morth's shop?

Matters were not as he expected. Buildings around the site were burned, charred, but the shop of Morth of Atlantis was a flat circle of gray ash. Whandall felt a fist closing in his chest. *Nothing* had survived.

Those were bones . . . skulls. Five skulls.

Maybe Morth was among them. Maybe Whandall's family was avenged.

Maybe Morth had bent the god's exuberant rage to his own will, to punish looters.

Whandall wouldn't know until he reached home. He couldn't make himself hurry. He couldn't go straight home: the strangler's Flower Market street-brothers hadn't had time to forget Whandall's face.

He saw a whooping Lordkin drop a howling dog into a well to die. That struck him as stupid, but there were four Lordkin and they were big. He left them alone. He found clumps of kinless holding off jeering Lordkin with makeshift weapons, and he left them alone too. In the back of his mind he could see himself and his kin, and in truth, the whole thing was beginning to look stupid.

Others might have thought so. Whandall saw more of caution than of Yangin-Atep's manic joy. The Burning was ending, though coals still burned.

The family cook pot had been stolen from the courtyard. The men hadn't come home.

They never came home. Even Wanshig had disappeared. Whandall at fifteen was the oldest man in the Placehold.

CHAPTER
24

The men were gone—and Mother's Mother never showed surprise. She'd lived in a world of her own for years. She came back to reality long enough to organize the household. The women took her orders, perhaps because they were terrified.

She took time to hold Whandall as she might have held a small child. "You're the oldest now," she said. "Keep the Placehold! I've always been proud of you. You saved your brothers before; now you have to do it again. Keep the Placehold!"

It was as if she had waited half her life for this. Now, tasks done, she slipped away, back to some pleasant place that no one else could see.

Elriss was pregnant. She wept for Wanshig and stayed in the women's rooms. Mother was more practical. In the first light of the morning after the burning she found Whandall.

"I have to leave."

"Why?" he asked. They had never been very close. With a new baby every year she had little time for him even though too many died. He'd spent more time with Mother's Mother. "Will you be back?"

"I'll come back if I can," Mother said. "Elriss will take care of the youngest. You and Shastern can take care of yourselves. Whandall, there's no food and no water."

"We need you to get food from the Lords," Whandall said.

"Elriss and Wess and Mother—three's enough. The Lords won't give any more than three can gather," Mother said. She lifted her carpet bag. "I'll be back if I can come back."

"But where will you be?"

She didn't answer. Whandall watched her go down the stairs. There she joined two other Placehold women, women who had both left babies in the Placehold's care. He watched them make their wary way out into the street, out into the Burning, and wondered if he'd ever see Mother again.

Three hours after first light Shastern and five younger boys came in pulling a cart. Each had an armful of stuff, clothing, enough rope to trade for a big cook pot if they could find someone who'd trade. There was a small cook pot in the cart. There was food amid the junk, but some of it was spoiled and the rest would have to be eaten in a hurry.

They traded whooping memories of the Burning. One by one they turned serious when they saw there were no men. The younger boys gathered around Whandall in the big room on the second floor. Girls came out to join them. They all stared at Whandall Placehold.

Shastern demanded, "Where are the men?"

"Gone," Whandall said. He didn't tell them what he suspected, that all including Wanshig had been blasted by Morth of Atlantis. Was there anything he could have done? If he'd stayed with Wanshig, would all the men have lived?

"But they'll be back," Shastern said. "They're just . . ." He saw Whandall's face. "What do we do?" Shastern asked. "When the word gets out, there'll be men come to gather the Placehold!"

"What do we eat?" Rubyflower asked. Her ten-year-old eyes were as big as dinner plates.

"How much food do we have?" Whandall asked.

Rubyflower shook her head. "I don't know. A week before Mother's Day we usually have more in the pantry than we have now."

"And it's two weeks to Mother's Day," Whandall mused. "Have you heard anything about Mother's Day? Will the Lords come? Will they bring the gifts?"

No one knew.

Whandall sent Ilthern to find out. "Don't talk," Whandall said. "Just listen. See what they're saying in Peacegiven Square. Listen to the Lordsmen and their clerks. Maybe they'll say something."

"It won't matter," Rubyflower said. "If they had Mother's Day tomorrow, we'd never get the cart back from Peacegiven Square! Someone would gather everything!"

The little girl was right, Whandall thought. Only four men in the Placehold carried knives; only two wore tattoos. Placehold itself might be defended by barricading the stairs. It wouldn't burn; the Burning was already fading. "Bring up rocks," Whandall told Rubyflower. "Get the other girls. Boys too. Ecohar, you go with them. Bring up rocks."

"Here?"

"Here and on the roof. Try not to look frantic."

"And what do we eat, Whandall?" Shastern asked quietly when the smaller children were gone for rocks. "Rubyflower's right—we'll never get a cart home."

"Whandall will think of something." Wess spoke from behind him, possession and pride in her voice.

Vinspel had been killed in a knife fight, ten days back. They'd had to tell Wess. No man would tell her, or tell any woman, that Vinspel had been fighting for another woman. The other Placehold women liked Wess too, but they *would* talk.

And now Whandall could only think that no man could keep her from him.

She was the oldest girl in the room. Mother's Mother was leader of the Placehold, but she was somewhere else inside her mind. Mother had been the real leader, usually, when she didn't have flasks and powders. But now she was gone. If Wanshig came back, Elriss would be leader. Now—

Now, Whandall's woman would have the job, honors and duties alike. It came to Whandall that he didn't really know what that meant. He knew that Mother's Mother, then Mother, had kept the keys to the pantry. Neither seemed to cook or sew or clean. Others did that. But without someone to make it happen, they didn't.

Two children began to wail. Wess grabbed the oldest, a six-year-old, and shook him. "Quiet. Let Whandall think," she said. "Go with Rubyflower and get some rocks. All of you, shoosh! Get rocks we can throw from the roof. Not you, Raimer. Get some water for the roof garden. Not drinking water; dirty water will do fine. Come on, all of you—let's get to work."

Whandall nodded. "Rocks. Good," he said. "Shastern, you help Wess. Find some way to barricade the stairway too. I'll be back as soon as I can."

"Where are you going?" Shastern asked.

"Pelzed."

He'd have to tell Pelzed how helpless the Placehold was. That would be dangerous, but Pelzed would find out anyway. Better to tell him straight off. Pelzed—Lord Pelzed—owed Whandall a favor. Would he remember? Would he care? But it was the only place Whandall could go.

Pelzed had led a band toward Lord's Town. Whandall couldn't follow there. He'd wait at Pelzed's roofless house.

But Pelzed was back.

Three of Pelzed's women were going through a stack of gatherings.

Pelzed shouted when he saw Whandall. "Whandall! Come have some tea!"

Whandall approached warily. He waved to indicate the loot. "From Lord's Town? Lord."

Pelzed grinned. "Not exactly," he said. "Sit down."

"Yes, Lord Pelzed."

"Heard you'd had some trouble," Pelzed said. "Wanshig's gone? Some of the other men."

"Yes, Lord. Lord, you once said you owed me a favor. We need help, Lord."

Pelzed poured tea and pushed the cup over to Whandall. "Tell me."

"All the men are gone, Lord," Whandall said. "There's only me and the younger boys. The women will try to find men, but . . ."

Pelzed nodded. There was no expression in his eyes at all as he sat lost in thought. Finally he said, "Are you asking for my protection?"

"Yes, Lord."

"Why not ask the Lordsmen?"

"Lord, there are lines a hundred people long in front of every clerk in Peacegiven Square," Whandall said. "And what good would it do? Men come to gather the Placehold. We send for the Lordsmen, and maybe they come and maybe not, but they won't come in time to do us any good. We have our own Lord here. Why go to the Lords of Lordshills?"

"You learn fast," Pelzed said. "All right. We'll protect your cart on Mother's Day and I'll get the word out that anyone gathering at the Placehold will have to answer to me. And I'll speak to the Lord's clerks in the Square. You'll be all right."

"Thank you, Lord."

"You'll have to control the Placehold. Don't make any new enemies. I can't fight new enemies," Pelzed said. "You remember that."

"Yes, Lord."

"How many boys do you have at Placehold?"

"Eleven, Lord, not including Shastern."

"They'll all join Serpent's Walk," Pelzed said. "Join knowing they owe us."

"Yes, Lord."

"Good." Pelzed sipped more tea. A crafty smile came to his lips. "Don't you want to know what happened?" he asked.

"Oh, yes, Lord," Whandall said. "I saw you going toward the Lordshills."

"So did the Bull Pizzles," Pelzed said. "They were following us. We couldn't shake them and there were too many to fight, so there we were, going out gathering with a bunch of Pizzles following right behind. I had a good plan—wear forester leathers. Wear leathers and make sure we didn't leave any dead behind. They'd never know it was us. But when we got closer we saw Lordsmen. Twenty, maybe more. They had armor, swords, spears, big shields, and we weren't about to get past them. Kraemar and Roupend were feeling Yangin-Atep's power. They wanted to run in and gather. I couldn't control them much longer."

"Is that where you got all that?" Whandall asked. "Lord's Town?"

"No, what I did was let the Bull Pizzles get past me, then go back to the Pizzle streets," Pelzed said. "With our leathers on. Struck a bargain with the kinless there. Kraemar and Roupend got to burn some old houses and stores, the rest of us gathered all this, and the Bull Pizzles never came back. I may even have a new street for Serpent's Walk."

"Lord—was Chief Wulltid killed, then, Lord?"

"No, you know what he's like; he didn't go with his men. He stayed to take his pleasures in his own houses." Pelzed laughed. "I hope he enjoyed himself. He won't like my new arrangements." The grin was wider. "But the Lords will. Bull Pizzle isn't very popular with the Lords right now."

Whandall sipped tea and listened. He tried to imagine himself as Lord Whandall of Serpent's Walk. It was a good picture, and the more he thought about it, the more he liked it. It was a big job and he didn't know how to do it, but he could watch Pelzed and learn.

Wess had moved all his things into the big northeast room. Resalet's clothes were gone. His other things, bronze mirror, drinking cup, were laid out for Whandall's approval.

Wess was wearing a short wool skirt and a thin blouse that opened down to her navel.

Where did you get that? He knew he shouldn't ask. *From Vinspel?* His hands were on her shoulders. "Nice," he said, and repeated himself: "Nice. Wess, you're beautiful." She must have used the mirror, he thought, and he reached out for the magical thing and looked into it.

There was no trace, now, of that ring-shaped scar. The serpent tattoo was magnificent . . . alien.

"What did I look like?" he asked. "I stayed clear of you while I was healing." He'd let her see him once. The look in her eyes.

"That scar. I never thought it would heal."

"I found magic," he said. "Wess, I've got to talk to the rest of the house, but first, what have you got done?"

The children were being taken care of.

There was food. This evening's dinner would be huge: they were cooking everything that wouldn't keep. They'd eat as much as they could. Tomorrow, who knew?

Stashes of rocks were on the roof, and children on guard. Invaders would expect rocks. There should be something else too, something to startle a gathering band. Boiling water? Too complicated; too much work, and where would they get water? *Think* of something. Fire would burn *on* a roof.

The Placehold was nearly empty. Was there some way the place could look busier? All that showed from the street was a blank wall and a wide gate. What men he had, he could move them through that gate more often.

"And I couldn't think of anything else," she said. "You?"

"I've got Pelzed's protection. The only idea I had. Dark Man's Cup will do us some good, I think. Pelzed killed some friends for not keeping his promises there."

CHAPTER
25

W handall was busier than he had ever been in his life.
He'd forgotten that everyone went hungry following the
Burning. There wasn't enough food outside: too many gatherers and not enough to gather. Hunger, then feasts when anyone could
gather food. They fought over the dishes, and everything tasted so good,
he remembered that. Now he knew why: they were starving.

Whandall's elder half sister Sharlatta came home with Chapoka.
Chapoka was an adult male, and there was no more to be said for him. He
never gathered except from a friend, he complained about everything, and
he never shut up. Whandall knew him well enough to throw him out.

Chapoka wouldn't be thrown, and Whandall was harassed and hungry.
He decided his household of children could use entertainment. The fight in
the courtyard left Chapoka with scars he would have to explain for the rest
of his life. The gaudiest were on his back.

Afterward the Placehold's survivors treated Whandall like a Lord. During this time, lack of respect was one complaint he never had.

He hadn't realized—he had to leaf back through his memories to understand that *everyone always complained to a Lord all the time.*

Even Wess. Loving Wess was wonderful, and she held the Placehold
together as much as anyone. But . . . living with a woman took new skills
at accommodation and ate time he didn't have. It wasn't like living with a
roomful of brothers, and he hadn't *liked* that very much.

He saw his former life as a long dream of idleness. He came to understand why fathers disappeared. Maybe he wouldn't have stayed with it. But he knew. . . .

He knew where the men had gone. Whatever befell the Placehold now was his doing.

Whandall's mother brought Freethspat home four weeks after the Burning. Everyone was astonished. He was a heavily scarred man around thirty years old, from so far across town that nobody knew anything of his clan. "Sea Cliffs," he said, and he showed a finely tattooed sea gull in flight.

When Whandall came home that afternoon, Freethspat and Mother had the northeast room. Whandall's things were in the north room that Shastern had taken because no one wanted to move Elriss from the southeast room she had shared with Wanshig.

Wess moved in with Elriss. She was avoiding him again. Once they met on the stair, and Wess spoke rapidly, before he could open his mouth.

"You could have *asked* me to stay."

"What if I asked now?"

"Stay where? Whandall, I would have followed you. You never said anything. It's like I came with the northeast room, or with your being the oldest man!"

"I wasn't sure," Whandall said. She'd left him once before. She had come to him when his status changed, and it might change again. For those reasons and one other, he'd dithered.

That other reason . . . "Wess, if I had you *and* the Placehold to take care of, that would be my life. Guard you and the rest of them until I am dead. I know how to do that. Be Pelzed's right hand. When Pelzed wants to slack off a little, years from now, I'd *be* Lord Pelzed. Lord Whandall," he tasted the name, "except when Lords or Lordsmen can hear me. I . . ."

She waited for him to go on, but he didn't know how to say it. He hadn't even tried until now. *I don't want to be Pelzed! Pelzed bows and scrapes and flatters, and sets his people against each other, and lies, and kills, and tells other people to kill friends. And with all that lives not a half as well as the real Lords in Lord's Town. What I want, it isn't here—*

Wess brushed past him and was gone.

Coals still burned.

The killing of firefighters had got up the kinless's noses. Now they wanted to carry knives.

For months after the Burning, the talk was of little else. There was no fundamental disagreement among the Lordkin. How could a conquered people be permitted weapons? Of course the firefighters shouldn't have been killed . . . not *killed*. But fire was Yangin-Atep's. Wait, now, Yangin-Atep suppressed fire too! So it wasn't blasphemy. Yes it was, but they could have been driven off . . . taught an unforgettable lesson, scarred or maimed, *then* driven off . . . but they'd *soaked* those blankets to smother the fires—that was *drinking* water. . . .

In the street-corner gatherings, Whandall tried to stay out of the arguments. They could get you killed. A teller from Begridseth was beaten for asking the wrong questions, and again Whandall didn't participate.

At home the women were in quiet mourning, but Mother's Mother left no doubt about how she felt. The Lordkin had become no better than animals.

The kinless couldn't see reason. They had been attacked while rescuing horses—yes, and fighting a fire too. Attacked and murdered. The kinless wanted the killers' heads. Hah! No hope of that, of course, even without the protection of their street-brothers. You'd have thought half the city had watched the firefighters die; they were willing to describe what they thought had happened in minute detail, but nobody could remember a face.

But the kinless wanted to carry knives or clubs, to fight back next time!

Many Lordkin would have offered them the chance, for amusement. A bad precedent, though, a reversal of ancient law.

But nothing was being built.

Lords and kinless were holding talks; Lordkin spoke at every intersection; and every mouth was dry. The Deerpiss carried water an uncertain distance and then stopped, because smashed aqueducts were still smashed.

Garbage wasn't moving. The Lordkin began to see that it would not move itself. Rats and other scavengers were growing numerous. Ash pits that had been stores and restaurants now began to serve the Lordkin as garbage dumps.

Mother's Day came and went. Nothing was distributed in Peacegiven Square because there was nothing to distribute. Scant food was coming into the city; too much was disappearing on the way. Great fire, would the Lordkin have to take up driving wagons them*selves?*

That, Whandall decided, was an interesting notion.

Now Freethspat and Whandall and Shastern were the only men in the Placehold. Freethspat fit in well enough. He didn't often beat the younger children and never seemed to beat the women at all. He was respectful to Pelzed and spoke well of Serpent's Walk. Mother never yelled at him, which was unusual.

A week after his arrival, Freethspat was gone all night. Whandall wondered if he'd disappeared. Mother had no doubts, and in the morning he brought home a pushcart full of food, some of it fresh. There was enough food to last a week and no one mentioned the blood on the cart.

Freethspat was a provider.

Freethspat might have had a little Lords' blood in him too. Over the next three weeks, rooms nobody would walk in barefoot became jarringly clean, and the Placehold girls smiled proudly when Freethspat praised them. Six Placehold boys who had been old enough to gather in the Burning, but too young for anything so serious as robbing a wizard, now brought home gold rings and wallets from looker pockets and produce from kinless markets. And Whandall—

"Now it's your turn," Freethspat said.

They were in the courtyard, gathered for dinner. Heads turned as Freethspat spoke. They'd heard this conversation before.

Whandall asked, "Mean what?"

"Mean it's time you earned your keep, Whandall," Freethspat said. "Sure, I can get more to eat, but what happens to your mother if they get me? And your sisters? Your turn."

"I don't know where to get food."

"I can show you, but your mother says you know a lot," Freethspat said. "You've been to Lordshills. Take me there."

Whandall shook his head. "The Lordsmen will kill us both. Me for sure. Lord Samorty told them last time I was there. Here, look at my arm—it grew back crooked." Whandall pulled off his shirt. "Here—"

"Then somewhere else. You know the forest, but there's nothing to be had there, is there? No. Then somewhere you went with your brother— what was his name?"

"Wanshig," Elriss said, glaring. She was nursing Wanshig's son.

"Wanshig," Freethspat said. "They tell me you hung around with him a lot, Whandall. He must have showed you something. They say Wanshig was smart."

"He was," Elriss said.

"So show me."

Whandall could have liked Freethspat. But the man was just an inch taller and just an inch wider than Whandall, just a little too obtrusive in his strength. He called him *Whandall,* as a brother would. He lived in Whandall's room.

There had been no need for Whandall's gathering skills in the time since the Burning. (Eleven weeks? *That* long?) There was no need now.

But Whandall was getting restless, and Wess was unobtrusively following the exchange, and it wouldn't take much of a coup to shut Freethspat up. "I did have a notion," Whandall said. "I just couldn't see a way to make it work. Freethspat, what do you know about wine?"

Well back from the road and screened by growths of touch-me vine, Whandall and Freethspat watched the vineyard. The noon sun was making the workers torpid. Their patient drudgery hadn't changed since he and Wanshig had watched them nearly a year ago. The grapevines were glossy green; the buildings behind them showed no sign of scorching. The Burning of two months back simply hadn't happened here.

The Lordkin guards did seem more alert. A youth passed Whandall walking upright and noisily, far from the comforts offered by that big house. Woodsman's leathers made him clumsy, and still he avoided the morningstar bushes and beds of touch-me, steering wide of the hiding place Wanshig had found for them.

Whandall had been surprised to see how much Freethspat knew about leathers and the chaparral. Freethspat knew about a lot of things.

And here came a pony, a local pony with a fleck of white bone on its forehead, pulling a wagon with a single driver.

"That one," Freethspat said. "No. It's empty."

"Wait," Whandall whispered. He watched the wagon go by. Just watched this time.

He was not bored. In Serpent's Walk, *there* he'd been bored. The same limp justifications—"What do the kinless want of us? When Yangin-Atep takes us, we do these things! It's not us; it's the rage!"—until they believed it themselves.

It was hard to believe in that empty wagon. Wasn't the bed a little high? Easy to picture a false floor with flasks of wine under the boards. The kinless driver tugged at his yellow silk noose. A little besotted, was he, rolling a little with the wagon's motion? A big one, he was, with shoulders like boulders; maybe you needed that to control a pony. It hardly mattered. A kinless wouldn't fight.

The guard was a Lordkin, Whandall's age, fifteen or sixteen. Older men had sent him out, and stayed to drink in comfort, no doubt. In armor he'd be helpless. Whandall could take him.

Then the wagon, much closer now—have to sprint to catch it—and the driver. Arms like a wrestler. The big hat shadowed his face, but the nose was flat. Hard to believe in him too. He was still tugging at the yellow silk tied loosely around his thick neck. He wasn't used to it.

Damn! The hat shadowed his nose and ears, but—

"That driver is Lordkin," Freethspat said. His voice was filled with disgust. "Working like a kinless!"

"You're right."

"What could you pay a Lordkin to make him work like a kinless? What could he gain that another Lordkin couldn't take away from him?"

Whandall thought about it while the wagon receded. "Wine, maybe, if he drank it right away. Secrets, things nobody else knows. This isn't going to be so easy, is it? We may have to kill the driver."

"Have to kill the guard anyway. Your turn, Whandall."

CHAPTER
26

The next wagon didn't appear until near sunset. The same guard had been out there for all that time, pushing through branches, wearing a path, sweating into his leathers, and bored into a stupor. The wagon distracted him.

"Now," Freethspat said without turning.

It was Whandall's scheme. All it needed for completion was some way to avoid killing. Freethspat was a skillful gatherer. He knew things. He had brains.

Freethspat turned to look at Whandall. "He's too far now. When he comes back, take him."

"I brought you here," Whandall protested. His voice never rose above the sound of the breeze in leaves. "Isn't that enough?"

Freethspat studied Whandall with interest. "You're not scared?" he whispered.

"No."

"I understand. But Whandall, this is what we are. This is what a Lord-kin is. Here and now. Right now. With me watching."

Whandall took in a deep breath. The guard was coming toward him again. His forearm and wrist brushed a morningstar. He grunted in pain and shied back, and then Whandall slammed into his back. And cut his throat.

It was his first kill, and it went much better than he'd expected. Whandall had several seconds to get into place before the wagon arrived. He didn't look back at the corpse.

He thumped into the wagon bed while the wagoneer was scanning the trees for the guard. The wagoneer half stood, turning, slicing blind with his long knife in a move he must have practiced for years. Whandall blocked the blade with his own and threw with his other hand.

Pebbles spattered the pony's head and ears. The pony screamed and surged forward. The wagoneer stumbled, tried to stab out anyway, and was cursing as Whandall's blade slid in under his armpit.

The road curved wide around, down to the streambed. The turns weren't sharp and the pony knew the way. Whandall had time to put on the hat and coat—and figure out how to move the complicated knot to get the noose off the corpse and onto his own neck—before the gatehouse came in view. Bile was rising in his throat. He let the pony slow. It wouldn't do to be seen vomiting over the side.

He heard Freethspat climbing in behind him. There was a rustle as he hid under the tarp. "Well done," came the whisper. "Couldn't have done it better myself. Whandall, I'm proud of you."

Whandall didn't care to speak.

Freethspat examined the dead man, then cursed softly.

"What?"

"He's a Toronexti," Freethspat said. "So was the other one. Why didn't you tell me?"

"Tell you what?" Whandall demanded. Suddenly he remembered Wanshig's words: Alferth had hired Toronexti to guard the vineyards.

Freethspat sighed. "You have a lot to learn, boy. You don't gather from the Toronexti. Ever."

Whandall pointed to the dead man. "They're not so tough—"

"No, they're not. But there are a lot of them. You kill one, others come looking for you, and *you won't know who they are.*"

"So what do we do?"

"We get out of here with this stuff." Freethspat frowned. "We get rid of it as quick as we can. Maybe they gathered the wagon. No Toronexti marks on *that.*"

"What do they look like?"

"Never you mind."

It was tempting to think in terms of secrets: of hiding. The wine under the false bed was in little flasks. *Those* could be hidden. It was what you did with wine. But how would you hide a wagon?

They discussed it after they'd cleared the gatehouse. They reached home in a stony silence.

Whandall began moving garbage.

Friends offered suggestions: get shovels, line the wagon with hay. Some of the Serpent's Walk men helped him do that. Others helped move garbage away from where they lived, until they got bored. Freethspat stayed with it. If any part of the scheme had collapsed, Freethspat would have gotten Whandall out alive and then never let him forget it. But he became good with the shovel, and he stayed with it.

Four more were good enough at it, and stayed long enough, that Whandall and Freethspat shared wine with them. They stayed as a core, to gather other men.

Four days of that, and everyone was tired of it. Serpent's Walk was full of men from Alferth's quarter who knew very well where and how Whandall got that wagon. Whandall left the wagon abandoned. It disappeared, with a few flasks left under the boards as a gift.

There was wine for Mother and Mother's Mother; for his sister Sharlatta and the man she'd brought home after Whandall evicted Chapoka; for Elriss, who had known no man since Wanshig disappeared, and Wess, whose man had taken to vanishing at night. Wine served as a don't-kill-me gift for Hartanbath, the man he'd cut. That was Freethspat's suggestion. Whandall and Freethspat shared two bottles with Hartanbath and some of his Flower Market friends, and were gone before Hartanbath had drunk very much.

Dusk in Tep's Town. Whandall stood at the western edge of the Placehold roof garden to watch the sun fall into the sea. The landscape below softened, hiding the garbage and the filthy streets. A few kinless hurried home, eager to reach shelter before darkness gave the world over to gatherers and worse.

There were Lordkin with no place to go. Some found shelter with kinless. That could be tricky. Kinless had no rights, but some were protected. Pelzed and other Lordkin leaders put some streets off limits. The Lords didn't permit a breach of the peace, but they never said what that was. Armed Lordsmen might come to help a kinless house under siege. Sometimes Lordsmen squads swept through Tep's Town and rounded up any Lordkin unlucky enough to get their attention. They took their prisoners to camps where they were put to work on the roads and aqueducts for a year. That didn't seem to happen in Serpent's Walk. Pelzed? Luck? Yangin-Atep?

Probably not Yangin-Atep.

And you didn't steal from the Toronexti. But only Freethspat could recognize them, so now what? And how did he *do* that?

The day faded, and now the city was lit with a thousand backyard cook fires.

Whandall took out three flasks of wine. He drank the first in three gulps. He was halfway through the second when he heard the scream.

He listened long enough to be sure it didn't come from the Placehold. He sipped more wine. Not his business. The scream ended with a strangled gurgle. Someone had died of a cut throat. Whandall wondered who it might be. Someone he knew? A kinless who resisted? More likely a Lordkin knife fight.

Freethspat was proud of him. He'd killed the guard. His first kill. Some would add to their tattoos, or wear an earring. It was what Lordkin did. This was what it meant to be Lordkin.

His belly spasmed and spat the last swallow of wine straight up into his nose and sinuses. He doubled over, coughing and snorting and trying to get the acid out of his windpipe, and more wine came up. Stupid. He knew what wine did. He got himself under control and took another swallow.

There were torches over by the new ropewalk. The scream had come from that direction. Could someone be gathering there? Who'd be such a fool? The ropewalk was in Pelzed's forbidden zone. Two Lordkin families lived among the kinless rope makers. Whandall had been inside that area only once, during the Burning. Rebuilding of the ropewalk started the day after the Burning, and Pelzed himself came down to supervise and make it clear that the kinless working there were never to be molested. Rope was important, both to use and to sell. Once Whandall had been curious about how it was made, but no Lordkin knew that.

Hemp held many secrets. Where hemp was grown, how the fibers were stripped from it, always at dawn after a night of heavy dew, but no one knew why. Tar was brought from the Black Pit. Hemp fibers and tar were taken to a long narrow building, and later they came out as rope, some tarred, some not, to be used and sold. Ships used rope. Rope left Serpent's Walk, gold and shells came back, and every step of that was protected by Pelzed here and the Lordsmen elsewhere.

A dozen torches now. Whandall began the third flask of wine. It was his last. The screams had stopped. The torchbearers went out of sight. Whandall thought he saw shadows moving near the ropewalk.

The next morning a Lordkin from the Hook was found with his throat cut. Someone had gathered his clothes and shoes, leaving him naked on a trash heap.

CHAPTER
27

Thus Whandall—who already knew how to fight and how to run—learned how to gather a pony-drawn vehicle and *really* move out. One day he might be glad.

And he had a hell of a story to tell, if the chief flasker ever wanted to make something of it.

That was unlikely. Alferth worked with (never *for*) certain lords. Whandall had robbed *them*. Alferth would defend his status, but he would never defend property. To Alferth, Whandall and Freethspat had only demonstrated their skill.

A great many Lordkin were part kinless, as many kinless merchants were part Lordkin. Only kinless would defend property. And Alferth's nose was a little too pointed, and he didn't have enough earlobe, and in fact any fool could see (as any wise man would forget) that Alferth had kinless blood.

But somewhere a Lord had been robbed. Whandall wondered about *him*, and about the Toronexti that Lord had hired to guard and move his wine. What would *they* do? The Toronexti guarded a path to nowhere, and nobody knew who they were. Alferth knew who had killed two of them.

Whandall was coming to realize that no one ever felt safe in Tep's Town.

He stopped worrying about Alferth, though. Alferth wouldn't talk to the Toronexti *now.* They'd want to know why he hadn't spoken earlier. They'd lost a wagon they were guarding; they'd never want anyone to know that! If Alferth spoke, he would only embarrass himself and the Toronexti. Nobody did that.

* * *

They were still talking, somewhere in the higher circles no Lordkin had seen save Whandall, up there where the Lords set the taxes and the kinless made their futile protests. On the street corners there was talk of compromise. Whandall heard the rumors and wondered what to believe.

Tep's Town was to have a troop of guards.

Whandall laughed when he heard that, but the rumors piled up details, and the laughter faded. Someone in the councils was serious.

Several hands of kinless men would be given weapons, never to be concealed. Most would be allowed hardwood sticks and torches.

Torches? A mad suggestion. Fire belonged to Yangin-Atep. Darkness belonged to any gatherer in need.

Rigid rules were laid down. The guards might use their sticks in carefully described circumstances, but never otherwise. Only officers (their numbers restricted) might carry blades, and those no longer than a hand. Guards would wear conspicuous clothing. They must never approach a Lordkin by subterfuge. From time to time their behavior would be reviewed by the Lordkin and the Lords.

Whandall wondered what the kinless thought they had won. Hedged about with such rules, they'd be more helpless than ever. The Lords themselves, and the loudest voices among the Lordkin, might have agreed to this nonsense, but if Lordkin saw fit to take a stick away from some kinless guard, they would!

But water and food were moving again. Garbage was leaving the inner city, though a few of those ash pits turned garbage pits were being made to grow food. Structures began to rise to cover the scars of the Burning.

Everyone was happy about that, but Whandall remembered the Lordshills and wondered.

Rumor flowed down from Lord's Town. There, Lordkin and kinless lived together and worked for mutual benefit. Garbage still moved. The fountains were turned off, most of them, but the date and olive trees weren't dry. Flower gardens still grew.

How was it done? Who were these Lords to have a city and a life when Tep's Town was dying?

It was death to go and look.

There had been a living god who gave fire to men. Nobody could doubt that. But Alferth, who started the Burning when Whandall was seven, hadn't been possessed by Yangin-Atep. He'd laughed when Tras suggested such a thing. The fires he'd set didn't seem to be motivated by anything bigger than the whim to watch a fire.

Whandall was losing faith. Yangin-Atep must be mythical by now.

Morth of Atlantis was gone.

The Placehold women didn't want Whandall to take a woman. He was the last man born in the Placehold. Yangin-Atep forbid he should leave—the house would have *no* trusted protector—but one more woman would be a hardship.

Wess came to share his bed sometimes, so he should not have been lonely. Wess had reconsidered. Freethspat wasn't interested in a second wife, and Whandall was as good a catch as Wess was likely to find. She made it clear to Whandall that she would move in anytime he asked.

Whandall refused. It rankled that she had moved out of his room when she thought Freethspat might be available. . . .

And other men came to visit. Wess was never unfriendly to any man who might have power. Freethspat was here, and his sister Ilyessa brought home a man . . . and it didn't feel like his family anymore.

One day Whandall would bring home a mate. The women would presently accept her. He would sire children. He was a fighter—or the rest of the city thought he was. He would rise in power among Pelzed's counselors, and a few would whisper that Pelzed thought of him as his heir. In later years he would sometimes collect taxed goods to supply a feast. He would speak with the Lords to shape civic policy. The Placehold and the city expected these things of him.

They didn't know that fire had claimed the Placehold men because Whandall stayed behind to get laid.

He was leery of making decisions for others. He held his opinions to himself and shied away from being too persuasive. And he watched the city rebuild.

PART FOUR

The Return

CHAPTER
28

Two years after the Burning, Elriss had blossomed into a very handsome woman, desired by nearly every man who saw her. She worked in the roof gardens and tended Arnimer, the son born months after the Burning. She taught all the Placehold children. She worked with the other women, and she was respectful to Freethspat; but except to go to Peacegiven Square on Mother's Day, she never left the Placehold, and she never spoke to men, visitors, or single Placeholders, except for Whandall.

She treated Whandall like Wanshig's little brother. Even wine hadn't tempted her. Presently even Whandall thought of her as a sister.

Whandall was dressing. Presently he would go to the meetinghouse to drink tea with Pelzed, carry out any errand Pelzed might have, watch how power was used . . .

Elriss came shouting to his door. "Wanshig is back!" she cried. "I see him! He's coming up the street."

And moments later Wanshig was there. He looked older, thinner, and a great deal stronger. Whandall had only moments to greet him before Elriss swept him into the room she had held from before he left. She showed him her son. Then the infant Arnimer was sent out to play with the other children, and no one saw Elriss or Wanshig for a long time.

Whandall went to the roof.

Wanshig knew! Whandall could have come to help the Placehold men, but he stopped for Dream-Lotus. Wanshig was back, and Wanshig knew.

* * *

They sat drinking weak hemp tea after dinner. Everyone listened as Wanshig told his story. He was looking at Whandall as he said, "I ran just as fast as I could and I was still too late. I saw an old man running away, looking back. I wondered if it was Morth."

Whandall realized he'd been holding his breath.

"The shop was full of Lordkin," Wanshig said. "I could see them through the door and a big window: at least ten, and they were all Place-holders, Whandall. Enough Placehold men to drive anyone else away.

"Things were burning inside. Resalet was possessed of Yangin-Atep! I saw him wave at a shelf, and a whole line of pots puffed into flame. He picked up something big in both arms."

"What was that?"

"I never knew. Understand, I was moving at a dead run. Legs like soggy wood. All I saw of anyone was a shadow backed by fire. I knew Resalet by the way he moved, and his arms were wrapped around a heavy round thing about as big as . . . as Arnimer."

The babe looked up on hearing his name. Wanshig stroked his back and said, holding his voice to an icy calm, "I tried to scream 'Get out! Get out!' I went, 'Whoosh!' No breath. I sucked in air to scream. Whatever was burning in that shop caught in my throat. I went into a coughing fit.

"Cousin Fiasoom staggered through the door, clawing at his throat, and fell to his knees. Resalet was coughing too. I could see him hunch over, just inside the doorway. He gestured the edge of his round thing into a tiny white flame, very bright. He plucked off the lid.

"Everything went white."

"The box exploded?"

"No. I saw just that much. *Resalet* exploded. *Resalet* was one great glare like looking into the sun at noon. It was like daggers in my eyes. I screamed and threw my arms over my eyes and curled up around myself. I felt Yangin-Atep *breathe* on my back, one long blast, and then he went away.

"I was blind. When I could move, I waited a bit. Maybe someone from the Placehold would see me, see? Nobody did, so I started feeling my way around. I stayed back from the heat that must have been Morth's shop. I could hear the riot around me.

"My sight came back with edges and white spots. I could see people around me gathering and burning. I wanted out. You understand? *Out.* No more Burning. No more Serpent's Walk, no more Tep's Town."

"Sure, Shig."

"Nobody's called me that in a long time."

"What then? The women were guarding the Placehold—"

"I didn't even think of that. I went to the Black Pit. I couldn't see; I couldn't fight. I needed a place to hide, and you told me ghosts couldn't hurt me, remember? I thought they'd scare away anyone else, so I went there. Spent the night.

"In the morning I could see more. My good white tunic was charred all across the back where Yangin-Atep had breathed on me. My hair came off in handfuls. It was *crisp*. There were a lot of fires far away, east and south. Whandall, I never wanted to see fire again."

Whandall laughed.

Wanshig didn't. He said, "I went to the docks. I played sneak-and-spy past a few Water Devils. There were ships. I went to the biggest.

"The entrance to a ship, they call that a *gangplank*. Two men were on guard there, not Water Devils. I told the big one, the older one, 'I want to sail on a ship.'

"Both men laughed, but I could feel them separating a little, you know? To put one behind me. The big one said, 'Well, that's not a problem, boy,' and I turned fast and caught the other one's arm.

"He'd tried to hit me with a little wood club they call a *fishkiller*. You know, Whandall, we *practice* this kind of thing. I broke his arm and let him dangle over the water, holding him out with my one arm—you know, showing off. I told Manocane, the big guy, the officer, 'I want *his* job.'

"That was Sabrioloy. His job was guarding the Lordkin. When the Lordsmen wheel up a cart full of gatherers, Sabrioloy knocks them on the head, shows them who's boss. He tried that with me. After that, I was boss, boss over the Lordkin sailors, anyway. Sabrioloy showed me the rest of what I needed to know. He trained me, and I didn't throw him over. Whandall, he couldn't swim."

"A ship's man? I thought even Water Devils could swim."

"Most sailors can't swim."

Their doubt must have showed. Wanshig said, "We were just pulling out of the bay. The officers wanted more sails up, so Sabrioloy and I drove the men aloft to raise them. Jack Rigenlord was an old hand, and he was up there above us all. Then a *mountain* of water stood up out of the sea and hit us broadside. It must have been magic, Whandall. I never saw anything like it before or since. Waves come in lines, rows, but this just stood up and curled over and *wham*. The ship heeled over and the mainmast bowed like a whip. Jack flew into the sea. He waved once at us and was gone. That made me a believer.

"I made Etiarp teach me to swim, first time we docked near a beach. Etiarp was a Water Devil who tried to gather from a merchant ship. We taught a few of the Lordkin. If a Lordkin could swim, I promoted him. We taught Sabrioloy too."

CHAPTER
29

It was a night of storytelling, and it ran nearly to dawn.

Freethspat told how he and Whandall had gathered a wine wagon. He still had a flask to pass around; only Yangin-Atep might know where he'd hidden it all this time. Whandall let him describe the escape. Then he told how he'd turned himself and Freethspat and the wagon into a garbage hauling business. He much enjoyed Wanshig's open amazement and Freethspat's determined grin.

Wanshig let the flask pass him while he told a story of being chased by a snake-armed monster bigger than the ship. When Freethspat called him a liar, Wanshig only shook his head.

The old Wanshig would have had some clever riposte. The new one saw how they stared, puzzled, waiting.

He said, "We sailed into Waluu Port eighteen days after Jack Rigenlord drowned. A woman came down to the dock asking for Captain Jack.

"Now Jack, he didn't have more than one woman in any one port, and some of them thought he was captain, I guess. Fencia, she had a marriage contract. When Jack didn't appear, she found us at the nearest saloon.

"Manocane knew her. He made her sit down, and bought her a mulled ale and made her drink, and then he said, 'Jack married the mermaid.' "

Freethspat was delighted. "I've heard of mermaids when I was a boy—"

"Oh, the merfolk are real enough," Wanshig said. "They're wonderful! They like to pace a ship, ride the bow wave. Where the magic's weak they take the shape of a big fish, but they breathe air, not water. There's a nostril *right* on top. Where the magic's strong you see a man or woman with fishy hindquarters. We don't offend the mers. They can drive fish toward a fleet or away, and show you where the rocks are when it's thick with fog. We like the merfolk.

"But it's just a sailor's way of speaking, 'He married the mermaid.' Jack Rigenlord *drowned*. We don't like to say *drowned*. But Fencia of Waluu Port didn't know that. She was furious. 'He was going to marry me! I waited through six years and four voyages for him to get enough money, and now he's married a *mermaid?* How does he expect to get *children?*'

"We'd been drinking. She was *so* angry, you know, and I guess I thought it was funny. You know: *married!*" Laughter rippled. Wanshig didn't smile. "Manocane opened his mouth, but I cut in first. I said to Fencia, 'No, wait, they aren't married *yet*. He says he wants your permission.'

"I saw every head turn. I heard a lot of laughing choked back.

" 'My permission!' she screams, and she makes me tell her all the details. What was he doing when she popped out of the water? What did the mermaid look like? Did she cover her breasts? Did she sing him down into the water or did he just see her and jump? Did Jack even remember Fencia? I made it up as I went along. By now we were surrounded. Sailors have a deadpan way of telling a story, so they kept straight faces. If Fencia heard any cackling she must have thought they were laughing at her because her man left her.

"I thought we were about to get some real entertainment. Sometimes an angry woman can remind a sailor why he left the land."

Whandall waited. When Wanshig didn't speak again, he asked, "Then what?"

"She gave it," Wanshig said.

"What?"

"She didn't do any more screaming that night. She just turned around and stalked out, head high. The next morning Fencia came to the dock and announced to a big crowd that her engagement to Jack Rigenlord was at an end and he was free to do as he liked. If she cried, it wasn't where anyone could see her. Manocane and I got all the other sailors to hold their tongues. I heard what they said afterward, but me, I thought she was brave.

"I've lied since," he told them all, "but I don't *like* it. People get hurt. And I'm home now, and I won't lie again."

On subsequent nights, Shastern listened quietly to Wanshig's tales of the sea. He concealed his thoughts, but when Wanshig spoke, Shastern always came to listen. Whandall noticed, and wondered if Shastern's thoughts resembled his own. If Whandall was fated to leave Tep's Town . . . despite Morth of Atlantis, might it be by sea?

CHAPTER

30

Wanshig found Whandall on the roof garden. Whandall had developed the habit of seeing to the health of the plants. Wanshig said, "I want you to know that two of us couldn't have done any more than I did. You could have got there in time to be blinded, that's all."

Whandall had found a few bugs already, so he finished inspecting the row of tomatoes. He stood up to find Wanshig watching the sun fall into the sea.

"What are you watching for, Shig?" Whandall asked.

"Green flash. Just as the sun vanishes, sometimes, when it's very clear, you can see a flash of green." Wanshig said.

"Have you seen it?"

"Twice, but never from shore," Wanshig said. "Just when we were at sea. It's very good luck. The weather is always great the next day." Wanshig stared westward, at the darkening hills. "Sunsets are better when the sun falls into the sea."

"You liked sailing," Whandall said.

"I loved it."

"So why did you come back? For Elriss?"

Wanshig looked around to be sure they were alone, and still he lowered his voice. "That's what I told her," he said. "But Whandall, they put me ashore."

"Why?"

Wanshig didn't answer that day.

He'd been home for nearly a week, then, and Whandall hadn't seen him taste wine.

Wanshig wobbled home long after dinnertime. Whandall found him washing in the courtyard tub, in the dark. "Shh," he said. "I don't want Elriss. To see me."

"What happened? You haven't had a drink—"

"Three weeks and a day. A teller found me, Whandall. Somehow he heard. A Lordkin went sailing and came back. He had some flasks."

Whandall nodded in the dark. "What did you tell him?"

"Stories."

"Why you came home?"

"Nonono! Not that."

Whandall waited.

"They liked me, Whandall. I did them some good. Taught most of the crew to swim. Protected the merchants. Nobody gathered from our passengers! They really liked me."

"B—"

"Shipmasters trade," Wanshig said. "They don't want to be known as pirates. Pirates aren't welcome. Condigeo keeps warships. They can afford them because they hire them out to other towns, to hunt pirates, so you never know when you sail into a harbor whether they might have pirate hunters ready to come inspect you. Ships get a reputation." He paused to stare at the first stars. "So they don't want gatherers on board."

Whandall thought about that. "And you didn't know this?"

"I knew it. They told me the first day I was aboard. No gathering in port. Ever. Of course I didn't believe them, until the first time they caught me. Took everything I had and gave it back, and gave my pay to the people I'd gathered from. Taught me a proper lesson, they did."

Whandall didn't say anything.

"But then I got drunk. There's a town below the Barbar Mountains, three days' sail west of here. Stuffy place, but lots of magic. Silks, arts, crafts. And I was coming home; I'd be here in three days! First time we'd put in here since I shipped out. Whandall, nobody wants to come here! Not often, anyway. So there was this shop, with a dress that would look terrific on Elriss."

"You thought she'd still be here?"

Wanshig looked around again. Elriss wasn't about.

"Her or someone. But I couldn't afford it. That was all right, I'd get it another time, but then I went down to the docks and some of my buddies had bought a whole keg of beer. We sat drinking all night, and come morning—" Wanshig shrugged. "Well, it seemed like a good idea to go get that dress. Of course they caught me. The captain didn't say anything about it, not then, but when we got here he put me ashore and told the other captains."

One morning Shastern was gone. When he didn't come back the next day, Whandall told Pelzed. Patrols were sent out, and a formal question was sent to Wulltid of Bull Pizzle. Shastern was a loyal soldier of Serpent's Walk.

Wulltid's answer was polite but brief. No one had seen Shastern of Serpent's Walk. If anyone did, he would be well treated and delivered to his home.

Three days after Shastern disappeared, Whandall sat with Pelzed in the Serpent's Walk meetinghouse. Pelzed had made a complicated trade of services and protection. Now a kinless crew showed up to put on a new roof. Whandall thought he recognized two of the older workmen as woodsmen he'd seen with Kreeg Miller, but he didn't speak to them. They'd never know him!

A runner came to the long table where Pelzed sat most days. "Shastern is back, Lord," he said.

"Where?"

"Peacegiven Square. There's a wagon with a Lordsman in armor and a Water Devil."

Pelzed frowned. "The Lords are bringing Water Devils to Serpent's Walk?"

"Lord, he's a boy. Small tattoo, no knife. He asks to speak to you, and there's a Lord's clerk there too. They ask you to come, Lord."

Pelzed looked around the meeting room. "Miracos. You'll stay here. Whandall, come with me." Pelzed selected two more guards. Whandall thought Miracos glared at him as they went out. Everyone wanted to stand near Pelzed when he spoke to the Lord's clerks, and Miracos thought of himself as Pelzed's chief advisor. Lately Whandall had been favored. . . .

Shastern lay on a litter in front of the Witness table. A helmeted Lordsman stood next to him. The wagon was nearby, driven by a kinless teamster and drawn by kinless ponies, not the big horses Lords used for their own business.

The Lord's Witness, with his tight-fitting cap and robes, sat at the table. He didn't rise when Pelzed arrived with his retinue, but the kinless clerk stood and bowed to Pelzed, then intoned formally "Witness, we see Pelzed of Serpent's Walk."

The Witness stood. His voice was thin and dry, very formal. "Pelzed of Serpent's Walk, I am instructed to convey the greetings of Lord Samorty of the Lordshills. Lord Samorty wishes you well." He sat again.

The clerk turned to the Water Devil, an unarmed boy of no more than sixteen with hand tattoo only. "Speak, Lattar of the Water Devils."

"Witness, we return Shastern of Serpent's Walk to his people," Lattar said. "He was cast onto the docks by ship's guards at *Womb of Pele*'s gangplank. Let the record show that his injuries are not of our making. We found him, we tended to his wounds, and he is now delivered to his people."

The clerk turned to Shastern. "Do you dispute this, Shastern of Serpent's Walk?"

Shastern mumbled something. The clerk frowned, and Whandall went over to his brother. He could see that Shastern's mouth was swollen, and there were bruises showing through his tattoos.

Shastern saw Whandall and tried to smile. "Greetings, big brother," was what he tried to say, but only Whandall understood it. "Lost a tooth."

"Did Water Devils do this?"

"No." Shastern tried to move his head. "Shif'sh crew," he managed to say. "Devils sen' me home. Not their fault."

Whandall turned to Pelzed. "He doesn't dispute it, Lord."

Pelzed nodded. "Serpent's Walk is satisfied. Return my thanks to Samorty of Lordshills."

The clerk smiled wryly. "Witness, all parties are satisfied," he said.

The Witness spoke without rising. "Read the proclamation."

The clerk took a parchment from under his robe. "Proclamation. To all those who hear this, take heed, for it is the law.

"Many shipmasters are unfamiliar with the customs of the Lordkin of Tep's Town. This has resulted in unfortunate incidents causing disrespect and injury to Lordkin. Therefore, for the protection of the Lordkin, henceforth all Lordkin who wish to approach any ship in the harbor of Tep's Town must first obtain permission from the Lordsmen officer of the harbor watch. We regret the necessity of this ruling, but it must be strictly enforced. By order of Samorty, Chief Witness of Tep's Town and Lordshills Territories."

The clerk turned to the Witness. "The proclamation has been read. We will read it again each hour this day and the next."

The Witness nodded.

The clerk turned back to Pelzed. "Pelzed of Serpent's Walk, you have heard the proclamation of the Lords. Take heed. Your kinsman Shastern of Serpent's Walk has been returned to you. The wagon has been hired for the day and is at your disposal. Witness, our fees were paid in advance, and there is no more business to be done."

Shastern healed fast. One tooth was gone, and his sisters fed him soup for a week while the swelling in his jaw subsided, but no bones were broken. At dinner Shastern told everyone he'd tried to gather from a harbor tavern, met a crewman and went aboard, and was beaten when the other crewmen saw him.

But he spoke with Whandall on the roof, alone. "I thought if Shig could go to sea, so could I," Shastern said. "But they wouldn't let me on the ship at all. The whole crew beat me. I kept saying I knew they didn't want gatherers, that I'd never gather, I didn't come to gather, I just wanted to go to sea, and they kept kicking me. If the Lordsman hadn't come, they would have killed me, I think."

Shastern fingered his tattoo. "Whandall, Pelzed of Serpent's Walk is a name with power. They don't call him Lord, but the Lordsman knew his tattoo. There was some kind of meeting with the Devils chief and the Lordsmen, and then they sent for a Lord."

"Samorty?"

"Yes, they called him that."

Whandall nodded. "He goes on watch himself. What did they meet about?"

"About me," Shastern said. "I just wanted to get home. I was dripping blood, and I needed a drink. When the Lord saw me, he got angry. 'Clean him up,' he said. His voice was real low and mean. 'Are you blind? Don't you see that tattoo?' So they got me a basin of saltwater and another of fresh, and a cup of wine. Good wine. Then they went in another room, but the big Lordsman wouldn't let me go. He got me another cup of wine, but he went with me when I had to piss."

"Deciding what to do with you," Whandall said. "I'm guessing, but it's like them. They cleaned you up so if they let you go, you'd tell about that. Then they decided whether to let you go or feed you to the crabs." Whandall put his hand on his brother's shoulder.

"Maybe," Shastern said. "They were nice enough when they came out. Made the ship captain apologize. He gave me a bag of shells and two silvers." Shastern held out a coin stamped with a hummingbird. "Then the Lord said, real slow and careful, that he regretted it but Lordkin had to stay away from the ships, and they'd draw up a proclamation. That was when he said nice things about Pelzed and Serpent's Walk, like he didn't want Pelzed mad.

"But we can't ever go to sea."

Whandall nodded and looked out over the Valley of Smokes.

CHAPTER
31

He was twenty before the Burning came again. And this time *everyone* was ready.

Hartanbath was more bison than man. In the Serpent Street region of Tep's Town—Flower Market, Bull Pizzle, Serpent's Walk, and several lesser bands—he was the man a fighter must defeat.

His missing ear-and-a-half contributed to Whandall's own reputation. Whandall could never have hurt him if Hartanbath hadn't been powerfully distracted. Hartanbath seemed to have learned *that* lesson. He was never seen fornicating in public again, with or without a woman's consent.

Whandall did not want a rematch. Few did. Hartanbath didn't lose.

At seventeen Whandall had taken to driving Alferth's wine wagons. Two years later he was present when Alferth held a street-corner drinking party.

A half-naked, dark-skinned, heavily armed looker ambled up and took a flask of wine with each hand.

Hartanbath objected.

The looker mocked Hartanbath's ears.

The looker was younger. Hartanbath was an inch taller and a stone heavier. Both could hit like logging axes. But Hartanbath ran out of strength first, sat down, and covered his head until the looker was satisfied.

Then the looker finished the wine and consented to tell stories.

He was Arshur the Magnificent. Some tremendous mountain range east of the Valley of Smokes had birthed his people. To the child Arshur, all was vertical, and all vertical faces were slippery with snow and ice. Arshur could climb any wall, enter any building, bypass any trap a householder might set for a thief (as if kinless would dare!).

There were cities where a thief might be imprisoned, others where he might be hanged, and cities where no thief could escape the King's magicians. Arshur had gathered fortunes in these places and others. He had fought monsters and magicians with his good sword—a huge clumsy mass of spelled bronze, thrice the size of a decent knife. A seer had predicted that he would one day be a King. When Arshur explained what a king was, the laughter angered him.

"So tell us, *Majesty*," Shastern asked, "what brings your magnificence to Tep's Town?"

Arshur's face clouded only a moment. Then he downed the last of the flask and struck a pose. "I spent my last gold coin on a party," he said. "This was up the coast, to the north and west, Great Hawk Bay they call it. They do have hawks, but mostly they have merfolk."

"Merfolk?" One of the younger onlookers was willing to admit ignorance.

"Werepeople," Arshur said. "You hear of were*wolves?* These are sea creatures. No? Shape changers. People who become animals."

"Old tales," Alferth said. "Not told much anymore. Are you saying they're *real?*"

Arshur nodded vigorously. "Real, yes. You would not doubt my word?"

No one did, of course.

Arshur said. "Bear men are the worst. Not as much sense as a wolf, and when they want to—" He made motions with his hips.

"Rut," someone shouted.

"Rut, yes. When they want to rut they rut anything. Anybody. They're big and hard to kill, so when they want to rut, most people get rutted. Sea people are easier to deal with. They like people. Especially the girls. *Great* rutting. And the merfolk at Great Hawk Bay set the best table in the universe. There's a restaurant in the harbor, an island with a bridge to it. Rordray, that's his name—Rordray owns the place. Sometimes cooks himself but usually leaves that to others. He built the place to look like the top of a castle because that's the way his last one looked, somewhere else where the sun rises out of the sea."

The sun rises out of the sea. Wanshig had *seen* that.

"You spent all your money, Your Magnificence," Shastern prompted. It wasn't obvious to anyone but Whandall that Shastern was set to run if Arshur came after him.

Arshur laughed instead. "It's sad being in a place of magic with no money. Rordray didn't need me! Neither did anyone else. If you steal—"

"Gather."

"—gather, they have magic to catch you. Besides, I like the people at

Great Hawk. I could steal—sure, I can steal from anyone—but they'd know who did it! Then Rordray said he'd pay me for hemp and sage leaves, and the best comes from a place he calls the Valley of Smokes. That's here."

Whandall asked, "Don't they have hemp and sage other places?"

The barbarian looked at Whandall. "Other places they grow too strong. Something to do with magic. Wizards can change the taste, but Rordray says they never get it as good as grows here naturally."

"Hemp tea," Alferth said. "I've been told that before—that you get good hemp tea here."

"You sure do," Arshur said. "Wish I had a cup. Storytelling is thirsty work."

"Later," someone shouted. "How'd you get here?"

"Took ship," Arshur said. "Fought off pirates, big canoes of them at the cape. They turned and ran after they saw what I did to the first canoe! More pirates out of Point Doom—fought them off too. So when we got here I figured I had some drinks coming. Only thing was, I hadn't been paid yet, and the tavernkeeper wouldn't give me any credit."

"Tavernkeeper?" someone asked.

"Boy, don't you know anything?" Arshur demanded. "But you know, I see how you wouldn't. No taverns here! Just down at the docks. It's a place where they sell hemp tea, ale, wine sometimes. Tables and benches. Good roaring fire at night, only not here; here, the fire's always outside.

"Anyway, I was drinking good ale in peace when the owner demanded his money. He called the watch when I couldn't pay. By the time I explained to them, they'd beaten me upside of the head. The ship captain gave my pay to the tavernkeeper for damages and sailed on before I woke up! So here I am. I'll ship out one day, but I thought I'd see the country."

"How do you like Tep's Town?" Alferth asked.

"Not so good. No magic. Not that I know much magic, but a little magic makes life slide by a little smoother. And the women! Down there by the harbor there's a nice town—Lord's Town, they call it. They sure didn't want me there! Anyplace I'd go, they'd send for the watch. Chased me right out of town, they did. So I get here, and the women all run away when I try to talk to them! One of them pulled a knife on me! On *me!* I wasn't going to hurt her. They tell me you can rut anytime you want to here, whether the women want to or not, but I sure didn't find it that way."

"Burning," Shastern said. "That's during a Burning. You just missed it."

"Arse of Zoosh! I never have any luck. When do you do it again? Next year? Maybe I'll stay a year."

"Maybe in a year," Alferth said. "And maybe longer."

"It'll be longer," Hartanbath said. Tenderly he touched his remaining shred of ear, notched by Whandall and now torn by Arshur. "Maybe a lot longer. Seems like more years between Burnings than when I was a kid."

Alferth climbed unsteadily onto the wagon and stood on the seat. He swayed just a bit as he shouted to the crowd. "What say? Is Arshur a Lordkin?"

"Yeah, who says I'm not?" Arshur demanded.

There were shouts. "Not me!" "Lordkin he is!" "Hell, I don't care." "Hey, this could be fun!"

Arshur was treated as a Lordkin from that day. Hartanbath disappeared for a season—healing?—then came back to pound the first fool who referred to his loss. He and Arshur were seen drinking together. . . .

It was an endless, pointless dance; but you had to keep track of who was on top. Arshur fitted into Lordkin society. For a few months he stole what he willed and carried his loot about, until he realized what older children knew almost by instinct: that a kinless might as well tend and carry property until a Lordkin needed it.

And one day Arshur got in a fight with the town guard.

His companions chose not to involve themselves. "They just kept hitting him and hitting him with those sticks," Idreepuct told them later, with secondhand pride. "He never gave up. They had to knock him out; they never made him give up."

Idreepuct was speaking in an intersection of alleys, to people already angry. Voices thick with rage demanded, "What was he *doing* to make them do *that?*" and, "Are the Lords *crazy,* to give them those *sticks?*"

Doing? It seemed almost irrelevant, but the tellers kept asking, and Idreepuct presently confessed. Ilsern—a tough, athletic woman who had never admired a man until Arshur came—had heard somehow of Alferth's secret wine wagons. Of course she told Arshur and Idreepuct.

They snatched a wagon. It was piled with fruit and it didn't look much like Alferth's wagons, but they took it anyway. They drove down Straight Street, whipping the ponies into a frenzy. Ilsern pelted passersby with fruit while Dree tried to pull the floorboards up and the kinless driver clung to the side and made mewling sounds.

By now the town guard didn't just have sticks and vivid blue tunics. They had built themselves small, fast wagons to put them where there was trouble. Wagons weren't part of the Lords' agreement, but they weren't exactly weapons either.

A guard wagon chased them. Then another. Kinless scattered out of the way. Dree got the floorboards up. "Nothing but road down here," he told Arshur, and Arshur swore and drove the ponies even harder. They nicked a fat Lordkin lady carrying a heavy bag; she screamed curses as they sped away.

They were fire on wheels until one pony fell dead, pulling the other down too.

And that was the end. Idreepuct and Ilsern stayed where they had fallen in the road, kneeling in surrender, and that stopped the guard, of course. Rules were rules. You knelt, they had to freeze. It could be very funny to watch their frustration.

But Arshur was still jittering with berserker joy.

He broke one guard's ribs and another's shoulder, and a blow to his head left another unconscious for two days. When Whandall came on the scene, they were carrying Arshur away strapped to a plank, laughing and insulting the guards, with a broken leg and bruises beyond counting. "And one of 'em hit him in the head," Idreepuct complained. "They can't *do* that, can they?"

Tarnisos said, "Big deal. Arshur's got a head like a rock—" as Whandall strode briskly out of earshot, and then ran.

There was Mother's man Freethspat on a corner talking to Shangsler, the big-shouldered man who had moved in with Wess twenty days past. Whandall stopped to describe the situation. He ran on, gathering whatever Placehold men he recognized. All of them were near strangers. Some would defend the house; some would celebrate the Burning instead.

The Lordkin believed they could feel it when Yangin-Atep stirred. Whandall felt that now. He intended to be guarding the house when the Burning began.

Days later, nothing at all was burning, and the Placehold men were letting him know it.

Whandall felt foolish. He *might* have noticed that Idreepuct had spilled the secret of the wine wagons to a score of loose tongues. Some had seen Alferth's wagons moving regularly along the Deerpiss. . . .

The vineyard was said to be totally destroyed. Now the most excitable among the city's Lordkin were out of action, nursing their first real hangovers. A gray drizzle had driven them indoors. The town guard had virtually disappeared, tactfully or prudently, carts and sticks and all.

The Burning remained a smoldering potential. It was only a matter of time.

PART FIVE

The Last Burning

CHAPTER
32

It had been raining hard for two days.

The Placehold would have camped in the courtyard for safety, but you couldn't have a Burning in the rain, could you? So the women and children were inside and the men were guarding the door in rotation.

But twenty-year-old Whandall was elsewhere, dripping wet in a windless rain, surrounded by seven sullen Lordkin in their thirties. A very bitter Alferth described what followed Arshur's beating:

A gathering horde of Lordkin flowed upstream along the Deerpiss and through the meadow, the Wedge. They damaged the gatehouse but couldn't be bothered to take the bricks apart. No mention was made of Toronexti guards: they must have joined the crowd.

Laborers saw human figures straggling out of the forest. Ten; twenty. They alerted Alferth. All the vintners, Lordkin and kinless, prepared to protect their holding. Only Tarnisos on the roof noticed the dust plume as *hundreds* of invaders surged up from the gatehouse.

They stomped the vines into mush. A few stopped to taste grapes for the first time. The rest stormed the wine house. It was deserted: Alferth and his people were fleeing through the forest, weaving a path among the deadly guardians of the redwoods, guided by what they had learned from Whandall Placehold.

The invaders found the vats in the basement and drank everything that would flow.

Alferth waited two days before he took his people back.

In the woods they found corpses slashed and mottled and swollen. Many who took that shortcut never reached the vineyards. Two hands more of bodies lay among the vats, killed by bludgeons and Lordkin knives, by wine and each other. The living had returned to town.

Whandall wasn't sorry to have missed that! Still, he gave thought to his own status. Alferth had been important to Pelzed and Serpent's Walk. Pelzed might see Whandall as more than Alferth's man, but Pelzed might equally consider that Whandall had held the Placehold with Pelzed's help, that all debts were paid.

Alferth was in his midthirties. Most of the boys he'd grown up with must be dead by now. What would it take to put him back together?

Whandall raised his voice above the rattle of raindrops. "Alferth, they didn't take what you *know*. You've still got that."

Alferth only looked grim. He was thinking like a victim. Freethspat found that disgusting and was starting to show it. Tarnisos was ready to kill someone. Anyone.

"You know how to make vines grow," Whandall said. "Alferth, you know how to make juice turn into wine and the wine into . . . well, *respect*. I don't know any of that. Almost nobody does."

"Kinless. They know it all," Alferth said.

"Find some land somewhere else."

"Time, you kinless fool. It takes time and work to make wine. A *year* before there's anything to drink, and that's after you have vines. Longer to grow vines. I'll be forgotten by then. Without wine I'm nothing."

Alferth was thinking like a kinless. "That's how we grew up," Whandall pointed out. "We have nothing except what we gather." He looked for support and saw smiles flicker. Not enough, and it wasn't quite true either. The child Alferth had had nothing, but he hadn't been *old*.

It came to Whandall that he had done what he could. Leave now. . . .

A two-pony wagon came trotting up Straight Street.

Alferth and his men watched from the curb. It came near, through several silent minutes. The little bone-headed ponies were pulling hard: the wagon was heavy, though the bed held only a few coils of rope.

Whandall cursed in his mind. He smelled blood. They were next to a butcher shop, but Whandall could recognize an omen. *Go home; get everyone into the courtyard. It's still raining, but the Burning is on us, I feel it. . . .* But he'd shouted of the Burning six days ago, and *nothing*.

Tarnisos trotted a few paces west to an ash pit, a shop for farm gear five years ago. The rebuilding hadn't touched it. He came back with an arm's length of fence post charred at one end.

Alferth stepped casually into the road. Freethspat followed, then the rest. Whandall hadn't moved. Without willing it, he became the fixed end of an arc across Straight Street.

The driver might have been dozing or hiding his face from the rain. He looked up far too late. Pulled on the reins, tried to turn the ponies. Far too late, as seven Lordkin swarmed over his wagon and wrestled his ponies to the ground.

He fought. He shouldn't have done that. Alferth took a solid blow to the head, and then the rest were on the driver, beating him.

"Aye, enough!" Whandall said. Louder, "Enough!"

Nobody chose to hear.

Whandall couldn't watch, couldn't interfere, dared not show his anguish. He turned to the cart instead. The bed was high, maybe too high. It carried coils of tarred rope, but not a lot of that. Had someone else taken to driving wine? Wine would distract them. He felt for a loose board, found a corner and lifted.

Eyes.

Three small faces. One mouth opened to scream. A child's hand covered the smaller child's mouth. Whandall put a finger to his lips, then set back the board, having seen very little . . . but at least three children.

Tarnisos set himself as if in a whackball game and swung his fence post at the driver's head.

They were killing him. He'd been curled around himself on the ground, but at Tarnisos's blow he sprawled loose and sloppy. And Whandall felt a rage burning outward from his belly. Not since he'd cut Hartanbath had he felt like this . . . but he was helpless as Tarnisos wound up for another blow.

Whandall raised his hand and set Tarnisos's weapon afire.

Tarnisos dropped the flaming beam with a yell and a backward leap.

Yangin-Atep was real. Yangin-Atep was in Whandall as a jubilant rage. He pointed into the butcher shop and it caught with a flash and a roar. The men still kicking the wagoneer looked around at the sudden light, and knew.

The Burning had begun.

The butcher shop burned merrily in the rain, flames cradling the apartment above. Tarnisos picked up his torch and tried to set the shop next door alight. It was wet, and Whandall held his power back. The rest were kicking smoldering wooden walls into slats to make more torches.

The kinless driver looked dead. Moving him might kill him if he wasn't, but he wasn't safe here. Whandall crossed the man's arms and enclosed the man's elbows and torso with his own arms. Resalet taught his boys to do that, to hold in damaged innards. He eased the man into the wagon, nesting him in a coil of rope.

He got onto the seat, found the whip, and used it. The wagon lurched away.

Tarnisos yelled and came pelting after him.

The last Burning had happened in a drought. This time everyone had stored food. A handful of kinless children would not discommode the Placehold, Whandall thought. They could tend the house while the Burning lasted and then go home, if they still had a home.

But four strangers were now pelting along behind Tarnisos, and Tarnisos had caught the wagon and was pulling himself aboard. What did the man think he was doing?

Tarnisos pulled himself over the benchback and next to Whandall. "You felt it!" he crowed. "Yangin-Atep! Alferth thought I was crazy, but you *feel* it, right? Right?"

With the weight in children the ponies were pulling, Whandall wasn't going to outrun anything. He waved behind him. Six followed now, and one had swept up an armful of faggots. "Who're they?"

Tarnisos looked back. "Nobody. They saw you start the Burning, maybe."

Maybe. Maybe they recognized a false-bottomed wagon. They thought they were chasing wine! Better distract them.

It was like being drunk. Not words he never wanted to speak, but *fire* leaked from the joyful rage at his core. The bundle of sticks flamed at both ends, and the man carrying them whooped. He began passing them out in some haste.

This next turn would take him home, but Whandall drove straight on. Behind the running men, fires were catching. He could not lead this merry mob to his own front door! Let Freethspat warn them of what was coming.

"Why'd you take the—" Tarnisos rapped the probable corpse's skull. "Him?"

"Anything on him?" Best not to let Tarnisos know what he was hiding.

Tarnisos inspected the man. "Nothing anyone would want. He's dead. Why did you want the wagon?"

"I've got something in mind," Whandall said.

A much easier turn came up. He could follow it west and north toward the Black Pit, then north along the Coldwater until it branched into the Deerpiss—a route Whandall knew well. Two of the runners dropped back, and then all of the rest in a clump, barring one. They'd stopped to gather at a store, it looked like. But the last runner was pumping hard. Monumentally ugly, he was, a barbarian. Whandall picked him for a teller just arrived.

He kept driving.

Markets and large stores attracted unwanted attention; they were looted too often. Feller's Disenchanted Forest was big for Tep's Town. Now, ahead of the Burning and first of the local looters, Whandall pulled up in front and got out.

"Coming?"

"Whandall, what is it you *want?*"

"Dunno. I've never been in here before."

A squinting clerk approached them. Behind him, kinless customers were moving briskly out of the store. The nearsighted clerk lost his smile, turned, and ran.

Whandall ignored them all. He selected two big axes, two long poles tipped with blades, blankets. Rope was already in the wagon. Thick leather sheets loosely bound by laces: one size fits all, adult or child. Wooden masks with slits for sight. He piled some into Tarnisos's arms and some into his own and led the way out into the rain.

The teller had caught up. He blocked Whandall's path and tried to speak, but he could do nothing but heave for breath. Whandall's look sent him stumbling back.

Tarnisos stopped in the doorway. "Nobody would want this stuff, Whandall!"

"I said I had something in mind." He dropped his load into the wagon and returned.

Tarnisos pushed his own load into Whandall's arms. "There's a stash of shells somewhere in there, and I want it." He jogged back in, pushing past the gasping teller.

Whandall dumped the stuff into the wagon. He'd watched woodsmen at work, long years ago. What had he forgotten? He had rope, severs and axes, sleeping gear, armor . . .

Lightning played through the black clouds. In this light the driver looked very dead. Whandall lifted the man out of the wagon bed and set him under the awning. Poor kinless, he'd gotten in the way at the wrong time. Other kinless would heal him or bury him.

Whandall boarded the wagon. A clattering approached . . .

A wagon rounded the corner on two wheels. Voices hailed Whandall to halt.

Whandall reached for his rage. The guard wagon flapped one great sheet of flame. Town guards screamed and baled out, hit the dirt and rolled.

The teller tried to talk to a fallen guard. The guard's stick whacked his shin; the teller danced. Whandall laughed, a sound like a maddened bird, startling himself.

Two guards were on their feet, running toward Whandall, waving sticks. The ponies were running better now, but they still wouldn't outrun men on foot.

Whandall's wave turned their regulation sticks into torches.

He waved behind him, setting one end of Feller's Disenchanted Forest on fire. The stairs had been at the other end. Tarnisos would have his chance to get out. Whandall didn't want him hurt; he wanted only to be rid of him.

It was quiet beyond the houses. Lightning flickered in black-bellied clouds. Whandall listened for children rustling beneath the wagon bed, but he heard nothing. It worried him. They could be suffocating. Whandall cursed. Being wet bothered him unreasonably.

He made for the Black Pit.

CHAPTER
33

The Pit was changed. Only the stink was the same. The gate was open, but much of the fence was in ruins, half rebuilt, but not as neatly as Whandall remembered. As he pulled the ponies to a stop, he found no mist around him, and no misty monsters. He was alone but for the black and silver pools that made up the Pit, and a scrawny coyote pacing the shore not far away, eyeing him distrustfully.

Here was no protection at all. Whandall kept an eye for rioters and rivals and city guards. But the coyote would have fled such invaders.

He found the wagon bed's loose corner and pulled it up. He thought of the long knife he hadn't drawn, and the way he'd seen rats react to being trapped.

The children didn't move. By the wave of body odor, they'd been in there for some time. Their big eyes watched him in wariness and fear. They snorted at the alien stench of the Pit. Seven of them were packed in with hardly a wine flask's worth of empty space to share.

The youngest might be four and five. Two were hardly children at all. The older boy might have been a Lordkin of nineteen; the girl, sixteen; though Lordkin would have been at Whandall's throat by now. The girl was trying not to meet his eyes.

She was as beautiful as any woman he'd ever seen. She was slender, tall for a girl, her legs long and smooth. Surely there were Lordkin among her ancestors. The lines did blur between Lordkin and kinless. Sometimes the results were wonderful. His whole body and mind were ready to drown in the dark deeps of her eyes.

He held back. He could guess how he must look to a kinless. She was already terrified.

"I'm Whandall," he said. "The man who was driving you was killed."

The girl's shoulders slumped. "I knew it," she whispered.

Whandall couldn't take his eyes off her. She started to cry, tears welling despite her efforts at control. The man must have been her father, but of course Whandall couldn't ask. He desperately sought for something to say that wouldn't offend her, wouldn't scare her away. Nothing came to him so he turned to the boy.

"Who are you?"

"Carver Ropewalker," the boy said.

"Your sister?" Whandall asked.

Carver Ropewalker nodded and sat up. "What are you going to do?" He was trying to sound brave, but the fear came through in his voice, and he kept glancing at Whandall's big Lordkin knife.

"I'm not sure. I got you out of the Burning," Whandall said. *I saved you! You could at least thank me! But now what?* "You could wait here—"

"Here? This is the Black Pit!"

Whandall was listening to the boy, but he was watching the girl as both climbed out of the wagon. The younger children stayed in the compartment, their eyes enormous. The girl was crying but trying not to show it, afraid but not terrified. And who wouldn't be afraid of the Black Pit? "Stay here with me. I can't go back yet. I'm possessed of Yangin-Atep."

Carver Ropewalker looked at him in disbelief and a scorn he was trying to swallow. The girl seemed more frightened than ever. "We'll be all right here," she said. She wouldn't meet Whandall's eyes or even look at him.

Whandall realized she was more afraid of him than the Pit. A kinless girl, unmarried, her father dead, the city burning despite the rain. Now she faced a Lordkin babbling that he was possessed of the fire god!

"I didn't hurt the driver," he said, in case she feared that too. "I tried to save him, but he was dying before I could get him in the wagon." He didn't think they believed him. Yangin-Atep's anger rose in a surge. Who did they think they were? These were kinless, kinless at his mercy, and the Burning had begun!

"You can leave us here," Carver said. He wasn't quite demanding and not quite pleading. "Don't worry about us. We'll get back—"

"There'll be nothing to go back to!" the girl wailed. "I smelled hemp smoke after we got in the wagon compartment." She peered through the gloom and rain toward the city she couldn't see. "You should hurry back," she said. "You'll be missing the fun."

Yangin-Atep's fire rose higher in Whandall Placehold. She hated him.

They all hated him. She was his if he wanted her, and he did, as he had never before wanted a woman.

They were all staring at Whandall now. Carver tried to get between Whandall and the girl. Brave and futile, a silly gesture. Carver Ropewalker was no threat, none at all. Yangin-Atep or someone laughed within him, and Whandall moved forward, his control stretched to its limits.

Something growled behind him. Whandall turned gladly to face a new threat.

There was no threat. There were only these pools of black water, and the snarling coyote.

Not water. It was waveless black stuff that didn't reflect, and scattered silver pools of water on top, and a deer's head . . . no, a terrified deer struggling neck deep, its antlers jittering. That was what held the coyote's attention: the coyote was trying to decide whether to go after the deer. It snarled at Whandall: *Mine!*

Yeah? Whandall focused on the far side of the black pool, where the coyote was glaring at him like a rival, and let a little of his rage leak out. He thought the coyote's fur might puff into flame. He wasn't expecting what happened.

An acre of black goo flamed and rose into a mushroom of fire.

The deer screamed and thrashed. The coyote ran. Shadows in the flame formed a pair of dagger-toothed cats who menaced the drowning deer.

Carver Ropewalker gaped at the fireball.

"I'm possessed of Yangin-Atep," Whandall repeated. "What will the Burning be like if I'm not there? It might—I don't—" Whandall's hands were trying to speak for him. He kept secrets better than he told them.

The girl wouldn't meet his eyes. Whandall felt the girl's fear. He suddenly understood what Arshur the Magnificent had tried to tell them: the women of Tep's Town wouldn't play at sex. They were afraid to be noticed.

He forced out, "I don't *like* burning down my *city* every few years. It makes a mess. People *die.* Mother's Mother says they never used to, but they do now." Again he was speaking to Carver, but he was watching the girl. Did she look just a little less afraid? But she still hated him.

"Father is dead, then?" Carver Ropewalker asked.

"The driver? Carver, I'm not sure. I left him where he could get help or burial."

He could see Carver swallowing that: dealing not just with his father's death but his own new responsibility and the ambiguous, dangerous presence of a fire-casting Lordkin. Presently he nodded.

"Father got in trouble," he said. "The Lordkin, you know what they've been like since the guards beat up that barbarian. We have a ropewalk in the Pond District—"

"Yeah?" The Pond had once belonged to the kinless. Now the populace was mostly Lordkin; the only kinless were those who couldn't afford to get out. They must have felt like mammoths in a roc nest.

"And Father lost his temper."

"How do I name you?" Whandall asked.

Willow Ropewalker was the older girl, Carver's sister. She finally elected to look at him but not to smile. Their brother Carter was twelve or so. His hand was hidden, certainly holding a weapon. The younger ones were children of Carver's father's sister: Hammer, Iris, Hyacinth, and Opal Miller.

Carver and Willow and Whandall got the younger children out of the wagon. Two were crying without sound. Willow looked around her and into the Pit.

The fire-cats had become shadow-cats in smoke. They were stalking a dead tree, like house cats the size of houses. Whandall said, "They won't hurt us. They're only ghosts, but they'll scare everyone else off. This is a good place to wait."

"This is the Black Pit!"

"Yes, Carver, I know."

Carver said, "All right, Whandall; it's nothing *I'd* have thought of. I guess those fences will keep the kids out of the tar—"

Oh, *that* was it. The Black Pit smelled ferociously of rope! It was *tar,* not magic, though there must be magic here.

"Tar," the boy Hammer said. "Carver, we—"

"Stay away! These ghosts—don't you know how they *died?"* Whandall didn't; he listened. Carver said, "The tar sucked them down! Prey and killer together. Thousands of skeletons all down there in the tar, their ghosts in battle until the end of time."

The rain fell more heavily. The tar fires went out, but black smoke hung over them, and the rain was sooty. Willow tried to cover the children.

Carver said urgently, "Hey, Whandall. These blankets, we can spread them for an awning? Tilt 'em so they can drip?"

"Go ahead."

For an instant Carver was at a loss. Then he and the children began to look along shore for dead trees, poles, props for blanket-awnings. His voice drifted back. "Then what, Lordkin? How long will the Burning last?"

Whandall didn't want to talk to them. It was enough to control the rage. But the boy deserved an answer. "There's no telling. Yangin-Atep could take someone else. You'll have to wait. If the sky clears up, look for smoke. If there's no smoke over Tep's Town, go home."

The boy Hammer Miller was still in the wagon. "The ponies have gotten bigger," he said.

Whandall had wondered if it was his imagination. The beasts had pulled more strongly as they ran toward the Black Pit. Now they shuffled with nervous energy. They'd eaten every plant in reach. They were bigger, yes, and the projections in their foreheads were horns long enough to hurt a man.

Hammer asked, "What *is* all this stuff you brought?"

Whandall spoke his heart's desire. "Or we could cut our way through the forest."

Carver said, "You're joking?" But Willow Ropewalker ran to the wagon bed and began running her hands through the loot.

"Carver, he isn't! Axes . . . saws . . . leathers . . . up the Coldwater would take us right to the forest edge. We *can*—we can *leave!* That's what Father wanted. The Burning was coming. He—" She glared at Whandall. "Oh, fine, and now we'll be taking the Burning with us! I don't suppose you know how to swing an ax?"

Whandall smiled at her. Her beauty would make him drunk if he let it. "I don't know, Willow. Kreeg Miller never let me hold an ax, but I watched. I can drive ponies, and I couldn't do that once."

But his plans—daydreams, really—hadn't run past this moment.

He said, "Lady." He tasted the word. Pelzed's woman liked to be called that. "Lady, there's a world out there. What do you think? Could we get through?"

"Father thought so," said Willow. "Your army came through the forest with the Lords leading you. Those old Lordkin must have chopped their way through. Whandall, you'd *better* learn to use an ax."

"You're both crazy," Carver said.

Whandall recognized the way Willow looked at her older brother: a contempt born of too much knowledge. "We can't stay, Carver! Whatever we have is all gone. There's a world out there—"

"I've been on the docks," Carver said.

Willow just looked. *Huh?* Whandall said, "My brother was a sailor. What's your point?"

"I've met sailors and lookers and tellers from all up and down the coast and farther yet. All they know is, this is the town they burn down. Willow—Whandall—they don't know kinless from Lordkin from Lords. *They can't tell the difference.* We go out there, we go as thieves. Forgive me—you say *gatherers,* don't you?"

It came to Whandall that he had never believed it in the first place. He wasn't disappointed, then, to know that Carver was right. That Wanshig had told him the same. Wanshig, who held a post for three years and was then put back on the docks in Tep's Town, because he couldn't stop gathering, because he was Lordkin.

But the blood was draining from his face, and he could only look at the ground and nod.

Morth asked, "What if a magician vouched for you?"

Whandall looked up. He felt that he should be startled, somehow.

Morth of Atlantis looked no older than the last time Whandall had seen him. His clothes were inconspicuous but finer than what he had worn in Tep's Town. His hair was going gray. White to gray, waves of orange-red running through it like cloud-shadows as Whandall watched.

"Morth," Whandall said.

"My word should be enough, I think," Morth said. "And it would be wise if we did not get closer together."

A magician. A water magician. Whandall felt Yangin-Atep's rage. Fear came back to Willow's eyes, and Whandall fought with Yangin-Atep. Morth must have felt the struggle. He moved away.

"So why would some random barbarian trust you?" Whandall shouted. "For that matter—" Something odd here. "Where did you *come* from?"

Bubbles in drifting smoke, a mere suggestion of huge dagger-toothed cats, were playing around Morth's feet.

"A lurking spell. It worked?" Morth looked around him, very pleased at the signs of astonishment. "There's still manna around this place. Good. We'll be safe here until we decide."

Whandall left his knife where it was, pushed through the leather sleeve in his belt, but he hadn't forgotten it. He said, "Morth, you don't just happen to be here."

"No, of course not. I came here because I thought you would. I almost followed you, but I guessed you must be in the middle of the Burning, so—" Smile, shrug. He saw no answering understanding, so he said, "The tattoo. I prepared it after I saw the lines in your hand. I can follow its pattern anywhere in the world. I'm hoping to follow you *out.*"

Willow exclaimed, "Out! Then you think so too! It's possible! Whandall—" She said his name almost defiantly. "Whandall, is he really a wizard?"

"Morth of Atlantis, meet the Ropewalkers and the Millers. Yes, Willow." Her name didn't come easily. "He's a wizard. Once a famous one. I mean, look at his hair. Did you ever see such a color on an ordinary man? Morth, where have you been since—since you lost your shop?"

"I moved to the edge of the Lordshills, as a teacher. It seemed to me that Yangin-Atep had cost me everything, Burning after Burning. I had better go to where a god could find no magic. I never built another shop."

"I saw the ash pit. Some burned skulls."

Morth must have sensed that there was more to this than curiosity. "Yes. And in the ashes did you see an iron pot with a lid?"

"No. Wait, my brother saw that. Is it important?"

"It was my plan to get out! It was my last treasure!" Morth's fists were clenched at his sides. "I thought cold iron was all I needed to protect it. The Burning City! It never crossed my mind that cold iron can be heated!"

The Ropewalkers and Millers were fascinated. Truly, so was Whandall.

"Well." Morth had regained control of himself. "I never sensed the Burning. I was fooling myself about that. That afternoon I was eating lunch at my counter when I looked out the door at eight Lordkin running straight at my shop! I saw the big one cast fire from his hand, and that was all *I* needed. I went out the back.

"My last treasure was two Atlantean gold coins rich in manna. Get those out of Tep's Town and I'm a wizard again. They would have lost all magic if I hadn't stored them in a cold iron pot with a spelled lid. It was too heavy for one man to carry. I cut the handles off and made myself believe that nobody could steal—sorry, Seshmarl—*gather* it."

Carver said, "Seshmarl?"

"It's Whandall," Whandall admitted.

Morth said, *"Whandall,* then. The Lordkin charged into my shop. I looked back. They weren't chasing me; I slowed and watched. The big man, he picked up my pot in his two arms. I just have trouble believing how *strong* you Lordkin are."

Whandall nodded. Morth said, "I'd seen him start fires. He was possessed of Yangin-Atep."

Carver and Willow looked at each other.

"I still didn't think he could get the pot open until he caused the iron to burn. Hot iron doesn't stop manna flow. I saw him lift the lid and look inside. Two gold coins must have been the last thing he ever saw."

He hardly needed to say, *And then all the magical power left behind by sunken Atlantis roared into a man possessed of the fire god.*

"You just don't seem to have very good luck," Whandall said, "with the Placehold men." And that was how he knew he was leaving: he had spoken his family's name among strangers.

CHAPTER
34

The rain stopped at evening, and by night the skyline had become a patchy red glow. The Burning continued without Whandall. The night seemed endless. Whandall made his bed on rock, wrapped in a blanket snatched from Feller's, far enough from the kinless children to make them stop *twitching*.

He half woke from a dream of agony and rage. His hands were fire that reached out to spread fire like a pestilence, by touch. The Placehold was burning. He was the Placehold, he was burning, and his shape was gone alien, a crab with a long trailing, looping tail and a terrible freezing, bleeding wound somewhere near his heart.

For a long moment he knew that fires were the nerves of Yangin-Atep. He sensed all of the fires in the Valley of Smokes and two ships offshore, one cooking breakfast, one aflame. He felt his life bleeding out through Lordshills where a Warlock's Wheel had eaten away all the magic. Then it all went away like any dream and left him chilled and wet.

He gestured and the half-dead fire flared into an inferno. At least it was easy to tend a fire!

He was very aware of Willow Ropewalker not far away. Desire rose and he held it back as he would hold a door, his weight on one side, enemies on the other.

Desire and excitement. They could leave, forever. Would they leave together? "Morth!"

The wizard was on the other side of the fire, and he stayed there. Whandall had to shout. Anyone might overhear. So be it.

"What will happen? You've seen my future. Is it with"—he gestured to Willow—"them?"

Morth considered what to say. "I haven't read their future," he said. "I don't know them well enough to do that. You may leave the Valley of Smokes. I don't know about the Millers and Ropewalkers. Further in the future, the line loops and blurs. You may return." He studied Whandall from the other side of the fire. "I can say this. You will have a more pleasant life with friends. With people who know who you are. Consider, Seshmarl—Whandall—you're choosing a new and unknown path. Easier to walk it with others."

"You know what I'm thinking, then?"

Morth shook his head sadly. "I know what *Lordkin* think. Actually, most Lordkin don't think at all. They just act. You're different."

"It's hard," Whandall said.

Morth smiled thinly. "I can't help. Anything I could do to calm you would probably kill you."

"As you—no, as *it,* your spell—killed my father," Whandall said.

Morth said nothing. Whandall wondered if he'd known all along. Wizard, liar, he'd killed Whandall's family. Yangin-Atep's rage boiled inside him, and Morth was gone.

Whandall heard a distant bush rustling. Flame shot high as greasewood ignited, and Whandall knew that *he'd* done that. He thought he saw a shadow beyond the flame.

"Morth!"

There was no answer.

"Whandall?" It was Carver, behind him.

"Stay away. I'm possessed of Yangin-Atep," Whandall said.

"Where's Morth?"

"I don't know. Running."

The night went on endlessly, and always there was the glow of fire over Tep's Town.

CHAPTER
35

Daylight. Whandall, dreaming fire, snapped awake as if he were guarding the Placehold with only children for defenders.

They were in the wagon, sleeping, most of them. One kinless boy was down by the fence.

Whandall went down to shore, walking wide of that black stuff that stuck to everything. The boy was Hammer Miller. Whandall hailed him from a safe distance.

Hammer turned without surprise, one hand hidden. The other held a milk pot. "I want to get some tar," he said.

"I can't let you go. Your sister would kill me."

"No, not Willow. Carver might. We can sell it."

"How do you know?"

"Everyone needs rope!"

"How much do you need?"

Hammer showed him a milk pot. "This much. I don't think I can lift it when it's full. I'll have to get Carver."

Whandall watched how they went about it.

First they talked the problem to death.

Carver and Willow tied a rope to Hammer's waist. Then, while Hammer danced with impatience, they tied another rope to the neck of the jar and let the rope trail.

Hammer went over the fence. He walked with some care and, twelve paces out, found his feet mired.

The coyote came out of nowhere, streaking for the mired boy. Whandall touched the beast with flame. A ring of flame flashed outward. Hammer shouted and ducked. The flame just singed him before it puffed out.

Carver was cursing him. Whandall said, "Didn't think. Sorry."

The coyote was gone. Hammer was still mired.

They pulled on the rope. He shouted. They left off long enough for him to scoop a mass of sticky black stuff into the jar, waist deep now and still sinking. They pulled again. It was hard work. Whandall joined them on the rope. Hammer tried to drag the jar after him, lost it, then caught the rope that tethered the jar and dragged it a little farther. When he could stand he braced himself and began pulling. Carver went over the fence, treading in the shallow footprints Hammer had left before he sank. Together they pulled the jar out half full.

"Enough," Carver said.

It wasn't that much different from a raid on some shop in Maze Walkers. Lurk, spy out the territory, test the defenses. Then go for it, gathering what you can. Anything unexpected has to be fixed on the fly. Settle for what you can gather in one pass; don't go back for more.

And this awful stuff, which had already ruined every scrap of clothing he could see, could be made into wealth by moving it somewhere else. How did they *know? That* was the hard part.

Now the wagon stank of tar, not of bodies long confined. The ponies pulled more strongly as they moved northwest. Whandall waited until he was moving up the Deerpiss before he made the Ropewalkers and Millers get under the floorboards. Tar pot on top. A guard would think hard before he lifted *that.*

The brick guardhouse was in sight, its gates closed. Opening them wouldn't be complicated . . .

A guard popped out, saw him, shouted, "Staxir!" Two more stepped out to study his approach. They all wore armor, but on this hot day none of them were fully protected, though they all wore masks.

They swung the gate open and retreated back under an awning.

What were Toronexti doing here? Though they looked edgy, weapons drawn, it looked like he could just drive on through. . . .

Nah. He stopped alongside the awning and, before any of them could speak, asked, "Staxir? What are you doing here? The vineyard's nothing but muck."

They laughed. They were older Lordkin, and wiser. "We're not here for Alferth!"

"We'll miss the wine, though, Stax—"

"This is the *path.* The Toronexti have to be here if the kinless want to leave."

Another surprise? Whandall asked, "The path goes right through the forest? Really?"

"No, but kinless still try it," Staxir said. "The Burning could start any hour, and don't *they* know it!"

"So we look in their wagons and take what looks good, and in a day they come back, and we take—"

"What're *you* carrying?"

Whandall said, "Stuff for cutting trees."

"What is that *stink?*"

"Tar. The woodsmen, they cover their hands with it to stop plant poisons. There're kinless out past here getting lumber, aren't there?"

"No," Staxir said.

Whandall scratched his head. "Well, there will be. The Burning is on, so I took this stuff. I can keep it in the wine house, day or two."

Men who might have taken some of his good tools a moment ago thought again. Eyes turned toward Tep's Town. Staxir said, "We gotta be here. Kinless'll be trying to get out again with everything they own."

"You don't need us all, Stax."

"Safer here. Dryer."

Sounds of disgust.

Whandall waved and drove on. He could guess the unspoken: a wagoneer who came this way with heavy gear to sell would be back with shells for a tax man's pockets. But Whandall didn't plan to come back.

Weeds were starting to cover the trampled vineyard. Whandall pulled the wagon behind the brick wine house. The roof wasn't brick; it had been timber and thatch, and it had burned. Whandall cursed. He was tired of being wet.

He got the children out of the wagon. Two youngsters were beginning to cry without sound. Whandall helped Willow out. Carver rejected his hand. He was still looking at Whandall like a dangerous animal. It was getting on his nerves.

A stub of blackened timber poked from the wine house roof. Whandall let a little of his rage leak into it. Against the black-bellied clouds it made orange-white light and a bit of heat.

Willow looked around her and said, "We're at the forest."

"What is this place?" Carver asked.

"Wine house," Whandall said. "The roof's gone, but the walls are still up." Shelter. But it was not yet noon, and he didn't want to stop. He looked at the malevolent forest across his path. Could they really get through that?

Carver walked toward the woods and into them.

"Careful!" Whandall called. He followed, with Willow just behind him.

The redwoods towered over them. These were young trees, though tall enough to cut the force of wind-driven rain. Deeper in, they would be much bigger. A hundred varieties of thorns and poison plants clustered protectively around their bases.

Whandall spoke to Willow, hoping that Carver and the children would listen. You didn't lecture a grown man directly if you could avoid it. "Stay clear of this thorny stuff. It's too dark to see how close you are. At night you wouldn't move at all. These pine trees, they won't hurt you. Almost everything else will. Even the redwoods make you want to look up when you should be watching your feet—"

"Where did you learn about the forest?" the twelve-year-old asked.

"I used to watch the loggers, Carter. I carried water for them. Carver, do you think we can cut our way through here?"

"You brought those cutting things."

"Severs."

"Severs. We can use those," Carver said. "But the plants can always reach farther than you think. You think you've got clearance, but—I'm worried about the children."

"These leathers'll fit the older ones. And us." *We could cut a path for children,* Whandall thought, *or a wider path for a wagon.* But how far did the forest go? "It took an army half a year to get through, two hundred years ago," Whandall said.

"We only need enough for one wagon," Willow said briskly. "We go around what we can, cut when we have to. Sell the lumber gear when we get to the other side, and the tar, if there's anyone to buy. Did you bring a whetstone?"

"Whatever that is, I didn't bring it."

Whandall hadn't thought in terms of buying and selling. Kinless would know how to trade, how to work, how to *find* work. On the other side of the forest, *Lordkin would not have license to take what they wanted.*

He hadn't missed that point, but he was starting to feel its force.

But he felt the warmth stirring in his belly, not unlike lust, not unlike the heat that rose from wine. Alferth was wrong to call it *anger.*

"This was Yangin-Atep's path."

His arm reached forward and the heat ran through his fingertips, feeling out the old path, far beyond what his eyes could see. Yangin-Atep's trailing tail. The dream held for an instant and was gone again.

Brushwood caught. Vines and thorn plants burned in the rain. An eddy swirled the smoke around them and made them choke. Then the wind steadied, blowing it north ahead of them.

CHAPTER
36

The land ran generally uphill. The flame-path didn't cramp them, but it wasn't quite a road. There were stumps Whandall had to burn out. The horses were grown visibly stronger. They pulled with little effort, but they shied at Carver's touch on the reins.

Whandall tried it. Both ponies stopped and turned to look at him along spiral spears as long as a forearm. Willow took the reins from his unresisting hands, and the ponies turned and began to pull.

That first night they stripped a dozen crabapple trees for their dinner. Children didn't need to be instructed to hurl the cores away: they did it by instinct.

Carver suggested that Whandall sleep between the wagon and the vineyards. Lordkin might follow the scorched path, he said. Carver was trying to protect Willow. Whandall went along with that.

But in the morning he told Carver, "We don't need a guard at night. Only a madman would walk through the forest in the dark." He pointed back down the trail. A blackened ruin, ash and mud, with a few flecks of green growing into it. It wasn't straight, and it certainly wasn't inviting.

"That's odd," Carver said. He pointed ahead. The trail remained black, no traces of green at all.

The redwoods stood like pillars holding up the black-bellied clouds. Their shadows made a twilight even at noon.

Where Whandall's fire had gone, they saw nothing of predators and nothing of prey. They had to strike out sideways to their path to find anything to eat.

Willow picked an apronful of small red berries for them. Delicious. Whandall watched her mind wrestle with itself before she warned him. "Whandall, don't eat these berries if they're growing near a redwood."

"I know. We need to keep the kids away from any berry patch. The poison patches look too much like redberries."

Carver made slings, a weapon new to Whandall. It would send a stone flying at uncanny speed. Carver was good with a sling; Carter was even better; Whandall developed some skill. They were able to feed themselves and the children and to fend off coyotes.

Kinless with weapons. Kinless *skilled* with weapons. He half remembered the Lords talking of an old war fought against the kinless. How had kinless fought? Had they used slings? Why had they lost?

He dreamed that night, of Lords with helmets and armor and spears leading a horde of Lordkin with knives. They fought a smaller, slimmer people who used slings and small javelins. The stones rattled against the Lords' shields. A few mad Lordkin held their hands out, and sheets of fire flowed into the kinless ranks.

And every one of the fire-wielding Lordkin looked like Whandall.

In rain they had slept under the wagon. They'd left the rain behind, and now they could sleep in the wagon, off the ground. Fire was easy: half-burned charcoal was everywhere. They dug a midden and laid a ridge of dirt from the midden to the wagon. In the dark a child could follow it by feel.

Whandall watched them, studying how the kinless worked, how the kinless thought. How they talked. Always they talked.

Their third morning brought them to the crest of the mountains. Downhill, the land was blackened and almost bare. Plants were growing back. Whandall hadn't done this; it was half a year old. But the going looked easy and the path was clear. Whandall's new burn switchbacked through the half-grown plants like a black snake.

"Whandall, this is easy traveling, and we don't need your fire. Let's go back for another wagon."

"Who, Carver?" he asked, knowing Carver would never leave Whandall with Willow. Lordkin men (some, anyway) guarded their women no less than Carver did.

"You and me. Willow, you can keep the wagon moving, can't you? The ponies won't mind anyone else anyway. If you get into trouble, just stop."

*   *   *

Green creepers were sprouting everywhere along the path, poking through the ash of Whandall's burning. Between dawn and sunset Carver and Whandall retraced their path through the burned woods.

A wagon had been left near the loading dock. One of the mares had wandered into view. She was smaller than the stallion ponies, and her horn was just a nub.

They watched the wine house through sunset until midnight before they believed that it was deserted. Then Carver approached the mare and was able to put a bridle on her.

They found hundreds of little flasks heaped against a wall. "Empty," Whandall pointed out.

"Well made, though. They won't leak. Maybe we can sell them on the other side."

They heaped the wagon with flasks and cut some grass for the mare too. They slept in the ruined wine house.

In the morning Whandall rode facing backward, wary that something might follow, while Carver drove.

Carver grumbled, "We didn't see anyone following us!"

"Lordkin know how to lurk." Some half-suspected danger tapped at the floor of Whandall's mind. He watched their back path.

It wasn't black anymore; it was green. "This ash must make wonderful fertilizer," he said.

Carver turned around. "You can almost see it growing!"

Ahead of them was only blackened dirt.

"Yangin-Atep," Whandall said, "wants us gone."

Carver snapped, "When did your fire god become a fertility goddess?"

"Not Yangin-Atep, then, but *something* wants us gone. The forest?" Whandall remembered days in Morth's shop, Morth reading his palm, mumbling about Whandall's destiny. Could a god read destiny too? "I think that's it. I'm carrying fire through a forest."

"We're being expelled," Carver said.

Whandall shook his head, smiling. "You're escaping. I'm being expelled." And even as he watched the trail behind seemed to grow more creepers.

Travel went fast. The mare grew stronger as they traveled, and larger, but she wasn't giving them any trouble. Behind them the trail's outline blurred with green.

Coyotes had discovered the travelers' abandoned middens. That was scary. That evening Whandall and Carver crawled under the wagon to sleep, back to back and armed.

A voice in the dark. "This magician who killed your father. Did you try to kill him?"

"No, Carver."

"Good."

Whandall believed he had nothing to hide from Carver: nothing so monstrous as the open truth of what he was. Still, sharing secrets outside the family seemed unnatural.

Into the quiet dark Carver said, "Did you know that *plague* is a kind of living thing? Wizards can see it. Wizards can kill it and heal the client. Otherwise it grows. Without a wizard, other people get sick too, more and more. We need wizards. But wizards don't like the Valley of Smokes."

" 'Course not. No magic."

The dark was silent a while longer. Then Carver asked, "Why not?"

"Kill Morth? Why?"

"Your father."

"Morth did what kinless do. Sorry, *taxpayers*. What we do too. If Pothefit caught a looker taking the cook pot from the Placehold courtyard, he'd've killed him."

It was too dark to see Carver's expression. Whandall said, "The Burning killed Pothefit. In the Burning you can have anything you can take. They couldn't take Morth's shop."

Silence from Carver. The woods stirred: something died violently.

"That's what I was trying to remember," Whandall said suddenly. *"Morth* could follow us. I keep forgetting Morth. Carver, we wouldn't *see* him. That lurk spell."

Near sunset of the next day they reached the crest of the mountains and found two dead coyotes near a dead campfire.

Carver ran.

Whandall watched him disappear into the rocks. He almost followed. Coyotes might menace Willow and the children! But Whandall was trying to learn kinless ways, and what about the wagon?

Unhitching the mare wasn't easy. She tried to pull the rope out of his hands. He hung on long enough to tie it to a tree stump. The length of it would let her reach forage. She had her horn if coyotes came back.

Then—but wait. What had killed these beasts?

He stooped over one of the corpses. Not a mark on them. Wide blood-red eyes, mouths wide, tongues protruding. He touched the slicked-down fur, expecting to find it wet, but it wasn't.

* * *

He caught Carver far downslope at the next dead campfire. There they slowed to a walk, blowing hard. Willow and the wagon must have taken a full day to cover this distance. Carver's hands held his sling and a handful of rocks cracked to get sharp edges. He said, "I wish I had a knife."

Whandall said, "With *that* you don't have to let them so close. I wish I had a sever."

Day was dying. They smelled meat cooking, and they slowed.

They saw the fire first, and a young looker standing tall and straight, backlit, with orange-red hair falling to his shoulders. Willow had the horses tied and a fire going. Then a whiff of corruption showed an arc of dead coyotes at their feet.

Willow saw two men coming at a grim half-run, Whandall's knife point, Carver's whirling sling. She leaped up from her cooking and stepped quickly to the man's side.

"He saved us!" she shouted. "The coyotes would have torn us apart!"

Carver's sling drooped. He said, "Morth?"

Morth smiled faintly.

"Morth, you're young!"

"Yes, I found this!" Morth held out a handful of yellow lumps. Whandall had never before seen the magician *gleeful*. "Gold!" he said. "In the river!" He stepped forward past Whandall's knifepoint and pushed the gold into Whandall's unresisting hand.

Whandall said, "This is dangerous, isn't it? Wild magic."

"No, no, *this* gold is *refined*. I've taken the magic," Morth said. "Can't you see? Shall we race? Shall I stand on my head for you? *I'm young!*"

Carver backed up a bit, and so did Willow. Here was no lurking spell. Morth *wanted* to be noticed. He babbled, "Gold *is* magic. It reinforces other magic. Look!" He leaped straight up and kept rising until he could grasp a branch twice Whandall's height above him. He shouted down, "Not just young! I used to *fly!*"

He dropped lightly. "Give gold to a wizard, most of the power leaches from the gold. After that it's refined gold, harmless. People use it as if it has value, but the original meaning was, *I gave gold to a wizard to touch. A wizard owes me.* Whandall, keep the gold. Morth of Atlantis owes you."

Whandall put the nuggets in the pouch beneath his waistband. He asked, "Why?"

Morth laughed. "You're guiding me out."

Whandall's fingers brushed his cheek: the tattoo he couldn't see. "And every wizard in the world can track me?"

"Every Atlantean wizard," Morth said, and laughed like a lunatic.

CHAPTER
37

Willow had roasted a half-grown deer and some roots Morth had found. The adults held back—even Morth, even Whandall, ravenous but following their lead—until the children were fed. Then they dug in.

Carver suddenly cried out. "Lordkin! Did you do anything about the other wagon?"

Whandall told him what he'd done. "But the mare doesn't like me, so you'll have to go get her yourself. Unless you think we should both go?"

Whandall enjoyed what Carver's face did then. Leave Willow with Whandall? or leave the wizard with Willow and no Whandall to guard *him?* or take Willow, leaving the children alone with the wizard *and* the Lordkin and nobody who could handle bonehead stallions? . . .

"I'll go."

"It can wait till morning."

"I should hope so."

The night was black as the inside of a lion's belly. Whandall had to imagine: Carver, Willow, Morth, the gently snoring Carter, and himself, arrayed in a five-pointed star in the dirt near the wagon, feet pointing inward, severs ready to hand. The children in the wagon. Hyacinth dropping over the side, sleepy and clumsy, *thud,* crawling away to use the pit.

"It's the biggest burn patch we've seen. It took us all day to cross it, and half of yesterday." Willow's voice in the dark, wondering and content.

Joking, Whandall said, "This fire wasn't mine."

"Lightning," Willow said. "Lightning hits the highest tree. It burns. Afterward the redwood grows in two prongs. Sometimes coals fall and a patch of forest catches."

"Why doesn't the whole forest burn? Woodsmen just go home when they see a fire."

She said, "Patches burn, then they go out."

Morth said, "Yangin-Atep spends most of his time in a death-sleep, but a big fire wakes him. Feeds him. Fire is Yangin-Atep's life."

A companionable silence. Then Carver said sleepily, "What if you don't believe in Yangin-Atep?"

Whandall raised his voice above Morth's laugh. "Carver, firewand seeds don't sprout unless there's been a fire. Neither does redwood. This land is fire's *home*. Tep's Town—"

"Valley of Smokes."

"Smokes. Would have been burned out before I was ever born if some power weren't snuffing the fires. Yangin-Atep is the reason fire won't burn indoors. There's a truce between Yangin-Atep and the redwoods, so they don't burn. I tried to tell Kreeg Miller . . . a taxpayer woodsman?"

Willow said, "There are a lot of people named Miller."

Whandall had nursed a hope that he was helping Kreeg Miller's relatives. There was an old debt he'd never acknowledged.

Willow said, "Outside the forest there's no Yangin-Atep. You could cook indoors. Get your food still hot. Yes?"

"Yes," said Morth and Whandall.

"Well, I never heard of such a thing, but we'll see." Willow turned and was asleep.

Whandall rolled his blanket tighter around him, wishing he could get up and stroll around, knowing that a thorn plant or laurel branch would surely slash him if he did. They had left the rain behind. The sound of the night was wind and sometimes a tiny cry of mortal agony.

CHAPTER
38

For a time the wagon moved easily downhill with Willow at the reins. Then they had to use the severs, sliding the poles under nettles and morningstars and lordkin's-kiss to cut the roots with the blades, to shape a path wide enough for children and a wagon. They could have used Carver's help, but Carver had gone back for the mare and second wagon.

Willow spoke: "This yellow blanket, *this* we use to clean the severs, to get the poison sap off. Use the rough side only. *You* don't *ever* touch it, right, Hammer? Iris? Hyacinth? Opal?" The children nodded. "This one blanket, because there's nothing else that color. The blanket hangs here on the wagon tongue, never moves, so anyone can find it."

They saw problems before they happened. Looked for them. They lectured each other as easily as they lectured a Lordkin male.

Carter and Hammer were assigned to hold the other children together. They moved fairly rapidly. Half a morning later, Whandall remembered part of the deer left in the wagon from last night. He dropped the sever, stood up—

"Whandall. Don't try to save work. Touch-me venom can stay on a blade and brush off on the wagon and then on a child. Someone could sit on it. It's clean when it leaves your hands, every time," Willow said. "Understand?"

A blank face hid his rage. Whandall picked up the sever and wiped the blade clean. Willow had treated him like a child, a bad child, in front of Morth and the children. Carter and Morth both had the grace to be paying attention to something else. If Carver had been here, Whandall might have had to hurt him.

In a later, calmer moment, it came to him that she hadn't spoken by chance. Willow had been watching, waiting for him to do what he did.

A stand of lordkiss blocked Whandall's scorch-path, its leaves barely singed. Morth called, "Whandall! Don't burn it! You'd strangle us all. The smoke is poisonous."

Whandall had reached for Yangin-Atep's rage and found only a dying ember. The fire god was leaving him.

They had to dig a path around the lordkiss. He thought of it as showing off his strength, to make it feel less like work.

In early afternoon they broke through the undergrowth above running water.

Through sparse branches Whandall saw a far distant mass floating in the sky: a cone with its base in cloud, gray rock and green-tinged black capped with blazing white.

Morth gaped. "What is *that?*"

"The legends said it would be there," Carter mused. "Before the Lordkin came, there was a path through the forest."

"Mount Joy," Willow whispered. "But the story said you could only see it if you were worthy. One of the heroes—"

"Holaman," Carter said.

"Yes. He spent a lifetime searching for this vision," Willow said. "Are we blessed?"

"With good weather," Morth said. "But I think my path leads there." He held his arm out, palm down, and looked along it, first with his fingers together, then spread.

"Magic?" Carter asked.

"No, navigation. If your stories are right, we won't see this again, so I'm looking for landmarks in line with it."

"Looks hard to reach," Carter said. Whandall was thinking, *Impossible. But for a wizard?*

Morth said, "The world's most inaccessible places are the places where wizards have never used up the manna. I have to go there. Gold would keep me alive, but the magic in gold is chaotic. I was too long in Tep's Town." Morth ran his hand distractedly through his hair. "I need the magic in nature to fully heal. Too much gold would drive me crazy."

He looked at the fistful of red and white strands he was holding and whooped laughter. "Too little is bad too!"

Willow led the stallions. The wagon lurched, and sometimes the children had to heave up on the downside to keep it from rolling over. Still, matters had improved: nothing ahead of them seemed to need cutting. The vegetation grew right up against the shore, and it was touch-me all the way. But the river ran shallow at the edges, and the wagon wheels would only run a few hands deep.

Willow said, "We'll find easier traveling if we follow the river."

Whandall waited for Morth's reaction. He'd been treating Morth like a friend who sniffs white powder: a dubious ally. This might be the chance to be rid of him. But Morth only said, "You can't stay with the river long."

"No, of course not. Wagons don't go on water, do they, Whandall?"

Surprised to be asked his opinion, Whandall said, "Willow, people don't go on water either."

The way she looked at him, he flushed. She asked, "Whandall, can't you swim?"

"No. My brother can."

"I meant," Morth said gently, "that the sprite can't get to me right away, but he must know I'm here. Let's see how far we can get."

The river continued shallow. The wagon bumped over rocks. They had to run slow, where the still growing ponies wanted to *run*. Carter and Willow couldn't leave them without their becoming restive. They'd grown large and dangerous, as big as Lords' horses, with horns that would outreach Whandall's Lordkin knife.

"I could spell them," Morth said. "Gentle them."

"No." Morth was as twitchy as the ponies; Whandall didn't trust his magic.

"Well, at least I can dispel the stink of tar!" He gestured, but nothing happened. The smell was still there. Morth frowned, then danced ahead, vanished out of sight. A fat lot of help he was . . . but it could be said that he was scouting terrain, springing traps that would otherwise wait for children and a wagon.

The ponies and wagon plodded on, veering around deeper pools, rolling over rocks, wobbling, tilting, held from rolling over only by a Lordkin's strong shoulder, whenever Whandall hoped to leave this snail's trek and follow the magician.

Carver wouldn't have much trouble catching up, Whandall decided. He'd find a path carved ahead of him.

They were halfway down the mountain when Morth came bounding back, bellowing, "Don't any of you lordspawns get *hungry?*" He gestured and sang, and suddenly Whandall's clothes were clean. Even the tar stains were gone. "Now to eat!"

The children chorused their agreement. Morth roared laughter. "I could eat . . . the gods know what I could eat!" He faced the woods and raised his hands as if they held invisible threads. "Let's just see. Seshmarl, a fire!"

Whandall gathered an armful of dry brush and set a few fallen limbs on it. His touch raised no more than a wisp of smoke.

It was not that he enjoyed being ordered about like a kinless! But Whandall preferred to hide how weakly the power of Yangin-Atep ran in him. And Morth's hands still waved their messages into the forest, while white chased red in waves down Morth's luxuriant mane and beard. Whandall coaxed the smoldering kindling until flame rose toward his fingertips. When Morth turned from the woods, there was fire.

Animals came trooping out of the wood. A gopher, a turkey, a fawn, a red-tailed hawk, a half-starved cat as big as Hammer, and a family of six raccoons all filed up to Morth and sorted themselves by size. The cat was smaller than the ghosts of the Black Pit, and it didn't have those huge dagger teeth.

Whandall made a sound of disgust. An animal might be meat, but it should be hunted! Altering its mind was—

(Hadn't Morth said that once?)

But the animals were strangling. All but the raccoons were reaching for air and not finding it, thrashing, gaping, dying. The bird tried to reach Morth, and would have if he hadn't dodged, and then it was dead too.

Drowned. And a burbling chuckle leaked out of Morth.

Whandall reached for his knife. It wasn't needed. He and the kinless watched as two adult and four half-grown raccoons stripped the feathers from the bird and butchered the drowned animals with their clawed hands, skewered the meat and set it broiling. The children watched in fascination.

The raccoons all spasmed at once, *looked,* and instantly disappeared into the chaparral.

Hawk had a miserable taste, but everyone tried it. Willow convinced the children that they'd brag about this for the rest of their lives. Turkey and deer were very good, and gopher could be eaten. They had safe fruit Morth had found, with his ability to see poison. It struck Whandall that he had not eaten this well since Lord Samorty's kitchen.

In early afternoon Morth suddenly said, "Here!" and waded into the stream. Whandall was startled. "Morth? Aren't you afraid of water?"

"We've hours before the sprite can get here." Morth bent above the purling water with his arms elbow deep, fingers spread just above the river bed. Whandall saw golden sand flow toward him, merging into a lump.

"Ah," he said. He picked up a mass the size of his head as if it were no heavier than a ball of feathers. For a time he stood holding the gold against his chest, with his eyes half closed and the look of a man breathing brown powder smoke from a clay pot. Then he handed it to Whandall. "Again, for my debt. Put this in the wagon."

Whandall took it. He wasn't prepared for its weight. It would have smashed his toes and fingers if he'd been a bit less agile.

Morth was helpless on the ground, laughing almost silently, *Hk, hk, hk.*

With every eye on him, Whandall set himself, lifted, hugged the gold to his chest, and carried it toward the wagon.

Morth rolled over and stood up. Mud covered his sopping wet robe. He'd lost weight: his ribs showed through the cloth. His hair was red and thick and curly. His long, smooth, bony face wore a feral look, like a young Lordkin about to test his knife skills for the first time.

"That's better," he said. "Little more of that." He walked back into the river and began wading downstream.

Willow repacked the wagon, Whandall helping, while the children put out the fire and wrapped the remaining deer meat in grass. Whandall said, "He never helps."

Willow looked startled. "You don't either."

"I'm helping now."

"Well, yes, thank you. You don't do it often. Well, it's because the ponies don't like you."

"What I meant was, you don't seem to notice," Whandall said. "Morth has lived in Tep's Town longer than I've been alive, but he's a looker. Do you see him as a . . . ?"

"Yes. Maybe." Willow laughed uneasily. "He's a funny-looking Lordkin? Crazy and dangerous, and sometimes he can do something we can't."

They set off with the wagon. They saw Morth rock hopping downstream until the river turned.

Late afternoon. Whandall heaved upward while the ponies pulled. The wagon lurched, rolled, and was back into riverbed that was shallow and flat.

"I quit," Willow said.

Whandall looked up. She was riding, he was walking . . . but she was exhausted. The restive ponies had worn her out.

"We have to get the wagon on shore," he said.

"Do we really?"

"The water thing that hunts Morth, it's coming up the river. We don't want to be in the way. And there isn't any shore yet . . ."

So they wrestled the wagon through another eighty paces of rough water. Then there was a strip of sand and a sloping bank they could push the wagon up, and Willow could sleep forty feet above the water.

Whandall had worked hard too. Had worked. He was new to that.

It was good to lie down on warm earth. The children lay about him, all asleep. Willow was curled up with a tree root for a pillow, comfortably distant from the Lordkin, with ponies tethered on either side, one rope strung between two trees. Whandall watched her for a time, his mind adrift.

The ponies looked up at him. He felt the heat of their stare.

They stood. They pulled in opposite directions, a steady pressure. The rope parted silently. They walked directly toward him.

Whandall scrambled to his feet, already choosing a tree to climb, but a stallion trotted to block it. He picked another and that was blocked. The rocks? Yes, the rock slope behind him: he ran toward it ahead of a pair of ponies charging at full tilt, their horns lowered.

It all had a dreadful familiarity. He knew exactly what to do because the ponies behaved exactly like a pair of Bull Pizzle bullies, and if he couldn't get around them he'd be dead. He was climbing the rocks before they reached him, and then the rocks impeded their hooves. But the slope was steep. Stones rolled—a pony screamed—he kicked a few loose on purpose, and now he was high above them. He'd have taunted them like frustrated Bull Pizzle Lordkin—

But ponies didn't act like this!

Ensorcelled?

He reached into his pants, into the concealed pouch, and found Morth's handful of gold dust. He tossed a cloud of gold over them.

The ponies went mad, scrambling at the slope, risking their hooves and their bones and their lives. Then they paused . . . looked at each other . . . turned and trotted, then galloped back toward the wagon.

Wild magic would strengthen a spell but disrupt it too, Morth had said. But who could have spelled these ponies if not Morth of Atlantis? Whandall scrambled down the slope, chasing the bonehead ponies.

Willow was standing in the wagon bed holding a sever. Morth stood out of range, laughing, ignoring the ponies who were now menacing *him*. The air around him seemed to sizzle.

Whandall called, "Willow!"

She was near tears and glad to see him. "He wanted—I don't know what he wanted, I didn't let him get that far."

Morth was offended. "No woman would have reason to be insulted! I'd never have offered if I hadn't seen something of lost Atlantis in you. I have gold!" He held a yellow chunk the size of a child's head in each hand. He stood as if bracketed by suns.

"Willow Ropewalker, I have power! I can protect you from whatever dangers await us. Can you hold a man when you lose your youth? You don't *have* to get old! And I don't either!"

The heat rose up in Whandall, but only the merest flicker. He reached for Yangin-Atep, but Yangin-Atep was gone. He drew his knife. He saw Morth's hands rise. Willow raised the sever as if she would throw it. "Stop!" she commanded.

Morth turned toward her, his back toward Whandall. "What must I do to convince you I mean no harm? Willow, forget what I spoke—"

"Leave her mind alone!"

Morth laughed. His hands wove invisible threads. A great calm settled on Whandall. He knew that this was the spell that had killed his father.

Smiling gently, he strolled toward Morth. Morth watched with interest. Whandall was well within range. Now . . . but first he gave warning.

"Morth, do you think that I can't kill a man without getting angry first?"

"Seshmarl, you surprise me."

"Leave us. We've helped each other, but you don't need us anymore."

"Oh, you need me," Morth said. His eyes flicked away and back, and he laughed again. Whandall held his pose. Morth would be dead before he had spat out the first syllable of a spell.

"You need me elsewhere, Seshmarl! So, here is more gold, refined." Morth dropped the gold and danced away. He was ten paces uphill from Whandall's reflexive lunge, dancing between bouquets of swords and slashing laurels faster than the plants could move. In the gathering dusk he paused on the rocky crest and shouted downstream.

"You!"

A wave was rolling up the river.

Tidal bore, a later age would call such a thing. It followed the river's meandering path, growing taller as it came. It would drown this camp. Morth watched it and laughed.

"You! Aquarius!" Morth was tiny with distance, but they heard him clearly. "You great stupid wall of water, do you know that you've made me rich? Now see if you can follow me!" And Morth ran.

The fastest Lordkin chased by the most savage band had never run so fast as Morth. The wave left the river's course and tried to follow him, straight up a hillside and along the crest, dwindling, slumping. Morth's manic laughter followed him down a hill and up another, straight toward the distant white-topped cone of Mount Joy, until he was no more than a bright dot on the mind's eye.

They waited until evening before going to the river for drinking water. The river roiled with white froth and weird currents even where there were no rocks.

CHAPTER
39

At dusk Whandall tried to start a cook fire, but the power had left him. There was plenty of cooked meat from Morth's feast, but there would be no more cooking until they could learn to make fire.

The absence of Yangin-Atep was loss and gain, like a toothache gone and the tooth with it.

Carver rejoined them by the light of a setting half-moon.

Whandall was ready to kill him even after he knew that the sound of a mare and wagon thrashing through brush wasn't a dozen coyotes. Fool kinless! Maybe the mare's magic led him through that maze of death.

Willow spoke before Whandall could. "Brother, have you been traveling through chaparral by dark?"

"Willow! I was worried—"

Her voice was low and her speech was refined, and Whandall listened in awe and dread. He never wanted to hear her speak to *him* that way.

Carver lay between them. In the night, when Willow might be asleep, he rolled toward Whandall and said, "I was afraid for her. I was afraid."

Whandall whispered, "I hear you."

Silence.

"You missed all the excitement. I'll tell you tomorrow."

* * *

There were stretches of narrow beach. Elsewhere they could rock-hop or wade. But the moment came when they reached a deep pool with vertical walls on either side.

Carver said, "I'm going to teach you to swim."

At first it seemed the cold would kill him. Its bite eased quickly. The bottom was soft mud, a delight to the toes. The water came to his chin. He couldn't really drown. Still, for a time it felt like Carver and Willow had decided to drown him. Sweep your arms to *push* the water back and breathe in while the water isn't in your face. Breathe out anytime. . . .

He began to feel the how and why of it. But already the trees hid the sun, and he was exhausted and shaking with cold. And ahead was the river, with no way up the bank. They would have to go on. How far Whandall didn't know.

There was no fire. They ate cold meat and berries by the light of a growing moon.

The night closed down while the elders described their river trip, and the swimming lesson, amid much laughter.

Presently Whandall asked of nobody in particular, "What do you think is out there?"

"We never get lookers from the other side of the forest," Carver said. "Maybe there's nothing. Maybe nothing but farms or herdsmen."

"Or more forest, or nothing at all," Whandall said.

"No Lordkin, anyway," Willow said.

"Doesn't mean there can't be . . ."—Carver searched for a better word, then gave up—". . . thieves. Or old stories about Lordkin. We don't *know* that they don't know about Lordkin. Tomorrow you stay with the children, Whandall. They couldn't keep up anyway—"

"Carver, I can swim! You taught me!"

"You learned fast too," Willow assured him. Her hand was on his arm; she hadn't done that before. "Now you know how to swim in a pool, Whandall. If you ever fall in the water, you might even get out alive. But we'll be wading in a running river—"

"You shouldn't come anyway," Carver said. "You shouldn't be seen."

"We'll take Carter and the severs . . . better leave you one sever for the coyotes, Whandall. We'll come back when we know where the river goes."

Whandall wished he could see their faces. He was just as glad that they couldn't see his.

For two days Whandall kept himself and the children busy widening the path to the river, giving them more safe space to roam. Whandall and Hammer found unwary prey at the edges of the scorch. Hammer knew how to fish. He tried to teach Whandall, and Whandall caught two. They ate them raw.

Feeding the ponies was difficult. They couldn't be let loose to graze, because no one but Willow could catch them. Whandall gathered anything that looked like grass or straw, and the children carried the fodder up to where the ponies were tethered. They had to carry water as well. If Whandall came near the ponies, they menaced him with their horns and strained at the ropes holding them to trees. More than once Whandall was grateful that the Ropewalkers knew their craft.

But all three of the Ropewalker family were gone, leaving him with the four Miller children and one of the wagons. The wagon with the bottles and the gold.

Whandall knew nothing of kinless families, loyalties, infighting, grudges. It worried him.

Carver and Willow and Carter Ropewalker might cease to need him very soon. It might have happened already. A Lordkin with a knife would be all he was and all he had, for whatever that might mean to strangers on this side of the forest.

In Tep's Town, a Lordkin with a knife need be nothing more.

He could go back. What could stop him?

But strangers guarded the Placehold, men brought home by Placehold women during the past few years. They could protect the house if they had the nerve; they might have lost it already; they had little in common with Whandall Placehold. Elriss and Wanshig were friends, but they were together with their children most of the time. Wess had another man, and another after that, and never came back to Whandall. Other women were friends for a day or a week, never more. Alferth's wine wagons had nothing to carry. What was there to hold Whandall in Tep's Town?

Here on the other side of the forest, Lordkin might be unknown.

He did not know how he would survive where he could not simply gather what he needed. But kinless knew how to make things happen; it wasn't all luck and a Lordkin knife. They could teach Whandall, as they'd taught him to swim. He'd brought them out of the burning city. They owed him.

And there was Willow. If only. A Lordkin could have a kinless woman, but only by force, and he could not force Willow.

He could treat her—he *had* treated her—with the respect he would give a Lordkin woman. She seemed to have lost her fear of him, and he was glad of that. But why would Willow look at a Lordkin male?

It was not too late to go back. Take the Miller children. Give them over to the first kinless he met.

These thoughts played through his mind while he hunted food for the children and tried to keep them out of trouble.

At the next noon the Ropewalkers were back.

"A road," Willow told them. "And a long way up the road are some houses."

"How far?" Whandall asked.

"We can be to the road tomorrow afternoon if we start now."

Whandall thought about that. "What are the people like?"

"We didn't see any people," Willow said.

"We didn't want to be seen," Carver said. "So we didn't get very close."

"What are the houses like?" Whandall asked.

"Squarish, made of wood. Solid looking, well made. Roofs like this." He held his hands to indicate a peaked roof, unlike the flat roofs that were more usual in Tep's Town. "Very solid."

"Interesting," Whandall said. "Like Lords' houses? Made by people not afraid of burning?"

"Yes!" Willow clapped her hands. "I never thought of that, but yes!"

Whandall got up. "I'll load the wagon. You'll have to hitch the ponies."

PART SIX

The Bison Tribe

CHAPTER
40

The ponies were as big as Lords' horses now, and each had a spiral horn, larger than a Lordkin knife, growing from his forehead. Outside conditions had bleached them: they were as white as chalk, with long silky manes. They looked nothing like the kinless ponies they'd been. The mare was nearly as big as the stallions, but her horn was smaller, and she hadn't lost the gray coloring. She was tame.

The stallions were not tame. They went frantic when Whandall or Carver approached them. They wouldn't attack the children, but only Willow could bridle them and hitch them to the wagon. If she tried to ride on the wagon they stopped and waited until she walked ahead again.

One more night on the river. Whandall sat and stared at the water. What would they find ahead? What would Willow do? She lay asleep next to her brother. Her straight black hair was a tangle and she slept from exhaustion, and Whandall thought her the most beautiful woman he had ever seen. He wondered at that. Magic?

They started early the next day, and at noon they came to a bend in the river. Carter pointed excitedly. "The road is just up there." He pointed up the steep slope.

There were trees in the way. Whandall scouted out a route to the road. By going around they could avoid most of the trees, but finally there was no choice. They'd have to cut two trees to get through.

Neither tree seemed to be guarded by other plants. There were few plants in the forest, and those were just bushes and leafy plants, without thorns. They didn't move when approached.

This tree was broad-leafed, the trunk thinner than a man's body. Whandall bowed to it as he'd seen Kreeg Miller do, then chopped a deep notch on one side in the direction he wanted it to fall. Then he and Carver chopped on the other side until it fell, not quite where he wanted, but out of the way.

The other, larger tree dropped exactly where Whandall aimed it, and they were free to go to the road. Willow brought up the horses and wagon. "You bowed to the tree," she said.

Whandall shrugged. "Woodsmen do that."

Willow giggled. "To redwoods," she said. "Not to all the trees. Just redwoods."

"There aren't any redwoods here."

Willow's smile faded slightly. "I know."

"You care?"

She said, "Grandmother loved them. I think we protected each other, humans and redwoods, before the Lordkin came. Here they're gone."

"Maybe we'll find more," Whandall said. He looked at the trees he'd felled. "We won't run out of wood, anyway. Maybe someone will have a fire."

"I hope so," Willow said. "Bathing in cold water. Ugh."

Kinless women took baths every day, Whandall had learned, even when there wasn't soap or hot water, nothing but a stream. It seemed a strange custom. He'd jumped in himself, and whooped and thrashed like the others, to show that he too could stand cold.

The road was no more than a deeply rutted track, but while the river itself wandered in sweeping curves like a snake, the road was straight. Here and there the river had changed course to undermine the road. There the road curved away from the river, then straightened out again.

They had jerked meat, and bread they'd baked when they had fire. Evening found them on the road. Just after dusk Carver looked at the night sky. "We're going north," he said.

"How do you know that?" Whandall asked.

"Stars," Willow said. "Father taught Carver how to read stars."

"It's hard," Carver said. "I looked last night, and I couldn't tell. There are more stars here. Lots more, too many to recognize! This early in the evening it looks right. But when it's dark there are thousands and thousands of stars."

"What are stars?" Carter asked.

"Dargramnet . . ." Whandall hesitated. "My mother's mother. She said the stars are cook fires of our ancestors. Cook fires and bonfires to Yangin-Atep."

"You hesitated," Willow said. "You do that when you speak of your family. Why?"

"We—the Lordkin—don't talk about families to strangers," Whandall said. "Or even close friends."

"Why not?"

Whandall shook his head. "We just don't. I think part of it is certainty. You know who your mother is, but not always your father, and your mother might go off anytime. Even when you think you know—but *you* know, don't you? How?"

"Whandall, girls don't sleep with men until they're married," Willow said.

Sleeping wasn't what made babies, but this seemed to be a language thing. Did she *really* mean . . .? Whandall asked, "What happens if they do?"

"No one will marry them," Willow said. Pink was flooding into her neck and cheeks. "Even if it's not their fault. There was a girl, the daughter of a friend of Mother's. Dream-Lotus was a few years older than me, old enough to be . . . attractive, during the last Burning. Some Lordkin men caught her. They almost killed her. Maybe it would have been better if they did."

Whandall's voice came out funny. "Why?"

"She had a baby," Willow said. "It wasn't her fault—everyone knew that—but she had a baby, and no man would have her. Her father died, and then her brother drank himself to death."

"What happened to her?" Whandall asked. He didn't dare ask about the baby.

"We don't know. After Mother died we lost track of Dream-Lotus. She always wanted a job in the Lordshills. Maybe she went there."

They came to the edge of the town at noon the next day.

First there were the dogs. They ran barking toward Willow. One got too close, and the rightside pony lowered his horn and lunged. The dog ran away howling. The barking and howling brought two townsmen.

They were big men, dark of complexion, each with long straight black hair braided in a queue hanging down his back. One held a leather sling in one hand and a rock in the other. The other man had an ax. They shouted something unintelligible, first at Whandall, then at the howling dog. The dog came over to them, and the man with the ax bent to examine it. He spoke without getting up, and the other man nodded. Whandall's thumbnail brushed the big Lordkin knife at his belt, just to know where it was.

The men looked from Whandall on the wagon to Willow walking ahead of the horses, frowned, and one said something to the other. Then they pointed to the horses and one laughed.

"Hello," Whandall said. "Where are we?" No response. He repeated himself in Condigeano.

The man with the leather sling said something, saw Whandall didn't understand, and pointed up the road. They called their dogs and watched until Willow had led the wagon out of sight.

Whandall counted twenty houses before he stopped trying to count them. There were at least that many more, strung along three parallel dusty streets. The largest house was about the size of a good Lordkin house in Tep's Town, but they had flower gardens in front, and a few had fenced yards. They didn't look as elegant as Lords' houses, but they were not crude, and they were clearly built to last a generation and more, some wood, some baked clay, none stone.

At the far end of town was a wagon camp, a dozen or more big covered wagons drawn into a circle. Just before the wagon circle there was a wooden rail corral holding a hundred or more great shaggy beasts. They seemed to have no necks. Their eyes stared out of a big collar of fur, and they had short curved horns and lashing tails. They stood in a circle, the biggest ones on the outside, smaller ones inside, and they munched on baled hay while staring malevolently at Whandall and his wagon.

When Willow tried to speak to a gaudily dressed lady on the dusty town main street, she didn't seem unfriendly, but she only laughed and pointed to the wagon circle.

"My feet hurt," Willow said.

Two boys came out of the wagon train circle and shouted something. Whandall gestured helplessly. They laughed and went back inside, and in a moment a large man of around forty came out. His face was weathered and he had a bit of a squint.

He was lighter of complexion than the men they'd seen earlier. He was dressed in leather, long trousers, long-sleeved pullover tunic, soft leather boots. A big red moon was painted on the left breast of his tunic. Red and blue animals chased each other in a circle around the moon. A dark red sun blazed on his back, and below it, warriors with spears chased a herd of the same ugly beasts they'd seen in the corral. His hair was black with some gray at the temples, plaited into a queue that hung halfway down his back. There were feathers in his hair, and he wore a bright silver ring with a big blue-green stone. Another silver and blue-green design hung on a thong around his neck. His belt held a very serviceable-looking knife with a fancily carved bone handle. The blade was not as long as Whandall's Lordkin knife.

"*Hiyo. Keenm hisho?*"

Whandall shook his head. "Whandall," he said. "From Tep's Town."

The man considered that. "Know Condigeano?"

"I speak good Condigeano," Whandall said excitedly.

"Good. I don't speak your tongue. Not much contact with the Valley of Smokes," he said. "How'd you get here?"

"We cut a path through the forest," Whandall said.

"I'm impressed." He looked from Whandall to Willow, looked at the ponies, looked at the children on the wagon. "Don't think I ever met anyone who got out that way. There's a few harpies in Condigeo, but they got there by ship."

Willow looked back at Whandall. "Harpies?" she said.

"I guess he means us," Whandall said.

Willow shuddered. "Tell him—" She caught herself.

"Fine-looking one-horns," the man said. "Looking to sell them?"

"No, I don't think so," Whandall said.

"Well, all right. That your sister?"

Whandall choked back the automatic rage at the impertinent question. "No."

"Um. You hungry? My name's Black Kettle, by the way." He patted his ample paunch. "But everybody calls me Kettle Belly." He swept his hand to indicate the wagon train. "This is the Bison Clan."

"I am Whandall." Clan? That was too complicated. "And that's Willow. Her brothers Carver and Carter. The children are cousins," Whandall said.

"Ah. Your girl?"

I already told you more than you have to know! But the question seemed innocent enough. Maybe people here talked about such things. Tras Preetror had.

Willow wouldn't understand him. Whandall said, "I hope so."

Kettle Belly smiled. "Good. Fine-looking girl. Here, follow me. We'll get you something to eat."

"Thanks. We could use fire too."

Kettle Belly laughed heartily. "A Valley of Smokes harpy can't make fire?"

Whandall wanted to resent that, but Kettle Belly seemed so friendly and well intentioned that he couldn't. Instead he laughed. "Never learned how. Never needed to."

"Guess I understand that all right," Kettle Belly said. "You come on with me, then." He turned to one of the children. "Number Three—"

"I'm Four."

Kettle Belly roared laughter again, and gave instructions. He turned back to Whandall. "I told him to let Mother know we've got company. And he'll look up Haj Fishhawk's wife. She came from the Valley of Smokes; she'll be able to talk to your friends. When you're ready to trade those one-horns, let me know; I'll give you a good price and show you how to drive bison."

"Why would I want to sell them?"

Kettle Belly smiled indulgently. "Well . . . something might come up."

Ruby Fishhawk was at least fifty, a kinless woman with soft eyes and long fluffy hair gone white. As soon as she met Willow she began asking questions about family. Who was Willow's mother? Who was her father's mother? In minutes she found that Willow's father's mother had married Ruby's aunt's brother, and Willow's mother's brother was Ruby's cousin.

"But you're tired. Kettle Belly says you don't have fire! How long?"

"Three days," Willow said.

"You poor thing! Come with me; I have a bathtub. I love my husband, I love the trader folk, but they don't bathe properly! Sweat lodges are all very well, but there's nothing like a proper bath! Come on; I'll show you—"

"What about the horses?" Willow asked. "Whandall can't handle them . . ."

Ruby grinned as if Willow had made a good joke. "We'll take care of that." She spoke rapidly to Kettle Belly.

He nodded and pointed to a second and larger corral beyond the circle of wagons. There were two of the one-horned stallions. Each stood in his own part of the corral. One had the company of two gray shorthorn mares. The other was alone. They eyed Whandall's team and snuffled. Whandall's mare whinnied.

Girls younger than Willow carried fodder to the corral. One of the girls was watching the strangers with evident curiosity. Kettle Belly gestured and she came over to them. She was shapely, a little younger than Willow and just beginning to show as a woman. Whandall found her pretty in an exotic way. Her hair was long and straight, tied with a bow of orange ribbon, and she smiled at Whandall.

Kettle Belly spoke rapidly, finally saying "Whandall." The girl smiled, and nodded to Whandall. "Her name translates to Orange Blossom," Kettle Belly said. "You'll learn to say it, but not now. I think she likes you."

Orange Blossom smiled shyly.

"She'll take care of your one-horns. Your wagon will be safe enough here next to mine."

Orange Blossom began to unhitch the horses. Whandall watched, wondering what to do. The horses and wagon were all they owned. He saw that Kettle Belly was watching him with wry amusement.

"It'll be all right, lad," Kettle Belly said. "Think about it, we're Bison Clan wagon traders. Everyone knows who we are. If we were thieves, would any town trust us? It's not like we could run! Not with bison pulling the wagons!"

Orange Blossom slipped a bridle on the mare. She didn't bother with the stallions. She led the mare toward the corral, and the stallions followed docilely.

"Young colts," Kettle Belly said. "Give them another year, they'll fight. Right now they won't be any problem."

Ruby was still talking. "Well, that's all settled, then. Come, Willow." She led Willow off into the circle of wagons.

"She hasn't heard her own language since the last time we went to Condigeo," Kettle Belly said. "She has kinfolk there. Kinfolk as she reckons them, anyway. Well, come on, lad, there's better things than bathtubs! Tell the youngsters to go with Number Four there; he'll find them something to eat."

"Number Four?" Whandall asked.

"Ho, we don't give boys names like they do in the cities," Kettle Belly said. "When they're old enough, they find their names. Until then we just call them by their father's name, unless there's so many they have to have numbers. Anyway, Four will see the kids are fed. You come with me."

Whandall explained to the Ropewalkers and Millers who had been listening without comprehension.

Carver thought he should stay with the children. Carter had a different idea. He wanted to go with Whandall. Whandall was about to say it was all right with him when he saw that Carver didn't approve. "You'd better help your kin," Whandall said.

"All right, Whandall," Carter said.

Kettle Belly led Whandall to one of the big wagons. The wagons were roofed over with hoops covered with some kind of cloth. The roof was high enough that Whandall thought he would be able to stand under it, but they didn't go inside. Kettle Belly led him around the wagon and into the circle.

An awning had been attached to the top of the wagon and led out to poles, so that it made a high-roofed shed to shade them from the sun. Large boxes made low walls around the covered area. The area under the roof was carpeted, and there was a bench just outside it. Kettle Belly sat on the bench and began pulling off his boots. He indicated that Whandall should do the same.

"We mostly take off our shoes before we go in," he said. "Saves the women some work."

Whandall considered that. It was a new way of looking at things.

The carpet felt strange to his bare feet. He had seen carpets in Lordshills, but he'd never walked on one. These were brighter in color and seemed sturdy. He thought the Lords would pay well for one. "How are these made?" he asked.

"What, the carpets? Woven," Kettle Belly said. "From wool. This one was done by hill shepherds. They weave them in winter." He turned back a corner of the carpet. The underside was covered with thousands of small knots.

"It must take a long time."

"It does," Kettle Belly said. "This one probably took eight or ten years to make. You can get cheaper ones in towns. Weave won't be as close, flax and hemp threads in the wool. There may be some for sale here when the market opens tomorrow. Have a seat."

They sat on wool-stuffed pillows. The pillows were woven of a coarse material like the carpets, but they had different designs. Kettle Belly sat with his legs out, his back against one of the wagon boxes.

If you had to live out of a wagon, carpets were a good idea, Whandall thought. "Do they sell good carpets here?"

Kettle Belly smiled. "Well, I wouldn't want the Firewoods Town people to hear me say," he said. He watched Whandall react to that and grinned. "Marsyl carpets look all right, but Marsyl Town doesn't get cold enough in winter. Sheep here don't have the best wool. We buy Marsyl carpets when we're headed south and we don't have a full load. They sell all right down Condigeo way."

"You're not going south," Whandall guessed. Tras Preetror had said that Condigeo was six days' sail south of Tep's Town.

"Right."

Kettle Belly clapped his hands. A woman about his age came out from behind the wagon boxes. She was darker than Kettle Belly and considerably thinner. Her skirts were leather with designs tattooed on them in bright colors. Some of the tattoos were emphasized by colored thread sewn into patterns. Her dark hair was pulled back and tied with a ribbon but not plaited like the men wore theirs.

Kettle Belly stood when the woman came into the enclosed area, and after a moment Whandall did too.

"Whandall, my wife Mirime. I'm afraid she doesn't speak much Condigeano." Kettle Belly spoke rapidly in a tongue that meant nothing to Whandall, but he thought he heard the word *harpy*. Mirime didn't look happy with her new guest, but finally she nodded and went out between the boxes to what must have been another room. In a moment she returned carrying a tray with two cups and a bottle. She set it down on the carpet, bowed slightly, and left.

Kettle Belly waved Whandall to the cushions. He filled both cups and handed one of them to Whandall. The cup reminded Whandall of the thin-walled cups the Lords used, and like the Lords' cups it had figures painted on it. There was a ship on one side, and a woman with a fishtail on the other.

It was filled with a wine that smelled wonderful. Whandall was about to gulp it down when he saw that Kettle Belly sipped at his, then watched Whandall. Whandall sipped too. It was smooth and sweet, nothing like the wines he'd had in Tep's Town. He sipped again. In moments the cup was empty.

Kettle Belly refilled the cup from the stone jug. "We saw big smoke last week," he said. "Burning?"

Whandall nodded. "Yes."

Kettle Belly clucked. "Never did understand that. Why would you want to burn your city down?"

"Not everyone wants to," Whandall said.

"Sure. Ruby Fishhawk told me. There's two kinds of harpies, ones like her who put the fires out and the other kind."

"Kinless and Lordkin," Whandall said.

"Yep, that's what she called them."

"Lordkin follow Yangin-Atep," Whandall said. "When the fire god takes a man, the Burning starts." The wine cup was empty again. Kettle Belly filled it without being asked. Whandall drank more.

"Lordkin do other things," Whandall said morosely.

"Thieves, aren't they?"

"We gather. In Tep's Town that's not stealing. Not for Lordkin."

"It is here," Kettle Belly said.

"Willow is kinless," Whandall said. He hesitated. The wine burned in his stomach. "So are the others. But I'm Lordkin."

"Well, of course you are," Kettle Belly said. The laughter was back in his voice, and his smile was broad.

"You knew?"

Kettle Belly roared with laughter. "Whandall, Whandall, everybody knows."

Whandall frowned. "How?"

For answer, Kettle Belly called out, "Mirime! Bring the mirror."

The woman came back in carrying a bronze mirror that Kettle Belly polished with a clean soft cloth, then handed to Whandall. "You don't have a mirror, do you?"

Whandall looked.

He saw a bright feathered serpent with a man's face under it.

"Other places, other customs," Kettle Belly said. "Tep's Town isn't the only place that has tattoos. But they're said to be gaudier among the Lordkin harpies, and Whandall, no place have I seen anything like that! It's why no one was afraid of you, you know."

"I don't understand." Whandall found the wine buzzing in his head and heard his speech thicken. "The tattoo, it's prob'ly Atlantis."

"Atlantis! But you're not from Atlantis."

"No, no . . . made friends with an Atlantis wizard," Whandall said, wondering why he was talking so much to this stranger.

"Well, he did you proud. But Whandall, anyplace you go, anything you do, it'll be known all up and down the road in weeks," Kettle Belly said. "You're the easiest man to describe on the Hemp Road!"

"Is it ugly?" Whandall asked.

"Takes getting used to, I'll say that," Kettle Belly said. "But once you do, it's sort of pretty."

Whandall drained his cup and held it out again. Kettle Belly leaned over to fill it, then stopped. "Sure?"

"No. Dumb." Whandall's fist closed, hiding the cup. "But this, my brother was looking for this."

"Meaning?"

"Good wine. Wanshig was *sure*. Never tasted anything like this, but he was *sure*. Like I was *sure* there's a way out an' I finally found it."

Kettle Belly nodded understanding. "Question is, can you hold it?"

It wasn't a familiar term to Whandall. It? Wine. "Sure."

"I hope so," Kettle Belly said. "Lad, I hope so. You're not the first, you know."

Whandall frowned the question.

"Other Lordkin harpies come out. Why do you think we call you harpies? Most don't last. The lucky ones get put back. Most get killed when it's too much trouble to put them back."

"What happens to the rest?"

"There aren't many. You met Ruby Fishhawk. There are two harpy guards with Lonesome Crow's wagon train, and I hear tell of a harpy leathersmith up in Paradise Valley. Not sure I know of any others. Maybe a few more women."

Whandall thought about that. "There's no way to put me back."

"I knew you were smart. You can control yourself too. Sober, you can, anyway."

How would he know that? What magic did they have here?

"Tell you what, let's have some water," Kettle Belly said. "More wine with dinner. First let me show you around."

CHAPTER
41

The wagons weren't like Whandall's. They were well designed and bigger. There were cargo wagons and wagons to hold bales of hay and fodder, but every family had one that was like a house on wheels. Those were covered by a roof of closely woven cloth held up by metal hoops, and they had a complicated harness arrangement to attach them to the weirdly shaped bison.

"Keeps our Greathand busy," Kettle Belly said. "The blacksmith. And lots of leatherwork. But there's no magic needed. Lots of people on the road. Magic runs thin along the Hemp Road. Best not to depend on magic too much."

Whandall nodded. "There's not much magic in Tep's Town."

"That's what they tell me," Kettle Belly said.

"You call it the Hemp Road."

Kettle Belly shrugged. "There's other commerce. Probably as much wool as anything else. But hemp's a stable product. Always a demand for good hemp. Fiber, rope, smoking flowers, hemp tea, hemp flower gum. You can always get a good price for good hemp."

"Doesn't it try to kill you?" Whandall asked.

"What, *hemp?*"

"Maybe it forgot how," Whandall muttered. Kettle Belly looked at him strangely but didn't say anything.

The wagons they lived out of were bare inside. Kettle Belly explained, "We don't so much live in the wagons as just outside of them. The wagon boxes nearly fill the wagons when we're on the road, and make the walls when we're in camp. See, some of the boxes open from the side, some from the top. Stack the boxes, spread the canopy roof, spread the carpets, lash everything down, and you've got your travel nest. We can be done an hour after we make camp if everyone works together."

It was all new to Whandall. No Lordkin, no kinless. Just people who worked like kinless but kept what they made. . . .

"Who owns all this?" Whandall asked.

"Well, that's complicated," Kettle Belly said. "Lot of this stuff is owned by the wagon train. Most families own a cargo wagon; a few own two; I own three. And every family owns a housewagon and team of bison. That's the bride's dowry." He grimaced. "Five girls I've had. Married off two. Three to go, three more outfits to buy! But my girls get the best. You should see what I'm having made for Orange Blossom. There's a smithy fifty leagues up the road, makes great wagons. Like this one. We'll collect hers next time we're through there, sometime this summer. She'll have to beat the boys away with a stick after they see that rig!"

Like kinless, Whandall thought. Kinless men took care of their daughters. Lordkin men seldom knew who their children were. A boy could look like his mother's man, and then it was pretty clear, but you never knew with girls.

Dowry. A new word, and Kettle Belly talked so fast Whandall wasn't sure of everything he had said. There was too much to learn. And yet. Whandall grinned broadly. He had learned one thing—he had a chance here. A real chance.

The market area was a field beyond the town. There were tents and wagons with platforms, and an air of messiness as townsfolk and wagoneers hastened to set up the fairgrounds. "It'll look pretty good in the morning," Kettle Belly said. He led the way to a large tent at one corner of the field. Orange Blossom supervised as four children worked to lay out carpets, set up tables, and generally make preparations.

"So, Whandall, got anything to sell?" Kettle Belly asked.

"You can see the wagon's empty—"

"Mostly I see it's got a false bottom." Kettle Belly chuckled. "No telling what you've got in there. Of course that's the idea. Anyway, I won't charge you much to set you up a table in my tent."

"Is this a good place to sell?" Whandall asked.

Kettle Belly shook his head. "Depends on what you're selling. Oh, well, not really. Not a lot to buy here, either, other than food and hay, leastways not going north in spring. We'll buy some berries. Crops ripen here quicker than they do up north; sometimes you can turn a good profit moving berries north while people are sick of winter food. But they won't have much, and you have to be careful. Berries spoil fast if you hit a stretch where the magic's weak."

"Then why do you stop here?"

"Heh, lad, we don't have any choice. The bison go only so far, then they stop for a couple of days. Have to let them rest up and fill their bellies. That's most of this town's excuse for existence, wagon stop on the Hemp Road." He eyed Whandall critically. "And now we have to come to some agreement."

"What does that mean?" Whandall turned wary, and crouched slightly.

"Knife fighter. Lonesome Crow tells me you harpies are good at knife fighting," Kettle Belly said.

"Good enough," Whandall said. "What kind of agreement?"

"Boy, you keep asking for information. It cost me to learn what you want to know. Should I tell you for free?"

Whandall considered that. "Wizards trade information," he said. "Tellers trade stories. I studied with a teller."

"Yes, but you don't know anything I need to know," Kettle Belly said. "Leastwise I doubt you do. Stories are good. You can eat off good stories. Any night you have a good story, dinner's free. But what do you know that I need to know?" By now he must have seen Whandall's grin.

"Great Hawk Bay," Whandall said. "They'll pay well for herbs and spices."

"Depends on the spices," Kettle Belly said. "We don't get that far west. There's a market in Golden Valley that pays better than Great Hawk, for that matter. Great Hawk's on the sea, they get ship trade. Whandall, do you have Valley of Smokes spices in that wagon bottom?"

Whandall considered his options. None of them seemed very good. Might as well tell the truth. "Some."

"Hold on to them. Golden Valley's the place to sell those. If you can get there."

"Why would that be a problem?" Whandall asked.

Orange Blossom giggled behind them. "It won't, if you stay with us," she said. She was using a broom to sweep off the carpet.

"It can get tricky," Kettle Belly said. "Bandits. Maybe you can fight them off, but generally there's more than one. Then there's the tax collectors. Every town wants a cut. They'll take all they can get from a lone traveler. You go alone, you won't get two hundred miles."

Whandall didn't say anything.

"You're tough," Kettle Belly said. "And damned mean looking to boot. But one man alone isn't enough to fight off tax collectors."

Whandall thought of the Toronexti. "Are you making an offer?"

"I'm thinking about it."

"Do, Father," Orange Blossom said.

"Yep. Whandall, you travel with us to Golden Valley. If there's fighting to do, you'll fight on our side. You pay your own travel expenses, that's food and fodder. We pay the taxes. You keep up with us. It costs you a third."

"Father!" Orange Blossom said.

"Hush, child!"

"A third of what?"

"Of the value of everything you have when we get to Golden Valley."

"What does everyone else pay?" Whandall asked.

"A fifth. But you'll be a lot more trouble than they are."

"Starting from Condigeo," Whandall guessed. "They pay that starting from Condigeo." He wasn't used to bargaining. But a Lordkin must have guile. . . .

"Well, you have a point," Kettle Belly said. "And besides, my daughter likes you. A quarter, Whandall, and that's my best offer. A quarter of what you're worth when we get to Golden Valley." He paused. "You won't get a better offer."

Supper was a big affair. A huge pot of stew bubbled over an open fire in the middle of the wagon camp. Carpets and cushions were spread out around it. Men and older women sat while children and younger women served out bowls of stew and small pots of a thin wine generously watered.

Kettle Belly waited until Whandall had finished a bowl of stew, then came over to introduce him around the wagon circle.

First he was taken to a wagon with a cover painted like the sky. An odd funnel-shaped cloud reached from the top of the canopy to the bottom of the wagon bed. It was so real that Whandall thought he could see it move if he looked away from it. If he stared at it, it stayed still.

The wagon was tended by two women as old as Ruby Fishhawk, and a girl about Willow's age. The girl stared at Whandall until Kettle Belly spoke rapidly, and one of the women went inside. She came out with a man.

"Hickamore," Kettle Belly said. He spoke rapidly, then turned to Whandall. "This is Hickamore, shaman of this wagon train. I've told him that I have invited you to join the wagon train."

Hickamore was ageless, his dark skin like the leather he was dressed in, his eyes set deep in his head. He might have been thirty or ninety. He stared at Whandall, then looked *past* him into the distant hills. Whandall started to say something, but Kettle Belly gestured impatiently for silence. They stood and waited while Hickamore stared at nothing. Finally the shaman spoke in Condigeano.

"Whandall Placehold," he said.

Whandall jumped.

"This is your name?" Hickamore made it a question.

"Yes, Sage, but I have not told it to anyone here."

Hickamore nodded. "I was not sure. You will have other names, all known to the world. You will not again have or need a secret name."

"You see the future."

"Sometimes, when it is strong enough."

"Will I meet Morth of Atlantis again?"

Hickamore stared into the distance. "So the story is true. An Atlantis wizard lives! I met one long ago, before Atlantis sank, but I know little of Atlantis. I would know more."

Whandall said nothing. A shrewd light came into the old shaman's eyes. "Black Kettle, am I an honest man?"

"None more so," Kettle Belly said.

"None here, anyway. Whandall Placehold, I make you a trade. Black Kettle will charge you half the traveler fee he demands, and you will tell me all you know of Morth of Atlantis."

"Now, Hickamore—"

"Black Kettle, do you dispute my right?"

"No, Sage." Kettle Belly shrugged. "He hadn't accepted my offer."

"He does now," Hickamore said. "One part in ten."

Kettle Belly howled. "One in eight is half what I offered!"

Hickamore stared at him.

"Robbery," Kettle Belly said. "Robbery. You'll ruin us all! Oh, all right, one part in ten, but you must satisfy the Sage, Whandall!"

It was all happening too fast, and Whandall still felt the effects of the wine. Were they stealing from him? Was all this staged? Pelzed had done that. And the Lords, with their circuses and shows. They were certainly treating him like a child, arguing over his goods.

His and Willow's. And the children. One part in ten would be half what anyone else paid. And they didn't know about the gold. A Lordkin must have guile. . . . "Thank you," Whandall said. "We accept."

Greathand the blacksmith was nearly as big as Whandall, much bigger than anyone else in the wagon train, with arms as big as Black Kettle's thighs. He eyed Whandall suspiciously and spoke mostly in grunts, but he didn't object to Whandall's joining the wagon train.

After Black Kettle introduced Whandall around the circle of wagons, Ruby Fishhawk took Willow and the others on the same tour. The evening ended with wine and singing, and Whandall fell asleep staring at the blaze of stars overhead.

The market tents were set up in a field next to the wagon camp. Not all the Bison Clan families had tents. Some shared, two families with tables in one tent. Everyone displayed something for sale; that was a rule Kettle Belly insisted on. Even overpriced goods made the fair look larger.

Across the field from the wagon train tents the townsfolk set up their own market. Their tents were less colorful than the Bison Clan's, and there were not many goods for sale. Mostly the town dealt in food stocks and fodder.

Kettle Belly went with Whandall to inspect the town's goods.

One tent sold rugs. Warned by Kettle Belly, Whandall inspected these closely. There were fewer knots on the underside of the carpet, and the patterns were not as bright or as well done.

As they walked away Kettle Belly muttered, "Overpriced. Far too high for this time of year. I wonder if they know something."

"What might that be?"

"Cold winter. Wind off the high glaciers. Have to ask Hickamore."

"We need rugs," Whandall said. "I don't mind sleeping on the ground, but Willow isn't used to it. The children aren't."

"Tell her to hold on a couple of weeks," Kettle Belly said. He pointed north. "Beyond the pass at the end of this valley we start up into the mountains. Not the real mountains, but they're high enough that the wool's better. We'll be in Gorman in two weeks. Look for rugs there. They won't be as good as mine, but they'll do. Use them on the road, buy better in Golden Valley, and sell the Gorman rugs in Last Pines next year. You'll get at least what you paid for them."

Orange Blossom had harnessed and bridled two pony stallions. Streamers flowed from their horns. In the scantiest of clothing Orange Blossom stood on their backs, one foot on each, and rode through the town to bring the townsfolk to the market field. A stream of young men followed her back to the market.

Willow caught him gaping. "She does that well," Whandall said.

Willow only nodded. Then she went to find her brother, and together they went to the Fishhawk tent. They came back with two of the Fishhawk boys and two posts twice as long as Whandall was tall. Carter dived into the hidden compartment of their wagon and came out with ropes. They stood the posts eight paces apart, and used ropes and stakes to hold them upright. Then they strung a rope from one post to the next and tightened it with a stick twisted into the rope.

Willow vanished into their tent. She came out wearing skintight trousers and tunic. "Catch me," she shouted to Whandall. Then she climbed agilely to the top of one of the poles and stood on it. "Catch me!" she shouted again.

Carter moved beside Whandall. "She wants you to stand beneath her in case she falls. If she falls, you catch her."

"Oh." Memories came back. "You're the ropewalkers!"

Carter stared.

"I mean I saw you before, before I knew what your name was," Whandall said. He remembered the man who had stood beneath the ropewalking girl during Pelzed's show. That must have been her father! Whandall moved out under the rope, his eyes fixed on Willow. She was both beautiful and vulnerable.

Willow smiled down at him. "I'll probably fall. I haven't done this in a long time," she said. "But you're strong."

"I'd suit up," Carter said, "only there's nothing to wear."

"Next time," Willow said. "I'll work alone today." She walked out onto the rope.

Whandall stayed under her. It wasn't easy. She did backward somersaults, stood on her hands on the rope, jumped and caught herself. She seemed less graceful than the little girl Whandall remembered, but she got the attention of the spectators.

A mixed crowd of villagers and wagon train boys gathered to watch. They all stared at Willow. She smiled back at them and did a forward somersault.

Carver was standing by one of the posts. "Wow."

Whandall looked at him.

"Forward's a lot harder than backward. You can't *see*," Carver said. "She's still the best—"

Willow attempted something complicated. She was falling before he quite realized that it wasn't an act. She had the rope and lost it, but it slowed her for a moment, and then Whandall was under her. Whandall braced himself.

She fell limply into his arms. He caught her and they both went down, knocking the wind out of his chest. They lay on the ground, Willow atop him. Despite the pain, it felt good to Whandall. She was well muscled, soft at the shoulders—his hands moved involuntarily.

Willow smiled and deftly got up. "Thanks. My hero." She said it half mockingly—but only half—and she smiled. Then she bowed to the crowd and went into their tent.

Kettle Belly came over to their wagon after dinner. "I feel better about the deal you made," he told Whandall. "You didn't tell me Willow could perform."

"Carter can too," Whandall said, remembering. "He needs practice, though."

"They'll have the chance. A good show is worth a lot, Whandall. They'll draw crowds out in Stone Needles country. Golden Valley too. Whandall, we're moving out tomorrow. How will you move your wagons?"

"The ponies—"

"They'll be slow. Willow can still lead them?"

"Well, I suppose so, I don't know why she couldn't."

Kettle Belly grinned knowingly. "Good. But it won't do. They won't move faster than the girls can walk. Most of the way is uphill. The girls will get tired and slow us down, even if Orange Blossom takes turns with Willow. Willow will be too tired to practice. And what about your mare?"

"Carver can still handle her. She'll pull a cart if he drives it." Whandall shrugged. "Not me. That mare wants me dead."

Kettle Belly grinned again. "Okay. Good. Carver drives the wagon with the mare. The other wagon's a different matter. I'll bring over some bison in the morning, and Number Three will show you how to hitch them up."

"What about our ponies?"

"They'll follow the girls. Willow and Orange Blossom can ride at the tailgate of your wagon, and all the one-horns will follow them. Darned things are more trouble than they're worth, but they're popular in Golden Valley."

CHAPTER
42

After dinner he left the Ropewalkers and Millers working on the wagon. Carver sent a dirty look after him, a look he was meant to catch. He stopped. He said, "Carter, maybe you'd better come with me."

Carter trotted to Whandall's side, but, "This is work," Carver said, as if Whandall might not recognize it on sight. "We need all the hands we can get."

"I made a bargain with Hickamore, the wizard," Whandall informed them all. "If I don't keep it, we'll be paying Kettle Belly a fourth of what we own. So I'm going to tell him stories about Morth—"

"But why Carter? He doesn't speak Condigeano!"

"Carter might have seen things about Morth that I didn't. The younger children would miss anything subtle, and you weren't *there,* Carver. While Willow and I were dealing with Morth, you were a day's walk away dealing with a cart and mare that you had left behind. But I could take Willow instead."

"Oh, Whandall, I think they need me here," Willow said with apparent regret. "Take Carter."

Carver began pounding a post into the ground. Carter and Whandall went to Hickamore's wagon.

The shaman and his family sat under the stars. They must have had first choice of campsites; the circle of rocks around his fire was almost too convenient as a conversation pit.

"My children, these are Whandall and Carter, surely the most unusual of visitors to our home." How had Hickamore known Carter's name?

Magic. "Folk, greet my daughters Rutting Deer and Twisted Cloud, and their friends Fawn and Mountain Cat."

Twisted Cloud was just turned fourteen, quite pretty in the local fashion, high cheekbones and arched brows and straight dark hair. She had Carter's full attention. Running Deer (the shaman *couldn't* have said *Rutting Deer,* could he?) was seventeen, with that same look, exotic to Whandall. Fawn didn't say, but she looked to be the same age. Fawn was pretty enough, but Running Deer was Twisted Cloud made mature: tall and lovely, with dark straight hair sculpted into a single braid. Mountain Cat was eighteen or nineteen and finely dressed. He was with Fawn or with Twisted Cloud—it was difficult to tell which—but he didn't want the barbarians near either of them.

Whandall sat aside. Even among lookers he knew how to avoid knifeplay.

The girls chattered. "Willow," Twisted Cloud said. "Why is she named Willow?"

"It's their way," Fawn said. "Like Ruby. Something precious."

Twisted Cloud nodded understanding. "It's hard to find. Maybe they don't have any in the Valley of Smokes?"

The old man offered Whandall wine. Whandall asked for river water instead. Twisted Cloud scowled, knowing she'd be sent to the cistern to fetch it, and she was.

Hickamore asked, "When did you first see Morth of Atlantis?"

"He was in Lord Samorty's courtyard below Shanda's balcony, talking to the Lords. He looked decrepit, then, and amused. I was only a little boy, but even I could see that he thought they were all fools. They saw it too, I think, but they thought he was *wearing* it. A wizard's attitude, like the Lords' attitudes they all wore like masks. But it wasn't."

"He did think they were fools, then. Why?"

"They used something that burned up all the magic right through their whole town. Magic didn't work there. Morth was dying for lack of magic—"

"A Warlock's Wheel?"

Whandall shrugged.

Hickamore was excited. "What did it look like?"

"I never saw it. What's it supposed to look like?"

But in the distraction of Twisted Cloud's return, the question got lost. Whandall drank, then thanked her, and Hickamore asked, "What was a Lordkin boy doing on a Lord's balcony?"

Whandall told of crawling over the wall, meeting Shanda, the exchange of clothes. . . . Running Deer, Fawn, and Twisted Cloud were listening, rapt. Mountain Cat had forgotten all his suspicions under the lure of a good story.

Hiding on the balcony watching an opera. The Black Pit at night. The magic forest: Hickamore wanted to know more about hemp.

"It wants to kill you," Whandall said. "Everyone knows that. You can't walk through a hemp field without falling asleep, and it will strangle you by morning."

"Not here," Mountain Cat said.

"Ropewalkers," Hickamore said. "How do they make rope if the hemp tries to kill them?"

Whandall looked to Carter. "Carter, the shaman asks—"

Carter said in broken Condigeano, "Old men know. Never teach me."

At Hickamore's urging, Whandall described taking Shanda through the chaparral, being caught by Samorty's people, the mock beating. Hickamore wanted to know more about maps. Whandall drew Tep's Town in the dust, by firelight. Hickamore gave him colored sand to improve it.

Then Hickamore added Whandall's improvements to a map he must have drawn earlier. Grinning, he watched Whandall's face as the map came to life. A green-sand forest bowed and rippled to a yellow wind-storm. Cobalt river tracks glittered. Bison no bigger than ants ran before the orange sparkle of a prairie fire. Within the fire a bird's beak showed for an instant, there and gone, and something else, a bird as large as a bison, ran ahead of the fire and vanished.

Carter was yawning, and that gave Whandall his excuse to depart. Bringing Carter had been a good idea.

Hitching up bison was a pain, but driving them turned out to be easier. The beasts were not very smart. They wanted to follow their leaders. They were hitched four to a wagon. As long as a team of bison could see the team in front of them they followed docilely. Kettle Belly drove the lead wagon.

The road took them steadily north. They crossed two small streams, then the road led steadily upward.

The first sign of the terror bird was a high, piercing shriek. Then a scream from a woman in the lead wagon. Then more of the alien shriek-ing. Then a coyote burst from the chaparral, followed by something bright green and orange, and big.

Whandall had never seen its like. It ran on two legs like a chicken, but the eyes were a head higher than Whandall's and it hadn't even straight-ened up! The head was too big for its body, mounted on a thick and pow-erful neck. The beak was most of the head, and it wasn't shaped like a chicken's. It was curved and hooked, built for murder. The legs were thick and stumpy, thighs nearly as big around as Whandall's, and covered with feathers. A plume of tail feathers fanned out behind it.

Whandall gaped. It was clearly a bird, but those weren't wings! The fore-arms ended in what looked like Lordkin knives, with no pretense at flight.

The coyote ran in terror. An astonished camp dog sprang after it just too late, and the beast shrieked again and charged the dog. The dog dodged by a hairbreadth. The beak snapped shut on nothing, striking timber from a wagon's side. The howling dog dove under the wagon.

The apparition darted after it.

Bison panicked. The lead wagon jolted as the bison broke into a cumbersome canter. Others followed. In seconds the orderly wagon train was a mass of stampeding bison pulling wagons, and the bird was in the middle of it.

Willow and Orange Blossom were seated on the tailgate of their wagon, clinging to ropes as the wagon lurched away. The bird hesitated, then charged them.

Whandall snatched a blanket from a wagon seat and ran forward, waving his Lordkin knife, shouting a wordless challenge.

Ponies tried to block the thing, but it evaded their horns and aimed a kick powerful enough to stagger the larger stallion. Then it ran toward Willow. It was faster than Whandall. Whandall flapped the blanket at its eye.

The bright blanket got the terror bird's attention. It turned to charge Whandall, its eyes fixed on the blanket. Whandall kept the blanket in front of him until it was nearly on him, then stretched out his blanket-covered left arm and raised it while turning to his left. The bird stretched out its neck and dove into the blanket. Whandall brought down the big Lordkin knife at the base of its neck.

The neck was too thick. The bird ran a circle around Whandall, blinded and trying to tear through the blanket, while Whandall sawed at the neck with his knife. Turning the edge forward got it under the feathers. Round and round, but that *had* to be bone, and he was getting through it, and then the head was bent back but the bird was still running. It ran Whandall into the side of a wagon. He spun off and lay dazed.

The bird was hellishly fast, but its head flopped loose now, and here came Carter and Carver with a rope stretched between them. The bird's random path veered toward them. They pulled the rope taut and tripped it. As it thrashed they ran round it, wrapping the legs so it couldn't get up.

The spear-claw forearms thrashed for ten minutes. By the time the beast was still, Kettle Belly and the other drivers had halted the wagon train. Now they all gathered around Whandall and the Ropewalkers and the dead bird.

"What in the hell is that?" Whandall demanded.

"Terror bird," Kettle Belly said. "They're rare."

"Let's keep it that way," Whandall said, but he was grinning. Victory felt good. And Willow was looking at him in a way she never had before. So were the other girls of the wagon train, all of them. That felt good too.

* * *

The terror bird made soup to feed the whole train, in a row of the big bronze pots that most of the wagons carried. The train gathered around Hickamore's ring of rocks to share it. The meat was tough, and *red,* less like bird than bison.

As they ate, Hickamore asked Whandall about his tattoo. Whandall had learned some of the local speech by now, but it went better with Ruby Fishhawk to translate from his own language.

"I know now that Morth of Atlantis made it for me, and enchanted it, so that he could follow me out of the Burning City. I believe it killed all the men in my family. . . ."

Gradually the folk around them went silent. Hickamore's daughters listened, and the Ropewalkers and Millers too, and Willow. They'd never asked him about the feathered snake tattoo. What had they known of Lordkin? They might not know *this* tattoo was unusual.

Whandall felt good. If Willow hadn't been there he might not have stuck to river water. The party broke up far too early.

The road led up to another pass. Orangetown was in a vale there, and unlike Marsyl, Orangetown had walls.

The town gates were set into stone gate towers, and the walls were stone for a hundred paces to each side of the gates. Elsewhere they became a wooden palisade, logs sharpened at the top and set into low stone walls, chest high to Whandall. Whandall thought Orangetown was smaller than Lordstown. It was certainly tiny compared to Tep's Town.

There were permanent corrals outside the walls, with pens for the bison and another fenced area for the ponies. A steady wind blew from the northeast and the pens were downwind of both the town and the campground. The campground itself had wells and fountains and stone-lined walks. There were feed stores and warehouses adjacent to the animal pens. A large field with wooden seats filled the area between the campgrounds and the animal pens.

Kettle Belly and a dozen of his younger relatives—sons, daughters, nieces, nephews, and cousins—came to help Whandall and the Ropewalkers unhitch their animals and set up camp. "You'll be here," Kettle Belly said, indicating an area among the low trees. "That's your well. The toilet trench is in the grove there. Use it, and clean up any animal droppings. They're sticky about that here."

Whandall smiled to himself. Not everyone had a well and a fireplace at his campsite. The area Kettle Belly picked for Whandall was nearly as large as Hickamore's, and certainly nicer than what the Fishhawks got. "The town looks organized," Whandall said.

"We'll pay for it, but yes, they're organized. One thing. Catch up on sleep. It's safe here. When we set out north again we'll stand night watches until we get to the Big Valley." He eyed Whandall's big Lordkin knife. "Wouldn't surprise me if you got a chance to use that again."

"More of those birds?"

"I'm hearing rumors of two bandit tribes in the hills."

Carter fingered the sling he wore openly around his neck and displayed a bag of stream-rounded stones. "We'll be ready!"

Whandall smiled thinly. He'd never seen a kinless with a sling until Carter took to wearing one. Carter had a knife too. He was clumsy with it, but the kinless were good with slings. More than ever, Whandall thought he knew why Lordkin turned up missing from time to time back in Tep's Town. . . .

"Bandits have seen slings before," Kettle Belly said.

"Bet they never saw anyone like Whandall before!"

Kettle Belly eyed the orange feathers Whandall wore in his plaited hair and the gaudy feathered serpent crawling up his arm and across his cheek and eye. "Now there you may be right."

"I heard Morth say, 'What if a magician vouched for you?' I had no idea he was there, and I wasn't even surprised. Morth called it a lurk spell," Whandall said.

He took a strawberry. The shaman had set out a platter of big red strawberries. Whandall hadn't seen anyone picking them. "Shaman, where did you get these?"

"Treeswinger Town, before we met you," Hickamore said. He saw Whandall's astonishment. "My magic preserves many kinds of food. One of the ways in which I earn my keep."

Whandall ate another strawberry, then drank. He lifted the water bottle to show Twisted Cloud. "Brought my own. You won't have to leave this time."

The girl giggled.

She did too much of that. Whandall didn't know how to deal with a giggler. He continued, "Two huge dagger-toothed cats made of fog and smoke were playing around Morth's feet. His hair was going white to pink and back again, like cloud shadows. He had magic to make him young, but it wanted power.

"I had to hold back. I wanted to kill him. No reason at all. Yangin-Atep was in me, and Yangin-Atep is a fire god, and Morth is a water wizard. Morth backed away. The kinless children were still giving me plenty of room . . ."

Hickamore held out the wine flask.

He had only made that gesture once, the first night of storytelling. After that, he'd kept the bottle. Whandall took the bottle and drank.

It wasn't watered. Better not do that again!

Mountain Cat reached. Whandall passed the bottle.

Whandall asked Carter for his own memories of Morth, and then Willow's and Carver's. Carter laughed. He said that Willow had thought Morth might protect them from the Lordkin who threw fire. Hammer had found Whandall awesome, because he frightened Carver; but Morth tended to lecture, like his father.

Whandall didn't take the bottle again, but he could feel its effect burning in his blood. He spoke on. The fire track through the forest, Morth suddenly among them . . . Tell them about gold in the riverbed? Not yet.

Twisted Cloud went to bed. Mountain Cat made his excuses and departed. Carter was asleep.

Whandall picked the boy up in his arms and made his farewells.

The campfire lit his way, barely. He became aware that both older girls were walking with him. One spoke in a teasing voice. "Mountain cats made of smoke? Is any of that true?"

Whandall kept walking, because Carter was heavy. He said, "I wouldn't lie. Also, I wouldn't lie to a shaman until I knew his power."

"Why do you bring the boy with you? You almost never ask him anything. Is he your ———?"

"He is under my protection. What was that word?"

"Stays with you so that a woman can't get you in trouble, so that another woman's dowry is safe. Does Willow Ropewalker fear for her dowry? She doesn't have one!"

"Running Deer, what *is* that word, *dowry?*"

But the girls were gone, so abruptly that Whandall wondered just how much wine he'd taken. One full swallow; it had burned his throat going down. Maybe some wines were stronger than others.

CHAPTER
43

The water in their camp well was cool and sweet. Whandall drank his fill, then splashed himself clean in the washing pool next to the well. The afternoon was hot. It had been a long day, starting before the sun came up.

He found shade in a thicket near the wagon and stretched out for a nap.

The sun was still high when he was awakened by someone moving. He looked out through the thicket, moving just his head. Old habits die hard.

Willow was tightening a rope four feet above the ground. For practice she liked it high enough that a fall would hurt, but not so high that she'd break bones. She tugged on the rope, nodded in satisfaction, and went into the wagon. Whandall waited for her to come out. He liked to watch her, although Willow didn't want anyone to watch her practice.

She came out wearing bright feathers. When they'd skinned the terror bird, Whandall had given the feathers to Willow. He hadn't known she had made a costume from them. It looked good on her, gold and green and orange feathers sewed into the cotton and linen cloth most townspeople wove and sold. It fit her tightly, showing the curve of her hips and breasts, and stopped short at the knees to show her perfect calves. Whandall stifled his approval. She might be angry with him for watching her. When Willow got angry, she got more and more quiet, and if he asked her what was wrong, she would mutter, "Nothing." It drove him crazy.

She vaulted onto the rope and did a quick back somersault, then a handstand, the feathered skirt tumbling down to show more feathers and a few

inches of thighs. Wagon train women and townswomen never allowed anyone to see them when they weren't fully clothed . . . unless they were
performing, like Orange Blossom riding the ponies. Then they wanted
everyone to see them. Girls were confusing.

Willow came off the handstand and dove forward. Whatever she
attempted, she missed, and nearly fell, just catching the rope. She used it
to swing upward and back onto it, then did a forward somersault.

"Bravo!" Carver came around the side of the wagon.

"You startled me," Willow said. "Coming up?"

"No. I've lost the knack," Carver said.

"Brother, you just need practice."

"No, I've really lost it. Besides, no one wants to see me do ropewalking. They want to see pretty girls."

"That was nice. Do you really think I'm pretty?"

"Yes. Whandall thinks so too."

"Maybe." She jumped lightly to the ground. "Well, if you aren't going
to be part of the act, I'll have to work out a new routine."

"You'll do fine," Carver said. "Mother always said you were really
good."

"I miss her," Willow said.

"Dad too."

"Well, sure, but—yeah, Dad too."

Carter and Hammer came out of the wagon. "Hi. Hey, you look great,"
Carter said. "Did you make that?"

"Well, I sewed it," Willow said. "Ruby Fishhawk helped."

Carter fingered the feathered skirt. "That sure was something to see.
Whandall saw that bird looking at you and *pow!* He was right there, that
big knife out, that blanket—did you see what that bird did to the blanket?
It would have torn Whandall the same way, only he was too fast for it. And
strong. You ever seen anyone stronger?"

"Will you stop with that?" Carver said.

"Why should I?"

Whandall lay still, wondering what to do now. Lurking was natural, but
this . . .

"Wasn't he, Willow?" Carter demanded. "Wasn't he wonderful?"

Willow nodded but didn't say anything.

"Ah, you think Whandall can't do anything wrong," Carver said. "But
what does he really know how to do? He can't tame ponies. Even my mare
runs away from him. He can't make rope. What can he do?"

"He can fight!"

"Lordkin can fight," Carver said. "And he's a Lordkin."

"He's not," Carter said. "He's not Lordkin and we're not kinless! Not out here."

"Then what are we?" Hammer asked.

"I guess we're just people," Carter said. "Rich people."

"Whandall's rich," Carver said. "We're not. Morth gave that gold to Whandall, not us. We don't even own the wagon, not if Whandall says we don't."

Hammer had been listening with attention. "But it's ours," Hammer said. "Well, yours. But one of the ponies was my dad's, so that makes it mine."

"Yours if Whandall says it is," Carver said.

"It's mine anyway!" Hammer said. "If that Lordkin harpy won't give it to me, I'll—"

Carter laughed. "You won't do anything!"

"I'll get help," Hammer said. "Carver will help. And the wagonmaster. And the blacksmith. They'll make him give me my pony!"

Carter laughed again. "You think everyone in this wagon train could take something away from Whandall if he didn't want to give it? He could kill everyone here!"

"Well, maybe not," Carver said. "But you're right—he'd be pretty hard to take out. They won't try it. The wagon train can't afford to lose that many people dead or hurt. Unless we get him in his sleep."

"You won't do that!" Carter said. "Why are you all mad at Whandall? He saved Willow from that bird! He saved us all. We'd never have got out of that forest. We'd still be in Tep's Town if it wasn't for Whandall, and he never did any of us any harm. Willow, you're the oldest; make him stop talking like that."

"We still don't know what happened to Father," Carver said.

"Whandall didn't hurt him," Carter said.

"He says he didn't," Willow said.

"You believe him?" Carver demanded.

"Yes. Yes, I do. Anyway, he was possessed of Yangin-Atep," Willow said slowly. "Yangin-Atep could do anything. It wouldn't be Whandall's fault."

"You believe in Yangin-Atep now?" Carver asked.

"Don't you? Morth does. You saw what Morth could do with magic, and Morth was afraid of Yangin-Atep!"

"Yangin-Atep can't take Whandall again," Carter said. "We're safe here."

"We don't know that," Willow said. "We don't know what gods there are, or what they'll take a whim to do. But I think we're safe from Whandall."

"He's still Lordkin," Carver said.

"Why do you keep saying that?" Carter asked.

"Because that's what everyone says. Everyone in the wagon train."

"Does Kettle Belly say it?" Willow asked.

"No—"

"Hickamore?" She was holding back a laugh.

"I never asked him."

"Who *have* you been listening to?" Willow asked.

"Yeah, who's everybody?" Hammer chimed in.

Carver was turning belligerent. "Rutting Deer. And Fawn, the blacksmith's older daughter. They say he's a Lordkin boor."

Willow laughed merrily, and Whandall's heart danced inside him. She said, "You don't know much about girls, do you, little brother?"

Carver gaped at his sister. That *hurt*.

"I already heard that story," Willow said. "Ruby Fishhawk told me. Rutting Deer—"

"Her mother had a vision," Hammer snickered. "Can you picture it?"

"Hush. Rutting Deer and Fawn are together all the time, and they both had their eyes on Whandall after he killed the terror bird—"

"So did you!" Carter laughed. "I saw you."

"So they tried to flirt with him." Willow forged on: "Carver, Fawn's not as good looking as Rutting Deer, is she? But she's not promised. Rutting Deer is promised to a boy in another wagon train. They both think it's fun to flirt. That poor boy, Mountain Cat—anyway, Whandall just couldn't believe that name!"

"I can understand that," Carver said. "I can hardly make myself say that in front of a girl. Even if it's her name."

"He thought he'd heard wrong. Whandall called her Running Deer. But he got them mixed up and called *Fawn* Running Deer. Now they both want his liver," Willow said.

"He's still a Lordkin," Carver said stubbornly.

"And Mountain Cat is still their toy doll, but you could take his place if you say what they want."

Whandall would have paid a high price to be somewhere else. No outsider should hear any of this.

"Us. The wagon," Carver said. His face was very red, and he was forcing the words out. "The team. Who owns any of this? Whandall already gave away one part in ten—"

"That was a good deal!" Carter said. "Everyone else pays more."

"Yes, but he made the deal for all of us," Carver said. "He didn't ask us. Like it's all his."

"So you'd give Kettle Belly twice as much. More. He wanted a quarter! You're very free with the family goods." Willow turned away. "It's time to start dinner. Whandall will be hungry. Carter, Hammer, go find us some wood."

Whandall crawled out through the thicket, staying with the shadows, sliding through branches without bending them. He knew how to hide from kinless. There was a lot to think about as he walked back to the main camp.

Rutting Deer. Fawn. Got them mixed up in the dark, Whandall thought. Names were important. In Tep's Town you never let anyone know your true name, so whatever name people called you wasn't real to begin with. Out here, your name was your *self*. *Rutting* Deer?

Flirting. Willow said Rutting Deer and Fawn were flirting. He didn't know that word. What had they been doing before they turned cold?

They'd been talking about dowries.

What's a dowry?

Whandall glanced up at the sun. Still high. Hours to dinner. Time to find out. There was a person he could ask. . . .

He bought half a dozen ripe tangerines in the Orangetown market. Mother's Mother had liked those when she could get them. He took them to Ruby Fishhawk's wagon. She didn't hesitate before inviting him into the wagon box tent for tea. It was automatic to take off his boots before going in. He'd learned that much.

Ruby fussed with tea things, poured a cup, and sat on a cushion across from Whandall. "Now. What is this about?"

"I need help," Whandall said. "I don't know anything about girls."

"A boy your age? I don't believe it," Ruby said. She grinned to make it clear what she thought.

"Girls *here*," Whandall said. "And Willow."

"Willow. Oh. Yes, of course. I keep forgetting that you're Lordkin."

"Forgetting?" Whandall leered out of a rainbow-colored snake.

"Well, it's more I forget what Lordkin are," Ruby said. "And you're not like the ones I remember. Well, usually you aren't. The way you went after that terror bird, now that's how I remember Lordkin. Fearless. Strong. When I was a girl I used to wonder about Lordkin men, what it would be like to have a protector like you." She grinned. "That was a long time ago. You like Willow, do you?"

"Yes." Whandall found it hard to speak about Willow. What could he say? "She's the most beautiful woman I ever saw."

"My. Have you told her that?"

"No."

"Why don't you?"

"I don't know how."

"You just told *me*," Ruby said. She chuckled. "Whandall, are you asking me how to court her?"

"What does *court* mean? Like *flirt*?"

"Well, courting is serious flirting," Ruby said. "If a boy only wants a girl's attention, he flirts. If he's thinking of marriage, he goes courting."

Whandall digested that. "Is that what girls do too? Flirting isn't serious? Courting is?"

"Well, yes. It's a little more complicated than that, but yes."

"Then I want to know how to court her."

"You can't," Ruby said. "No, wait, you're the *only* one who could, and she knows that, and girls like to think they have a choice. They usually don't, but they like to think they do."

Whandall repeated what he almost understood. "Why am I the only one who can court her?"

"She doesn't have a dowry." Ruby reached over and poured more tea. "That won't matter to you, but it will to all the other boys."

"Yes! What's a dowry?"

Ruby grinned mysteriously. "A dowry is a fortune. Money. A wagon. Rugs. Things girls bring to a marriage, Whandall."

"You mean boys court girls for what they *own?*" Whandall was being shown a whole new evil. "Lordkin would never do that!"

"They wouldn't, would they?" Ruby said, "I'd forgotten that too. The boys here don't think that way. Think on it, Whandall. A dowry belongs to the woman! If her husband mistreats her or throws her out, she takes it back with her. Ideally it will be enough to live on, to support any children she might have. And a husband thinks hard about getting rid of his wife if it means he has to hire out as a laborer." She laughed. "I had to have it explained to me, you know. Kinless don't think that way either. A girl's dowry in Tep's Town, some Lordkin buck would gather it."

"Oh—"

"Not you, dear. We don't have kinless and Lordkin here."

"That's what Carter says." Whandall mused. "What does Willow need to make a dowry?"

"A wagon and team, if she's going to live on the road. Money. Clothes. Rugs. The more the better, Whandall."

"The wagon is hers," Whandall said. "It always was, but I guess she doesn't know that. If she has a dowry, anyone can court her?"

"Well," Ruby said, looking at Whandall's thick arms and bulging muscles, "they can, but some will be afraid to as long as they think you're involved. But that's all right, Whandall. Willow will understand that." She chuckled. "Of course any boy might find his courage. And Willow is a lovely girl."

"What do I do after she has her dowry?"

"Give her presents—"

"I did. A dress, and a necklace. She thanked me, but she never wore them."

"Did you ask her to wear them for you?"

"No—"

"Land's sake, boy!"

"But—"

"You want her to wear them for someone else?"

"No!"

"Well, then, you have to ask her," Ruby said. "Whandall, Willow grew up kinless. Kinless never show anyone what they have. It took me a year before I wore my nicest clothes outside the wagon tent! It's not something you think about; it's just the way kinless live."

Kinless were drab; he'd thought it was their nature. Now he began to understand. "And if I ask her to wear the things I bought her, and she says no?"

"You'll know you need to do some more courting," Ruby said. She winked. "Give her a little time, Whandall."

"I will," Whandall said, but as he walked back to his—Willow's—wagon, he saw Orange Blossom smiling at him, and two other girls sat with their legs showing, and he wondered just how long he could wait. It had been hard, learning to be a Lordkin, but at least he'd understood what he wanted to be.

Supper was ready when he got to the wagon, and then Hickamore wanted a story. There was no chance to talk to the Ropewalkers and Millers.

CHAPTER
44

Orangetown wasn't truly a pass, but more a level spot on the way up to the high country beyond. The next two days led steeply up, with no good place to make camp. Everyone had to help ease the wagons through stony fields. The hills rose steeply to each side and ahead, and all were covered with brilliant orange flowers. Whandall had never seen anything like them.

"Beautiful," he said.

Kettle Belly grunted and put his shoulder to the other wheel of the Fishhawk wagon. "Ready! Heave!" Together they lifted the wagon wheel out of the hole. "The flowers are pretty enough, but there's another thing I like about them," Kettle Belly said. "They're too low to hide anyone sneaking up on us. Out here we don't have to worry too much about bandits, and tonight we can be in a safe campsite. I think we'll stop there to rest up." He waved his arm to indicate the trail ahead. "After that, though, we'll be back in scrub oak and chaparral, and rocks. There's bandits out there—I can smell them."

"You can *smell* bandits?" Whandall could have used that talent in Tep's Town!

"Well, maybe not. But Hickamore can. A good wizard can give warning, and Hickamore's good. Blast! Now Ironfoot's wagon is stuck—"

"Kettle Belly!"

The caravan chief looked around at Whandall's horrified shout. He said, "Ah."

Moving among the mountains, grayed by distance, was a vastness built to their mountains' own scale. Its legs were as tall as redwoods, but so wide that they looked stumpy. Its torso was another mountain. A forest of hair, piebald brown and white, hung down all around it. Ears bigger than any sail. An arm . . . a boneless arm where a nose might have been, lifted and fell as the . . . god turned to study them.

"It's Behemoth," Kettle Belly said. "It won't come any closer. Nobody's ever seen Behemoth close. Give me a shoulder here, Whandall."

Whandall set back to work. From time to time he looked up at Behemoth moving among the mountains, until the moment when he looked up and the beast god was gone.

The road became steeper, then leveled off. Whandall was glad of it. He and the blacksmith and Kettle Belly were the strongest men in the wagon train, and sometimes it took all three of them to get a heavy wagon over a bad place. "I'll be glad when this day is over," Whandall told Kettle Belly.

Kettle Belly glanced up at the sun. "Two hours and a little more. Only one place to camp tonight," he said. "Four! Run ahead and tell the scouts we'll camp at Coyote's Den. Not that they won't know it."

"All right, Dad!"

"Coyote's Den?" Whandall asked.

"The road forks just up ahead. The right-hand branch goes uphill. We'll take that one." Kettle Belly grinned as Whandall groaned. "Not too steep, and it's a good road. The Spotted Coyotes see to that. They've made a good place to camp, too. Of course they had to."

Whandall frowned the question Kettle Belly had expected.

"They had to because there aren't enough of them to be tax collectors without giving some service," Kettle Belly said. "Look around you. Nothing here but some pasturage, and not a lot of that. Over there, beyond that ridge, there's some better land, but no one ever goes that far off the Hemp Road. For some reason the Spotted Coyote tribe has to live here, something about instructions from their god."

"He told them to live here but he didn't give them anything to live on?" Whandall asked. "What does he do for them?"

"Beats me," Kettle Belly said. "Coyote's a strange one. Nobody really knows what he wants. Anyway, the Spotted Coyotes made the best of it. They found a big ring of boulders, and over the years they've made it into a rest stop. Here we go; that's the fork."

Kettle Belly's number three son ran out with a long curved cow horn. "Can I do it?" he asked excitedly.

"Sure."

Number Three blew six long blasts on the horn.

"That tells the Spotted Coyotes how many of us to fix dinner for," Kettle Belly said. "That's how it works. You tell them you're coming, and they cook up stew to be ready when we get up to the top. They feed us and watch out for us." Kettle Belly's lips pursed into a small tight grin. "And they don't charge any more than they ask for just to pass through their territory."

"Are there a lot?" Whandall asked.

"No, not really, but enough you wouldn't want to fight them, and you *really* wouldn't want them making the road worse than the winter rains do."

"Toronexti," Whandall said. When Kettle Belly gave him a blank look, Whandall tried to explain. "Tax collectors. Toll takers. But *they* never give you anything for what they take."

"So you organize a lot of people and go kill them," Kettle Belly said. "That's what we do. If a town gets mean enough, we get all the wagoneers together and go burn them out."

Whandall thought about trying to organize enough Lordkin to destroy the Toronexti. Nobody knew how many they were, where they lived, nor even who they were behind those masks. They were backed by the Lords, it was said. Nobody could fight the Lordsmen.

The top of the hill was a natural fortress. A spring bubbled up in the center of a ring of boulders that formed a natural castle large enough to enclose a wagon train and all the livestock. Over the years the Spotted Coyote clan had smoothed out the area inside the boulder circle and built corrals and pens and shelters, and big cook fire rings. The smells of bison stew wafted to the wagon train.

Kettle Belly and a small dark man about his age shouted and gesticulated at each other. Whandall thought they were pretending at passion as they went through a ritual. Kettle Belly would throw up his hands in disgust, and the Spotted Coyote leader would gesture outside the circle, grinning as he pointed out a small column of smoke a couple of miles away. Kettle Belly looked worried, then shouted again. . . . Eventually they came to some agreement, and money changed hands. By then dusk was falling and the stew was done.

They ate dinner around a big campfire. Logs had been arranged in a circle to form seats and backrests. It was pleasant to sit back and relax with the prospect of a night's sleep without need for guard duty.

Whandall pleaded exhaustion when Hickamore wanted to talk about Morth of Atlantis, and soon the wizard was deep in conversation with a man twice his age who wore a mantle of wolf skin. A Spotted Coyote boy came around to fill everyone's cup from a goatskin of wine. Whandall sipped appreciatively. It was not as good as the wine Kettle Belly kept in his wagon, but it was smoother and more pleasant than anything that made its way to Tep's Town.

A pleasant evening. Willow sat next to him, tired because the girls had been hopping on and off the wagon all day as the hills became steeper and they had to get out and push.

Flirting. Courtship is serious flirting. Flirting meant being amusing and funny, and Whandall didn't know how. He looked around to see how others were doing it.

Not far away Carver sat with Starfall, the blacksmith's dark-haired daughter. They sat very close together. Whandall couldn't hear what they were saying, but Starfall seemed to be doing all the talking as Carver sat listening attentively. That seemed like something Whandall could do, but Willow wasn't saying anything!

"Did you like the dress I bought you?" Whandall asked.

"Yes, very much. Thank you."

"You don't ever wear it."

"Well, I wouldn't want to wear it here, with all these strangers," Willow said.

"Kettle Belly says they're safe," Whandall said. "They're not—" He cut himself off.

"Thieves?"

"I was going to say 'gatherers.' "

"Oh." She looked at him with wide eyes. "I keep forgetting," she said.

"That's good."

She smiled softly. "Be right back."

Carver was still listening to Starfall. She moved closer to him. Whandall had no trouble imagining her warmth against his side. The boy said something, and Starfall laughed appreciatively. Other couples were talking softly, boys smiling, girls laughing. If only he could hear what they were saying!

Willow returned. She was wearing the blue dress Whandall had bought, and the gold-and-black onyx necklace.

"That's—wonderful," he said, settling for that, although he wanted better words. "I knew it would look good on you."

"And it does?"

"Better than I thought," Whandall said.

Her smile was haunting. She sat next to him, not as close as Carver was sitting to Starfall, but she had never been so close. He could feel her warmth radiating against his side, warmer than the fire. They didn't talk for a long time. Whandall kept trying to think of something clever to say, but nothing came to mind, and it was enough just to be close to her.

When Carver and Starfall left the firelight circle and went off into darkness, Whandall thought Willow was about to say something, but she didn't. He imagined standing up, taking her hand and leading her to privacy and secret places, but he did nothing, and he wondered if his legs had forgotten how to obey him.

Suddenly she smiled at him and touched his face. Her touch was light and smooth, as she ran her fingers along his tattoo, down his arm, still smiling. Then she sat close to him, and they stared at the fire.

Carver had a sappy grin at breakfast. It faded when he went to hitch up the mare. The pony reared and tried to trample him. Whandall watched, frowning, as Carver shouted at the pony. Someone in the next wagon party laughed loudly.

A few minutes later, Greathand the blacksmith came to Whandall's wagon. He wasn't unfriendly, but he seemed preoccupied. "Need a favor," he said. "Like to have Willow bring one of your ponies over to my wagon."

"Sure. Why?"

"Rather not say until I know," Greathand said. "If you don't mind." The blacksmith seldom asked favors. Whandall was pretty sure no one ever refused him when he did ask. And there was no reason not to do it. Was there?

Willow had heard. She led the smaller of the horned ponies over to them. Whandall had to look twice: it was as large as the larger one had been the day before, and without the black star marking on its forehead Whandall would not have known which one it was.

The ponies changed size sometimes. Whandall had asked Hickamore about it. "Magic changes along the road," the wizard had told him, then asked how Morth cured skin diseases.

Willow followed Greathand toward his wagon. Whandall watched her lead the pony for a moment and remembered her smiles last night. But there was work to do loading the wagon.

When Willow came back, Greathand and Kettle Belly were behind her. They waited until she led the pony back to join the others. Greathand stood back and let Kettle Belly talk for him. "These aren't your kin, but it's your wagon," he said.

"Willow's wagon," Whandall said.

"You're in charge," Greathand said. "That boy Carver doesn't have a father, and he's in your wagon!"

"Yes," Whandall said. It sounded like an admission but Whandall didn't know why.

"So we can talk to you about him," Kettle Belly said. "What's his situation? Profession?"

"He knows how to make rope, and sell it," Whandall said. "Why?"

Greathand frowned. "Why are you—?"

Kettle Belly held up a hand. "Ropewalking. Expensive to set up, but a ropewalk makes good money," he said. "Have to have a place to do it, though. Not on a wagon train." He turned to Greathand. "Starfall doesn't have a wagon yet. Want to think about a different dowry?"

"She can't take back a ropewalk!" Greathand said. "But she didn't want a wagon anyway. She's always talked about living in a town year-round."

"Well, we can work that out, then," Kettle Belly said. "How old is the boy?"

"Sixteen, I think," Whandall said.

"Little young," Kettle Belly said.

"Starfall's only fifteen," Greathand growled. "If the damn fool hadn't made such a big thing about not being able to harness that mare, maybe—anyway, Starfall's all excited, so I guess it's got to be. Whandall, we'll talk when we're over the pass, discuss arrangements, where the kids want to live, what it takes to set up a ropewalk. You tell Carver he's a damn lucky boy." The blacksmith went away, still muttering under his breath.

Whandall frowned at Kettle Belly. "I saw Carver and Starfall go off together, but they weren't the only ones last night!"

"They're the only ones that all of a sudden can't harness one-horns," Kettle Belly said. He grinned. "I always thought you were putting me on, but you really don't know!" He laughed at his enormous joke. "Whandall, *everyone* knows it! Nobody but a virgin can harness a one-horn. Yesterday Carver could harness the mare and Starfall didn't have any trouble with the stallions. This morning—"

"I've been stupid." Many cryptic things were becoming plain.

"Doesn't work that way in the Valley of Smokes, then?"

"No." Whandall thought about it. "Ponies are smaller, don't have real horns. It surprised us when ours grew those big horns. Magic! Kettle Belly, what happens now?"

"Well, you heard. Greathand will have to come up with another kind of dowry. I don't know if he can afford a ropewalk—he's got Fawn to marry off too—but he'll do what he can. Carver have any shares in your stock?"

Whandall nodded. "He's not poor. This is all new to me. What happens if they don't want to marry?"

"Come on—they knew there were one-horns in the wagon train!"

"Carver didn't know what that means."

"Starfall did," Kettle Belly said. "You trying to tell me that it's different in the Valley of Smokes?"

Whandall remembered Willow's story of what happened to Dream-Lotus. "No. Not for kinless," he said. Carver must have known what he was getting into. Whandall remembered incidents with Fawn and Rutting Deer, chances he had, things he might have done.

It was different here, because there weren't Lordkin here, and he could never explain that. "No," he repeated.

Kettle Belly squinted up at the rising sun. "Burning daylight," he said. "We have to get moving. Whandall, you'd better explain this to Carver."

"Yes. Does he have any choices?"

"Well, he can take a wagon as dowry, if he wants to learn this life. Being married to Greathand's daughter won't hurt him a bit."

"What if he runs away?"

"He'd better run damn far from the Hemp Road. Forever."

CHAPTER
45

They made camp in a boulder field. Large rocks helped form a natural rectangular fortress, nothing so refined as the place the Spotted Coyotes had built. Wagons filled in gaps among the big rocks. Whandall watched their placement—all wagons in sight of each other. They'd traveled until near sunset to find such an open place . . . an easy trek down the gorge to the river . . . but wouldn't any bandit know just where wagons would stop? And the boulders and the rising and falling ground around them could hide all of Serpent's Walk and Bull Pizzle together.

But Hickamore drank strong hemp tea and sang, and when he came out of his trance was satisfied. There were bandits near, but they only watched. They had no plan, no purpose, only their envy.

The sun had set, but the west was still red and orange. Whandall sent two of the Miller children to keep watch outside the wagon circle. "Stay very still, and if you hear anything, shout and run under the wagon. But yell first!"

Then he had Willow, Carver, Carter, and Hammer sit down around the fire.

"We need to talk," Whandall said. "Carver, you knew what was expected when you went off with Starfall."

Carver looked very solemn. "Yes. Well, I knew it in my head," he said. "I wasn't thinking much, though."

"Starfall was," Willow said.

"How are you so sure?" Carter demanded.

She shrugged. "Girls always are. In Tep's Town you might get away with being careful, but it's a big risk. Out here—believe me, Starfall knew what she was doing. So did you, I think."

"It's so—permanent," Carver said. "That's what I'm having trouble with."

Carter nodded in sympathy.

"So what do you want to do?" Whandall insisted. "I think I'm supposed to negotiate for you. Where do you want to live?"

"I can make rope," Carver said. "Well, if Carter will help. Carter, I'll teach you my part if you'll teach me yours."

"Greathand can't afford a ropewalk," Carter said.

They all looked at the wagon. Then they looked at Whandall. No one said anything.

Whandall grinned. "Depends on Willow," he said.

"Me! I don't have anything, except the dress you bought me. I don't have anything at all!"

And she was near tears. Dowries. Was that the problem? "The wagon. The ponies. Willow, they're all yours." He'd been thinking how to say that. He'd waited too long.

"One of the ponies is mine!" Hammer protested.

Whandall shrugged. "Argue that with Willow," he said. "But Kettle Belly says one pony is worth a team of bison, so Willow has a wagon and team."

"And the mare?" Carver demanded.

"I have a claim," Whandall said. "I helped catch her. The hemp and tar too—part of that's mine. I won't claim it, though. Willow can have my share."

"Why?" Willow asked. "It's very nice of you, Whandall, but why?"

"I know why," Carver said. "Don't you?"

She didn't answer, but she had the same vague smile that had appeared when Whandall said she owned the wagon and ponies. She looked quickly at Whandall, then looked away again.

"Don't forget, the wagonmaster gets a tenth," Whandall said. "Now about the gold."

"Morth gave that gold to you," Carter said. And Carver said, firmly, "Yes."

Whandall nodded. "I'll share. I needed you to move it for me. Still do. There's enough for your ropewalk, I think, if you and Carter stay together. I keep half. You, all of you, share the rest any way you decide." Half would still be a lot. "Half after the wagonmaster gets his share."

"Kettle Belly doesn't know about that gold," Carver said. "No way he could know."

"We could hide it," Carter said eagerly.

"No."

"Whandall—"

"No," he repeated. "We tell the wagonmaster."

"Why?" Carter demanded. "He doesn't know—he can't know."

Whandall tried, but words came slowly. "I said. I promised."

"A Lordkin's promise," Carter said. "Made to a thief!"

"Kettle Belly's not gathering," Whandall said. "He's—he's working with us."

Carter looked to the others. Some understanding flowed among them. Carver said, "All right," and shrugged.

Whandall felt like an outsider. There was a long silence. Finally Whandall got up and left the wagon. No one spoke until he was too far away to make out words, then Carter and Carver began speaking excitedly.

CHAPTER
46

"Come in," Kettle Belly said in invitation. "Have some wine."

"No, thank you," Whandall said. "I have something to show you."

"Yes?"

"Not here. At Willow's wagon."

Kettle Belly frowned at the setting sun. "Time to set the watch," he said. He began pulling on his boots. "Willow's wagon, you said? Not yours?"

"Hers after her father died," Whandall said. "In the Burning."

"Makes sense," Kettle Belly said. "I keep forgetting about the one-horns."

"The ponies are hers too."

"Well, of course." Kettle Belly tied off his boot laces and held out his hand for Whandall to help him up. They set off at a brisk pace with two of Kettle Belly's nameless sons following. "Good. Let's go. You and Willow getting along all right, then?"

Whandall didn't answer.

"And it is my business," Kettle Belly said. His tone was serious now. "Everything that happens in this wagon train is my business until we get to Paradise Valley."

"Pelzed used to say things like that."

"Who's Pelzed?"

"Someone I used to know. I think we ought to hurry."

Kettle Belly was taking two steps to Whandall's one and didn't have breath for an answer.

* * *

"Leave that alone," Willow shouted.

"Why?" Carver demanded.

"Because—"

"Hello, Willow," Kettle Belly said.

Carver turned quickly. He was holding a gold nugget in both hands. It was pulling him to the ground.

"That's what we wanted to show you," Whandall said. "We have gold."

"I see that," Kettle Belly said. "More than that?"

"What's in the wagon."

The wagon bed was open, and Kettle Belly looked. He said, "That's a lot of gold."

"I know. It's refined gold too."

"Where did you get it?" The shaman's voice. They turned to see Hickamore come out of the shadows.

"*Damn* that lurking spell!" Whandall shouted.

Hickamore grinned. "I wondered if you would tell the wagonmaster." He turned to Kettle Belly. "Now, Black Kettle, behold the skill of your shaman and the value of our bargain. Dowries for all your daughters in your share alone!" Hickamore cackled. Suddenly he stiffened. He went past Carver and reached into the false compartment of the wagon, now open.

"Stop that!" Carter shouted.

Hickamore ignored them. His skinny arms lifted, holding two nuggets both as big as his head, as if they floated up under his palms. "Refined, you said. A wizard absorbed its power. Morth? Is that who you meant? He didn't take it all, boy!" The old man's voice had gained in timbre and volume: it must have been audible throughout the camp. "Here." He handed a nugget to Carter (who dropped it) and one to Hammer (who staggered), took the nugget Carver was holding, and lifted it high. His face twisted in joy. His eyes rolled back into his head, and he stood entranced.

"Now what have you done?" Kettle Belly demanded of Whandall. His two sons stared at the shaman. In the shadows were Bison folk who had followed Hickamore's voice toward possible entertainment.

Carver and Carter had given over shouting at Kettle Belly. They watched the shaman. Willow ignored Hickamore to stare at Whandall, looking at him in a way she never had before, not unfriendly, certainly not angry, but as if she'd never really seen him. Before Whandall could speak to her, Hickamore recovered. He grinned wildly. "More gold calls. It's kin to this," he said.

"We're a long way from the river," Whandall said.

"Yes, yes, it was washed down to the river from above," Hickamore said. "The hills are alive with its music; I feel the power of it calling me. We must find it."

"Now?" Kettle Belly demanded. Hickamore nodded ecstatically.

"Is this wise?" Kettle Belly said. "There are bandits all about us."

"With the power in the gold, I will find and destroy them all!" Years had fallen from Hickamore's face, but they were creeping back again. His voice must have carried for miles; any bandit spy would hear him.

"You made a spell so you wouldn't get old," Whandall guessed.

Hickamore grinned craftily. "I have spoken many spells in my life, Lordkin. Kettle Belly, I must find that gold tonight. It wants me."

"How much gold?"

Hickamore shook his head. "As much as this, perhaps more. You want refined gold. I want—"

"The gold changed Morth," Whandall said slowly. "He became some-one else."

"Younger, you told me," Hickamore said.

"Yes, and crazy!"

"I am already crazy," Hickamore said with casual conviction. "Whandall, come. We will search together, and you can tell me more of Morth of Atlantis."

"But—"

"Recall our bargain," Hickamore said. "Black Kettle will count what is here. Come." Before Whandall could protest, the shaman took his hand and pulled him away from the wagon. Behind him Whandall could hear the others shout-ing as Kettle Belly inspected the false wagon bottom. He tried to go back. He'd left Kettle Belly surrounded by armed adolescents in an argument over wealth!

Missing the point entirely, the shaman said, "Your friends are safe with Black Kettle. He is an honest man. I have said so, and it is true. You!" He turned to one of Kettle Belly's sons. "Number Three. Run quickly to my wagon and tell Twisted Cloud that her father needs her instantly to go with him on a journey. Run!"

"Why Twisted Cloud?" Twisted Cloud was Hickamore's fifteen-year-old daughter, who giggled.

"We seek magic. Rutting Deer has no sense of magic. Her jawline is clearly mine, else I might be suspicious of my wife," Hickamore said.

Whandall looked sharply at Hickamore, but if the shaman noticed, he didn't react.

A half-moon peeked through scattered streamers of cloud, nearly over-head. The clouds stirred restlessly.

The older man strode on. Before they reached the wagon train, they saw Twisted Cloud running toward them, still fastening her skirt. Her black hair flew in the wind.

"You feel it?" Hickamore demanded.

"Something," she said. She wasn't giggling now. "Father, what is it?"

Hickamore seemed to sniff at the air. "This way, I think—"

"No," Twisted Cloud said. She cocked her head to one side. "More uphill, where the flood ran."

"Ah. Yes. It is very bright."

There was nothing bright ahead of them, but Whandall didn't say so. He'd seen Morth at work.

They were rushing ahead of him, running through poppies and scrub brush and over rocky ground. Whandall had trouble keeping up. A young girl and an old man were leaving Whandall in their dust. Hickamore might be enchanted—was enchanted—but how could Twisted Cloud outrun Whandall?

She saw him stumble—somehow, though she was far ahead—turned back and took his wrist, and ran again, pulling him.

She babbled breathlessly as she ran. "I squinted when I was little. My father made magic to strengthen my sight. It worked, a little. I've never seen so well as tonight! There are spirits about, but nothing dangerous. Follow me!"

"Oh, that's it. You're seeing—in the dark. Did Hickamore make himself—young too?"

A laugh in her voice. "Yes, but when he was younger . . ." She stopped talking.

The ground wasn't tripping him anymore. They were climbing a steep hill of bare pale rock. Twisted Cloud was steering him aright; but Hickamore was far above them now, outrunning them both. Power in the half-refined gold was taking him back through time; or else he was running over raw gold left by a flood.

Whandall gasped, "He doesn't need me . . . as much as he thought!"

Her answer was not to the point. "Rutting Deer is promised, you know."

"Doesn't like me."

"My dowry isn't the equal of hers, but—"

Whandall laughed. "Hickamore wants *us* together?"

"Just to *see* each other, it may be. To notice."

A man could be knifed for lusting after a girl this young. *Change the subject.* "When he was younger. What kind of magic . . . does a shaman cast?"

She laughed. "I'll tell you one he told *me*. Piebald Behemoth was dying. Father was his apprentice. A shaman must not be seen to grow ill and die. Father took the aspect of Piebald Behemoth and became our shaman." Twisted Cloud was pulling him uphill and chattering as if a fifteen-year-old girl had no need to draw breath. She'd never spoken so much in her older sister's presence. "The Bisons *wanted* to be fooled, you understand. Father let himself get well over the next year. Took a new name. And of course he blesses crops for the villages we pass and makes weather magic that sometimes works. The twisted cloud that was tearing up the camp the day I was born, Father dispersed it before it reached our wagon. Mother told me about that."

Their path converged with a small and narrow, swift-running stream. Hickamore was far ahead. Twisted Cloud raised her voice above the sound of rushing water. "And once he tried to summon Coyote, but the god wouldn't come."

The stream narrowed and was partially dammed, so that it formed a falls as high as a tall man. Twisted Cloud and Whandall reached the stream just as Hickamore was emerging from the pool behind the boulder. He was holding a nugget the size of his fist and grinning like a fool. Lean as a snake he was, and muscled like a Lordkin. Black hair fell to his shoulders. His eyes were ecstatic and mad.

All in a moment his black hair curled; a wave of gold ran through it, and then a wave of dirty white. Then most of the white mane was dripping into the stream, leaving bald and mottled scalp. Hickamore's face contorted. Gaunt and hollow, jaw more square, brows more prominent, it was not his face at all but the face of a dying stranger.

Hickamore fell backward into the water. His twisted features were a grimace of pain and horror. One eye turned milky, the other stared wildly.

"Father!" Twisted Cloud screamed. She held two smaller nuggets. When she ran to her father with them, he writhed in pain. She threw the gold into the water and reached to wrest the larger nugget from Hickamore's fingers. "It's the old spells!" she shouted over her shoulder. "Take the gold!"

Whandall ran to help.

The old man's arms had gone slack, but the gold would not release his fingers. Twisted Cloud touched it and yelped. She pulled her hands loose as if the gold were sticky and lurched back into Whandall, shouting an unfamiliar phrase.

He tried to get around her. Then his mind caught up: she'd shouted, "Don't touch it!"

Hickamore whimpered and spat teeth. The sound in his throat was a death rattle. Then he was still. The current dribbled water into his mouth.

Whandall asked, "Are *you* all right?" For Twisted Cloud was looking around her like a blind woman. This wasn't mourning; this was something else.

Her eyes found him and pinned him to reality. "I can *see*. I think I never saw before. Whandall Feath—"

"Girl, what happened to your father?"

"All the old spells. Did Morth of Atlantis know how to make a failed spell go away?"

"I have no idea."

"Father didn't know. Piebald Behemoth didn't know. Father took the old shaman's aspect on the night Piebald Behemoth died, before I was born. Stay *here,* Whandall."

The stream was icy on his shins. The shaman's daughter spoke *before* he started to wade to shore. He stopped, and looked, and saw the merest shadow of what was happening on shore.

Both sides of the stream were thickly overgrown with plants. It hadn't been like this earlier. You could almost see them growing. Whandall hissed between his teeth. He was not a man to take such a thing lightly.

"Father blessed crops," the girl said, "and made rain during drought. That didn't always work either."

Clouds were forming knots in the half moonlight, gearing up for rainstorms decades postponed.

"Should we be in a riverbed when the rains come?"

"No." Twisted Cloud turned and began to wade downstream. "We have a few minutes. It won't be like this farther down."

Whandall had lost all feeling in his feet. The bushes on both shores were closing above them. Behind their backs, the voice of a god laughed.

They whirled around.

The dead shaman was sitting up. His voice was strong, and louder than the falling water. "Cloud, dear, your father is dead. He lived a life very much to his liking, and no more can be done for him. Harpy–Seshmarl–Whandall?"

"Coyote."

"Hickamore once mimicked a shaman freshly dead. His spells have succeeded beyond his maddest dreams. And I am Coyote, yes." The voice of a god. Hickamore had tried to call Coyote. "But do you know who Coyote is?"

"A god among the Bison People. I've heard stories. My people may have known of you, Coyote. The stories make you sound like a clever Lordkin."

Coyote laughed. His throat was drying out in death. Whandall glanced aside: Twisted Cloud was basking in a state of worship. He'd get no help from her. *Don't offend a god,* he thought, and hoped it could be that simple.

Coyote said, "I must know more of this Morth. I see that you understand the notion of trading knowledge, trading stories. Will you trade with me?"

"That would delight me," Whandall said; and Whandall was gone.

CHAPTER
47

Whandall Placehold came to himself in black night, shadowed by a boulder, kneeling in pooled blood above a dead man. He was holding his Lordkin knife, and it dripped. He stayed quite still—more still than the dead man, whose heel still jittered against the rock—and listened.

He heard not city noise but campground noise. Running water. Forty beasts and a hundred children and elders and men and women settled down for bed. The campground must be just the far side of this rock. Sounds announced a dozen Bison gone to gather water. Nobody did that alone; there might be bandits about.

A smallish bandit lay right at Whandall's feet. His throat had been cut. His knife was better than Whandall's, and he wore a sheath too. Whandall took both. The moon wasn't up yet, but there was starlight and campfire light, and in the west a wall of black clouds sputtered with continuous lightning. In that near darkness he could see lurkers who moved too often. In just these few breaths he'd seen too many to be mere spies.

Would they attack the caravan directly? Or the little water-gathering party? Where was Twisted Cloud? Safe? *Where was Willow?*

How had he come here? Memory was there to be fished up if he could find any kind of bait.

So. The dead man . . . and a chest-high rock. Rocks everywhere, hiding places everywhere, but Coyote must have . . . *had* seen this rock as the best. A bandit or two *must* be hiding there, so Coyote had crept from shadow to shadow until this shadow gave up its lurker. Coyote cut his throat, and now it was *his* hiding place. Then—

Then nothing. Only Whandall blinking in the dark.

Ah. He'd been counting on the gold! And it all came flooding back. . . .

Coyote had become Whandall. Whandall had become Coyote. Whandall was gone.

Coyote held out his hand. Twisted Cloud took it and came into his arms with a laugh, her joy a near-intolerable glare.

Whandall shied back. That memory was too intense. It blinded him to the danger in the lightning-lit night. Women had loved Whandall for gifts, or for status, or for love alone, and one he had gathered; but he had never been *adored.*

Coyote expected it. He knew how to treat a worshipper.

Sending the girl into ecstasy was not the point. She might remain rapt, wandering in enlightenment while she grew old. He had to keep bringing her back, with humor, with sudden bursts of startling selfishness, or, for minutes at a time, by becoming Whandall Placehold, ignorant and lost, puzzled and horny. This Whandall was a mocking graffito, and the memory made Whandall's ears burn, but it snapped Twisted Cloud from nirvana into postcoital laughter.

Everything was funny to Coyote.

They'd loved in the freezing stream, an hour ahead of a flash flood, while plants went crazy all around the old shaman's body. Coyote loved the danger. Then they'd run downstream ahead of hard rain and a flurry of hail.

And while they ran, Coyote had run barefoot through Whandall's memories. Tracing Morth. Matching Whandall's life to sketchy tales he'd found in Hickamore's dying brain. Seeking more.

Whandall had guessed right. The shaman didn't know of a lurking spell. He hid in shadows like any Lordkin gatherer.

Coyote lurked in the same fashion, hiding in shadows, risking a too-keen eye. *Of course* a god need not be seen. But that was a cheat, as Morth's lurking spell was a cheat, Coyote thought contemptuously, even as he yearned to try Atlantean magic.

Whandall, remembering, saw what Coyote had forgotten: he must *teach* his skills. A god can't teach a god's power to his worshippers!

In Whandall only a trace remained of Yangin-Atep the torpid fire god, but Coyote sensed kinship. He saw a city of thieves and arsonists! And himself barred forever by his nature!

The stories. Coyote loved stories. He learned Wanshig's tale of Jack Rigenlord and the Port Waluu woman, and Tras Preetror confronting Lord

Pelzed's men, and others. The story he'd told Hickamore of a boy and girl on Samorty's balcony, Coyote balanced against Whandall's own memory.

He reveled in the *performance,* story and music and people pretending to be what they were not. He lived it again while his body ran blind. Plants lashed Coyote, unnoticed, and now Whandall felt scratches and swellings across every exposed square inch of skin.

What he left behind . . .

Coyote remembered walking from the frozen east across a wilderness of ice that had been ocean, crossing stretches of water he ensorcelled to buoy his followers. Then south toward the sun, he and his people, six hundred years moving south under pressure of starvation. Setting fires to drive game into reach and to leave the forests free of undergrowth afterward. He had become Coyote while they wandered, but he bore other names elsewhere, and he was there still. Tribes encircling the world's cap of ice shared a trickster god, and another lived in the tundra, and in Atlantis another. In the Norse lands he was Loki, who was also a god of fire.

Gods of a same nature shared a life, and memories and experience were contagious. Loki the fire god was being tormented. Prometheus gave fire and knowledge to men and was punished by Zoosh. Birds tore at his liver. Yangin-Atep felt the same agony: his life leaked through the gash that was Lord's Town, an emptiness made by Lords with a Warlock's Wheel. Whandall Placehold had felt their agony in his sleep.

Coyote had kept his bargain. Story for story.

Urgency added spice. Coyote had never forgotten the bandits. He and Twisted Cloud stopped and spread their clothes on bare rock and loved again, and again lower down.

He said presently, "They've come to attack your caravan. They'll do it while the shaman's gone. Twisted Cloud, return to your folk. I will stop them."

"Please," Twisted Cloud said, "don't let Whandall be killed."

"I won't," Coyote promised. He had no idea whether the Lordkin would live.

Neither did Whandall. Lordkin's promise! Still, Twisted Cloud's last thought for him made him warm inside.

Every few breaths he saw more bandits in the rocks, in the dark. They had some skill, he decided. Whandall alone would have seen less of these lurkers in their native turf, and they'd have seen him. But something of Coyote's skills stayed with him.

*   *   *

Coyote had intended more. He moved ahead of Twisted Cloud, lurking shadow to shadow.

Twisted Cloud moved toward the camp, slowing as she came. With skills taught by her father, she would remain hidden from bandits; but Coyote knew what would happen when she reached the caravan. Perhaps she did too.

Coyote passed lurking bandits and left them alive, save one who just wouldn't get out of the way. He passed through the caravan's ring of guards. They patrolled in pairs. The boy Hammer and the young man Carver were on duty.

The rest of the Miller and Ropewalker families were on guard around their own wagon.

By now most of them should have been asleep. Little Iris Miller was out like a doused flame, but the rest were up and edgy. This was going to be difficult. Twisted Cloud was perhaps twenty-five minutes away; Coyote would have that long.

He needn't escape with gold! Coyote only needed to touch it, but for several seconds. He needed a disguise . . . wait. Why not pass himself off as *Whandall Placehold?*

He slid out of their vicinity, circled and came back from the uphill direction, a Lordkin stumbling just a bit in the wild sputtering dark. "Willow, you still up? Carter? I saw Hammer on sentry duty."

She said, "Whandall, *good—*"

Carter broke in. "Yeah, well, the entire *caravan* knows what we're carrying, thanks to *you.* We don't just have bandits to worry about—it's *everyone.*"

Carter was disappointed in Whandall. Coyote was enjoying himself immensely.

"My first good chance to teach you how to hide what you've gathered, and I failed you. Poor child. *Now hear this,*" he said with the authoritative rasp Whandall Placehold had spent years perfecting. Heads snapped up. "We are not gatherers. If we were gatherers, we wouldn't know what to gather and what to leave alone, because we're among strangers. Town or caravan, we'd be caught and hanged the first time we tried. But none of that matters, because *we are not gatherers.*"

Willow was smiling radiantly; Coyote saw that without looking at her. The smaller children looked mutinous, but Carter's jaw hung slack. Coyote held his eye until he nodded. Then he went to the wagon.

They'd closed up the floor. Coyote made as if to inspect it. "Did Kettle Belly count this?"

"Yes, Whandall," Willow said.

"Good!" But he was reaching for the manna. No need to open the false bed. Wood planks wouldn't stop the flow.

No need indeed. Two wizards had sucked all the power out of all that gold. It was as dead inside the wagon bed as so many rocks.

Twisted Cloud was ten minutes away.

Any attempt to delay her would eat his time too, and *he* didn't have time. Coyote-as-Whandall stalked away saying, "I'll go patrol. I bet Hammer's ready for a nap."

Willow stared after him. "Be careful," she called. "Be careful."

Out beyond the firelight, he melted into the shadows. He'd needed wild gold! Coyote was going to miss the battle! And all he could do now was set this fool Lordkin in place.

CHAPTER
48

By now Whandall knew where most of the bandits were, at least those nearby. Fifty or so. There might be many more. A messenger was moving among them, but whatever his words, they were not "Attack!" Even a stranger's body language told him that.

They weren't waiting for anything in particular. They watched and envied. The shaman had known that in hours, or a day, they would run out of patience.

But Coyote had been waiting, and now Whandall knew why.

A pony whinnied. Then the others. Then the firelight showed Twisted Cloud walking proud and erect, with nothing to hide.

The ponies would have screamed their anger if she had lain with a man . . . with, say, Whandall Placehold. But Twisted Cloud had lain with Coyote. She was carrying Coyote's child, freshly conceived.

The ponies went mad. They began to destroy the corral.

The bandits knew a distraction when they saw it. Without Twisted Cloud, their attack might have come at any time. They'd already marked the locations of most of the caravan's guards. They charged in a scuffling run. The scouts ran about whacking laggards to get them moving.

And Whandall was behind them.

First things first. The nearest man was slow, and his back was turned. Whandall could have swung wide, but the man ahead of *him* had a fine knife with a big shiny leaf-shaped blade. Whandall would have to kill the first man before he fought the second.

The bandit never heard him. A backhand slash at a leg, draw across the thigh until it spurted blood, then bring the knife around and high and straight down to the join of neck and shoulder. He barely croaked as he fell.

But the second must have glimpsed something. He whirled around to see in the half moonlight a silent giant with a dripping knife. He screamed when he should have fought, and then the point was in his throat.

But Whandall's knife stuck in the bone. And again he'd been seen! The bandit to his left turned and charged and ran himself on the knife Whandall had taken from the man Coyote had killed. Whandall left his own knife where it stuck. He had two bandits' knives, each long and heavy, the hilt grooved for fingers, and with a guard! Treasure indeed in Serpent's Walk, and worth his life out here, maybe, because four or five bandits were spreading through the boulders to surround him.

Again! What were they seeing? A Lordkin should know how to lurk!

Elsewhere the bandits were converging on the wagons, yelling like Lordkin, each pretending he was a mob. Whandall had been told they would do this. Among the rocks, who could know how many there were?

Kettle Belly stood in the center of the wagon camp, surrounded by his sons and a dozen others, the trained young men he called his army. Others, men and women and adolescent children, went to defend their own wagons. Younger children scrambled under wagons.

Kettle Belly shouted orders—and was obeyed. At his command fifteen young men with spears and javelins formed a line and threw their javelins at the bandits they could see. The wrong band, the disorganized gatherers. Kettle Belly couldn't see the bandit lord, but Whandall could.

That one. His brighter colors flashing in moonlight, a burly bandit shouted orders to twenty companions who wore colorful sashes. Those hesitated, awaiting his word. The equivalent of Pelzed's guard, Whandall thought. But most of the horde were rushing toward the wagons, paying no attention to the big man.

Those were no threat. They were gatherers who would run if faced with real force. It was the bandit chief and his henchmen that the Bisons ought to fear.

Memories flooded through Whandall, riding the shouts of the bandits. Coyote had run with bandits too, and he knew them. Bandits didn't want to destroy a wagon train. They wanted loot, women, and a wagon to carry it all. Eight or ten bandits could snatch a wagon and pull it into the dark, if other bandits stayed to harry pursuit. Men could outrun a bison team.

Five bandits were coming at Whandall, spreading out to surround him. Not enough to slow the horde. Yelling wouldn't even be noticed, but—"Snake feet! Snake feet!" he screamed. He danced between two men and turned on one with slashing doubled blades and left him with both arms bleeding, then whirled to find the other *much* too close, stabbed him through the heart, and delicately plucked his blade. "Serpent's Walk, you ignorant lookers!" and he ran.

Three still chased him. He was lucky to get any attention at all! He was only one man with a few corpses around him; over there was a wagon train rich with loot. These savages were going to kill a lot of people unless he could distract them.

Four of the front rank of gatherers went down before Bison Clan's spears. Two got up and limped away from the battle. Kettle Belly's army hefted spears in both hands and advanced toward the charging bandits. They hadn't seen the bandit chief and his guard moving toward the caravan at a jog, holding formation.

Whandall ran to intercept them. He'd guessed their target.

He could hear panting behind him. He turned once and slashed and was running again. Three behind him now, one wounded, and none of them really wanted to catch him. In the caravan, some of the defenders had noticed Whandall.

From somewhere behind them came a high-pitched song that sounded of rushing wind, of storms and joy and death. Twisted Cloud! Her voice carried courage to her friends, fear to her enemies, and more.

Gold! She would be carrying some of the river gold, empowered by its wild magic. What had she learned from her father? Her spells would be uncontrolled in the best of times, and now—Whandall didn't think he should put much trust in Twisted Cloud's spells. Still her song rang out, and a few of the rear rank of bandits melted away into the night behind them.

A wind was rising. The storm that had gathered above Hickamore was coming to Bison Clan.

Carver stood on Willow's wagon, Carter just behind him, their slings whirling. There wasn't much light, and if their stones hit anyone there was no sign of it.

It was a game. Coyote would call it a dance. The bandits wanted loot, women if they could get them. The wagonmaster wanted to limit his losses, keep his people safe, inflict enough damage to make the bandits think again before attacking his wagon train. He would risk men to save women. He would risk all to save all the wagons, but he would not risk many men to save only one.

The bandits would choose the wagon least guarded, the lightest and easiest to move. Willow Ropewalker's wagon was small and near, defended by children.

And Whandall Placehold was behind them.

Coyote memories and Kettle Belly's training were overlaid on what he could see. What Coyote knew of bandits and raids was all scrambled up with memories of possession by Yangin-Atep. That was different. He'd been possessed of Yangin-Atep, but he had *been* Coyote. Coyote had opened his memory and doused him with knowledge and stories. Whandall would be days sorting out his own memories from Coyote's.

Three of the chieftain's score had been cut down by the caravan's defenders, but other freelance bandits were gathering around that core of men, increasing their number.

The corral splintered. The bonehead stallions ran mad through the camp, horns flashing in moonlight. Twisted Cloud ran behind them, flapping her arms, howling like a coyote, guiding them into the attackers. Bandits scattered ahead of them. One rose on a horn and was thrown flying, and one ran straight into Whandall's knife, stopped in mortal shock, and screamed only when he saw Whandall's face. Whandall moved among them, slashing. The ponies broke free and ran screaming from Twisted Cloud.

The bandit chief shouted more orders. Five of his guard and half a dozen other bandits heard, thought it over, and converged toward Whandall Placehold. About time they noticed him! Whandall backed away from the horde that was coming at him; whirled and struck down the tired man at his back; turned back and saw them stop as if they'd hit a wall. Then half of them came on.

Too many. Too many were coming at him at once. If they swarmed ahead, they'd have him before he could deal with more than two.

The bandits knew that. No one wanted to be one of the two.

Whandall snatched up a cloak that a dead bandit had gathered from a wagon. He wound it around his arm with the skirt dangling, just in time to shield himself from a knife thrown from the shadows. It was still turning, and struck the cloak without penetration. Whandall leaped forward to slash and felt the *chuk!* of his blade striking bone.

Then he leaped atop a boulder.

Kettle Belly shouted orders. His spearmen moved forward at a trot, spears held waist high in an underhand grip. The bandit chief was between Kettle Belly's spears and a maniac dripping blood and marked with a serpent. His companions closed around their chief and shouted in a language Whandall had never heard before. He understood every word.

"Look what I got, Prairie Dog!"

"Fool! My brother is dead. It's not loot I want, it's blood."

"Drink alone, then."

"His *face!* His *face!* You said their shaman was dead!"

"Run away!"

* * *

They were pursued by worse than Kettle Belly's laughter.

Some had snatched clothing that Ropewalker wagon had set out to dry. A gale wind pulled at the cloth like sails, and they ran off balance and half blind. Whandall ran after them, striking down the slowest, who fell with a scream.

Two others turned, releasing what they carried, drawing knives as their loot flapped away like ghosts. Then one fell without a sound. The other dithered an instant, then came on alone. Whandall killed him.

He looked around to see a whirling sling, a triumphant grin. "The moon's come out!" Carver shouted.

His sling whirled. A bandit with a wooden chest in his arms cursed as the stone hit his back. He turned, dropping the chest. It shattered. Whandall caught up to him. Slash the leg, chop to the shoulder, run past, take another.

"Whandall!" Kettle Belly's voice, well behind, too far behind to be any help.

Carver laughed beside him. "Whandall! Do you know what your *face* is like?"

He'd seen himself in Morth's mirror. But Carver didn't wait for an answer. "You light up! Every time . . . you kill a man . . . the snake lights up . . . in blue fire! Just for a breath, but . . . it scares them out of their *minds!*"

There must be magical power—*manna*—in murder. It was lighting up his magical tattoo. But only for an instant, and now each running man perceived Whandall in the dark behind him. A man clutching a big wood bucket with a handle turned and saw him, and shrieked. Whandall's utmost burst of speed still couldn't catch him, though his staccato scream was announcing his location all across the plain . . .

Enough. "Carver!"

"They're getting away!"

"Leave some to tell the *tale,* Carver," Whandall commanded. "Come back to the wagons."

He had two fine new knives. He'd left his crude Lordkin knife somewhere on the plain, stuck in a man's throat. Coyote spoke to him, from memory or from the shadows, not in words but in pictures, of a pack of coyotes running away to regroup and fall on a pair of pursuing dogs. He urged Carver into a run.

CHAPTER
49

Nobody slept. Conversations clustered around the wounded. There was wine. Whandall was treated as a hero, except that nobody offered him wine. He said nothing, and looked.

Many were heroes that night, and great was the praise they received, but only the wounded were drinking wine. That actually made sense, he thought. Wine dulls pain.

Everybody had a story. They all wanted to hear Whandall's, but they didn't want to shut up.

"We've been counting on you, you know. We wanted to see how a harpy would fight." This from a man who remained cheerful as his wife bound up a deep slash across his back. He'd never spoken to Whandall before. "After Hickamore went off with you, we were all twitchy, waiting for the attack, wondering when it would come, why Hickamore would leave us *now*, why he'd taken the harpy. Thinking he must be crazy."

"He was crazy," Whandall affirmed.

"Yeah?"

"Gold fever."

"Ah." The wounded man found his train of thought. "Then the *ponies* all went crazy. We near jumped out of our skins. We saw Twisted Cloud come back alone, and bandits running out of the dark, and guards running ahead of them to get into position. Everyone armed was running some-where; anyone else was looking for weapons. Twisted Cloud saw what was happening, and she ran around flapping her arms at the ponies—"

"They were running away from me," Twisted Cloud said, "and I thought I could steer them into the bandits. It worked, a little, but they wrecked a lot too, and I wouldn't count on their coming back." She seemed unhurt. She smiled at Whandall, a sudden bedroom smile, and he couldn't help leering back. She told Kettle Belly, "I carry Coyote's child. That's what they were afraid of."

Fawn and Rutting Deer were tending Mountain Cat. That looked like a near miss, a wide bloody knife stroke across his ribs and chest, an inch above cutting his belly open. His arm was bleeding too. Fawn glared at Whandall (and, interestingly, Rutting Deer didn't) but Mountain Cat didn't notice.

"You saved me," he said, "know it or not. That son of a broke-horned pony cut me and was going into his backslash. That would have opened me like a salmon. Then, out there on the desert, you pulled your knife out of some poor bastard and looked at us like a hell-blue glowing snake, and he just couldn't look away. And I did! I think I sliced up his eye. Anyway, he ran."

Rutting Deer seemed bewildered. She caught Whandall looking and shrugged helplessly. "I never saw anything. Just you killing someone in the dark, and poor Mountain Cat fighting for us."

"I can't see it either," Whandall told her.

By midnight it was over. Kettle Belly's men took a tally by dim firelight and intermittent moonlight, not straying too far and never separating.

The score was twenty dead bandits against one old man who died of a heart attack and one young boy who was out after stream water. They found him facedown in the water, his head bashed in and his bucket missing. Some rope, clothing, a few pots, one mirror, some harnesses, a couple of spears; they lost very little and got some of it back. Most agreed that it would be a while before *these* bandits attacked the Bison Clan again.

"But there are other bandits," Kettle Belly said, "All along the trail." As Whandall crossed between fires, the man had moved smoothly into place beside him. "Winning this kind of fight can be really expensive. It wasn't, but it could have been."

Whandall waited.

"Hammer saw you and Carver running into the dark and out of sight! We thought they'd killed you!"

"We chased them."

"You have wagons to defend. You could get lost. They could double back around you!" Kettle Belly studied him. "It doesn't make *sense* to risk everything like that. We couldn't go after you, you know, and then you wouldn't be there next time.

"Look, harpy, this is how it's supposed to work. The bandits give up trying to get a wagon as soon as we show them some blood. Then they grab anything they can and run. Typically you'll see a couple of bandits facing off against a wagon family, and nobody really wants a fight. The owners shout for help. A couple of neighbors come, and the bandits run away and hit some other wagon."

Whandall began to doubt. Had he broken some law? "Kettle Belly, do we have some kind of bargain with them? A treaty?"

"With bandits? No!"

"Then it doesn't make sense to follow *their* rules. We gave them no guarantees, right? They're not holding back to keep some bargain, are they? Let's shake them up a little. They want rules? Let them come and ask for rules."

Kettle Belly sighed. "Hickamore said bandits wouldn't know what to make of you. He was right. You're more interested in killing them than in protecting the wagons. Now you're telling me you were following a *plan?*"

"Plan. Well. I did what I've been taught. The Placehold never makes half of a war."

Whandall dreaded the moment when he must face Willow . . . but when the moment came it didn't matter.

Hickamore's storm swept over Bison Clan. They were soaked and blinded. The rain was gone as quickly as it came, leaving them in a howling hot wind.

Kettle Belly and Twisted Cloud drove them to work. The flood was coming just behind!

The wagons were already on high ground, trust Kettle Belly for that, but everything had to be tied down, anchored. There was the risk that bandits would strike again under cover of the storm . . . and in the midst of all that, he and Willow could only glimpse each other at a half-blind run.

In a moon-shrouded moment they almost ran into each other. Willow blinked, then gripped his shoulders and bellowed, "Was it the fire god?"

"No, it was Coyote! You heard—"

"I was afraid she might be wrong!" She was gone.

Dawn showed the wagons on islands in a flood. Bandits would drown before they could gather anything. It seemed safe to sleep . . . and everyone posted a guard anyway.

Iris Miller had slept. She started to complain, but Willow touched her cheek and asked, "Who else could we trust?" and Iris went.

And they slept.

* * *

Whandall woke near noon. Traces of breakfast remained: the rest of the caravan hadn't been up long. He could see several of them out on the damp plain finding treasure the bandits had dropped.

Whandall had been thinking. Willow certainly knew, as the whole caravan knew, that Twisted Cloud was pregnant by Coyote where the only living man-shape was Whandall's. Whandall was prepared to spend months or years explaining to Willow that it was Willow he loved. He would be patient. He must satisfy her brothers too: not just Carver—who had fought beside him joyfully, who might be ready to accept him—but Carter too. It might take forever. So be it . . .

But Twisted Cloud was pregnant by his doing, and that was another matter. Whandall had heard too many Lordkin say "possessed" and known it for a threadbare excuse. If Twisted Cloud claimed him, he must marry her.

Two wives were rare among the Bison people.

But while Whandall was thinking, Kettle Belly acted.

At high noon Kettle Belly led Twisted Cloud to a table, helped her up, and joined her. Whandall saw no other signal, but conversations chopped off. Bison Clan gathered around them.

Kettle Belly's voice rolled like a Lord's. "Twisted Cloud will bear the grandchild of our shaman and the child of Coyote himself!"

Twisted Cloud glowed with pride.

Willow Ropewalker stepped up beside Whandall.

"What man is worthy of raising such a child? Coyote's son or daughter—"

"Daughter," Twisted Cloud shouted happily.

"—will be powerful and willful and prone to mischief. Twisted Cloud's man must control the child long enough to teach her—"

Willow called, "Kettle Belly? Wagonmaster?"

A ripple of discontent. Kettle Belly looked down, displeased.

"I claim Whandall Placehold as mine."

Whandall turned to look at her. Willow met his eyes, forcing herself.

Kettle Belly said, "Fine," and dismissed her.

Whandall couldn't think of an intelligent question. But if she didn't mean it, he was going to die.

"Women talk about being *courted,*" Willow told him carefully, "and I liked that. And you gave me a dowry so I'd have a choice. And it's been fun, Whandall," she held both of his hands now, "you courting me and not knowing how, and of course my *brothers* had to get used to you, but—"

"Willow—"

"—but I thought she might claim you! You made her pregnant!"

"Listen, that was—"

"So I got in first."

Whandall couldn't stop grinning. He dared squeeze her hands, then pull her into his arms. They turned thus to watch the ceremony. She clung to him, stroked his tattoo, ran her hand down his left arm to touch the misshapen wrist bones. Then she looked at him and smiled again.

After a long time, Whandall became aware of the rest of the world. What was Kettle Belly doing? Holding an auction?

"She does *not* seem eager to claim me," he observed.

"You're disappointed? Because I just—"

"No!"

"—just realized. You can't see your own tattoo glowing? Rutting Deer can't see it either, but anyone else must be keeping his mouth shut, because it means he doesn't have shaman's blood. *You* can't raise Coyote's child."

"Oops."

"But Orange Blossom— Hello, Carter. Did you—"

"I heard. My shy sister. Now I suppose you never will teach us how to gather," Carter said to Whandall.

Whandall said, "No."

"But you can teach us how to fight."

"You do fine."

Stag Rampant, a young man of Leathersmith Wagon, claimed Twisted Cloud. Whandall had seen the man's doubts, but they were gone now.

She would certainly be Bison Clan's religious leader until her daughter had gained maturity, and maybe beyond. And the rustle of activity was Bison Clan gearing up to travel. Late as it was, they could still make First Pines by evening.

BOOK TWO

WHANDALL FEATHERSNAKE

Twenty-two years pass . . .

PART ONE

The Raven

CHAPTER
50

Whandall just missed the bird. He was rooting around in the back of the cart while Green Stone drove. He heard Green Stone cry out. He wriggled backward out of the luggage space.

Whandall's second son was lean and rangy, taller than his father. He was standing precariously on the wobbling bench while the bison plodded ahead. "There! Did you see it? It was wonderful, a bird colored just like your tattoo, Father! It's behind those trees now."

"Watch where you're driving, Stone." The trees were bare, but Whandall still saw nothing. He didn't stand up. The winter wind cut like a forest of knives.

The Hemp Road continued north and east along the base of the low western hills. Whandall had set New Castle on one of those. Ahead was an open plain and river valley, where the Hemp Road ended.

Whandall fished out bread and cheese for their lunch. He could see dust ahead, at the horizon or beyond. He would not see more for another hour.

There was a fair-size town at the far end of the Hemp Road, a place for supplies and refitting, a market center for all of the caravans. Roads came together there, the coast road that led west to Great Hawk Bay, and another that wound through mountain passes north and east to valleys Whandall never expected to see.

In midwinter Road's End was six hours' travel from the New Castle. It would be faster in summer, slower in the spring mud. Nobody would travel that distance twice in one day. Willow wouldn't expect him back for three or four.

There were just under a hundred wagons in the wagon yard. Forty bore the fiery feathered serpent that had become the sign of Whandall Feathersnake. The count was uncertain: some wagons were only components. Wheels lay everywhere.

Mountain Cat lifted an axle into place for a Feathersnake wagon that had come home on skids. He'd have used the pulleys, but with Whandall watching, he preferred to show off his strength. "Whandall Feathersnake," he asked, "how runs your life?"

Whandall hefted the other end of the heavy beam. "No excitement."

"We want to thank you for the rug. Rutting Deer set it in our gossip den."

"Good." The public area. Unspoken: he would never see it there. Though the women stayed polite, Willow did not visit Rutting Deer.

Sometimes Whandall wondered. Had Rutting Deer gone to Mountain Cat's tent in fury because Whandall misused her name? Or was it the night of the battle, with Mountain Cat a wounded hero and the bonehead ponies all fled into the dark? Did she expect her father to bargain with unicorns for her? But Hickamore died, and still she might have married the man she was promised to; but one of the ponies had come back after the battle. . . .

So she'd married Mountain Cat. Without a wagon for a dowry, they'd settled in Road's End and found what work was there.

He could never ask. The Feathersnake family had to get along with a man who built their wheels and a woman who served their food. He said, "I just got here. What are the hot stories?"

"Plenty of work." Mountain Cat waved around. He told what he'd heard, a Bison Clan wagon lost to bandits this year and found in pieces. Pigeon's Wagon had lost control on the long hill from High Pines to the Great Valley and disintegrated; only the metal parts had come home.

"Did you see the bird? Rainbow colored. It circled us for hours. Looking for something, I think."

"No."

"Are you in a hurry for anything?"

"No, but tell me what's finished."

Whandall spent three days inspecting his own wagons, trading goods and tools and lore, trading stories too, as he had for a dozen years, and planning the summer's route with his firstborn son. Saber Tooth was just twenty. He'd been leading the wagons for three years now.

Whandall found himself wishing he were going too.

He had long since given up traveling to raise and guard his family, to build and maintain the New Castle, and to manage the details of trade. All of these matters he delighted in, but . . . if only he could be two men. Let him set *Seshmarl* in charge of the New Castle while *Whandall* ran off down the Hemp Road with the caravan for one more summer.

They kept telling Whandall about the flame-colored bird. It had circled the sprawl of partly repaired wagons at Road's End three times, then flown off down the road. Whandall grew tired of hearing about the bird. Everyone had seen it but him.

Past the New Castle's entry sign, a horde of younger children came running to greet him: not just his and Willow's children and grandchildren, but Millers and Ropewalkers and servants' children too. The New Castle was getting crowded, Whandall thought, and then he heard what they were calling.

"The bird! The bird!"

"Well, what?" He scooped up Larkfeathers, Hammer Ropewalker's girl, who named herself for the startling yellow hair she had seen in a trader's mirror. "Did I miss the cursed thing again?"

"No, no, look up!"

Nothing.

"At the sign, the sign!"

Behind him. He'd passed right underneath it.

The New Castle buildings were square-built, roomy but a bit drab. Willow didn't like to display their wealth. But she had let him sculpt and paint that sign, a great gaudy winged snake in all the colors of fire, and mount it high above the main gate as a signature and a warning.

The bird was perched on its head. Against those colors it was almost invisible. But the children were shouting, "Seshmarls! Come down, Seshmarls!"

The great bird took flight. It wheeled above them, flapping hard. Shadow-blackened with the sun behind it, it was clearly a crow. It cried, "I am Seshmarls!" in a voice that was eerily familiar.

It was too big to perch on a child's arm. It circled, thwarted, until Whandall lifted his own left arm, hardly believing. The bird settled crushingly.

The children cried, "Say it! Say it! 'I am Seshmarls!' "

By its shape, by its flight, it was a crow. Magic must have changed its colors. It could hardly be covered in paint and still fly! It turned its head to study Whandall, first with one eye, then the other.

It said, "Help me, Whandall Seshmarl! My hope lies in your shadow."

Whandall whispered, "Morth?"

The wizard's voice said, "Come to Rordray's Attic and Morth of Atlantis will make you rich!"

"I am rich," Whandall said.

The bird didn't have an answer for that. "I am Seshmarl's," it said. This time Whandall heard the possessive. The children gurgled in delight.

"What else does it say?" Whandall asked them.

"Anything we want it to!" Larkfeathers shouted. "And it knows us by name! I can tell it to carry messages, to my sisters or to Glacier Water's Daughter Two, and it does, in my voice!"

"Where does it sleep?"

"Here, mostly, but Aunt Willow lets it in the house if it wants to come in. It's ever so nice a bird, Uncle Whandall."

It would have to be, Whandall thought. He turned back to the bird. "Morth of Atlantis?"

"Help me, Whandall Seshmarl! My hope lies in your shadow."

"Help how?"

"Come to Rordray's Attic."

"Why should I?"

"Morth of Atlantis will give you wealth and adventure."

"How?"

"Help me, Whandall Seshmarl! My hope lies in your shadow. Come to Rordray's Attic."

Green Stone laughed. "Not very smart."

"It's a bird."

"I meant the wizard who sent it," Stone said. "Offering you wealth and adventure! You're almost as rich as Chief Farthest Land, and you've had more adventure than a man can stand!"

"I suppose," Whandall said. He'd said it himself often enough. He looked back to the bird. "When?"

"Another messenger comes," the bird said. "Wait."

The kinless didn't like to display their wealth. The wonderful dresses Whandall had bought her Willow had at first worn only for him; then only when playing hostess inside her own house. What wealth showed was in the private areas of the house.

Willow met him at the door. She led him through toward the back, the bird on his shoulder, Willow draped softly along his other side.

She'd set up a roost in the bedroom. She must consider the bird immensely valuable. And they both knew what would happen next, but in front of the bird? He said, "You know it can talk."

"Just what someone teaches it. *Oh.* Seshmarls, should we cover its ears? Love, do birds have ears?"

"Willow, I think you'd better hear this." To the bird he said, enunciating, *"Why should I?"*

The bird croaked, "Morth of Atlantis—"

"Morth!" Willow exclaimed.

"—will give you wealth and adventure. Help me, Whandall Seshmarl—"

Willow moved the roosting post out into the hall and they returned to the bedroom. A sense of priorities could be a valuable thing.

During the next few winter weeks their discussions formed a pattern.

Morth wanted to enter their lives again. Morth was not to be trusted! His wealth wasn't needed! As for Whandall leaving the New Castle, "Do you remember the last time you went with the caravan?"

"We nearly lost the New Castle," Whandall admitted. "I nearly lost you."

"Well, then."

During those first six years a legend had spread up and down the Hemp Road, of a grinning giant who wore a tattoo that flared with light when he killed. Then Whandall Feathersnake had retired. Three years later he'd led the summer caravan south. He returned to find invaders in the New Castle. A new tale joined the old, but Willow had extorted a promise.

Now he said, "Well then, they died. The story's all along the route. The farther you follow it back toward Tep's Town, the bigger the numbers get. Whandall Feathersnake was gone three years, seven, ten. Snuck back in as a beggar, covering *this* with mud," Whandall slapped his tattooed cheek, "depending on who's talking, or even shaved the skin off, leaving a hideous scar. Killed twenty, thirty, forty suitors who wanted to claim his wife and land—"

Nobody would dare try me now, he didn't say, but Willow heard the words between the words. She changed the subject. "I never liked it, you know. Sending you in *that* direction after I was pregnant. Back toward Tep's Town."

"Oh, that. No, love, I promised. But Rordray's Attic is on the coast, due west of us. Puma Tribe sends wagons every few years."

They'd told him of Rordray's Attic. It was a mythical place inhabited by shape changers, unreachable save by magic, the food touched with a glamour unequaled anywhere. That food was mostly fish, it seemed, and Whandall had not been much tempted.

Later, as the caravan route was extended, he met a few who had seen the place. Then a pair of Puma who had spent a few days there and been served from Rordray's kitchen. Sometimes another wagon's primary heir rode with Puma. They didn't go to make themselves rich. Despite the difficulties of crossing two ranges of jagged hills, it was a training exercise, a lark, an adventure.

Now Whandall said, "I'd add a wagon to their train and take just Green Stone. Bring back fish, spelled or just dried. I never liked fish myself, but some do. Take . . . mmm . . . rope, everyone wants rope—"

"Dear—"

"Maybe Carver's feet are itching too."

"Whandall!"

"*Yes,* my most difficult gathering."

"*I?* Do purses leap out to claim you the way I did? But you *do* remember Morth. Ready to make me immortal, his for eternity, like it or not? Crazy as a bat Morth? Running up Mount Joy with a fat frothy wave struggling uphill behind him?"

Whandall soothed her. "*Two* bats."

"But you got us away from him. Now let's keep it that way!"

"Yes, dear." Wagons couldn't move in the winter anyway.

•

CHAPTER
51

Two flaps and a space between made up the Placehold's front door. A man going in or out would not take all the Placehold's warm air with him. They didn't build that way in the Valley of Smokes because it never got that cold . . . and because too fine a house made too fine a gathering.

On a fine, clear, cold morning, Whandall stood in the double door and looked past the outer flap.

It looked like you could start *now*, take the wagons and *run*.

From the gate floated the voices of Saber Tooth and Green Stone. Whandall heard "Tattoo . . ." and tried to ignore the rest.

"Morth! Gave Father . . . us too!" That was Stone.

"Not us. You, if you like." Saber Tooth.

Whandall sipped from a dipper of orange juice. The air was clear and cold; the animals were not quite awake. Sound carried amazingly well.

"What if Morth . . ."

". . . wizard *wants* something. Know that. Pay with a tattoo?"

"Mother won't let him go."

Whandall grinned.

Willow spoke at his ear. "Our sons are misinformed. Whandall Feathersnake doesn't obey worth a curse."

Whandall didn't trust his voice. She'd startled him badly.

"Why does Stone want that tattoo so much?" Willow wondered.

He cleared his throat and said, "It's not just the tattoo. Stone would be my second in command on that trek. He could talk to a wizard. See the ocean. Taste food Saber Tooth has only heard about. At the end he'd have something his brother doesn't. Saber Tooth, now, *he* thinks he doesn't want a tattoo, but he *knows* he'll be riding toward the Firewoods with the caravan come spring, and nowhere near the ocean, wherever his brother might be."

"I wish he'd give it a rest. Talk to him?"

"And say what?"

"The only thing that ever scared Morth was water! And now he claims to be at a seaside inn? It's some kind of trap! *Seshmarls!*"

The bird was on her shoulder. "I am Seshmarl's," it responded.

"I finally remembered. Seshmarl is the name you used to lie to Morth! *Morth of Atlantis!*"

"Help me, Whandall Seshmarl! My hope lies in your shadow," the bird croaked. "Come to Rordray's Attic and Morth of Atlantis will make you rich!"

"He's afraid," Willow said.

"Sounds like it." Whandall sipped at his orange juice.

"Afraid of what?"

"It's hard not to wonder."

Wagons couldn't move in the spring mud, either. Two ranges of hills stood between New Castle and the sea, but the plain between was flat and well watered. Life was giving birth to life all up and down the Hemp Road. The tribes worked on the wagons and waited.

The Lion's messenger was a small man with an odd look to his jaw. He came alone, making his way downhill wearing nothing but a backpack. When the Placehold's men had come to meet him he had dressed in a breechcloth and a short-haired yellow hide.

"You're Puma Tribe, aren't you?" Green Stone asked him.

"That's right."

"Well, Puma's got five wagons in repair at Road's End. This's the New Castle. That higher hill south, that's Chief Farthest Land."

"New Castle, right. I'm to see Whandall Feathersnake," the stranger said. "Got a contract for him, and you ain't him."

"You're hard to fool. I'm his second son."

"You're not wearing his tattoo. I talked to the guy that gave it to him."

"Wait here at the gate," Stone said, and ran for the house.

The pack bore thick straps intricately knotted about his shoulders. It would be difficult to remove, Whandall thought, if you only had paws to work with. The tattoos on his cheeks—"Puma?"

The man grinned at the ambiguity. "Yes and yes."

The tribal names had been more than names once. From time to time a shape changer turned up. Saucer Clouds, Twisted Cloud's first son, was claimed to be a *were*bison. Wolf Tribe had thrown up a werewolf; they were watching him grow with some unease.

"That'd explain why you travel alone . . . ?"

"Why *and* how. Name's Whitecap Mountain, and I'm here to offer a contract."

"With . . . ?

"Rordray, called the Lion. He's a were too—they all are at the Attic, but they're seaweres, they're mers. Can you read?"

"No."

"Rordray sends refined gold." Whitecap Mountain reached into his pack.

"Hold up," Whandall said. "My wife should hear this." And others should not! Whandall led him down the path and through the main double door.

Willow greeted him and served hot lemon water. She was punctilious if not, perhaps, cordial.

Whitecap Mountain generally traveled with Puma wagons, he said, but this trip he'd been sent for Whandall Feathersnake. The refined gold in his pack was a flat sheet with the letters of a message pounded into it. "Yours. More on arrival; depends on what you bring. Shall I read it to you? Rordray wants a noonmarch of rope. Two sides of bison, smoked. Mammoth if you can get it anywhere near fresh. Black pepper, sage, basil, rosemary, and thyme. Wood for construction. He'll send back fish raw or cooked. Rordray's the best cook known to men, weres, or gods. Also, he has sea salt, and the mers sometimes bring him treasure from lost ships."

"Sea salt," Willow mused. "We're nearly out." She caught herself. "But—"

Whandall nodded, grinned slightly. Salt was rare enough on the Hemp Road, and the salt found in dry lakes didn't have the proper savor. Something was missing that was found in sea salt, according to Twisted Cloud. Without it your throat could swell up, or your children could grow up stupid or twisted.

It sounded like two wagons' worth of goods. *Better take four,* Whandall thought. Rordray was paying enough, and Whandall didn't know the traveling conditions. Two of his own traveling with two of Puma's should be safe enough. Pay them whatever it takes. *If* he was going at all. He looked at Willow, but she wasn't sending any kind of signal.

So he negotiated. "But fish, now, what if I can't sell it? Not a lot of us eat fish, and those that do, they say they like it fresh."

"Absolutely fresh and spelled to stay that way," the Puma said.

"You've got a wizard?" *Innocent smile, think Seshmarl,* but cups rattled on Willow's tray.

The Puma said, "I only saw him once. He never comes down the mountain."

* * *

Green Stone made a nuisance of himself during dinner. The children had been hearing about Morth of Atlantis since they were little. Stone wanted to know *everything*. The Puma obliged.

"I went up with the talisman box filled with Rordray's cooking, and brought the box back down next morning with the spell renewed. I never slept at all that night. That wizard, he *really* wants to talk. And he's got stories! I can't figure why he stays up there."

Whandall only nodded. If Morth hadn't told him about the water sprite, the tale wasn't Whandall's to give away.

They took Whitecap Mountain to their guesthouse and settled him in. When they moved to the bedroom, Whandall expected to talk all night.

"Now we know," he said. "That poor looker. The water thing has him trapped on a mountain, all alone. He told me once how lonely it was to be the last Atlantis wizard in Tep's Town."

"Why would he think you can help?"

"Had a vision? Magic. No point trying to guess *that.*"

"You wouldn't miss Hawk In Flight's wedding?" The household was gearing up to marry their eldest daughter to the second son of Farthest Land: a major coup.

Whandall said, "That's in spring. We could leave right after. The ocean, it's only a third as far as the Firewoods . . ." at the other end of the Hemp Road.

Willow nodded.

Whandall said, "Daughters and sons are different problems. I think Night Horse will ask for Twisted Tree. Do we accept?"

"We'd best. She's ready."

"She's young."

"This isn't Tep's Town. Girls aren't afraid to be girls where people can see them. They grow up faster this way."

Whandall had never quite believed in this form of cause and effect. He said, "Sons are easier. Saber Tooth will be wagonmaster. Green Stone is shaping up nicely. Twisted Tree is a little young—"

"You had a point?"

"Yes, dear. Fourteen Miller and Ropewalker boys, ten of 'em nephews. We may get more. Half of 'em work the Feathersnake wagons. Half of *them* are married already. The Ropewalk is only so big. So is the Hemp Road, love, though that's not so easy to see. There won't be work for everyone by . . . by the time we're fifty."

"They'll find lives. We raised them right." Willow looked at him coolly. "Or are you thinking of taking over some of Puma turf?"

"No! That's not the right answer, but I think I should look at extending the caravan route. Travel with Puma for guides. *See* another route. *See* if I could tell them how to do it better. It might give me ideas for cooperation."

"I suppose I'll have to let you go," Willow said. "Stone won't let me rest until I say yes."

"No, love, you don't have to put up with that. It would be very easy for me to say that this tattoo—*look* at me?—*this* tattoo is *mine,* and no other soul shall wear it. I could make that stick. Do you . . . you like it on me, right? You're used to it?"

She stroked his cheek as if smoothing feathers. He had to shave often or his beard would cover the tattoo. He said, "Because maybe Morth could take it off."

"No!"

"But maybe you just hate the thought of seeing it on Stone?"

"It's more like he's growing up too fast. I know that's silly. Men wear tattoos. But if he comes back with a tattoo that good, he'd better be bringing one for Saber Tooth, or there'll be trouble."

"Point taken."

"I asked Twisted Cloud about this."

"You did? What did she say?"

Willow's eyes unfocused as she tried to remember *exactly.* She said, " 'In the old drowned tower your people will find what they need of sustenance.' So she says you're going."

"Yes, dear."

CHAPTER
52

Whandall had heard of ancient highways built by magic to serve ancient empires in other lands. The Hemp Road was a wilderness compared to those; but it was a highway compared to the route to Great Hawk Bay.

It was hard work going uphill, harder going down, with everyone hanging back holding ropes to keep the wagons from plunging to their doom. The ground was rough in the valleys. They lost wheels.

The bird spent most of its days in flight and returned to the wagons at night.

Whandall had been a young man when last he guided a team of bison. He swung back into caravan routine with surprising ease. His Puma guide, Lilac, was a good driver and bison tender. There was work to be done, but in between you could be lazy as a Lordkin.

Along the Hemp Road they told stories of places where a simple summoning spell would bring all the game you wanted, meat every night. Partridges, rabbits, deer, they came when summoned, and old men remembered those times, or said they did.

Lilac sang in the evening dusk. Three rabbits came and sat on their haunches, waiting patiently for her to wring their necks. One short scream as the rabbit understood . . .

The track led through high grass, past stands of scrub oak trees. The air hung heavy in the mornings, heavy dew and swirling mists.

"No rain here," Lilac said. "The dew is all. Good for garlic and thistle, not much else."

From time to time they encountered a flock of crows. Seshmarls wheeled up to them, squawking in crow language, and they would fly away in terror. Sometimes the bird chased them, but he always returned to Whandall's arm in the evening.

On the Hemp Road even a lazy Lordkin had to watch for gatherers from other bands: for bandits. On this route, bandits couldn't survive. There weren't enough wagon trains to support them. Towns were few, little more than hunting camps. Farming and hunting communities could survive . . . and if a badly guarded caravan passed, why, farmers might gather some opportune treasure. One must still keep watch.

No one had ever heard of him here. The Feathersnake sign guarded his wagons on the Hemp Road, but not here.

On the tenth day he saw a restlessly stirring black mass ahead of the caravan.

He tried to guess what he was seeing.

He was driving. The bird Seshmarls perched beside his ear, gripping the edge of the roof above the driver's bench. From time to time it took wing to hunt. They were both enjoying themselves, and Whandall didn't want company. But after a time, reasoning that anything he couldn't identify might be dangerous, he called down into the covered wagon bed.

Lilac poked her head out. She was a pretty nineteen-year-old of Puma Tribe who had made this trip as a girl, twice. She traveled in Whandall's wagon rather than Green Stone's, at her mother's insistence. Those two found each other too interesting.

She watched for a time. She said, "Crows. Ravens. Something like that."

The bird rose from the roof and flapped toward the black mass. A crow colored like a flying bonfire, he had driven away half the flock when the wagons came in range. What the crows had hidden was the white-and-red bones of a beast bigger than any wagon.

Looking over Whandall's shoulder, Lilac said, "Mammoth."

"Are they common around here?"

She was awed. "Tribes around here dig pits for 'em. It's dinner for two days for a whole tribe and any guests. I heard of a war that stopped because Prairie Dog Tribe trapped a mammoth and invited the Terror Birds to share, but it doesn't happen often. No, they're not common. Nobody I know ever saw one alive. You?"

Fool Turkey, who drove the Wolf Tribe wagon for many years, told a tale of riding a mammoth for nearly the length of the road before slaughtering it to stave off a famine . . . but Fool Turkey was a champion liar. Whandall said, "No. You'd think they'd be too big to miss."

Lilac nodded.

"A pit could trap one, not just kill it."

"Got to dig them deep. If it lives through the fall it could climb out, and it comes out angry."

"So? I mean, it's big, but—" But the girl smiled and made an excuse to go back into the wagon.

Every tribe has its secrets, Whandall thought.

They rolled on toward the sunset. Then one night they could hear the sea, a sound Whandall had not heard for twenty-three years.

CHAPTER
53

A wave broke in white spume and rolled toward the children. Lilac and Green Stone danced back, not quick enough. Foam and seawater rolled over their legs. The wave receded and they followed it. Dancing with the ocean.

Whandall watched from well back. He could swim in a river, but this . . . he could almost sense the mass of water ready to roll a swimmer under.

Far across the calm waters of the bay, a score of boats bobbed about a cluster of drowned towers.

"There's a fair-size city down there under the water," Lilac told Green Stone. She turned and called to Whandall. "Wagonmaster? I suppose you could find drowned cities along *any* coastline after Atlantis sank . . . ?"

"My brother would know." Whandall hadn't thought of Wanshig in many years.

What poked above the waves was a handful of ruins solid enough to moor boats to, and an extensive flat roof, crenellated, that stood four stories above the water. Waves had smashed the southern edge; a new wall had been bricked in.

Any storm would make the lower levels unusable, Whandall thought, but that left two stories and an extensive floor plan. He could see gardens on the roof, as with the Placehold.

It had been four years since Puma Tribe sent wagons.

He should stop thinking of these two as children. Lilac had proven an excellent guide. . . . "Lilac, we brought twice as many people as the Attic is used to. How do you think they'll handle it?"

"Simplest thing is just not to send a boat," Lilac said.

Green Stone asked, "Why didn't you send the bird ahead, Father?"

"I want to know if they fluster easily."

Behind them the sons and nephews and grandsons of Puma and Bison tribes were making camp, tending beasts, pulling the wagons into a defensive ring, working the spells that would give them safety and clean water, all under Carver Ropewalker's direction. Lilac and Green Stone went to join them. Whandall left them to it.

There were mountains in view. Any of those largest three . . .

"Are you really thinking of climbing a mountain?"

It was Carver. Whandall didn't answer.

Whandall was master of the caravans. Carver Ropewalker stayed home and made rope. This trip had firmed him up a bit. He bore marks of the kinless: round ears, pointy nose. Once these differences had been life itself. He looked across the water for a time before he spoke.

"Whandall, I've lost two belt knots and I'm stronger than I've been in years. I *am* glad I came. But do you believe Twisted Cloud?"

"Prophecy works as well as it ever did."

"The magic goes away. Prophecies go vague and cryptic. They tell you less. Twisted Cloud *didn't* say, 'Eat at Rordray's Attic and you'll be rich again.' " Carver closed his eyes to remember *exactly.* " 'In the old drowned tower your people will find what they need of sustenance.' Whandall, it's fifty years since Atlantis went under. Can you imagine how many drowned towers there are along this coast?"

"Be fun to search them out."

"They're sending us a boat."

Rordray's Attic, kitchen and restaurant, was the top floor of the old Carlem Marcle Civic Center's south tower. The roof could house an overflow. The next floor down was all guest rooms, Lilac said.

The restaurant was full of fishermen. Rordray and his son directed some of them to push tables together to accommodate Puma's thirty-three travelers. The sudden influx hadn't bothered Rordray and they hadn't run out of food or drink.

Thone had met them with the boat: a big blond man, Rordray's son. His smooth round strength and perpetual smile suggested one or another sea mammal. He described what his father had prepared for the noon meal, as if it were a string of amazing discoveries.

Thone's enthusiasm was infectious. Whandall took a bite of swordfish with only the slightest of qualms. Lilac was watching him with a grin. She laughed loud at the look on Whandall's face.

"Good," Whandall said in amazement.

All the mers were watching him.

He said, "I don't think I've ever really tasted fish."

"Try the vegetables too."

In midafternoon the place was still half full, though most of Whandall's travelers had been rowed ashore. Rordray's customers liked to take their time. Many must be were creatures, Whandall thought. The huge, smoothly muscled guy *had* to be a mer whale. He had eaten twenty headsman crabs; he had picked up a table for ten all by himself.

Carver and Whandall loved the Attic on sight, but of course it was too small—

"Now, wait," Carver said. "You don't doubt Rordray can *feed* a caravan, do you?"

"After a meal like that? And I saw the size of his ovens. But—"

"Rooms? Most of a caravan would stay in the wagons anyway to save money. And he's got storage in those other buildings."

"Did you notice that everything came from the sea?"

"Spices. He's got spices from as far back as Beesh, and some root vegetables too."

Whandall said, "Caravan passengers demand every variety of diet known to man or beast. We get vegetarians. We get fat going for thin, thin going for fat, weird going for wizardry or lost youth or moral dominance games. Some won't touch fish. Some think fish is poisonous—Lion!" Their host was just emerging from the kitchen. Wait, now, Lion was a *nickname!* "Rordray, sir, can you favor us with a minute of your time?"

The Lion stopped by their table. The bird on Whandall's shoulder suddenly said, "Morth of Atlantis greets you, Rordray, and begs a favor."

Rordray laughed. "Whandall Feathersnake. I see the wizard's message reached you."

Whandall said, "Yes. Carver Ropewalker is my partner; Green Stone, my son. Lilac—"

"Good to see you again, Sir Lion," Lilac said.

"A pleasure, Lady Puma. You've grown well."

"Is Morth here?" asked Whandall.

Lion—Rordray—laughed. "Not likely! He was here twice. He loves the sea. He stayed a day too long, nineteen years ago—" Rordray's eyes questioned. What secrets should he spill here?

"The water sprite," Whandall said.

"It came on us here. Morth fled uphill. The wave washed away part of the restaurant." Shrug. "None of us drowned. Gentlemen, what have you brought me?"

Whandall showed him what spices would ride in a pouch. Rordray pinched, sniffed, tasted, approved. Carver described the rest. Cured deer meat, bison on the hoof, no mammoth. Sage. Rope. Brandy; the Puma scout hadn't asked for that. "Of course you can inspect all of this in the morning. What can we take back?"

They discussed it. Rordray could sell them sea salt. Morth needed a fishing net; Whandall was to pay for it—Rordray didn't know why. Rordray's crew could never get enough rope. Could the Bison Clan increase their shipments? But Puma had slacked off because of a dwindling market.

Perhaps a market could be developed along the Hemp Road, for fish? Shipping fresh and fresh-cooked fish east would require another talisman box. Morth of Atlantis would be the only possible source for that. *We do need another trade route,* Whandall told himself. "Is Morth hard to reach?"

"I wouldn't try it myself," Rordray said. "He settled on the peak of Mount Carlem, there to the south and east. No wagon can climb that. Whitecap Mountain can guide you, if you can climb."

Carver laughed. "What Whandall can't do is turn down a challenge."

Rosemary? Thyme? Bison Clan didn't know a source for those. Morth might. Whandall wouldn't even recognize these plants. Rordray fished out tiny brown paper pouches, pinched out samples, and rubbed them under his nose.

Lilac exclaimed, "Thyme? *I* know that. We passed it coming here. I've smelled it near the Stone Needles."

Meat of a terror bird? Puma had a hair-raising tale, and so did Whandall, but the point was made: Butchering a terror bird was a matter of happenstance . . . not a delicacy one could fully recommend, either, but as a curiosity . . . as jerky? Or carry Morth's back breaker of a cold iron talisman box.

"The Hemp Road runs from the Drylands near Condigeo north past Firewoods opposite Tep's Town, down into the Great Valley past Farthest Land to Road's End, and back," Carver said. "Now we want to extend the route."

"You're successful, then."

"Until recently," Carver said, and Whandall said, "Fire's *sake,* Carver!"

Carver glared at him. "Yes. Successful. Our problem is, shall we build up the route west to Carlem Marcle and the Attic, or northeast for whatever we find? The rumor of Rordray's Attic would bring us custom all by itself, but it's not enough. And there's a road to build."

Rordray nodded, unsurprised. "I would never have room downstairs for so many, not unless the sea sinks by a few floors."

That wasn't likely. Was it? Morth would know. Without Morth, there was no trade route. They would have to speak with the wizard.

A man and two women emerged from the kitchen, all built on Rordray's own heroic scale. The older woman reached past Carver, set down a tray with a pitcher and eight small cups. Rordray waved. "My wife and daughter, Arilta and Estrayle. You've met Thone." They were pulling up their own chairs. The table had been roomy a moment ago.

Carver poured for them all, then sipped. Whandall sipped from his own cup, carefully. It was the brandy they'd brought from Zantaar Tribe, and it was deadly stuff.

He said, "Well, Carver, the prophecy holds. We've found sustenance." He saw his partner's glare and made haste to change the subject. "Rordray, when I was a child I learned to trade information and stories. Shall we talk about Morth? If he led a water sprite to you, I'm surprised you're still friends."

"Well, you know," the Lion said, "it was Morth who warned us out of the old castle in Minterl. Do you recall that there were two sinkings of Atlantis?"

The caravaners looked at each other. Talk eased off a bit among the remaining customers.

"Where you've lived, maybe you never knew. The ground shakes, then stops? Near the sea, we notice that," the Lion said. "We knew of Atlantis in Minterl. We knew when the land shook and the wave covered whole towns. I set up my first inn in the tip of a sunken tower in what was once Castle Minterl.

"We have always traded with Atlantis. Naturally the ocean is no barrier to *us*. There is little of trade in goods, but stories travel along the whale path. Word of that side of the world comes half a year late. We heard that the east side of the island had settled, drowning beaches and beach cities a third of the way around the island. These were fishing communities, so there were mers to rescue land dwellers. Not many died. The King declared a disaster and raised taxes.

"The second quake came half a lifetime later," Rordray said, "when nobody remembered Castle Minterl as anything but Rordray's Attic.

"Mers still ran the fishing industry around Atlantis, but ashore we'd lose the shape of men. Fishing requires boats, harbors, warehouses, weather prediction, and a little judicious guiding of the currents. The fishers' local wizard was a man nearing his thirties, named Morth.

"Word came with a pod of whales. Morth had foreseen a tidal wave that would wash away whole civilizations. Morth's warning went to many more than just my little Attic, but he saw the Attic's doom."

"Did he know that Atlantis would sink to make that wave?"

"Wizards can't see their own fate. But *I* guessed."

"So you left."

"No, no. We had barely heard of Morth! We consulted local shamans and performed our own spells. We saw enough to convince us. When the wave and the quake came, we were facing a different ocean."

The Lion poured Zantaar brandy. Whandall put his cup in his pocket. Lion said, "The wave had to circle the world to reach us here at Great Hawk Bay. Then came Morth in a ship that floated above the land, but so low that it must circle trees. We made him welcome.

"He told us of the magical thing that hunted him. I recalled the Burning City. We were loading his ship with provisions when a mountain of ice came floating toward us. Morth sailed away inland, the ice sailed south, and we knew no more for half of a man's lifetime."

"I assume he filled you in later," Whandall said.

Rordray grinned. "He claims holes in his memory after he found gold in riverbeds. You may still have tales to tell."

The evening had grown dark, and it seemed to be story time. A pointy-eared fisher ordered a round of beer for the house. "I am Omarn," he told the newcomers. "When Atlantis sank I was near Minterl in dolphin form. I saw water humping up behind me. I swam like mad, and when the wave passed me I was going fast enough to ride it. The ride of my life! I rode the wave almost to the mountains. I saw the Lion's old Attic smashed all in an instant. Mers don't drown, but if anyone was still in there, Rordray, I think he must have been smashed under the rocks."

"No, we were all clear," the innkeeper said.

Whandall asked, "Shall I tell what Morth of Atlantis was doing in Tep's Town? I saw some of that."

"Wait now, Whandall Feathersnake," the innkeeper said. "A tale has come to us of a tattooed caravan lord who came home to find himself pronounced dead and his wife attended by a host of suitors. Can you tell us the truth of this?"

So, Rordray would trade tales with a stranger, but he wanted to name the tale. Whandall hesitated . . . and saw instantly how they would take that. He *must not* seem to be hiding old murders.

He said, "I used a protection. If I tell you what I had, do not ask where I kept it."

He had everyone's attention now. Carver and Green Stone had heard his tale, but the rest had not. Whitey guessed: "A dagger?"

"No, it was a handful of gold sand. Raw gold right out of a river. Once upon a time I used it to save us from . . . well, *Morth*. Raw gold turns Morth crazy. I always carry raw gold with me."

They sipped and listened.

"This was nine years after I married Willow Ropewalker, and three years since I rode with a caravan. I set up my life so I could stay home and raise my children. I visited nearby towns from time to time, and if anyone wanted me, he could find me.

"Burning Grass and Three Forks came to tell me that men on my wagon had cheated them. I asked around and decided it might be true. I told Willow I must ride with the caravan again.

"Angry Goose was running a game that uses a gold bead and three nut shells, and two friends sat in the game to protect him. It was a cheat. I threw them off and divided their goods. But Goose and his men should never have been allowed aboard.

"There was more. Everything went loose and sloppy when Black Kettle had to leave the caravan. I saw them camping in flood basins. I saw a man badger Twisted Cloud into changing a prediction. The guards held gambling parties.

"I saw that I'd have to ride the whole circuit. We were a long way back from the Firewoods at the southern end of the route before I was sure I'd straightened things out. I had some bruises. Caravaners are mighty fighters, and it must be easy to forget that what's given them to rule isn't theirs—"

"Did you have to kill anyone?"

"No."

"Good."

"Not then. I left the caravan at Warbler Flats. I stopped a couple of nights with friends, then rode on through Hip High Spring and home to the New Castle.

"My son Saber Tooth met me at the gate. He was only eight then. He carefully explained that the house was full of men who wanted to marry Mother, and Mother was afraid of them.

"I sent Saber Tooth in to find my wife and, if he could talk to her, tell her Father says to get ready to duck under something. Then come and tell me where everyone is. I told him where I'd be."

Whandall laughed and gestured at his cheek, shoulder, twisted arm. "I can't remember the last time I thought of disguising myself. There was nothing for it but to go right in, but I didn't have to go in the front door. I came by the hay chute—"

Rordray laughed. "What, is your house a barn too?"

"Yes. In by the hay chute, talk to the bison a bit so they don't raise a ruckus. I wasn't sure Saber Tooth could do it, so I wasn't going to wait very long. But he came to the hayrack and told me. Willow would be in the hidey closet with the four youngsters. Four men were terrorizing the kitchen staff.

"I gave Saber Tooth a knife and hid him in the hay. I went into the kitchen fast. Four men, right. Three were from Armadillo Wagon—Passenger Pigeon and his father and uncle—but the fourth was a stranger in Lordsman armor.

"I started to say, 'Welcome to the New Castle, gentlemen.' But they went for weapons as soon as they saw me. Not meaning to be surrounded, I slashed first at the ones who didn't have armor. Bussard's Shadow went down spraying blood everywhere, and I slashed Pigeon's knife arm. Then the armored man stepped between them and me. The ones still standing snatched Bussard's Shadow and ran backward pulling his arms, while the Lordsman came at me.

"That was scary. But Lordsman armor doesn't cover everything. I got a chopping block between him and me, thinking I'd jab at his ankles. But he pushed it over and ran after the others.

"I got outside, carefully, not wanting to be ambushed. They were running into the Ropewalk, the two Armadillo Wagon men carrying the third, and the armored man walking backward after them. I started to wonder who of the Ropewalker family was in there, but the only thing to do about that was run in and look.

"Rordray, my wife's family doesn't let me in there. I saw it once, when it was new and near empty. It looked no different from a barn.

"Years had passed since then. The place stank of hot tar. The Ropewalk was stacked to near the ceiling with spools of rope, each about as big as a man. The Ropewalkers stack them on end so they won't roll. The aisle ran down the center. Back of it, at least five Armadillo men were getting themselves out of the way. Somebody yelled like a Lordkin on wine. It was Carter Ropewalker. He was lying down and wriggling. I guessed he was tied up.

"But mostly, *three* men in Lordsman armor were facing me in that pose they use with the shields locked edge to edge. I saw that once during a fair in Tep's Town. *Nothing* can get through that.

"Rordray, I sure couldn't fight them. I could outrun them, even moving backward, but they had Carter. What I did was climb the bales of rope and hop to the back of the building. The Armadillo men were still just staying clear. The armored men ran toward me, got close, and lockstepped their shields again. That gave me time to cut Carter loose and send him up the spools. He got a rope anchored in the smoke hole to the roof. He was pretty battered and not climbing very fast. I waited until he was through, then climbed up after him.

"Then I sprinkled my gold sand down into the Ropewalk.

"I kept a hand on Carter to keep him from looking into the smoke hole. We could have gone down the outside then if Passenger Pigeon hadn't been below us with a long knife. Left-handed, though. He yelled up and threatened to burn down the Ropewalk if we didn't surrender. I told him he should move the rope-weaving device out first. That's the actual Ropewalk, the most valuable single thing at the New Castle.

"We got some of the story out of him while we all circled around and waited for developments.

"The way Pigeon tells it, this all happened because three Lordsmen took ship to escape the Lords in Tep's Town. Pigeon didn't know why. They took their armor with them. They offered to protect Armadillo Wagon on the Hemp Road, but Pigeon told them about a Lordkin gone missing, so they attacked the New Castle instead.

"Armadillo Wagon wouldn't have done this to anyone *but* a Lordkin. But, see, I'd been married nine years. Now I was going off. Lordkin don't come back! Everyone knows it. So Passenger Pigeon and his tribe set forth to marry the abandoned widow. Willow Feathersnake wasn't going anywhere until she agreed. There were the children for hostages. Pigeon told us he never threatened them. Later, Willow told me he did.

"By and by Carter and I decided that nobody was coming out of the Ropewalk. I went over the roof fast and slid down the other side and was in fighting stance before Pigeon could come around. He ran for the Ropewalk doors. They were closed. Carter and I blocked his path, but we let him pull a door open and look in.

"He backed away gobbling like a turkey."

Rordray's family were nodding. Mers were sophisticates in magic. And Whandall's family knew the tale, but horror looked out of Lilac's eyes.

"They were all strangled," Whandall said. "Pulled into shapes no sane man ever thought of. Nobody but Pigeon left to tell the tale. He sits at the south gate of Hip High Spring and warns you about hemp, even if you don't ask. Hemp is like that, you know? It wants to soothe you to sleep and lose you in dreams and then strangle you. And hemp rope on wild magic is a thing of nightmares."

Nobody seemed to want to top that story. It was full dark by now. The remaining fishers went up to the roof, and Whandall heard splashing. Then Estrayle led them down to their rooms.

The room was clean, the bed a bit damp. Still, it was luxury. He could not fall asleep at first, and could not think why.

Presently he realized that they didn't turn off the ocean at night. The *shh, sss* of the waves went on forever . . . and presently carried him away.

CHAPTER

54

They left for Morth's mountain after two days of feasting.

Whandall was inspired. "People come to Road's End tired and ready to be pampered. They want fish from Rordray's Attic. They just don't know it yet! If we can bring this to Road's End, we have goods to trade."

"Find Morth," Rordray said.

They took one of the wagons. Green Stone *had* to come, that became clear, so Whandall made him drive. Whitey couldn't drive because the bison didn't trust him. Lilac—Whandall wasn't sure why they were taking Lilac. He and Green Stone had decided sometime last night. Someone had to guard the wagon while the others were climbing. Why Lilac?

Willow would have his head.

Or not. Lilac might be just the girl—woman—for Green Stone. A link to Puma Tribe could solve some problems for the family, and the trade to Great Hawk Bay would never be vast, but it could be lucrative.

They hadn't brought a one-horn, but every woman knew she would confront one eventually.

They rode for four days, taking their time, hunting, letting the bison graze where they would, before the ground grew too rough to go nearer. Whitey spent an extra day leading them around the mountain to the shallower eastern slope. They stopped where bison could still forage.

Mount Carlem stood above them all that night, intimidating.

They started at dawn, leaving Lilac in charge of the wagon. They climbed in shirts, kilts, and packs. When the bird settled on Whandall's pack, Whandall chased him away. The bird rose with an angry squawk, found an updraft, and kept rising out of sight.

Green Stone carried a flat box of cold iron, a rectangle with the corners cut off, flat enough to ride a strong man's back. This one was empty and not yet ensorcelled. Whandall had the heavier talisman box loaded with provisions from the Attic kitchen. They left the heavy fishing net on the wagon. If Morth somehow needed that to get down, someone would have to go back for it.

The packs held water, blankets, and clothes. Why so many clothes? Because Whitey insisted.

The day grew hot. Shirts came off early. At noon Whitey let them stop to drink. By then Whandall knew he was an old man beyond his strength. He had never climbed like this. Everyone else was making his decisions for him . . . had been for years, without his realizing it . . . and he was just beginning to resent it.

When Whitey and Green Stone went on, Whandall made himself follow. He was at the edge of making his son trade burdens with him . . . but now the way became easier.

They'd found reserves of strength, Whandall thought, but it rapidly became ridiculous. They'd been climbing toward a scary, near vertical bare rock slope. The tilt seemed less now; it had flattened out. But the horizon eastward was tilted up like a dandy Lord's hat! It looked like anything loose should be sliding west toward the sea.

Green Stone said nothing of this. He must have thought he was going mad. Whitey watched them both with that Puma grin.

Whandall bellowed, "Mooorth!"

He just glimpsed a man-shaped streak zigzagging at amazing speed among tall stands of lordblades, near naked and all knobs, red braids flying. "Whandall Placehold!" Glimpsed and already here. "You came!"

Whandall looked him over. Morth wore only a sun-bleached and ragged kilt, and the bird now settling on his shoulder. He was tanned near black. His feet were bare and callused hard. The Morth of twenty years ago had dressed better but was otherwise little changed. Lean, with stringy muscles and prominent ribs; high cheekbones; long, curly red hair washed and braided. He was grinning and panting like a dog . . . and even so, he did not seem *mad*.

Whandall said, "Right. You know Whitey. Green Stone, this is Morth of Atlantis. Morth, my second son. Willow's second son."

The wizard gripped the boy's hand. "Green Stone, I'm very pleased you could come! May I see your palm?"

The boy looked at his father, got a nod, and let Morth turn his hand palm upward in the sunlight. Morth said, "I haven't done this since . . . Early marriage. Children branch off soon, here. Twins. Both girls." The wizard pointed with a fingernail that needed tending. "No, don't squint, you can't see your own future. More children down the line, I think, but your path gets fuzzy . . ." Morth looked up with satisfaction in his eyes. "Come. I live on the peak."

"Can you fly us?"

"Whandall, those days are long gone mythical! But I wove a spell for easier climbing so the Lion's people can visit me."

He babbled as they climbed. "The way I left you and the children, I'm embarrassed. Of course gold fever had my mind, and I still had to lead the water elemental away from you—"

"We saw that."

"—just kept going into the mountains. There's manna untouched by any wizard, but there's also wild magic, virgin gold. I have no idea how long I was out of my mind. I wound up on some tremendous height in the Vedasiras Range, with no gold around me, just a magical place with a view of half the world. Like this place, really, but even farther from any decent hunting. By the time I had my senses back—why do they always say that?— I was sensing *everything,* no path blocked within my mind, no way to concentrate on any one thing, like eating or bathing, digging a jakes, raising a shelter, tending a wound. Scatterminded. *That* was what had me so crazy.

"Where was I? I was stuck on a mountaintop, sane but starving and tanned like Sheban leather. Only my own spells were keeping me alive. I found meat and firewood downslope and spent some time building my strength back. Built a talisman to get me through, then set out north for Great Hawk Bay."

"Rordray told us."

"I thought I'd lost the sprite. All that wild gold should have had it totally confused. I was careless. When that wave humped itself, I just went up the nearest mountain as quick as I could. I've been stuck here ever since."

They put their shirts back on. It had grown cold. Morth didn't notice.

The mountain's peak was a fantastic lacework of stone castle. *Indefensible,* was Whandall's first thought. Any Lordkin tribe could have pulled it down with their hands. *What's holding it up?*

He looked in vain for supporting beams. There was no wood to be seen anywhere. It was as if rock had melted and flowed into place. There were no corners, no straight lines. Rooms and chambers and corridors spilled over and under and between each other like the insides of a careless knifefighter, rising up into a bulb of clear glass, a wonderful wizard's crow's nest.

Morth led them in.

In a roomy ground-floor chamber the rock walls humped into chairs around a fire. Four people, four chairs, and a high ridge for a bird to perch. Dark rocks were burning in the fireplace.

Whitecap Mountain set out both talisman boxes. He didn't open them. The Attic's provisions were for Morth alone. But Morth had prepared a meal for four, a stew of mountain goat, herbs, and roots. Whandall realized that he was ravenous; he saw the look in Green Stone's eye and waved him on.

When they had slaked their hunger a bit, the wizard said, "You came at my asking. I can pay that debt now, in refined gold." He waved at the fireplace. "Take what you like."

Had Morth been using wild magic? But the gold he was pointing at had drained out of the fireplace and formed a flat pool before it froze. Whitey and Green Stone wiggled it loose, used an edge of rock to break it in roughly equal halves, and slid it into packs.

"Energy wants to be heat," Morth said. "The simplest thing you can do with any kind of manna is help it to become heat. I can burn gold ore without its hurting me, and the expended gold just flows out."

Whandall nodded. *Uh huh.*

The wizard pointed to Whandall's crotch. "What is that?" Morth caught himself. "Secret?"

"Supposed to be. I'm not surprised *you'd* see it." Whandall eased a flat metal flask out from just above his groin. "What does it look like to you?"

"A dead spot. I can show you how to see the blind spot in your eye, but this is a bit more obvious. Nothing else looks like cold iron."

Whandall held it up without opening it. "Coarse gold right out of a riverbed. You wouldn't remember when I threw gold at ensorcelled ponies? But—" Whandall waved away Morth's attempt at an old apology. "But it broke the spell. So I carry raw gold, just in case, and it did save me once."

"That must be an interesting tale," Morth said, "but I want to hear a different one. Whandall, tell me about the last time you did violence."

Whandall looked at him. "Violence?"

"We last saw each other twenty-one years ago. I don't quite remember, but I think I tried to take a girl you wanted. I think you tried to kill me," Morth said.

"No. Not tried. I thought I might have to."

"Now I hear tales of a wagonmaster whose sign is a feathered serpent. He keeps his oaths and enforces honesty with a knife of spelled bronze. Whandall, I have to know what you are."

"The last time I did violence."

"Was that it?"

They were all waiting. Whandall said, "No, it was the last time I saw Tras Preetror. Do you remember him?"

"The teller."

"Six years ago. I was up on the house with my sons, fixing the roof. A servant came to tell me I had a visitor.

"It was Tras Preetror and a big man in part Lordsman armor who stood behind him and didn't say anything. They'd got past the guards. Willow was serving him tea. I got her aside and she wanted *me* to explain what he was doing here."

"Hospitality," Morth said.

"He hadn't asked for food and fire and shelter from the night," Whandall said. "I made sure of that. He'd just barged in, invited himself as if he belonged there.

"I had tea with them. He told us his tale. He's a *good* teller, Morth, you remember. He'd taken ship up to Great Hawk Bay to get tales from the mers at Rordray's Attic. I'd heard of this place from the caravans, but Tras told us a lot more.

"He'd heard rumors from the Puma wagons about a new head man in the caravans. He tracked the tales of a snake tattoo, east and south. Morth, I *have* to know that a traveler can reach me if my wagons have cheated him. The caravan tribes guided Tras straight to my house.

"Now he's waiting for *my* story, right? I showed him my cold iron case, and opened it, and blew a bit of gold dust on him and his man. I didn't see any result, Morth, but I *hate* your damn lurking spell and I thought he might have used it on my gate guard.

" 'Raw gold,' I told him. 'It distorts magic spells.' "

Morth barked a laugh.

" 'And it saved my life once,' and I told him just enough of the fight with Armadillo Wagon to hook him. 'Come with me, if you like, I'll show you where the bodies are buried.' And I stood up and led him out, still talking. 'Tras, every time I think I've given up violence, something pops up.' That got him moving, and his man jumped up and went ahead of us.

"He didn't seem to speak the local tongue. I switched to Condigeo. Tras's man didn't know that either, but hey, I hadn't practiced in a while. I was just finishing the Tale of the Suitors when we reached the graveyard.

" 'We bury all our dead here,' I said, and I took them among the graves.

"The Armadillo wagon ghosts came out to play. They couldn't touch us, of course, but they tried to attack *me*. Tras was used to ghosts. He forgot that his Lordsman guard wouldn't be. The guard was shivering and whimpering and trying to back through a boulder. Tras tried to interview one of the ghosts. I drifted behind three trees growing together, went between them and up, and hid myself.

"I talked through the treetops. 'Tras, there's something I should tell you, because you'll have to translate for me.'

" 'Where are you?'

" 'Behind you, Tras, always behind you. We know how to lurk. Tras, do you remember starting a riot? I tried to shut you up—'

" 'No, Whandall Feathersnake, you can't blame me for that!' And he laughed.

"His man had his nerve back. Tras spoke to him and he began circling around. He had me placed pretty quick. He pulled more armor from his pack, shin guards and stuff. Morth, I think there must have been some kind of turnover in Tep's Town. There's too much armor floating around in the great wide world. The gatherers from Armadillo Tribe had armor too.

"I said, 'Let's test your memory again. You know how Lord Pelzed's men left me. Do you remember?'

" 'That's not my fault either!'

" 'Tras, you will be in the same condition when I leave here. If you tell your man to protect you now, there won't be any living man to carry you away. I'll bury you here in the graveyard. If you tell him to step aside, he can take you someplace to heal.' "

Morth asked, "Did you think he'd do it?"

Whandall shrugged. "I gave him the chance. I don't know what he told his guard. When I dropped from the tree, the guard moved on me. I thought I'd have to kill him. He took some cuts and some bruises, and then he backed away protecting himself, and then he ran. Tras was gone.

"I tracked Tras down to the crypt and, well. I kept my promise. Then I slapped him awake and gave him some water, and I told him that if his man didn't come back for him by sunset of the next day, well. But if he did, there were stories I didn't want to hear. 'If I ever hear anyone describe how my household is arranged, or what kind of tea I serve, if I hear about a flask of gold sand' "—Whandall rapped his groin—" 'I will know who they heard it from.' I told him I travel everywhere, from Condigeo to Great Hawk Bay—I was lying, of course. I told him people are entitled to privacy, and some will kill for it. I'm not sure he heard any of that, Morth. I was raving. That diseased looker invaded my house. Nobody but the Armadillo Clan ever did that. Ask their ghosts."

Morth was silent.

"Tras wasn't hurt any worse than Samorty's men hurt me, but of course he's older. I don't know if he healed. He was gone at the next day's sunset."

And to hell with what Morth thought of him. Coming here wasn't Whandall's idea.

The night had turned cold, fire or no. They wore the cloaks Whitey had insisted they carry. Morth donned an impressive robe.

Whitecap Mountain broke the silence. "I know why the town of Fair Chance came to be deserted."

"That's a good story, but a partial truth," Morth said. "I sense a tribal secret at its heart. You won't tell *that*. As for me, my tale hasn't happened yet. My tale is that I must destroy the water sprite that wants my life. Living here is driving me mad."

"Go inland," Whitey said as if he was tired of repeating it.

"When I came here I was running from a wave. I climbed, thinking that water could not flow up so steep a slope. Water doesn't have to! A wave isn't a moving block of water, it's a pattern moving *through* water. The sprite can flow like a wave. It came to me through the ground water. It lives below me. When I go down to the spring, I go fast. I'll show you tomorrow, if you like."

Green Stone asked, "Is that safe?"

"Oh, you can watch from above. Get a view of the immediate danger. Whandall, what I want from you and your caravan is transport. Take me inland, out of its reach. Take me to the Hemp Road."

"You'd settle there?" Willow would love that!

"Oh, no," Morth said. "I'm going to *finish* this. I'm going to kill the water sprite. I think I have to return to the Burning City to do that."

Whandall said, "You're been trapped on a mountain for twenty years. This thing has hunted you for more than forty, and now you've decided to kill it. Is that about the size of it?"

Morth grinned in the yellow light of burning gold. "I can't tell you all of it."

"Morth, you can't even tell me *part* of it. You can't even get off this mountain!"

"That I might manage. I'd have to outrun the elemental. Water's natural path is downhill. I might run myself to death. But with transport to carry me farther, I might make it."

"And then you might just think you'd done all a man could do!"

"Once upon a time I thought I could rob Yangin-Atep's life. Steal the fire god's manna."

Nobody but Whandall laughed. The others had barely heard of Yangin-Atep; they couldn't know his power. Whandall asked, "What stopped you?"

"I saw less evidence of the god every decade. Yangin-Atep must be almost mythical by now, and I could never find where his life is centered. But the hope kept me there much longer than I should have stayed."

Whandall knew he was staring. "Why didn't you *ask*? Yangin-Atep lives in the cook fires!"

And he knew Carver's look: appalled and amused. Whandall had never learned to hoard information.

Morth paled. "In the fires. I'm a fool. I never asked the thieves!"

They were still arguing when it became impossible not to sleep. Whandall didn't remember whether he saw flowing rock, but the stone chairs were all stone couches in the morning.

CHAPTER
55

M orth stopped at a shallow rain-etched dip in the rock, damp at the bottom, to pick up a bucket. Then he led them to the edge of an abrupt drop. He pointed down along a bare rock face.

"See the streak where the rock changes color? That's overflow from the spring."

Whitey said, "Right."

Morth dropped over the edge.

Whandall could have caught his robe—would have, were he a child or a friend. But Morth wasn't falling. He was running down the mountain's side, weaving through the rubble. Once Whandall would not have believed what he saw. Morth dropped as fast as a falling man, zigzagging toward the gleam of water that marked the spring. He ran past it, dragging the bucket, and was already moving uphill, laughing like a maniac.

Water splashed up after him. Morth led it, still faster than a man, but he had been moving faster yesterday.

The men threw themselves backward as the wave came over the crest. Morth ran across the dip, emptying his bucket halfway, then turned and gestured. The wave crashed into the dip.

Morth was panting hard as they came up, but he was laughing too. Water half filled the dip. It lay almost still, rippling as if in a strong wind.

Whitey asked, "Wouldn't you love to be watching, *first* time he tried that?"

"I take it you can't trap it?" Whandall asked Morth.

"No, and enchanting the spring doesn't trap it either. A water elemental is a fundamental thing, and exceedingly slippery."

"All right. If this works, you'll owe Puma Tribe and my family too. Puma you can pay in refined gold," Whandall said. "Right, Whitey?"

Whitey nodded. "But ask Lilac. We change any oaths by mutual agreement only."

"My family might ask other things," Whandall said. "Tattoos, for instance. If we can get you as far as Road's End, the New Castle will ask three boons."

"I don't believe I can duplicate that tattoo."

Green Stone's disappointment didn't show at all. The boy was a natural trader. Whandall said. "We'll think of something. You pay in magic. Three tasks."

"I offered one."

"Did I accept? It got pretty sleepy last night."

Morth looked into Whandall's grin and decided not to make *that* claim. He said, "One when I'm free of the mountain. One at Road's End. One when the sprite is myth."

"Morth, you have no reason to think you can myth out a water elemental!"

Morth said nothing.

It's two wishes, then. "Done. It's . . . midmorning? And the sprite wouldn't stop us from going down? Whitey?"

"It stops Morth. Only trouble I ever had," the Puma said, "I tried to stop at the spring for a drink. Wagonmaster, I still think you should have taken gold. Wizard, we'll be down before nightfall. The wagon will move at first light, north to the trail and then east. *We don't stop.*"

"If I don't get down alive, the talisman box is yours, and the provisions in it. I renewed the spell. I'll enchant this one too before I go down."

Whandall said, "That's settled. Now tell the bird. Seshmarls?"

"Help me, Whandall Seshmarl—"

"Good bird. Morth, you tell the wagons—"

"Whandall, let me teach you how to make the bird carry your messages."

Whandall listened. He mimicked the bird's secret name, then spoke a few words. The bird looked at him in disgust.

Whandall grumbled, "My children learned all by themselves. Why don't I?"

"You have less magical talent than anyone I ever met," Morth said. "Interesting that your children don't share that disability."

"Disability."

Morth grinned. "You're an emptiness any god can fill. You just can't keep them out. Feathersnake Inn! And you'll never be a wizard, of course, but *this* you can learn."

Whandall practiced the bird's secret name, blowing the syllables out with puffed cheeks, then curling his tongue for the shrill whistle that ended it. He spoke his messages. "Tell the Puma wagons to return at their own pace. Whitecap Mountain has gold to pay them for their trouble. Rordray will get his boxes late. Late and loaded with red meat—mammoth if we can get it, elk or antelope or bison otherwise—and spices. Maybe we can find spices in the Stone Needles—"

"Keep messages *simple*," Morth said.

"Was that—"

"It's getting too long. Say, 'Message ends. Seshmarls, go.' "

"Message ends. Seshmarls, go."

"My hope lies in your shadow," the bird said, and took flight.

Whandall and the others began their descent. The sooner they were down, the better.

Lilac drove. Brush grew everywhere and the land was uneven. She had to be exceedingly careful until they reached flat ground, and wary after that. They wouldn't reach the trade road until after noon. A man on foot could run circles around them, Whandall figured, let alone a wizard.

They saw a column of mist drifting down the mountain and guessed at the waterfall within it.

Near the foot of the mountain Lilac made out a dot moving just enough to catch her attention. Whandall said, "Whitey? He might need help."

"Shall I hold his hand while he drowns?"

Whandall swung down from the wagon.

"I'll go. Tend your wagon." Whitecap Mountain dropped beside him and jogged away. Whandall lost track of him in some brush, and after that he was harder to see and moving faster.

There was something about weres, Whandall speculated. Did their magic—did *all* magic—work better when nobody watched? There must be things, processes, that an observer could not watch without altering them. . . .

Morth would know. Whandall jogged back to the wagon.

Sometime later Whitey strolled up carrying Morth's pack. Whitey stowed it and loped off to rejoin Morth.

Whandall wasn't sure they'd reached the trade road until late afternoon. Several times he was minded to ask Lilac to stop. The closer Morth got, the more those dots moved like a pair of cripples.

No danger showed. But Whandall could picture water flowing out of the ground into a mountainous bubble, over the wagon, bison drowning, Lilac and Green Stone drowning. . . . They should have brought a mer. A mer underwater could still act.

They came closer. Morth leaned heavily on Whitecap Mountain.

Whitey wasn't enjoying this at all. Morth looked like an old man dying of exertion. Dirty gray hair and beard, skin like cured leather, eyes too weary to look up. He was still moving faster than the wagon, but enough was enough. Whandall told Lilac to stop and let the bison graze.

They laid Morth in the wagon bed.

The sun was setting, but a full moon had crested the horizon. Whandall remembered a stream within their reach if they could keep going by night.

They were trying to reach water while they fled a water elemental. The irony did not escape Whandall's attention. Men could carry water, but bison must have a pool or stream. The path to Great Hawk Bay followed the water sources.

Ask Morth. . . . Morth was looking better already, but best to let him sleep.

CHAPTER
56

Rordray's massive dinner fed them all during the next day. Morth didn't eat much. His strength was slow returning even though he had packed *something* in the second cold iron box. *Talisman,* he said. *Don't look.* He reached in from time to time.

That night he slept like a dead man.

The next day he was fizzing with energy. Lilac taught him something of how to guide a bison team, just to keep him occupied. Later he went off with Whitey to hunt. They came back with half a dozen rabbits.

They camped and set the rabbits broiling while there was still light. Morth lifted a clay-capped vessel of wine, the last of what Rordray had packed, and offered it.

Whandall said, "Not for me. Morth, we should know more about what's chasing us. Who hates you that much? Where did they get something that powerful?"

"Oh, *that* was easy. They just diverted the nearest water sprite and sent it to kill me. It was moving an iceberg—" Morth laughed at their bewilderment. "The wells in Atlantis ran dry a thousand years ago. We used to send elementals south to break off mountains of ice and bring them to Atlantis for fresh water. The southland is all ice and untouched manna, because wizards can't survive there. Elementals gain immense power.

"But that's the real question, isn't it? *Why?* They were in a rage. They'd been in a rage for nearly a year. We all were."

"Why?"

"The Gift of the King." Morth carefully cracked the clay stopper and drank before he went on.

"We were the lords of magic. Our wealth made us targets for every barbarian who might hear tales of us, and the very land beneath us was trying to return to the sea. Every twenty, thirty years we'd lose a daywalk of beachfront. If Atlantis lost the skills of magic, it was all over.

"King Tranimel came to decide that the power of magic has no limit. It's as crazy as thinking a tribe of bandits can steal from each other forever—no offense, Whandall."

Whandall said, "After all, we don't *see* wealth being made. It just appears, always in somebody else's hands. We only need to gather it."

"You still say *we?*"

"*We Lordkin*. It's been a long time. So the King decided . . . ?"

"If wizards had held Atlantis above the waves for all these years, it must be that we can do anything. The King decided to make everything perfect."

Whandall could hear him grinding his teeth. Then, "Nothing is ever perfect, but Atlantis came closer than any nation on Earth. One day a King of Atlantis would achieve perfection. Tranimel would be that King.

"We wizards learn to use spells that do their work without showy side effects. Spells fail as time passes," Morth said. "A palace doesn't need to rise from the earth in a blaze of light. Better plows and crop rotation make fertility ceremonies more effective. You see? Less gets you more, if you do it right. But magic always looks too easy!

"The King, though willing to admit that water must run downhill, never seemed to understand that it must someday reach the sea. He passed laws that left us no clear avenue to refuse *any* act of magic that would improve the general well-being.

"Our first act was to give homes to the homeless folk of Atlantis. Thousands of architects, wizards, supervisors from the court, created housing across one whole mountain range: the Gift of the King. They needed *everyone*. For the first time in my life, I had enough money to live, money even for a few luxuries. I began seeing a girl. *Ah.*"

"Ah?"

"I just realized. It's been thirty years and I just . . ." Morth blinked, sipped wine, started over.

"Whandall, what the King intended would use the same manna that was keeping us above the waves. To use too much was the doom of Atlantis. *It's so simple.* How could the best wizards in the land be unable to explain what was *wrong* with the Gift of the King? I only *just* realized that we weren't trying very hard. The Gift of the King was employment for everyone. Wizards would get rich, architects would get rich, every court-appointed supervisor had a nephew who needed work."

"You weren't actually one of the best wizards, were you, Morth?"

"What? No. I served the southeast coast fishing industry. The mers catch all the fish; they herd them into nets to be pulled aboard boats. The men bring the fish in and store them; other men distribute them. We're needed to make weather magic and command the elementals, and the spell that floats a ship above the water sometimes needs reworking. It's all spelled out in books a thousand years old. Doesn't pay much. The Kingsmen didn't offer a choice, mind, but they offered twice what I was getting.

"Where was I? We built the Gift of the King. Along the north Atlantis loop a few farms drowned, some docks and warehouses slid beneath the water. But the homeless now had homes, more than they could ever use, we thought. And when a homeless person got in some citizen's way, or a thief, he or she was conveyed to the Estates.

"In the Estates a criminal class evolved within, it seemed, hours. Rape, armed theft, extortion, casual murder, all flourished in the shadows and corners. Bad enough, but the people of the Estates didn't stay there! Their hunting grounds expanded to all who lived nearby.

"The King couldn't have that! He ordained that there be light. Whandall, I would have lost my home without these magical projects. Glinda would have left me. I kept my mouth shut. I participated in the spell that caused every outside wall in the Estates to glow."

"Sometimes I have trouble thinking like a kinless," Whandall confessed. "Why did the King think that light would stop a gatherer?"

"Thieves, rapists, killers—*Lordkin*," said Morth, "don't commit their crimes in daylight if they think they'll be seen and punished. But the King stopped the punishments. He would cause no pain to his subjects. It was part of the Gift of the King.

"The Estates taught them that they did not need darkness to do whatever they wanted. This lesson they practiced the length and breadth of Atlantis, retreating to the Estates before anyone could hamper them.

"The King couldn't have that!"

"Calmly, Morth."

"Sometimes I miss my home." Morth fished the wine flask out of Whitey's hand and drank.

"It's under water, I take it."

"Taken for taxes. The King paid slowly. He couldn't collect taxes fast enough, and of course if we did get paid, some of it went for taxes; we never touched it. The mers used to pay in fish, but at least I got to eat the fish! The King's men who paid us also wanted to tell us how to do our jobs! And write down everything we'd done in crazy detail! And wait for payment until each and all were satisfied!

"I was ashamed to see Glinda. With all my heart I wished I'd never taken money from the King! It was too late. We were in thrall. And now the King had another idea.

"We were summoned for one massive, magnificent spell: a compulsion of novice's simplicity, but of huge effect.

"Every violent criminal—*not* every thief. One courageous wizard rightly pointed out to the King's advisor that no spell can make the subtle, vague distinction between a thief and a tax collector. On a good day, I honor him. On a bad day, I wish that the thieves and tax collectors had all been ensorcelled together."

"You're rambling."

"But that would have been fun." Morth handed the wine flask to Green Stone and drank from the water bucket. "We cast the spell, Whandall. On a morning nine days before the Lifting of Stone, every violent lawbreaker went to the City Guard to make his confession. And on that morning it was as if all Hell had let out for a holiday.

"Every guard station was surrounded. The criminals of the Estates outnumbered the guards forty to one. No natural inclination could have brought them together in any such cooperative venture, but they were here, and there was nothing to drink or eat or steal, but none who would dare interfere with them. The screaming of confessions alone drowned any cry for help. When they had satisfied their compulsion, they did what they felt like . . . and their will was to tear down the doors and murder the guards.

"At dawn any pair of guards found themselves surrounded by a score of . . . of *Lordkin* who first shouted their crimes in gory, hideous detail, more bragging than confessing. A guard told me that. *He* escaped by being a better climber than any burglar. By afternoon there was not a living City Guardsman outside the Guard stations themselves.

"The King was very angry with the wizards." Morth picked up the flask of wine with exaggerated care and drank.

"Was that when you left?"

"How could we leave? We had to collect the money the King still owed us. But first we had to correct the ill we had done. The King's men didn't have but the vaguest idea how that might be done, but they'd know it was done when the King showed himself satisfied. Then again, the Lifting of Stone was only six days away, and the Achean navy was preparing an attack—"

"Any Lordkin would have left *right then!*"

"I did."

"You did?"

"Do I look *stupid?*"

"Ask me if you look *drunk.*"

"I could see what was coming. We couldn't ever satisfy the King, but any wizard who wasn't seen trying would be axed. Seen trying had to mean something even a King's councilor could see, using manna we couldn't spare. The Lifting of Stone takes manna. The manna would be gone and the wizards would be exhausted. This year the Lifting of Stone just wasn't going to work.

"They'd taken my house and I didn't have anything to save except Glinda. I went to visit; I hinted at what I had in mind. Her brothers threw me out. She didn't stop them.

"I went down to the dock. Finding work was easy; all the other wizards were working for the King. The *Water Palace* had been sitting in dock for weeks—"

"A ship?"

"Right, one of the old ships that floats above the water. That style can cross land and ride above the big waves, but there are windows and cargo hatches on the underside, so it can't go anywhere at all without the occasional blessing. Over four days I convinced Captain Trumpeter to keep me aboard and get himself gone ahead of the Achean navy. I'd bless the ship at sea. We'd have been gone and free if the Acheans had been a little faster. I was half a world away before I knew what the priests had done to me."

Over many days they all exhausted their fund of stories. Communities were sparse and tiny and the tales they told were local gossip. A few memories stood out:

Farmers roasting a pit-killed mammoth and a harvest of spring vegetables. They were eager to share. By the smell of it, the meat had gone pretty high. Morth told them they were wizards cleansing themselves for a ritual. None could eat meat, except for (at his request) their driver. Watching Whitecap Mountain devour a mammoth kidney, Whandall thought that Puma must be part scavenger.

An elk challenged their wagon. They killed it, then wrestled it into the wagon bed. That afternoon they presented it to a loose cluster of a hundred farmers. By nightfall a meat and vegetable stew was ready to serve. A widow told of her late husband's year-long duel with what was believed to be a werebear. Lilac traded children's stories with the old wives' clique. Whandall told the tale of Jack Rigenlord and the Port Waluu woman.

It was a long, lazy time for Whandall. Responsibilities were bounded. At one town Whandall was tempted by a woman's offer. Dream of Flying was lovely by firelight, but he pictured Green Stone wondering where his father was sleeping, and then going to ask Lilac . . . and he told Dream that his wife was a powerful shaman and a mind reader too. She said that many husbands were sure of that; he agreed; the moment passed. The next morning he learned that offers had been made to each of them.

A good place to come back to.

On another night Whitecap Mountain told how the town of Fair Chance came to be deserted . . . and he found that all of the locals wanted to help him tell it. The tale went to babbling, then became a kind of throw-and-catch game . . .

They dug a pit to trap a mammoth.

They dug it well away from the town. No mammoth would come near dwellings, and if it did, there was no telling what damage it would cause.

They dug it big enough to hold such a beast and deep enough that the fall would kill it, and they covered the pit with redwood boughs and went home.

But before dawn they heard monstrous noise and felt the ground shake. When they spilled out to look, Behemoth itself had wedged its foot in the hole!

Houses were falling as the mountainous beast tried to tear loose. It saw the crowd arrayed to look, and it turned and bellowed at them. Its nose reached out and out, a day's walk long, and flung villagers left and right, windward and lee.

They ran in a tumble of falling houses, and they never came back, said Whitey. Two boys went back to look, another said. The company argued about what they found.

These farmers entertained guests rarely. Wizards were rarer still. They pulled Morth's story out of him, of how he had crossed the continent . . .

"We were safe at sea when the sea roared and sent a wave under the *Water Palace*'s windows. When we reached land there was no shore where men still lived. Making landfall where that monstrous wave had killed so many would not be prudent.

"The *Water Palace* sailed inland. We traveled for many days and ultimately set down at the town of Neo Wraseln, along a southward-facing shore. We rested less than a day before I stole the *Water Palace*."

A murmur rose from the farmers. "Gathered," Whandall said.

"No, I saved them all! I saw a wave of mist coming out of the ocean, and perceived an iceberg within the mist, and the elemental within the ice. I ran for the ship. I didn't have time to stop for any of the crew. I took it west to lure the elemental away from the town, then north, inland.

"At least I had someplace to go. In a dream I'd seen a tremendous wave smash the old Attic to rubble and roll onto the land, left and right as far as I could see. I recognized the Attic from the mers' description—"

Whandall said, "You sent word. Rordray told me."

"You'll be thinking I should have guessed the rest? But I can't foresee my own paths. The sinking of Atlantis took me completely by surprise. But I dreamed where Rordray would settle at Great Hawk Bay, and I sailed there. Ultimately they guided me to the Burning City, where magic doesn't work and a water elemental can't survive."

"And a wizard can't either," Whandall said, but Morth only shrugged.

CHAPTER
57

On the evening of the twenty-eighth day they camped in reach of a stream narrow enough to step across.

The water elemental had not shown itself since a waterfall followed Morth down Mount Carlem. "It prefers the sea, I think," Morth said. "Its time within the mountain must have been uncomfortable."

They had been approaching a range of hills for several days now. Whandall recognized this stretch. They would pass north of those hills. Another eight to twelve days, they'd be home. Now they were close enough to make out the spires that gave the place its name.

At night the Stone Needles glowed with manna, the wizard said, but only he could see it.

They moved at first light, Whandall driving.

Morth stirred. He scrabbled about in the wagon bed. Wrinkled around the eyes, white beard, gray-white hair, until he reached into the cold iron box. Then . . . well, nothing much changed. The talisman he'd made on Mount Carlem must be fading.

Around midmorning Lilac suddenly gasped, "Behemoth!" and pointed into the Stone Needles. The distant, misty heights ahead and right showed nothing.

Morth's head popped into sunlight. "What are you looking for?"

"I saw him! Behemoth!" Plaintively Lilac said, "I never saw him before."

Whitecap Mountain, strolling alongside the driving bench because it seemed to make the bison walk a little faster, was looking back down the road. "Wagonmaster, you may want to see this too."

Whandall stood up on the bench to look over the hood.

Dots in their wake, seven or eight men scattered across the road were watching the bison-drawn wagon. Now two jogged off in opposite directions.

"Could be farmers going about their business," Whitey said. "Could be bandits. A lone wagon makes a tempting target."

They were too distant, too slow to be seen moving, but dust in the air showed that they were following the wagon.

"They'll be a while catching up, won't they?"

"Oh, yes. They'll take their time. Sunset. We don't have any food, Morth."

They couldn't hunt with bandits about.

Whitey asked, "You know something of bandits, don't you, Whandall Feathersnake?"

"Yes, Whitecap Mountain. The first rule is, never separate the wagons or let them be separated."

"Better skip to the second rule."

Whandall stood to look back along the road. Men followed, far back and in no hurry. Those others who went jogging off would be bringing reinforcements or weapons or some stored magic, maybe a lurking spell.

"Never make half of a war," he said. "What do you think? If a Puma wearing a backpack and a man hideously scarred by a mad wizard's tattoo came loping back to meet them, would they run? Could we deal with them before anyone else comes? Kill them, frighten them, buy them off?"

Whitey said, "I think they can probably run almost as fast as you. If I run ahead, it's just me and them. Together we wouldn't catch them before nightfall, and if they've got friends they'd be right there to meet us. And if they sent friends ahead, who would defend the wagon?"

"All right. My third plan is, when they get close enough, I'll take off my shirt."

"Oh, *that* should scare them . . . you know, it might," Whitey acknowledged. "They might have heard of you."

Morth spoke. "Get me to the Stone Needles before they get to us, then leave the rest to me."

"That'll be tight," Whandall said.

"Try."

By noon the five had become a dozen. Whitecap Mountain drifted into the brush and was gone. Any bandits circling round might meet a Puma where it was least wanted. But a Puma could not attack a dozen farmers!

By midafternoon Stone Needles wasn't ahead anymore, it was a sixth of a circle rightward. The band following the wagon numbered around twenty. They were close enough that Whandall could make out hoes and scythes and less identifiable farm implements.

There was time to discuss it. If they turned off the path now, despite the rougher ground, it would tip bandits to where they were going. If the bandits broke into a run, attacked short of the Stone Needles, arrived panting and breathless, and fought in daylight—bad practice, but they'd win.

Lilac was driving. Whandall, watching the bandits, heard her say, "I saw it again!"

Morth exclaimed, "So do I!" and Whandall's head snapped around.

Behemoth, blurred by mist and distance, stood halfway up the Stone Needles. Mountains should have collapsed under it. Behemoth was even bigger than Whandall had seen it twenty-two years ago, all crags and angles, as if it had not fed well. Tusks to spear the moon. The shaggy hair that hung down everywhere was snow white, not piebald.

"That's not the same Behemoth," Whandall said. "There *must* be two. At least two."

Morth said, "I don't sense a god. Some lesser being."

It stood steady on legs like buttes, studying the tiny wagon. The long, boneless arm of its nose lifted in greeting or acknowledgment.

Lilac turned the bison straight toward Behemoth.

Whandall watched her do it. She didn't look at any of her companions, didn't invite comment.

Whandall stood up on the driving bench. He stripped to the waist and stood for a time, visible above the wagon's hood, in the near horizontal afternoon light.

The bandits were black shadows well beyond fighting range. Body language showed them in excited conversation, but they were still coming.

Whandall sat down. "I believe you have a family secret," he said to Lilac. "And that's fine, but does it threaten us?"

She said, "No."

Whandall let his eyes half close. He could relax for just a little longer.

Lilac said, "But we might be safer if I could tell someone."

"Speak."

Nothing.

"Does Whitecap Mountain know?"

"He might. He's of a different family. We haven't spoken of it," she said. "But I could tell my husband."

Green Stone jumped as if stabbed. "If you have a husband, I—"

"No! No, Stone."

Stone collected his tattered wits. "Should I be driving?"

Lilac shook her head violently.

"Green Stone, I believe I should speak for us now," Whandall said. "Lilac, would you accept my son as your husband? As wagonmaster I can declare you mated."

"Yes, subject to trivia related to dowry."

"Before we deal with *that* . . . are you taking us where you want us?"

Lilac smiled. Dimples formed. She hadn't looked back; she couldn't know exactly how close the bandits were. She was steering straight up into the mountains. "I thought Behemoth might frighten them off. *You* tried that."

Whandall stood to look back. "Well, they might be slowing down. You have a dowry?"

"It's mostly in goods, of course. We're not wealthy, Wagonmaster." She described possessions worth the price of a pair of good bison and a one-horn. "If you were to add"—about three times as much—"we could buy a wagon with that."

"Or I could buy a wagon for Green Stone. If you left him you'd still have enough to live on."

"But I wouldn't have a wagon," she said coolly.

On the mountain above, Whandall had marked out an imaginary line. Cross that line and he would be where Behemoth could crush his tiny wagon in one step, but they hadn't reached it yet.

"Our *children* and I wouldn't have a wagon," she mused.

He said, "Lilac, it's not easy to set a price on your family secret until you describe it. As for the rest, do your other suitors have families so eager as mine? We'll be at Road's End in twelve days or so. You could ask around. The wagons won't return from the Firewoods for another fifty, but you might get some sense of what offers await you. Come to me then."

He didn't say, *Have you other suitors?* He didn't say, *And we'll see what the one-horns say.*

But Lilac was glaring. "Does it strike you that a one-horn might improve *my* bargaining position?"

The truth was, it hadn't. Whandall sensed how much Green Stone wanted to speak. He did not look at his son. "I can mate you under two oaths. One or the other will bind us all, depending on what the one-horns say."

"Have we *time* for this?"

Big as he was, Behemoth shifted uneasily. The wagon had crossed that imaginary line and was within his range. Whandall stood up for a quick look back. The bandits had stopped in the road.

He asked, "Do you understand the term *glamour?* Appearance altered or enhanced by magic? Some women cast a glamour by instinct, with no training at all. Others are accused unjustly. It's why lovers don't bargain for themselves if they have family."

"You know I've cast no glamour! After seventy days' traveling? Look at me!"

Lilac was a good-looking woman, and no illusion, with the road's dirt under her nails and in her hair. If they hadn't all been so afraid of water these past forty days . . . curse! They'd all have been better traders!

"Suppose I just suggest," he said, "that mammoths also can cast a glamour. Hugeness is theirs, but they cast an appearance even more vast. Dead, they lose that power. A live mammoth trapped in a pit might seem to be Behemoth struggling to free his foot—"

She stared straight ahead, her face set like stone.

"But a mammoth could still crush this wagon, and if he's as close as he seems distant . . . Did you say something?"

"Where are the bandits?"

He stood and looked back. "Just watching." And ahead. "So's Behemoth. Lilac, I accept your terms." After all, it wasn't an argument he wanted to win. The Feathersnake wagons could not afford to look cheap! "I'll buy you a wagon. Your family can buy the team. You are a fine trader." *Even though you haven't fooled Feathersnake!*

"Thank you." She smiled: dimples again. Behind them, Green Stone whooped.

"But now I'd *really* like to extend the trade route. There are getting to be just too cursed many of us."

Morth jumped down from the wagon. "We're high enough." He straightened and was taller than he had any right to be. Behemoth backed up a step, then cocked an ear to whatever Morth was bellowing in throaty Atlantean speech.

Then the god-beast's arm uncoiled, reached out and over the wagon and down.

The farmer-bandits scattered, tripping over each other. Their piping screams rose up the mountain.

Morth was dancing on the hillside. "Yes! See that, you apprentice bandits! I'm a wizard again!" He saw his companions staring. He said, "I persuaded the beast that those rural Lordkin are bushes covered in cranberries."

The vast rubbery arm rose up and coiled back across the sky holding . . . a bush torn up by its roots, or the illusion of one. Not some luckless sodbuster-turned-bandit. Those were scattered the width of the path and further, running west.

Behemoth fed itself, chewed, found nothing in its mouth, bellowed, and reached again after the running bandits.

Something called from far above: a distant trumpet plaintively played by a madman.

Behemoth turned to answer. Whandall slammed his hands over his ears. A madman's trumpet screamed inside his head, the sound of the end of the world, or the end of all music. Behemoth turned away, toward the peak, and started to climb.

CHAPTER 58

There was water, but no stream was close enough to be a danger. It seemed a reasonable place to make camp.

Morth opened one of the talisman boxes and took something out, faster than Whandall could shield his eyes. "Used up," he said. "I can't even reenchant it."

Lilac was looking too. The doll was crude, of barely human shape. It had a wild white beard and long white braided hair, blue beads for eyes, and something like Morth's color.

Whandall asked, "Does it lose magic if too many people see it? Is that why you didn't want to show it?"

Morth didn't answer.

"Or were you just embarrassed?"

Morth laughed. "I'm no artisan." He tossed it away. "I'll make another tomorrow."

Around sunset an animal stalked the camp half seen; and then Whitecap Mountain stood among them.

"You're in time," Whandall said, and among the company assembled, Whandall Feathersnake declared Green Stone Feathersnake mated to Lilac Puma. At this time he exercised his first wish, and Morth wove a blessing of good luck on the marriage.

Afterward he told Whandall, "You know the spell won't work except in the most barren of places."

"Then they'll know where to go when things go wrong. If Willow and I had known *that*, that first year . . ."

Morning. Morth bounded from his blanket, lean and bony and agile as a contortionist, and howled in joy. Whitecap Mountain snapped awake with a hair-raising snarl. Green Stone and Lilac came running to see what the commotion was. They'd made their bed in a thicket last night.

"No problems," Whandall shouted. "Just Morth—"

"Whandall! See this? Rosemary." Morth pointed out the plant he meant.

Lilac shouted, "We'll collect some, Father-found!" and they ran off.

Morth said, "I'm going up. Climb with me. Maybe we'll find thyme too."

Whandall looked up. The mountain seemed to rise forever, and this time there would be no magic to make it easier. "How high?"

"Not far. Manna's blazing all over this mountain. I'll be back before noon." Morth was bouncing around like a happy ten-year-old. As a hiking mate he would be a pain.

"If you find thyme, tell us. I'll pick what's here."

The wizard began running. Whandall shouted, "Hold up, Morth," and pointed to a plant. It seemed to be growing everywhere, knee high and pallid white. "What's this? How can a plant live if there's no green to it?"

"I don't know it." Morth picked a leaf and nibbled the edge. "It's nothing Rordray would want, but I taste magic."

Whandall half filled a pack with rosemary. No need to keep spices in a talisman box. He didn't doubt Green Stone and Lilac would collect more in their copious free time. Maybe he'd try it in his cooking. They'd have more than Rordray needed.

From time to time he ran across a stone spire. They were all over the place, growing thicker uphill.

Noon, and Morth wasn't back.

This wasn't the wild magic that drove Morth crazy. No gold around here. Was there? It didn't *look* like places where he had seen gold.

Whandall began climbing. Morth might have gotten lost or stepped on.

The view was wonderful. The breath in his lungs was clean and rare. Stone pillars stood about him. This was heady stuff even for a man with no magical sense.

He shouted, "Morth!" and "Morth of Atlantis, are you lost?" but never with real concern. He didn't think that anything here could hurt a wizard in his full power . . . except that any other magic thing would be in *its* full power. Behemoth, say, or last night's trumpeter, which might be another Behemoth.

A thousand huge stone spires protruded through the ground. They didn't look like natural formations. Here and there stood a stone ridge looking almost like the rib cage of something ages dead. Bone-white primitive-looking scrub grew everywhere. Sage and rosemary grew too. Whandall picked some sage.

Once he looked down and was shocked at how high he'd climbed. Yet the peak pulled him on.

The way grew more difficult. Then insanely difficult. Whandall kept climbing. It just didn't occur to him to turn back. The mountain grew more wonderful as it rose. Now he was finding steps in the most difficult places, stairs hacked at seeming random into the naked rock. No, not hacked: rock had *flowed.*

A man was watching him from high above.

The sun had burned him black . . . like Morth on the mountain, Whandall thought, though his beard and hair were wild gold and he wasn't wearing any clothes at all. The Stone Needles Man watched in silence, and Whandall wondered what he would sound like.

"Thyme," he called up. "There's a plant called thyme, but I don't know what it looks like."

"Who are you?" The Stone Needles Man sounded raspy and unpracticed, a voice unused for a long time.

Whandall started to tell him. His mere name didn't seem adequate, so he told more; but wherever he tried to start his story, something earlier was needed—Morth, the Hemp Road, the caravan, the Firewoods—until he was babbling about kinless woodsmen in the redwoods around Tep's Town. He climbed as he spoke, and that had him gasping. The man watched and listened.

Even close, Whandall couldn't guess his age, wasn't even sure he was human. Something odd about his nose, or his scowl. Maybe he was were.

"Thyme," the old man said, "there," and pointed with his nose. "All through that patch of dragon nip."

"That's the white stuff?" Whandall had to go back down by a little to reach it.

"Um. I could call it mammoth nip; they like it too. Thyme is grayish green stuff, grows low to the ground. Yes, that. Rub a leaf in your fingers and sniff. Never forget *that* smell."

"Nice."

"I used it in the stew. Come eat." The old man started to climb higher yet. He turned once and said, "I want *your* lunch."

"Agreed."

"Um. I get tired of goat. Keep changing the spices—it's still goat. What've you got?"

"Nothing."

The man turned on him a look of baffled rage. Whandall felt ashamed. "I didn't know I was going to keep climbing," he said, and that led him to wonder, *Where do they think I went?* He should do something about that. The wagon was a fantastic distance below him, and the sun was halfway down the sky.

But they'd climbed to the top of the world, and here was a small neat garden and a fireplace and an animal skin shelter set on poles. Stew was simmering. Whandall was suddenly ravenous.

Morth lay by the fire. He looked dead.

The Stone Needles Man pulled the stew off the coals. "Don't try to eat yet. Burn yourself."

"Morth?" Whandall knelt by the wizard. Morth was snoring. Whandall shook him. It was too much like shaking a corpse.

"What happened to him?"

"Got curious. You got a bowl? Cup? Good." He took Whandall's cup and scooped stew into it. Whandall blew to cool it. Tasted.

"Good!" Meat, carrots, corn, bell pepper, something else.

"Sage and parsley, this time. It's always the same except for the spices. I have to grow the parsley. The rest is all around us." And the old man chuckled.

"Feels like I've known you forever," Whandall said. "I was trying to remember your name."

"Born Cath—no, *Catlony.* Barbarians called me Cathalon. Later I called myself Tumbleweed. Just kept rolling along, following the manna. Wound up here. Call me Hermit."

"I was Whandall Placehold, and Seshmarl. Now Whandall Feather-snake. What happened to Morth?"

At the sound of his name, Morth rolled out of his sleep. "Hungry!" he said. He scooped a bowl of Hermit's stew. Whandall tried to talk to him, but Morth paid no attention.

Hermit said, "Came up here this morning. We talked. He's a braggart."

"He's got a lot to brag about."

"You know, I may be the safest man in the world. The oldest love spell in the world is parsley, sage, rosemary, and thyme. I grow the parsley and the rest of it covers the whole mountain. You're inside a love spell."

Whandall looked around him in surprise. "Great view too!"

"I never learned to talk to people. Reason I kept moving. Never liked anyone I met. They never liked me. Anyone who can reach me up here, he's welcome."

"I'm lucky you didn't send me back down for your lunch," Whandall said. "I'd have gone."

The old man's face twisted. "Idiot. You'd starve on the way! And be climbing in the dark!"

"Hah. You're inside a love spell too!"

The Hermit stared, horror widening his eyes. Whandall laughed affectionately. He asked again, "What happened to Morth?"

"Hungry!" said Morth. "Burm my mouf. Curf!" He went on eating.

"Morth of Atlantis wanted manna," the Hermit said. "And food. I *did* eat *his* lunch, so I started some stew. But he wanted manna, so I said, 'Climb one of the fingers and touch the tip. Get yourself a real dose.' "

"Fingers?"

Hermit waved at a stone pillar twelve feet tall. "Morth heaved himself up to the top of that. When he floated down I could perceive the manna blazing up in him. He said, 'Yes! There's a god in there. Under. Feel a little sleepy.' And he curled up and stayed that way till now."

"Fingers? What's going on?" Suspicion . . . wouldn't come.

"Giant with ten thousand fingers. I've tried to feel its thoughts, but I can't. Too self-centered. I was that way when I came up here, and it's been so long. If I lost touch with the manna hereabouts, I'd dry up like an Egyptian corpse."

"But there's a god under the ground?"

"Feathersnake, did a god touch you? There's a trace in your aura."

"Yangin-Atep and Coyote both."

"So another touch wouldn't kill you."

A giant under the ground?

Suspicion would have made sense, but the Stone Needles Man wouldn't let him hurt himself, would he? He couldn't believe it. Whandall climbed the stone finger and laid the palm of his hand on top.

The land was in a coma of starvation.

Once these expanses of narcotic white weed had lured dragons out of the sky, down to the ridges where they could feed. Then stone fingers closed on them and they were lost. The bones of dragons remained, ossified stone ribs.

But dragons were gone now. Ten thousand huge fingers poked from the ground, questing for prey gone mythical. Flesh alone was not enough to feed a near god. Mammoths were big enough and had magic too, but they ate the dragon nip and avoided the fingers. A mammoth's long nose was perfect for that.

The Giant had been dying for ages, in a sleep as deep as death.

"Sleepy," Whandall said, stumbling back to the fire. "Hungry," as a whiff of stew reached him. He scooped more stew from the pot, working around Morth's hand, barely aware that they were both burning themselves. He ate and then slept.

"I remember when dragon nip grew taller," Hermit said. It was morning, and he wasn't likely to be interrupted. Morth and Whandall were eating. "Thousand years ago. I think it learned to grow shorter than what dragons could pull up. Plants do fight back, you know."

The pot was clean. Whandall licked his bowl. He wondered if he was being rude, but the Hermit was amazingly rude, and so what?

Morth asked, "What did you tell them, down there?"

"Nothing," Whandall said.

"They'll be going crazy. I'd better send a message."

The rainbow-colored crow came at his call. It settled on his shoulder, listened to a whispered message, then winged away.

Morth said, "We should be going too." He didn't stand up.

Hermit picked up a hollowed-out ram's horn. He asked, "Want to ride down?"

"Ride?"

The Hermit blew into the horn. Morth and Whandall winced away from a blast of sound, the sound of Behemoth screaming. Faintly an echo rose from below. No, wait, that wasn't . . .

From behind a granite mass too small to hide him, Behemoth stepped into view, and *reached*. Whandall threw himself flat beneath nostrils big enough to swallow a wagon. "I believe I'll walk—"

"Yes, indeed," Morth babbled, "but thank you *very* much—"

"Come visit any time," Hermit said. "People *do* visit. They never hurt me or rob me. It's getting rid of them, that's the trick. They taught me to be rude."

"They did not," Morth said immediately.

The Hermit snickered. "Well. No, but I get tired. The cursed *language* changes every few years and I have to learn to talk all over again. I do get lonely, though. Come again."

The wagon was in sight, and Green Stone was closer yet and climbing. Morth said, "It wasn't just different customs. He's crazy."

Whandall smiled. "Likable, though. He keeps giving things away. Anyone who comes here for the spices will *have* to climb, I think, and be glad he did."

Then Green Stone, gasping too hard to speak, was nonetheless demanding where they'd been for two days and nights.

Three bison-drawn wagons were in view, way off down the road.

When Whandall's wagon reached the flats, they were closer yet. His own bison were glad to stop and graze while they waited. Whitey loped off west to make contact.

Feathersnake's other wagon and two Puma wagons pulled up around sunset. Carver told him, "We were worried. A talking bird isn't a message we could verify."

"Did bandits give you any trouble?"

"No. This last village, there wasn't anyone in it. You didn't—"

"I never touched them! They just ran away. Must have thought you'd bring Behemoth down on them."

CHAPTER
59

The two Puma wagons rolled past the New Castle's gate. The Feathersnake wagons stopped. Green Stone helped Lilac down. Whandall waved Morth back before Morth could join them.

Where was everyone? "We sent the cursed bird," he said.

"We'll take care of it," Green Stone said. "Go on, Father."

"Tell Willow that I have brought Morth of Atlantis and will take him to Road's End. He will not be coming in."

"Right."

Whandall set his own wagon moving and looked behind to see Carver's wagon following. They had left considerable cargo in Green Stone's care. He didn't intend to pay storage and tax on all of this!

Every wagon fit to roll was gone from Road's End. The two Puma wagons were on their sides, stripped of their covers and their wheels. Puma guarded stacks of cargo. Carver went searching for the repair crew. Chief Farthest Land's men had to be found to open the warehouses—

"I could do that," Morth said.

"Better if they don't know it. Hello, that's . . ." Whandall called, *"Twisted Cloud!"*

"Whandall Feathersnake!" Twisted Cloud made her way toward them, but she was limping. Two boys ran ahead of her. "You're back in good time!"

"Yes, but why aren't you with the caravan?"

"I broke an ankle. Patch of mud wasn't dry yet. It's almost healed, but I couldn't stand at all when the caravan rolled. I had to send Clever Squirrel." Her daughter, Coyote's daughter. Whandall's daughter, some would say. An obligation if Twisted Cloud cared to make it one, but she never had, beyond the wagon Whandall had bought for her daughter. "The wagon's hers, and she's old enough now."

"She was born old enough. Twisted Cloud, this is Morth of Atlantis, of whom you've heard tales. You're both wizards—"

"Yes, I can see the glow," Twisted Cloud said.

"And you, there's a familiarity. Like Whandall. A god has been in you?" She blushed. "Well . . . yes."

The boys watched and listened with interest. Boys would not be introduced until they discovered their names . . . as Green Stone found malachite in a cave, or as his father's tales of the Black Pit shaped Saber Tooth's dreams.

"Did you come to join the caravan?" Twisted Cloud asked.

Morth said, "Yes, to reach the Burning City."

Whandall said, "I fear Morth has been sniffing raw gold—"

"Whandall, I can't tell you more! Your mind is open to too many gods, and the gods of fire and trickery all seem to be related."

Twisted Cloud said, "But the wagons are all gone!"

Whandall said, "Yes. Morth, they left when we did, as soon as the Hemp Road became passable. You'll be here until spring. That gives you most of a year to come to your senses!"

"And then the caravan goes only as far as the Firewoods," Twisted Cloud said.

"Curse," Morth said. "I'd lose all the power I gained on the mountain."

Whandall noticed that the band around the Puma wagons had grown. "I need to do some business," he said.

"I'll scrape up a meal for us," Twisted Cloud offered.

"Here, I brought back some spices."

Chief Farthest Land's men made meticulous records as Whandall stored his gatherings. They took a percentage of the estimated value. It was worth it to most traders, and to Whandall too, up to a point. The New Castle was the only hold in these parts that could be called safer than the Chief's safehouse.

Then again, like the Spotted Coyotes, or the Toronexti in Tep's Town, Chief Farthest Land *insisted*.

No doubt the Chief knew—*very* likely his clerks knew—that not everything Whandall brought home came this far. He had never made a point of it, and Whandall didn't abuse the privilege.

Whandall completed arrangements for repairs on his own wagons. Puma had arrived first; their wagons would be repaired first. Give them

Morth's preserving box full of Whandall's spices to carry to Great Hawk Bay. They'd be back before the autumn rains.

He returned to Twisted Cloud's fire and a rosemary-flavored bison stew.

Morth's youth, restored in the Stone Needles, had gone to hale middle age. Twisted Cloud had put on some weight since their encounter with Coyote, and birthed six children too, four still alive. Still a good-looking woman, she had a round face made for laughter.

"The tribes just don't get it," she chortled. "They think I should have seen it coming and walked around the mud patch!"

"It's like looking at the tip of your own nose," Morth agreed. "Your own future is all blurred. I saw the great wave from the sinking of Atlantis and missed the sinking itself!"

"Got clear, though."

"Lucky. Fated. Whandall told you? But there are things he couldn't have known. . . ."

There were three guesthouses at Road's End: low pits with tents over them. Rutting Deer and Mountain Cat ran these and lived in one. In the absence of her wagon, Twisted Cloud was using one. Her boys had moved Morth's baggage into the third while he took care of some business matters.

Now the wizards were verbally dancing around each other, each trying to learn what the other knew, hoarding secrets for later trade. Whandall tried to follow their talk, feeling more and more left out. Presently he went off to his travel nest to sleep.

CHAPTER
60

Without a wagon and team it was only a four-hour walk home. Whandall and Carver didn't hurry. Evening fell, and a long twilight. It might be the last peace they saw in some time.

The pile of goods was gone from the New Castle's gate. They parted there. Carver went on to the Ropewalk. Whandall went in.

The New Castle was a household disrupted by sudden marriage. Willow had put Green Stone and Lilac in the guesthouse. Stone's room wasn't enough to house two, and the noise . . . well, newlyweds were *expected* to be noisy. It was hours before Whandall and Willow could retire.

The bird had returned to Willow. "He's a good messenger," she said, "but next time, *you* speak the messages. I still flinch from Morth's voice."

"I will. And we have a wish coming." Whandall grinned in the dark. "Yes, we have a wizard's boon. There were two, but I used one. You awake?"

"Tell it."

He launched into his story. "Morth blessed Lilac and Green Stone's marriage," he concluded. "Now we've reached Road's End, so he owes us a second wish. He'll find someone to take him to Tep's Town. He'll die there, I think. We should collect before he goes south, but that won't be before spring."

"What shall we wish for?"

"Something for Saber Tooth? If he was affianced I wouldn't even hesitate, but we've got a married daughter now. We can give the wish to Hawk In Flight, or her firstborn. Too bad we'll never get our third wish."

"*Our* lives are perfect?"

"Yeah."

"Just asking." Willow stirred in his arms. "I thought of asking Morth to leave our family alone forever."

"That's easy magic."

"A waste. Some gift for our children's children? Ask him if he can do that."

Hawk In Flight had never been happier than when planning her own marriage. Now, seven weeks a wife, she entered the field as an expert. She and Willow began planning a formal wedding for Lilac and Green Stone when the caravan returned.

The celebrants were seen only at mealtimes.

Whandall kept himself occupied.

The bison had been well kept, but they needed exercise. The men who worked the New Castle had complaints they could not bring to Willow. He must hear them out and make judgments. Two must be married. Two needed a shaman's attention (and six *thought* they did). A woman must be put on the road. Her man went with her, and now they'd need a new blacksmith.

Whandall went up to the graveyard by day to pull weeds and tend flowers. Willow visited the hives nearby. Whandall didn't go with her. Willow must keep treaty with the queen bees; they didn't deal well with men.

"But you didn't get stung?"

"No," said Willow. She showed him bees still exploring her hands.

"Well, rumor says the Tep's Town bees are above First Pines this year. They mate with local queens, and then all the worker bees grow little poison daggers. Twisted Cloud calls them *killer bees*."

He went to the graveyard again at midnight to keep his peace with the dead, lest they grow restless. It was always freshly surprising, how the dead accumulated over a man's lifetime. Old friends; two children; no other family, and that was rare.

Whandall talked to them, reminiscing, while they hovered around him. It was hard to tell their thoughts from his own.

The twisted ghosts from Armadillo Wagon had raged at him for years after that business at the Ropewalk. Tonight they were not to be seen. Ghosts did fade . . . or perhaps the fools had tired of his jeering.

Three days of that, and then Lilac joined her prospective mother and sister. The servantwomen were drawn into that circle. The servantmen and

Green Stone showed the same sense of abandonment that Whandall could feel nibbling at his own composure.

"The magic goes away," he told Green Stone. They were where the women couldn't hear. "It's the great secret of the age."

Green Stone said, "The honeymoon, we tell each other it fades. Father, it happened too soon."

"Maybe you started early? I'm not asking," Whandall said, "only musing."

Green Stone was silent.

"Hey, this place will survive without us. I should supervise repair of the wagons. Three days. Want to come along?" He could exercise the bison too. Hitch all six to one wagon.

The Puma wagons were upright again, looking almost new and ready to go. There were no bison about, nor Puma tribesmen either. They would be out finding fresh bison to catch and tame.

Two of the repair crew were about. He'd expected to find more. They tried to rag him about hitching six bison to one wagon. Whandall made up a story about a troll sometimes seen on the road. The troll was willing to bargain, a bison for two men. This time they'd missed him. Might meet him coming back.

Whandall spent several hours inspecting his wagons and arranging repairs, taking it as an opportunity to teach Green Stone.

Then he and Green Stone made their way toward White Lightning's workshop. Lightning wouldn't be awake in daylight, but it was near sunset and the days were getting long.

Most boys found their own names, but White Lightning had been named for the lightning blast that left his pregnant mother blind and deaf for nearly a year. The baby she bore had skin as white as snow. He was a good glassworker, strong and skilled, but he couldn't travel. The sun would burn him badly.

White Lightning was peering into a white-hot coal fire through the slits in a soaked leather mask. Stone and Whandall closed the door flap and waited, standing well clear. White Lightning pulled a gob of glowing glass out of the fire on the end of a long tube. He blew into the tube to make a globe, stretched it, twisted it. Now he had two lobes joined by a narrow neck. Lightning set it gently in a box of black powder and rolled the powder over it. Then he picked up the black double bottle with wooden paddles and danced it into an oven that was cooler, darker than the fire he'd been using, and closed the door on it.

"Dexterous," Whandall said. "You look good."

Lightning turned without surprise. "I never felt better in my life. Hello, Whandall Feathersnake. Ah—"

"Green Stone is now a married man."

"Boy, you all grow faster than I can catch up. Feathersnake, what's your need?"

"Lamps. Twenty, if you'll give us the quantity discount."

Lightning doffed his mask. His face was chalk white, but there weren't any sores, and his eyes looked good. "You need them before fall?"

"No."

"Then, sure, take eight for seven."

"Oh, *all* right, make twenty-four. What are you making now?" Whandall saw Lightning hesitate. "Don't tell me secrets—"

"He didn't say so. One bottle, but it has to be perfect. Glass glazed with iron. Wizards! But he's a *great* medicine man." Lightning stretched on tiptoe. "Every joint doesn't hurt! I can see again too!"

"He wants a *black* bottle?"

"Come see it after I've fired it. I'll get two this way. He can take his choice."

Rocks burned in a circle of rocks. Morth of Atlantis sat with his back to a small fire so that he could face Twisted Cloud. The medicine woman sat so far back that her face was in darkness. It looked awkward. Stone and Whandall joined Morth, backs to the fire.

Whandall asked, "Gold?"

"Right," Twisted Cloud said. "For years they've been paying me in river gold. Time comes when wild magic is needed; it's good to have, I suppose, but what can I do with it otherwise? Finally comes a man who can refine it for me."

"A pleasure," Morth said.

Whandall couldn't exactly ask after Coyote's daughter. When he had the chance he asked Twisted Cloud, "How's the wagon holding up?"

"That was Mountain Cat's work, wasn't it? Eight years, and we've only had that one broken axle, and twice a wheel. It's Clever Squirrel's first time out alone, but she'll be fine too. She's been running the wagon since she was fifteen," her mother said. "I just go along for the ride.

"It's *her* wagon. Her dowry, given by Whandall," Twisted Cloud said to Morth, "though she's Coyote's daughter. Feathersnake, I don't think she'll marry."

"Oh, she'll find her man," Green Stone said. Coyote's daughter was his weird half-sister; his tone was proprietary. "She's just—exploring. He'll have to be someone who doesn't listen to unicorns. He'll need courage, too."

Morth asked, "Wagonmaster, have you settled on a wish?"

"Not yet. Where can I find you when I do?"

Morth glanced at the shaman. "I'll be in the guesthouse while I take care of some business here. Then back to the Stone Needles. Plenty of manna there. I'll take things for the Hermit, make myself welcome."

"Fascinating place, it sounds like," Twisted Cloud said. "Maybe I'll visit."

"You'll *love* the Hermit."

Twisted Cloud laughed. "But he's very accommodating, you say."

"I'll wait there for spring," Morth said. "Travel with the caravan, leave them at the Firewoods, go on into Tep's Town. I'd like it if you came, Whandall."

Whandall shook his head. "I promised Willow, long ago. Promised myself too."

"Weren't you telling me," Morth asked, "that you want to extend the trade route? Find more customers, peddle more exotica, hire everybody's children . . . ?"

"I'm looking around, that's true. But my children are able, Morth. We raise them that way. They'll find another path, or make one." Whandall didn't look at Green Stone, but the boy was listening.

Morth said, "Puma holds the path to Rordray's Attic. No room for you. But the Lords in Tep's Town, what've they got that's worth having?"

Whandall held his arms straight out. The left was shorter than the right and a little crooked. "I'm not wanted in the Lordshills," he said, "and they did this to prove it."

"That was then. You'll go back as a looker—"

"I've heard this tale before."

"More than a looker. You have a reputation. After twenty years and more of ships carrying tellers, the tales are bound to have reached the ears of Lords and kinless too."

"Kinless won't deal with a Lordkin!"

"Then again, do *Lordkin* have anything worth trading?"

"Well, yes, if you'll allow that some kinless is carrying it for us, but you still can't think that Wolverines or Owl Beaks or Water Devils will deal with a man from Serpent's Walk!" Whandall didn't speak of the deaths in his own family, the ruin that had dogged Morth. Morth *knew* those dangers. Whandall couldn't yet believe the wizard was serious. "I'd be crazy to go back. You too. Get away from that—" He gestured behind him at the fire of gold ore. "Get your head right. Think it over then."

"Are you enjoying your return to domesticity?"

"Very much."

"All the same, didn't you leave debts behind you in Tep's Town?"

"Nothing I could ever pay," Whandall said.

Green Stone spoke for the first time. "What's it like?"

Morth spoke of running a shop among kinless and Lordkin. Somehow Whandall found himself telling of how he'd played with the ghosts in the Black Pit. Then Morth again. . . . Whandall's family knew his tales of Tep's Town, and had heard Willow's tales too, but Morth was speaking secrets he'd never known.

It was late before they slept.

CHAPTER
61

The next day Mountain Cat and three more repairmen were all at work on Puma wagons. Whandall and Green Stone watched for a bit, talked to them a bit. Then they worked on the Feathersnake wagons. They left both wagons on blocks, each with missing wheels.

Whandall had bought three new wheels to replace the old, not because they were ruined, but to show Green Stone how to dismount and then mount a wheel. Green Stone had to know this stuff!

But they'd mount the wheels tomorrow. If the mad wizard took it into his head to run for Tep's Town *tonight,* he would not ride a Feathersnake wagon.

It was rare that Whandall Feathersnake remembered Tep's Town. What would his brothers say, watching him make repairs ahead of a band of kinless so he wouldn't have to pay them as much?

Enough of the day was left for hunting. Hunting was better while the wagons were gone from Road's End. They bagged a deer and some onions and brought it all back to become the evening's dinner. Twisted Cloud and her boys and Rutting Deer set potatoes, corn, and bell peppers to roasting too.

Dinner would be late. It took time to roast a deer. They told stories of Tep's Town while they waited.

"Lookers blame the fire god," Morth said. "Kinless blame the gatherers, and a natural human lust for what others have. I believe the curse on Tep's Town is a pattern of habits, rather than the baneful presence of a moribund fire god."

Green Stone asked, "What do you do to break patterns?" When nobody had an answer, he asked, "What does it look like? Lordkin all stand around waiting for someone to set a fire?"

"Come and see," Morth said to him. Then to Whandall, "Was there treasure you couldn't carry away with you? Enemies who couldn't touch a caravan master? If there ever was a chance to set things right in Tep's Town, this is your *best* chance. You'd go with a wizard. You'll carry refined gold."

This was beginning to make Whandall uncomfortable.

"I'll invest some gold with you myself," Twisted Cloud said. "I like the trade possibilities."

"I bet you do, Coyote's woman." Her attitude had Coyote's touch! Any risks would belong to Morth and Feathersnake, but new trade routes would be shared by Bison Clan and every wagon served by the Road's End shaman. Whandall asked, "Gold refines itself in Tep's Town, doesn't it, Morth?"

"Yes—"

"The wild magic leaks away? And your wizardry won't work either. Whatever you have in mind, try to remember that. Dinner's starting to smell wonderful, Cloud—"

When Rutting Deer and the boys went to retrieve the food, some glowing lizard thing leaped at them out of the burning rocks.

Whandall Feathersnake got his blade between them and the threat. Something like a Gila monster stood up four feet high and screamed at him, and as it came at him Whandall wondered if he'd finally bitten off more than he could chew. But it tried to eat his knife, and died.

"I never saw a thing!" Rutting Deer cried. "Oh, curse—" A quarter of deer lay in the dirt.

"Something changed by the gold. A lizard, maybe," Twisted Cloud said. "Deer, it's not your fault."

Whandall thought of work to be done tomorrow. If he went to bed now he could rise early.

Whandall woke before dawn. Green Stone was not in his blanket. Voices from Twisted Cloud's dying fire—wood, for the gold had run out—suggested that they'd been talking all night.

For White Lightning it would be near bedtime.

He was still up. With pride he showed off a black glass bottle. Another firing had glazed it. There were rainbow highlights in the black finish. He'd made a glazed glass stopper in the same fashion.

"So, and this one is second best?"

White Lightning laughed. "Yes, second best for Morth! He chose the other one. Why, are you thinking of buying it?"

"Never crossed my mind."

The smith settled for a bit of gold half the size of his thumb.

By examining this thing, Whandall might learn Morth's purpose. What was Morth hiding from Whandall? The only certainty was that this bottle was intended for magical use.

Glass in a cold iron glaze. What would Morth perceive? To a wizard this would be a hole, a blank spot. Hide it under gold—even refined gold—and a wizard would see only gold.

Morth and Green Stone were packing one of the Puma wagons.

"I thought you were staying longer," Whandall said.

"I had a notion," Morth said. "It might be worthless. Fare you well, Whandall Placehold. When you decide what you want, I'll be in the Stone Needles, growing strong again."

"Time we went home too. Green Stone, come."

The sky darkened as they traveled. Cloud drew itself across the sky, but there was no smell of rain. The wind made a strange crying sound.

Green Stone understood first. He didn't warn Whandall. He casually traded away his place on the driver's bench and crawled under the roof to sleep.

White dung began to rain down.

There was no way to hurry bison. Whandall could hear muffled laughter from under the wagon cover. The wagon, bison, and driver were covered in white when the bison plodded through the New Castle gate in a sunset sky dense with passenger pigeons.

Everywhere outside of the Burning City, elders remembered when evening's dinner could be *summoned*. Where civilization grew dense, surviving animals learned to avoid people. Some learned to fight back. In these days of dwindling magic, seeking meat became an adventure. Meals were often vegetarian at the New Castle. But twice a year, birds would overfly the land. . . .

There was nobody to greet Whandall's return. Men, women, children were all over the landscape, all swinging slings, sowing a hail of rocks and reaping birds. Green Stone and Whandall arrived in time to share the plucking.

The evening was spent stripping feathers and roasting and eating pigeons. Everyone gorged. They all reached bed very late.

Late breakfast was cold roasted pigeons. Whandall and Willow spoke of mundane matters.

Green Stone had been days away from his new bride. No need to disturb *them*. As for the wedding, plans had firmed up; most of the arguing had stopped. With the caravan away, not much could be done to prepare. If only Hawk In Flight would stop blurting out new ideas!

Morth would be no bother until next spring. "He'll be on a mountain," Whandall said. "If we can pick a wish . . ."

"Something?"

"Mm?"

Willow said, "You were talking and you just trailed off."

"I can find him 'when I decide what I want,' Morth said. *Maybe* he meant the wish he owes us. *Maybe* he still thinks I'll come with him."

"You wouldn't."

She looked so worried that Whandall laughed. "He's off to fight a water elemental on *my* home turf, but that's okay, he's got a *plan,* only he can't tell *me* because the fire god won't like it!"

"So you won't—"

"But if I'm willing to make the effort, I could be standing *right next to him* when it all happens!"

"—won't go."

"Dear one, I will not go. A Lordkin's promise. Now, what shall we wish for? Something a magician can reasonably be expected to accomplish? Nothing outrageous."

"We have most of a year—"

"I don't think so. There was something in his voice. Willow, he won't wait. He's thought of something. Maybe Stone knows."

"Why would he tell Green Stone?"

"Well, we generally ate with Morth and Twisted Cloud, and told stories."

"We'll catch him at dinner," Willow said. "And now, Lordkin, will you go to encourage the kinless at their work?"

"In my dreams," Whandall said. He went out naked. It was appropriate for the work, and the weather was warm.

Where passenger pigeons had passed, every human hand was needed to clean the droppings from every human artifact. Women worked inside, men outside. Whandall Feathersnake in his youth had learned to climb. He spent the day scraping roofs alongside those few who didn't fear heights.

The New Castle men and boys spent day's end in the pond, trying to get each other clean.

But Green Stone wasn't there.

CHAPTER
62

The household was in an uproar again. Whandall's impatience died when he saw his wife's face, and Lilac's.

"I almost followed him alone," Lilac said. "We have bison and another wagon, why not? But I don't know enough. He tried to tell me it was for the children! I called him an idiot, and he packed and left. Father-found, what happened at Road's End?"

"For the children? *What* for the children?"

"He's off to see the wizard! Morth of Atlantis is going to the Burning City, and Green Stone will go with him!"

"Whandall," Willow demanded, *"what happened at Road's End?"*

"Ah."

He must sound like he'd been punched in the gut, the way they looked at him. And now the hard part was admitting his mistake.

"Green Stone was with me the whole time. Morth wants *me* to go with him back to Tep's Town. Didn't I leave anything there? Unfinished business, family, debts, grudges, buried treasure, live enemies? Some crying need for what a trader's wagon can carry? He can't tell me why he needs me. Can't tell me any of his plans. I am to take some wagons into Tep's Town and find a way to get rich, and Morth is to come along. *Right.*

"Willow, I've been an idiot. He was talking to Green Stone!"

Lilac said, "We'll get him back!"

"He's a grown man, you know." He was still speaking to Willow. "If I force him to stay, he's a kinless."

"What could Morth have offered him?"

Think! "At Road's End he learned enough to firm up his plans. *Then* he tried to get me involved. . . . Stay here. I want to show you something."

He needed a lantern by now.

The droppings-covered roof had been stripped off the wagon and was soaking. There was no trapdoor in the wagon's floor, but with the wagon empty, the boards would slide out. Whandall set aside the bags of gold in the hidden well to reach the glazed black bottle and stopper, then brought it inside.

"Cold iron," he said. "It must be for holding something magical. The one Morth took is just like it."

They looked at it, and him.

"He went to Road's End. He needed a glassblower. I have *no* idea why he wants it. All right, let's just *guess* that Morth also wants *me.* Thirty years ago he saw lines in my hand. He looked at Stone's hand too—"

Lilac's hard hand closed on his wrist. *"What did he see?"*

"Early marriage, twin girls, then nothing. A blur."

Her grip tightened. "Twins? But why would Stone's future fuzz out? Is that *death?"*

"No! No, Daughter-found. A wizard can't see a lifeline that's tangled up with his. Curse! He really is going . . . or else he's going to handle raw gold. That can screw up a prediction too."

You have less magical talent than anyone I ever met, Morth had told Whandall. Could *that* be why the wizard wanted him?

"All right. Morth has my son. Is that because I might go along to protect him?"

"Dear, you have to," Willow said.

"Haven't I heard that song sung with different words?"

"Whandall Feathersnake!"

"I know. *Curse* Morth!"

"Why are we standing here? We have to *catch* him!"

"Wait now, Lilac. It's too dark to load a wagon and take off. Did any kind of dinner get made?"

"We roasted another batch of pigeons," Willow said. "Last night."

" 'Course you did. So we can't leave until morning, Lilac, and that puts Stone a day ahead of us, but *that* doesn't matter, because Stone's on foot. He'll catch Morth. Morth is *two* days ahead in a wagon drawn by bison. You don't expect to *run* after them? Well, bison move at only one speed. We'd still be two days behind when our wagon gets to the Stone Needles."

They went behind the big house, to the stream, where an army of roasted pigeons had been buried in mud.

They talked as they ate. Presently Whandall said, "I think we shouldn't chase him at all."

The women waited.

"Let's give Green Stone's mind a chance to work. He's deserted his wife of, what, twenty days? A marriage blessed by a wizard. He's got fifty, sixty days to think about that, and then everyone he knows comes home and finds out what he did. You're pregnant, Lilac, and if he hasn't guessed that, Morth can tell him.

"Whatever Morth has in mind for Tep's Town, if he can't tell me, he'll *have* to tell Stone. Give Stone a few days to give Morth's intentions a hard look. They may be plain idiotic.

"In particular, I want Green Stone to feel good sense rushing back into his mind as he leaves a mountain-size love spell. It's unforgettable. On the mountain with Morth he'll be accepting everything he's told, but as soon as he gets to where they left the wagon . . . *heyyy!* Lilac, you've been there."

"Yes, Father-found. I didn't realize. I just felt . . . like, we'd been married about a day. Making love in a scent of crushed spices," Lilac said with a wonderfully lascivious grin that faded even as they smiled back. "But you try to share a blanket with him, when he rolls up there's nobody in there *but* him. And you'd have given me more than just a wagon, Father-found."

Willow asked, "Lilac, is Whandall talking sense?"

"That part."

"One more thing," Whandall said. "We can talk to them. We've got the bird." Whandall lifted an arm; the bird settled. Whandall said, "We should work out what we want to say."

"Anything to get them back here!"

"My hope lies in your shadow," the bird said.

CHAPTER
63

Every message was sent after considerable argument. It helped that Willow could write.

"I don't want them *afraid* to come here," said Willow, "with all of us waiting to jump him."

"Let's not make it too easy. Curse it, the boy betrayed me too. Let's just leave it that Green Stone is on a journey and we need to work out details. And keep it *short.*"

"Dear one, does it bother you that he doesn't obey?"

Whandall stared at his mate, then laughed immoderately. "Willow, can't you see I still have trouble saying 'My son'? No, Saber Tooth is a *good* wagonmaster, and I can't break up the Feathersnake wagons unless I've got two directions to send them! So what is there for my second son? He'd *better* be able to find his own directions."

She smiled. Then, "Does it bother you that he chose the Burning City?"

"Yes."

"You do all the talking, then, and you talk only to Morth, right? We women aren't speaking to Green Stone. We're furious. You, you're talking business."

Seshmarls, carry my words. Morth, my son is in your care. We need to know what you intend. Will you leave for Tep's Town this year? Message ends. Seshmarls, go.

* * *

The bird returned two days later with Morth's reply: *We hope to.*
Whandall sent: *Return before his autumn wedding?*

Three days later: *Hope to.*
Stop at the New Castle. The boy's wife and mother are concerned.

Four days later: *I've lost my transport! May wait for spring. Will come to New Castle whatever happens.*
"That's good!" Willow exclaimed, and made the bird repeat it.
Whandall said, "Let's keep up the pressure."
I remind you, you blessed this marriage. Disrupting that spell could be perilous.
"Dear, couldn't he take that as a threat? Oh, you mean *magic!*"
"I meant *both,* curse him!"

Four days later: *Understood. What we intend will make Green Stone and Lilac's children safe for a hundred years. Stone says Behemoth is on the Hemp Road?*

"I saw Behemoth once," Willow said. "But why does the wizard want to know about Behemoth? And the Stone Needles Behemoth, it was *white?*"
"That idiot. That utter idiot. Ah, *curse.*" The women were staring. Whandall said, "Lilac, Stone won't turn back now."
Shall we assemble provisions? Can you grant a second wish?

The bird returned in three days. They must be in transit. *I can't prepare your second wish if you can't describe it. We need . . .* There followed a brief list of provisions.
Whandall said, "Morth is keeping the weight down."
"Tell him to give us back our man!"
"If we wanted a kinless we could have raised one, Lilac. Son and husband, but not slave. Green Stone stands by his own decisions."
"Then carve out a wish that keeps him safe until we see him again!"
"Spells don't work in Tep's Town—"
"They can, you know," said Willow. "You saw ghosts in the Black Pit! And there's magic along most of the Hemp Road—"
"Try this, then: *Cast good fortune for travelers under the Feathersnake sign.*"

Done. Expect us in six days.

* * *

"There's one more thing I can try," Whandall said, "but we can't count on it. Willow, if Stone goes anyway, shall I go with him?"

"Yes!"

The wagon was in sight a good hour before it arrived. Morth and Stone stopped just under the Feathersnake sign, and there they prepared a brief ritual. As soon as Whandall realized he was watching magic, he went behind the house and waited until he heard the gong.

Green Stone guided the bison through the gate. Whandall made no move to stop or welcome them. This had been the topic of much discussion. But when they were firmly on his land, Whandall lifted the black glass bottle and silently showed it to Morth.

Green Stone reacted with wild laughter. *"Yes!* Father, it was wonderful! You should have seen it! Morth said you didn't know—"

Morth said, "I should have bought both bottles. Curse, why not? One might break!"

"Well, yes, but what is it? But if it's a good story, save it for the women." Whandall led them behind the house, to a table and chairs set under a great tree. Willow and Lilac were waiting there, and servants had laid out a lunch.

Willow could think of no way to talk to her son without letting Morth of Atlantis onto New Castle land. But he wasn't to come inside!

Whandall set the bottle on the table, waited until Morth was seated, and sat down himself. Green Stone was still standing, looking at Lilac. Lilac looked back.

"I *had* to wonder why you came to Road's End," Whandall said to Morth. "Nobody but White Lightning can make anything like this bottle. My guess is, you want to carry magic. Something like a talisman, in a cold iron glaze so nothing godlike can leach it out."

Morth said, "Very good—"

"Father, we've got a whole wagon load of them!" Green Stone caroled.

Morth swallowed a snarl. Green Stone saw that . . . but Morth waved, *Tell it,* and Green Stone did.

"Father, we set up camp by the stream, on a nice wide beach of clean white sand, on the eighth night. In the morning the wizard went up the mountain. I waited for two days—"

"I wanted to borrow Behemoth," Morth said. "The Hermit would have given him up, but I saw that the white Behemoth is the Hermit's only friend."

Lilac dropped her staring contest. *"Borrow* Behemoth?"

"I couldn't do that to him," Morth told her. "But at least I could deal with the bottles—"

Green Stone broke in. "Morth brought a chunk of cast iron with him, shaped like a heart with lumps around the rim, and *heavy*. We half buried that in the sand and he set the bottle on it. Then we went back to the wagon.

"Night came. We'd left Morth's bottle behind a stand of bushes. Lights made scrollwork in the sky above it, curving out like a thousand whirlpools. Morth wouldn't let me go and look. When we went back in the morning there were bottles, more than I could count. They weren't all the same size. They trailed off in arcs and spirals and little knots, getting smaller and smaller, no bigger than sand grains at the tips. We left most of them. I don't know how Morth picked which ones to take."

Morth shrugged. "I took the biggest."

"The iron was all gone. There was just a pit shaped like a lumpy heart."

"So," Whandall said, "you need a *lot* of . . . what?"

"Virgin gold," Morth said.

"Wild magic?"

"I can't tell you any more. I wish you didn't know as much as you do! But I can't go near raw gold, so I'll need help to collect it."

"Yes. Well," Whandall said, "I've examined that bottle. Then I wondered what you might not want me thinking when *Yangin-Atep* looks in there."

"You'd come?"

He let his eyes flick toward Green Stone. "I'd have to." Let the boy work out the rest.

"How often have you felt the touch of the fire god?" Morth asked.

"Yangin-Atep left me about the time you did. Just that once. I think." Earlier? The madness with Dream-Lotus? Easy to blame that on the god, but he knew better. "Just that once, with Yangin-Atep. A season later, Coyote had me for some hours. Both did me more good than harm."

"We should hire you out as an inn. All gods welcome at the Sign of the Winged Serpent."

So there it was. Taking Whandall into the Burning City might tell the fire god too much. If Morth refused to carry Whandall, he might leave Green Stone too . . . and Whandall saw now that that wouldn't work. He dared not let Green Stone go alone.

He said, "If rumor of the Feathersnake sign has reached Tep's Town, you'll be safer with me along."

"Yes, if you can go as a legitimate merchant! Your son and I have spoken of this. The caravan must be nearly to the Firewoods already. We'll meet them and assemble a few wagons. *That* will be easier with you along. . . ."

They'd finished eating. This would have been the time to invite Morth to stay the night, but of course that wasn't going to happen. "I'll ask some men to load your wagon," Whandall said.

"Good. Whandall, taking you into Tep's Town might be too dangerous now."

"Sorry."

"But I need you to persuade . . . curse. Curse! Come. We should get on to Road's End. We may not have much time."

Lilac said, "I'll come that far. Stone and I should talk. I'll walk back."

"Take the bird," Willow said.

They walked into the house to get the bird. Willow asked, "What's *your* intent?"

"As Morth says. Get some wagons from the caravan, and anyone who wants to come along, and goods to sell to the Lords in Tep's Town. Come back with tar for your brothers, if nothing else."

"You're going, then."

"Don't you see? Morth offered Green Stone a ride on the Piebald Behemoth! *No* boy of nineteen could turn that down."

She said, "Nor can a boy of forty-three." Seshmarls walked onto her arm and across her shoulder to Whandall's. "Let me know what's happening."

"I will."

PART TWO

Gold Fever

CHAPTER
64

Whandall drove with Morth beside him. Lilac and Green Stone talked in the back, and whatever they babbled of persuasions and recriminations was lost. Blue in the distance, a shape from the world's dawn ambled toward them.

Morth said, "Behemoth must be close to Road's End by now. I wish I could have warned Twisted Cloud."

"You know, this is the craziest thing I've ever done," Whandall said.

"I'm not crazy. Crazy would be waiting for a water elemental to find me. I don't know what the sprite is doing. I've *never* known how far it can come inland. I've got to keep *moving."*

Repairs, loading, rebuilding of warehouses, all had stopped while Twisted Cloud and four of the chief's men watched Behemoth come. The men gaped in awe. Twisted Cloud was wild with laughter and delight.

The shaman caught sight of Morth. "Wizard, is that yours? The beast should be here by morning."

"I wish it were sooner."

"Wizard's flattery?"

"Medicine woman's sarcasm? I feel the elemental's cold wet breath on my neck."

Behemoth drifted toward Road's End like a storm cloud. Twisted Cloud watched. "He looks to be covering a league with every step, but he isn't. Wizard, how does one summon Behemoth?"

"Like summoning a rabbit for dinner. You must know the prey in your mind. I have Green Stone's stories of Behemoth and his description of a dead mammoth. As you see, they were enough."

Lilac and Green Stone would have their chance to make peace, Whandall thought, in one of the guesthouses tonight. The magicians would have to share another. Rumor told that Twisted Cloud had given up men years ago. But she seemed to get along with Morth, and Whandall wondered. . . . Well, after all, who wouldn't?

By dawn light it was as if Road's End huddled at the foot of a small hairy mountain. Behemoth was still a morning's walk uphill and would come no closer.

Morth's bottles, and a parsimonious few of the goods Whandall had sequestered, rode in the wagon with Lilac, Twisted Cloud, Morth, Whandall, and Green Stone. The bison ambled straight toward the great beast. Behemoth's illusion was too *big* to worry them.

As they neared Behemoth, he seemed to dwindle.

When they stood beneath him, he was a living image of a mammoth. Not small! He stank like a whole herd of wild bison. His trunk took Morth's proffered hand, and Morth spoke Atlantean gibberish. Then the beast lifted Morth into place.

Morth sang and danced on its back. The point of that became clear when dead things began raining out of its hair: parasites in wild variety, from mites too small to see up to crustaceans the size of a thumb joint. Morth brushed more from under the beast's great flapping ears.

Under Morth's direction they girdled the beast's torso with the fishnet they'd carried from Great Hawk Bay.

The beast picked up the travelers one by one. Whandall managed not to scream. Green Stone lifted his arms and *hugged* the beast's trunk. It lifted their cargo up to them and they tied every item carefully in the fishnet, while the bird fluttered wide around them, screaming curses. Lastly Morth summoned the bird with a gesture. Behemoth turned toward the hills.

The beast climbed steadily up a ravine, brushing aside knee-high bushes and trees, until it reached the ridge line. This high, the wind was cold. Whandall imitated Morth: he huddled prone against the beast's back, gripping the net. It was like riding a furnace.

Compared to wooden wheels bouncing on a rutted road, this ride was wonderfully smooth. Their motion was barely felt. Whandall savored the awe and the thrill of riding a moving mountain, if not as master, at least as a guest. Was this anything like what Wanshig had felt aboard a ship?

Was this thing any faster than a bison team?

Traveling above the Hemp Road made landmarks hard to find . . . but *that,* already behind them, was Chief Farthest Land's high peak and lookout point, as the caravan first saw it coming home. Landscape drifted by much faster than it ever would at a bison's pace. Behemoth was *fast.*

Morth asked Green Stone, "Have you any idea where we might find gold? There must be rivers all along . . ."

Green Stone was shaking his head.

"I know a hillside covered with virgin gold," Whandall said, "if we can find it, if it hasn't been mined out. I went up it in the dark. Came down with Coyote in my head. But it's south of First Pines. Now you tell me, will we pass close enough to First Pines to know this place? Stone, you've actually seen First Pines more often than I have."

"I'll ask Behemoth." Morth crawled forward to speak into the beast's ear.

Green Stone waved to the south. "Those are the pines, there where the land starts to dip. It looks like Behemoth wants to go above them."

Morth returned. He said, "Behemoth believes that he goes where he will, but he's wrong. He can't *see* places low in manna. They're holes in his map. He won't go near towns."

"Just as well."

Green Stone said, "So when we run out of pines we just walk on down and get the gold, yes, Father? We've covered a daywalk already, two wagon-days. Morth, were you going to travel at night?"

"Better not."

They camped on the crest. Pines ran from the frost line right down into the canyon, hiding the canyon and the Hemp Road.

Morth summoned a yearling deer to roast. The bird hunted his own dinner. Behemoth ate the tops of young trees and pushed down older ones to get at their top foliage.

Next afternoon they ran out of pines. Now they could see down into the canyon. A beige trace was the Hemp Road, running almost parallel to a stream's blue thread, but higher. The ragged slope of the far hill, and the stream that ran down the gorge, were familiar. The caravan passed twice a year, but Whandall had never been impelled to climb that hill again.

Huddled up against the forest was the town of First Pines.

Morth and Whandall were lowering cargo from the mammoth's back. Green Stone looked from the chaparral-covered hillside across from them, down into the canyon, then at Morth's bags of bottles. He said, "You want *all* of these filled with *gold?"*

"Yes."

His son hadn't quite imagined the size of this job! Whandall grinned. "We're far enough from town, locals won't bother us. Bandits might. We've been attacked here more than once. We can take a first pass this afternoon. Camp tonight at the caravan campground, watch for bandits—"

"No! Come back up. Sleep here," Morth said. "Bandits won't bother Behemoth."

Sleep with Behemoth—sure, that sounds safe. "Couple of days, then, if there's any gold. Twisted Cloud has known about this place all along. She might have told anyone."

"How do I know gold?" Green Stone asked. "How do I know wild from refined?"

Whandall wasn't sure he would either. Gold ore wasn't always bright smooth yellow. He said, "You coming, Morth?"

Morth was torn. "You've seen what I'm like when I've touched wild gold. Do you really need me?" Hopefully. Resisting.

Whandall said, "I can't sense it, you know."

"Don't I just. *Ah!* Take the bird," Morth said. "Watch Seshmarls."

CHAPTER
65

S tone and Whandall set out with the bird wheeling above them. They'd half filled their packs with empty bottles. Those didn't weigh much, but they'd be heavy coming back.

The rising wind was to Seshmarls' taste. The rainbow crow flew with motionless wings, pretending to be a hawk. He had to flap more often than a hawk would.

Without that bird they might have come and gone unnoticed.

They reached the floor of the canyon in a ring of older children all chasing around under the bird, demanding to know whose it was, or swearing it must belong to Whandall Feathersnake.

Whandall introduced himself and his son and the bird. When he asked where they were from, they pointed up the valley toward First Pines.

They crossed the valley floor, and the stream, in a circle of children and a flood of questions. While they climbed, Whandall told tales of the bandit attack and of Coyote's possession.

A few of the smallest couldn't keep up and dropped out. An older girl went with them, complaining bitterly of the excitement she would miss. Green Stone apologized. "We can't stop. We have to finish before dark."

Now ten remained of the original fifteen.

He just couldn't tell. These might be from First Pines, the children of customers and friends. They might be bandits' children, or First Pines might include part-time bandits. Then again, it was a fine day for walking uphill in a gaggle of babbling tens and twelves, with bright noon light to guide them around malevolent plants that had ripped half his skin off one black night.

"Oh, look!" cried a black-haired boy, and he pointed up.

The bird was arguing territory with a hawk. What had the hawk so confused, what had excited the boy, was the brighter-than-rainbow colors flashing across Seshmarls' feathers. It hurt the eyes to look.

"Wild magic," Whandall murmured, and Green Stone nodded. They took note of where they were and continued to climb.

The stream ran to their right. The children's chattering had dwindled, but one boy—thirteen or so, with straight black hair and red skin and an eagle's nose—urged them on. Whandall spun them a tale about an Atlantis magician in flight from a magical terror. He did not speak of gold. He let the bird's display guide him up the hill.

Gold would not be found where Seshmarls kept his accustomed colors. Where colors rippled across the bird in vibrating bands and whorls, hurting the eyes . . . well, it seemed they were tracking a flood that might recur once or twice in a man's lifetime. Gold followed the flooding.

"Oh, look now!"

The bird sank toward the stream, darkening as he fell. The children ran.

Greenery thickened, blocking passage. Stone and Whandall forced their way through. And there in the water, with eight children all around it, sat the skeleton of a man. Seshmarls perched on his skull, jet black.

Whandall said to them, "Here rests Hickamore, shaman to Bison Clan, lost these many years."

"Gold," Green Stone said, and picked up two yellow lumps as big as finger joints. He put one in his pouch and gave the other to the oldest boy. "Here," he said, and pointed out more dully glowing bits of gold for the children to collect, until every child had a bit of gold and they were scattered all up and down the streambed. Green Stone and Whandall tried to find gold in places a child would miss, and thus filled their belt pouches.

Day was dimming. Whandall gave a tiny black glass bottle to the oldest girl. "Wait three days," he said, "then show it to your folk and tell them where to find Piebald Behemoth the shaman."

They all trooped down to the valley floor and parted there.

Whandall and Green Stone followed the last sunset light up toward the crest and Behemoth. "That was clever," Whandall said.

"Thank you, Father. I wasn't sure."

"No, it was brilliant! This isn't what Morth needs; it's refined. Valuable, of course, but Coyote used up all the manna in it. But it'll draw them."

* * *

Morth heard their tale, then asked, "Will the children wait?"

"Don't know. We still don't know if those are First Pines children or bandits. It doesn't matter. It doesn't matter if they tell their parents or go themselves. The way to get the refined gold around the shaman's skeleton is to go up the river. We'll cross lower down tomorrow and get the wild gold on the slopes. We know where it is now."

The bird settled on Morth's arm. "Reminds me," Green Stone said. "Keep the bird with you tomorrow, Morth. He attracts too much attention . . . oh, that'll do," as the bird on Morth's forearm turned glossy black.

CHAPTER
66

They crossed the valley at dawn. A lone black crow wheeled above them. They saw no children.

They filled some bottles with water. Water going up, gold coming down. They panned a little gold in the stream. It was only a powder here. They stopped again at the bottom of the ancient mud flow. Whandall thought he saw color in the mud, not yellow, but the odd tints of gold salts.

And he felt the pressure of a lurk's eyes.

They kept climbing. Whandall looked about him, taking it all in, letting his mind find patterns. He didn't look for a face among weeds. That was not how you spotted a lurk.

The bird wheeled above them . . . and suddenly blazed with colors.

Vegetation was low and sparse, leaving little cover to hide a man. Flooding had left whole river bottoms sprawled across this slope; then years of rain had washed away the lightest particles of silt, leaving what was heaviest; and that must have happened over and over. Gold was everywhere.

Following the firebird's path, Whandall began collecting nuggets. Green Stone couldn't perceive gold until they'd been at it awhile, but then he caught the knack.

Seshmarls flapped uphill in a wide spiral. He was black again. Was he seeking the mad magic in gold, or just his dinner? The bird dwindled until they almost lost him. Then they saw his rainbow flare and followed.

Now Whandall had no thought for watching eyes, nor for anything but gold. When their belt pouches were full they emptied the gold into their packs. By sunset every muscle was screaming. Their empty bellies cried for food.

A half-moon gave them little light. It was good they'd brought water, but that was gone now. Unable to see to collect more gold, they began sifting the gold sand into bottles in the dark.

By moonset most of the bottles were full. There was no gold left in the packs, and no light at all.

Green Stone hefted his pack. "That's heavy!"

"Put it down. We can't walk in the dark."

"It'll still be heavy tomorrow. I'm cold, hungry. Father, what are we doing here?"

"Gold fever. We should have been on our way hours ago. Now we'll be here the night." With their gold sealed in cold iron, Whandall was having second thoughts. He thought his sanity had returned.

Green Stone said, "I wish Morth were here. He'd summon something to eat."

"Gold drives Morth crazy! We don't dare build a cook fire anyway."

"Well, we got his gold for him."

"Why does Morth want it?"

"I'm not supposed to tell."

"Not Morth's plans, no, but do *you* have a plan? Or did you come just to ride Behemoth?"

"Maybe I can find my fortune in Tep's Town, or earn it. Maybe it's my blood calling to me."

"Let me tell you about your blood," Whandall Feathersnake said, "and about *Morth*."

And they talked.

Whandall had first seen Morth of Atlantis from Lord Samorty's balcony, when he was learning how to lurk. . . .

One night during the trek to find Morth, Green Stone had crawled into Lilac's blanket and gotten himself a long and heated lecture involving one-horns, rumor, custom, and the rights of parents. Lilac was still ticked at his father for suggesting otherwise. So was Green Stone. . . .

Whandall's father had died robbing Morth of Atlantis. The Placehold men had died because . . .

When the gold fever really did ease off, hours later, Whandall tried to remember the long mad night of laughter and horror. How much of this had he actually *said?* Things he'd *never* confessed.

But he *had* told his son how the Placehold men died while Whandall stayed to gather a kinless woman and mutilate the man who tried to strangle her. Told him about ruling the Placehold until Mother came home with Freethspat. How Mother's lover made him a murderer. How Whandall made Freethspat carry garbage . . . like a kinless . . . and why that was funny . . .

Green Stone was snoring gently.

Whandall wriggled around until his back was to his son's, head to foot, separated by backpacks stuffed with bottles. Dozing, he suddenly remembered a sense of being watched.

He swept an arm wide around, just above the packs. His hand smacked hard into a thin forearm, and closed. The arm tried to pull away. He followed through on the sweep, reached across, letting go to avoid a possible knife thrust, and had the other hand with a knife in it. Then Green Stone was twisting the intruder's head.

"Don't kill him," Whandall said quickly. The struggling shape went rigid.

Whandall took the intruder's knife. "Let me speak first," he said. "You're a very good lurk. We'll speak more on this. We need this gold for ourselves, but I can offer you something you'll *never* refuse. But I'm just not sure I want you yet. Let him speak, Stone."

A boy of twelve or thirteen cried out in anger and terror. *"Who have you killed?"*

"What?"

"You're Whandall Feathersnake!"

"Your face," Green Stone told his father. "It's glowing."

"That's wrong. I haven't killed anyone in six years!"

"Must be the raw gold," said Green Stone.

"Yes. I don't kill lightly, boy. What's your name?"

Silence.

"Make one up. Never mind; we'll call you Lurk. Are you a bandit?" He didn't say *bandit's son.* Give the boy his dignity.

The boy said, "Yes. Do you need all of those bottles?"

"If the wizard would just *talk* to me, I might have an intelligent answer. Green Stone?"

"Father, Morth doesn't *know* how many he needs."

"Stay with us, Lurk," Whandall said. "I'm going to let go. In the morning we'll talk. If we don't need you, I'll send you home with the smallest of these bottles and a tale to make you famous. But if we need you, you'll ride Behemoth with us. I'm letting go now."

He let go.

The boy went to his belly and backed away. Whandall had expected that; he could have caught him. The boy backed under a stand of thorns and was gone.

Again Whandall and his son stretched out head to foot and back to back. Green Stone said, "He heard everything."

"Yes."

"I'm not sure what you said. I must have dreamed some of that. Gold fever. Did you ever tell Mother any of that?"

"No! You don't either, right?"

"Right. Why do you want Lurk?"

Whandall wondered if the bandit boy was still out there. "I've been thinking. If ever we hope to trade in Tep's Town, we have to do something about the Toronexti. . . ."

By late afternoon they had carried those fearsomely heavy packs up to Morth and Behemoth. They slept the rest of the day and most of the night.

Then up and off at first light, down to the river and up the far hill before Seshmarls' colors flared. Gold madness had them again. They'd have carried more gold, and saved a smidgen of weight, by piling gold sand loose in their packs. Whandall convinced Green Stone that it would drive them mad: they would try to carry a mountain's weight of gold, and it would kill them.

Again darkness caught them, and again they filled bottles by moonlight.

The moon sank. They curled back to back with the gold between them.

From the darkness, from beyond a knife's reach, came the voice of Lurk. "I think you lie about riding Behemoth."

"As you like," Whandall said.

"He's not so big as all that," Lurk said, "but he could crush a man with his foot, or his nose."

"How close did you get?"

"I touched his hind foot." When they didn't answer immediately, Lurk added, "His skin is rough. His smell is very strong. He opened one eye, and I smiled at him, and he watched me back away. You've wrapped his belly in—"

"Why did you touch him?"

"I got that close. Isn't that what you want?"

That was perceptive. "I need a man who sees all and is never seen. Did Morth see you?"

"No. You didn't see me either." Lurk laughed. "When you think you're safe, you sleep on your back, feet apart, your arms for a pillow. Do you have trouble breathing?"

"No, but I did once." Story for story, Whandall spoke his memory aloud: "I was healing from what the Lordsmen did to me. Broken ribs, broken arm, bruises everywhere . . . knees, kidneys . . . they smashed my nose and cheek and some teeth. Had to breathe through my mouth. I'd try to sleep on my side and wake up suffocating, and when I tried to roll over, everything hurt. So I learned to sleep on my back. You listening, Green Stone? I tried to go where I wasn't wanted. It's *dangerous* in Tep's Town. Lurk, it's *dangerous*. You could stay here and be safe."

"What are you offering?"

"You'll serve the Feathersnake wagons."

"That's *all?"*

"What do you have now? If you like what you have, what you are, then go home."

In the morning Lurk was there. They knew him: a thirteen-year-old boy, the oldest of the children on the hill. Straight black hair, brown eyes, red-brown skin, nose developing a hawk's prow. He wouldn't pass for Lord or Lordkin or kinless.

Lurk carried his share of gold-filled bottles as they made their way across the valley and up. By and by Lurk asked Whandall, "What are the Tornex to you?"

"Toronexti. They're gatherers who place themselves between me and what I want, between me and the Burning City." Whandall told him what he remembered. He could paint a verbal map of the Deerpiss, the Wedge, the guardhouse at the narrows. But the Toronexti . . . "If the Spotted Coyotes never gave anything for what they took, if they took whatever they wanted and there was no way around them, that's the Toronexti. None of us knew them well. I think it's always been one family, like the Placehold . . . my family. They walked and talked like Lordkin. But Lordkin don't have their own wealth. Where do they shop? Where do they get their mates? It isn't a Lordkin who rises from his blanket and goes to a guardhouse because it's *time*. Be he sleepy, or horny and a woman nearby, be his throat sore and his nose running and some fool waiting to yell in his face, a kinless goes because his Lord expects him. Lords do that too. A boy on a roof does that when the bugs are on the plants, and so does a Toronexti guard. They're weird. Lurk, I need someone to spy on them."

"And why should I come with you?"

"That's if Morth accepts you. You say Behemoth already has?"

Lurk waited.

"If you live, you will have stories your tribe will never believe and never forget. You ride Behemoth's back with Whandall Feathersnake. A fire-colored bird wheels above you and waits to carry your messages. You learn what Whandall Feathersnake can teach. You'll watch me destroy the most powerful bandit tribe in the Burning City with your badly needed help. You'll help the last wizard of Atlantis destroy a water elemental. You'll get rich too, if everything goes right. I have never seen everything go right. You coming?"

CHAPTER
67

Lurk gripped the fishnet like a dead man in rigor mortis. His face was buried deep in a patch of lank and matted brown hair. But Behemoth's ride was smooth, and by and by he looked up.

By and by he was sitting upright. Then he was pointing out landmarks. When they stopped that evening, Lurk vanished.

Whandall set about making camp. He tried to think like a Hemp Road bandit. He wished he knew how far they had traveled. They'd come a good way ... *maybe* farther than a bandit's child might find allies. Did bandits still fear Whandall Feathersnake? Or was he legend going myth?

It wouldn't matter. Whatever the truth of the stories, whether First Pines harbored bandits in exchange for a share of their loot, none would risk robbing Whandall Feathersnake without assurance that the tale would never be told.

But Lurk returned unseen bearing rabbits and a fat squirrel, and a coyote that was only stunned. "Some folk hold to a coyote totem," he said.

Good point. "Let it go," Whandall said. The beast limped away.

Morth summoned. Raccoons came. Watching raccoons skin the other creatures cost Lurk his appetite, but it surged back with the smell of broiling meat.

"Languages," Whandall said. "If we are to trade in Tep's Town, we need more who can speak the language. Morth, can you teach Green Stone and Lurk?"

"Yes, but to what point? Magic doesn't work in Tep's Town. The knowledge would fade like dreams."

"But if you teach them here, and they practice here? They'll remember what they practiced, even when the magic goes away."

Morth nodded sagely. "Well thought. That should work. We need a safe place."

"Safe?"

"All three of you must sleep," Morth said. "Understand, there may be effects we do not know. They may gather some of your memories as well as your knowledge of the language."

"You know the language," Whandall said. "Use yourself as model."

"Never, and for the same reason."

"Oh." Whandall thought on it. "So be it."

And afterward, on the journey south, they spoke only the language of Tep's Town, but curiously, not as Lordkin and not as kinless. They sounded like Lords . . . almost.

Stone and Lurk were speaking as an eleven-year-old Whandall Place-hold understood Lords to speak. "Your mind does not accept that these two are Lordkin," Morth speculated. "Hah! But can they pass?"

"Not for Lords, not for kinless, not for Lordkin. Lookers. Lurk, Green Stone, you know enough to trade, or you might even pose as tellers. In a pinch, talk Condigeano."

The ridge had descended, but the company perched on Behemoth's back still had a god's-eye view of Firewoods Town.

Several new houses had appeared since Whandall Placehold came out of that forest. Sixty houses, half adobe and the rest wood, all built for mass and durability and looking much alike, like an art form, *planned,* were strung along three parallel dusty streets. Fenced yards. Flower gardens. All very impressive to a Lordkin boy.

All the townpeople were gathered at the north end of town, around and among fifteen big covered wagons drawn in a wide circle. There were tents. A hundred hands were pointing up, up at Behemoth.

Lurk whispered, "Do you think they see *us* as giants?"

Whandall said, "Morth?"

"I don't know. Ask."

The Firewoods Wheel was turning.

It was not much more than a wide flat disk mounted horizontally. Twenty children crowded onto it. Adults and older children were pushing it around.

"The first go-round wheels ran themselves," Morth said.

"But what's it for?" Lurk asked.

"Altered state of consciousness," said the wizard. "In the old days *anyone* could sense magic. It was everywhere, talking animals, gods in every pond and tree. Stars and comets would shift position to follow events on Earth. Our ancestors missed that sense, so they invented wine and stage magic and the powders and foxglove I used to sell in Tep's Town, and the go-round wheel. Now too much of the magic is gone. It only makes us dizzy."

They watched. The folk below watched back; the wheel slowed. Green Stone said, "Nobody's coming up to help us move this stuff, are they?"

The wheel had Whandall mesmerized. He could almost remember. . . .

He shook himself. "Morth, stay here with Behemoth. We'll go down and get someone to carry."

A crowd of merchants and townsfolk watched them come. The wheel slowed with their inattention.

Whandall shouted, "This is Lurk. He's with me." He moved through the crowd a little faster than anyone could talk to them, he and Green Stone bracketing Lurk. They jogged to catch up with the rim of the wheel and began to push. Lurk caught a handhold and pushed too.

Children piled on and crawled inward to reach the padded handles. Others took the easy way, crawling under the wheel, emerging in the hole near the hub. They sought to hang on, if only to each other, to resist being thrown off onto the grass, until they got too dizzy or the adults were worn out.

Whandall ran and pushed, showing off his strength. *Forty-three, but not frail.* But a memory came flooding back with a terrible sadness, and he said, "There was one of these in Tep's Town. . . ."

He told it in gasps. *Whandall and others of Serpent's Walk arrived while Lordsmen were anchoring the wheel. Kinless were already there. Lordsmen used bulk and muscle to start the wheel turning. Children surged onto it. The armored Lordsmen went back to guarding while older children and parents ran round and round the outside of the wheel.*

Now Serpent's Walk children bent their efforts to picking purses, because it would go hard for them if they didn't. But the day wore on, and the kinless were careful of their purses, and the wheel looked like fun.

It happened all in a surge: the Lordkin children moved in and piled on and chased the kinless children off the wheel.

And the wheel slowed and stopped.

"I wasn't *really* confused here," Whandall panted. The Firewoods Wheel was turning nicely. "They were pushing it." Townsfolk were still looking uphill toward Behemoth, but a few were starting to push again. "The Lords let us think that—magic was turning the wheel, and hey—I was just a little boy. But the kinless wouldn't push if there weren't any kinless on it. If nobody pushes, it stops! We barely had time to feel what it was like. So we went back to picking pockets—and the kinless took their children and went away."

There were plenty of hands turning the wheel now. From those who had run out of breath and dropped out, Whandall picked out a big woman from the Feathersnake wagons. "Hidden Spice, where's Saber Tooth?"

She wanted to talk. He insisted. She pointed.

That was Saber Tooth . . . and everyone wanted to talk. Hard to guess which had more of the crowd's attention: Behemoth, or Whandall Feathersnake sprung up suddenly in their midst, or the bandit boy. They forged a path through the crowd.

Above the noise, Saber Tooth demanded, "Father, how did you get here? *Why?*"

"I'm here to protect your brother. Green Stone is here following Morth of Atlantis. My son, what the wizard's doing is the really interesting part. But . . . you've heard me talk about new markets? I think I've finally got a handle on that."

"Father, you can't mean what I think you mean."

"We'll talk. Maybe I'll come to my senses. Maybe your brother will too. Meanwhile, Saber Tooth, I need some muscle," he said. "About six of your men to go up the hill to where you see Behemoth. They're to do what a red-haired wizard tells them. They'll be coming down with heavy loads. I need those bottles protected. They're glass, and what's inside is dangerous, so don't bounce them. Then we can talk, but this is urgent, and those bottles are valuable."

"I'll go myself."

"Thank you. And where's Clever Squirrel?"

Saber Tooth waved. "See the one-horns?"

"Right." The one-horns had all drifted into one corner of the corral. "I should talk to her. Lurk, Green Stone, come with me."

"The one-horns don't want to be near her." Green Stone laughed. "See, Lurk, this is *Coyote's daughter.* Special. As a little girl she got to know the one-horns. The young colts, they thought she was their older sister. One morning when she was fifteen—she's a season older than Saber Tooth, two years older than me—she went out to the corral and the one-horns freaked. She stormed right back at them. She's got them cowed. They don't like it, but if she had to ride one, he'd carry her. *Hi, Squirrelly!*"

"Stones! Have you been riding Behemoth? Father-found, I'm not surprised, but Stones?"

"I can ride Behemoth and you can't!" Green Stone cried. They hugged each other hard, then the girl turned to the others.

"Clever Squirrel, meet Lurk," Whandall said.

"My name is Nothing Was Seen," the bandit boy said shyly.

Clever Squirrel had deployed her travel nest, with her dowry wagon for one wall and boxes of trade goods for the rest. She even had a little fire going, and she set a teapot on it, with Lurk trying to help.

They found each other interesting, Whandall thought. Should he be protective? They should at least know something of each other.

So. "Squirrelly, he wouldn't tell *us* his name. Nothing Was Seen, how did you find your name?"

"I became the best lurk in Red Canyon Tribe." He told Squirrel how he had spied on Whandall Feathersnake and the wizard who rode Behemoth. He told a minimum of what he had heard that first night. Whandall was glad of that.

Squirrel asked, "Father-found, what are you *doing* here?"

"Waiting for Saber Tooth and Morth of Atlantis, just now. We're going into the Burning City to see if we can kill a water elemental and set up a trade route." She lit up and he said, "No, I *can't* deprive the caravan of their medicine woman, and I *have* a wizard."

"Mother-found Willow will kill you."

"We talked."

She had to raise her voice above a rising background murmur. Her travel nest must be surrounded by most of the caravan and half the townsfolk, all asking each other what Whandall and Green Stone Feathersnake were doing *here* riding Behemoth! "Back into the Burning City? With Stones and not *me?*"

"Sorry. If I can really get a trade route going—"

"Show me your hand. Curse! Stones? *Curse!* The lines all disappear!"

"Then we're really going!" Green Stone was jubilant. He must have had his doubts.

"Well, then, what is it like to ride Behemoth, Stones?"

Green Stone said, "You never feel a bump."

"We had to stop off to collect wild gold," Whandall said. "I have no idea why the wizard wants that, but what bothers me is, why was it still there? Your mother has known where that gold is since the night you were conceived."

In the roar of rumor outside the wall of cargo boxes, Clever Squirrel didn't even drop her voice. "I'll answer if you'll tell me about that night. *All* about that night."

"Done."

She laughed. "Mother tells everyone else she never found the place again. She was outside her mind with ecstasy. The gold wasn't there anyway. The whole story's fiction."

"She told me different. She's tried to refine raw gold. She gets some in payment for a cure or a prophecy. But she never learned to block the flow of . . . chaos manna?" Whandall nodded, Lurk merely listened, and she went on. "Gold fever does things to Mother. She always winds up getting laid."

Whandall said, "That—" and his memory felt his wife's fingertips brushing his lips closed.

Too late. Coyote's daughter laughed and said, "Yes, that explains how I come to have five sibs! Five times she's refined gold, five children plus me. A woman who *knows* can take a man without getting a child, but not around gold, not Mother! Even during her time of blood, the gold changes her. That's how she got Hairy Egg. After Father went away—"

Nothing Was Seen was staring at Whandall.

Clever Squirrel laughed. "No, no, not Father-found," she said. "I mean Stag Rampant. He knew Mother had conceived me before they were married. No one dared put horns on him for Coyote's child! But my other sibs were too much for him. And after he left, Mother gave up men entirely.

"Can you guess what would happen if Mother led a man up that gold-covered hill? There are stories only the men tell, but *I* know them. Now tell me of my siring."

"I first saw that hill in black night with your mother pulling me along at a dead run," Whandall began. *Are you listening, Lurk? I will not answer for advice not taken. She's Coyote's daughter and Feathersnake's too! Treat her well and warily.*

CHAPTER
68

S aber Tooth and five strong men came down the mountain carrying
heavy bags. Morth was with them. They brought the bags into Clever
Squirrel's tent, and then Saber Tooth sent them away.

Above the village Behemoth came to his senses, shook his great head,
and turned back to the mountains.

"Father, you'll have to talk to them," Saber Tooth said. No need to
explain who he meant. The crowd outside was larger than ever.

"How long have you been here?" Whandall asked.

"We came in yesterday morning."

High noon now. "You were just setting up the market?"

Saber Tooth nodded.

"Good. Finish doing that, set up the tightrope and get your sister ready
to perform, and set up a stage to talk from. Tell everyone to come in two
hours. Morth, can you show them Behemoth again?"

"Show? Yes, of course," Morth said. "As long as no one wants to ride
him!"

"Good. One more thing, I doubt anyone would try to steal from Clever
Squirrel . . ."

She grinned. There were tales from when she was five and six and eight.

"But just in case, have a couple of reliable men sit right here, next to
those bags. Squirrel, can we meet here for supper? Good. As soon as the
market closes. Now let's give these rubes a show."

"But Father, what will you tell them?" Saber Tooth demanded.

"I'm not going to tell them anything," Whandall said. "You're going to tell them how you brought them the greatest show ever."

"But what will you do?" Saber Tooth asked.

"Why should I do anything? It's your wagon train and your show," Whandall said. "Tell you what. I'll catch for your sister. I'm still strong enough for that. You do the rest."

Burning Tower had grown in the months since Whandall had last seen her. The terror bird costume Willow had made for her was tighter, and what it revealed was no longer a little girl. Whandall stood beneath her tightrope, a rope set higher than Willow had ever dared, and hoped she wouldn't fall. He was aware of the stares of all the young men, wagoneers as well as townsfolk.

They were going to need more jobs! No question about it.

Her mother had taught her well. Forward somersaults, back flips, and a grand finale that involved spiraling down the left-hand pole to land on one foot, back arched, high kick to her forehead. Then she was away to the changing tent.

Morth appeared on the platform in a cloud of fog. He gestured to the hills. Behemoth came over the brow of a hill far away, bigger than the hill, as large as the mountain beyond. He reared high, then stood on one leg, kicking high with the other in a hilarious imitation of Burning Tower's finale. The crowd went wild. . . .

Supper was local jackrabbit stewed with spices from Stone Needles. Whandall insisted they finish eating before they talked. Then he sent out all but family members, Morth, and Lurk.

Saber Tooth was relaxed and smiling. "I don't think we ever made this much profit at Firewoods," he said.

Burning Tower grinned. "We'll sell them more tomorrow when they come back to find out which story we told today is true. . . ."

"If any," Lurk said.

Whandall stood. Carefully he opened one of the bags and spread black glass bottles out with his fingers. Clever Squirrel gasped.

"You can tell what's in them?" Morth demanded.

"The iron is thin on *that* one," Squirrel said. She set it aside. "And I saw how heavy they were."

Morth looked worried.

"What are they, Squirrel?" Saber Tooth demanded.

She laughed. "Gold! Wild gold aflame with magic and chaos!"

"Gold?" Saber Tooth looked at the bags. "All of that? No wonder my arms ache! Father, this is more than we'll make in two years! Three, if the Leathermen keep moving their wagons ahead of ours! Gold!" He reached for the flawed bottle.

"No, son," Whandall said. "Listen first. I have a tale to tell." He laughed and said, "And I don't know the ending yet! I don't even know what the wizard intends with these cursed bottles, and you can't tell me, can you, Morth? We'll have to *make* an ending."

"But I need Lurk. I need the wizard, and he needs *all* of these wonderful bottles."

"What can you do that's worth three years' profits?" Saber Tooth demanded.

"A new trade route," Whandall said.

Saber Tooth frowned. "Like the one to Quaking Aspen?"

Whandall laughed. "I grant you that was costly, but we'll make it back."

"In about seven years," Saber Tooth muttered. "So where this time?"

"To the Burning City."

At least Green Stone had the wit to keep unspoken his *I'm going and you're not!* while Saber Tooth thought that through. "Wow. Are we taking the whole caravan?"

"Not worried about the profits?" Burning Tower asked innocently.

Saber Tooth struggled with his dignity before putting his tongue out at his sister.

"I can't risk taking the whole caravan," Whandall said. "Not this time. I need four wagons, and son, I can leave you refined gold to hire more, but I'll need the best traders and fighters you have . . . no, not quite the best. The most ambitious."

"Same people, curse you."

"We need trade goods, anything that can't get to Tep's Town by ship. Terror bird feathers. Grain. Cooking pots. Nothing magical, not for Tep's Town. We'll pick as many Miller and Ropewalker kids as we can get, because they've got relatives in there. I have more refined gold, and that's a lot more valuable in Tep's Town than out here."

"But what do the harpies have that we need?" Saber Tooth demanded.

Burning Tower giggled. "We're harpies too, brother!"

Saber Tooth grinned at her. "Sure, but it's still a good question."

"I don't know," Whandall said. "Whatever we buy, we'll have storage after we get rid of Morth's bottles. . . ."

After that, they all talked at once.

CHAPTER
69

L ate that night Whandall dismissed the others and went to Saber
Tooth's travel nest. They sat on ornate carpets in a wagon den of polished wood.

"You'll be wanting this wagon, of course," Saber Tooth said.

"Well—"

"It's yours, Father. I have my own."

"Who's in that?"

"Hammer Miller."

"Is his wagon here?"

"Yes, it's loaned to one of his wife's relatives." Hammer had married a girl
from a town in Paradise Valley and was content to be a wagoneer foreman.

"Complicated," Whandall said. "Think Hammer would like to come to
Tep's Town?"

"I think you would have to tie him to a wagon tongue to keep him out."

"And you as well?"

Saber Tooth didn't say anything.

"Son, I would rather have you with me," Whandall said, realizing that it
was true. "But Feathersnake can't spare you. It can spare me—"

"Father!"

"It can, so long as you're in charge," Whandall said. "And you know it.
You're a better trader than I will ever be."

Saber Tooth didn't answer. They both knew it was true.

"So I can be lost, and Green Stone can be lost, and Feathersnake goes on. Your mother will grieve, but she won't starve, and neither will your sisters and their kin. Number One, we need you out here."

Saber Tooth was a long time answering. Finally, "Father, I'll take the caravan on to Condigeo. Having a new opportunity doesn't make an old one less worthwhile. I've always wanted to be the Feathersnake wagon boss. Most never see their dreams in old age, let alone as young as me." He sighed. "I've always wanted to see Tep's Town, too, but that can wait. You go in. We'll travel light to Condigeo, and we may be back here when you come out. If not, you can wait here for us."

"Good plan. What are you carrying to Condigeo?"

"Marsyl poppy seeds. Gorman hemp. Some bad carpets that will still be better than anything they have that far south."

Whandall nodded to himself. The Feathersnake wagons didn't go all the way south unless they had cargo Condigeo would pay for, and time to reach Road's End before the snows. Storms chopped off the Condigeo leg two years out of three.

"And civet cat glands," Saber Tooth said. "Two jars."

"I want one," Whandall said.

"Did your nose die of old age? Or do they make perfume in Tep's Town?"

"Not that I heard," Whandall said. "Just an idea. I won't need a whole jar; two cups of the juice will do. Be sure it's sealed tightly."

Saber Tooth's nose wrinkled. "Don't worry about that!"

"So," Whandall said. "It's my wagon, and Hammer Miller's, and who else do I take?"

"Four, you said?"

"Four wagons if I can get 'em."

Saber Tooth poured tea. Sipped. "Not Fighting Cat Fishhawk," he said. "His mother's getting pretty old now; she'll expect to see him."

"How is she?"

"Sorry she retired, I think," Saber Tooth said. "But she was too damn old to be on the road!" He brooded, thinking of the first hard decision he'd had to make as a wagonmaster. Beaching one his father's oldest friends. The worst of it was that Whandall should have done it years before and hadn't.

"So who?"

"Insolent Lizard," Saber Tooth said positively.

Whandall nodded. Kettle Belly's fourth son. Reliable and skilled, if a bit of a smart-ass. "One more, then."

"You'll need a blacksmith," Saber Tooth said. "I can hire another for a while. Take Greathand. He'd follow you anywhere."

Starfall Ropewalker's brother, not her father. The son took the father's name when the first Greathand died six years ago, a skilled giant to his last day. He wasn't blood, but he was kin. "Good. I'll talk to them after we've left this town behind."

Saber Tooth nodded agreement. The less the townfolk knew of family affairs, the better he liked it.

"Sure you'll be all right letting me have this wagon?"

"Truth is, Father, I like my own better. This is the nicest travel nest on the Road, but—"

"But you designed and built yours," Whandall finished for him. "Yup. All right, now for supplies."

"This is going to be like herding snakes. We have to cut out four wagons, take all the Condigeo cargo off them, put anything you want for Tep's Town onto them, and get it done out of town without making camp before the damn Leathermaster caravan catches up and sees us!"

"No doubt you are competent—"

Saber Tooth took on a cagey look. "This will be tricky, and tricky is expensive."

"Never knew I'd have to bargain with my own son," Whandall said.

"Sure you did." Saber Tooth looked thoughtful. "It's Morth who needs the gold in those bottles."

Whandall nodded.

"I do not exactly see why we need Morth."

"There's me and there's Morth, and nobody else on this expedition knows a cursed thing about Tep's Town."

"And we need him that much? I could sell everything we have and not come up with that much gold."

Whandall sighed. "Son, it's wild gold. Unrefined."

"But contained. There are wizards in Condigeo who would be more than pleased to refine it for us."

"It's not mine. Morth helped gather it. It's a matter of our word," Whandall said.

"Oh. I take it this is entirely a Feathersnake enterprise?"

"Yes, if we can keep it that way."

"Do that," Saber Tooth said.

CHAPTER
70

Every wagon owner expected to call at Whandall Feathersnake's wagon den, to present respects and get a glass of the best wine or tea or both, to meet the wizard who was Whandall's guest, to learn why Whandall Feathersnake kept a boy from a bandit family as guest, to test bargaining skills. Had Whandall Feathersnake gone soft from living in town?

Fighting Cat Fishhawk hailed Whandall with a glad cry. Ruby Fishhawk's son was four years older than Whandall, a touch of his mother's kinless ancestry in the ears.

"Give my warmest respects to your mother," Whandall said.

"Won't you see her yourself?"

Curse. "Perhaps not. I will not go farther than the Springs this trip," Whandall said. "Tea or wine?"

"Both, please, but little of the wine. The Springs? So you believe the stories of gold in the hills above?"

"Lurk, make us some tea." Whandall had taught him how. It was best to have something to do to cover a social gaffe. And Burning Tower was eager to be hostess for her father, but Whandall had sent her on errands. She wanted to help, too much.

"Condigeo is getting soft," Fighting Cat said. "I sold a Marsyl carpet, used, for seven sea turtle shells."

"Good price. Are sea turtles so common now?"

Fighting Cat grinned. "No more common than ever."

Whandall sensed a story. "How?"

"I don't talk so much."

Whandall grinned and waited . . . and Fighting Cat grinned back. Whandall said, *"Excellent!"* and they moved on to what Whandall needed, which was two repaired wheels, water jars, root vegetables, and dried meat.

When Fighting Cat left, Whandall told Lurk, "My first trip, the caravan had just found out we had a wagonload of refined gold. I'm passing Fighting Cat's wagon, he pulls me into his travel nest by the arm. Shows me a necklace that would look wonderful on Willow. I admired it. He wanted nine thumbweights of gold. Far too much, but it really was a beautiful necklace, and I was—I wanted very much to please Willow. He showed me each turquoise, blue to match Willow's eyes, tiny gold flecks. He pointed out the absence of cracks, that there was no yellow or green, which are flaws, but I didn't know it then.

"I kept looking. It was clear I wanted it, but the gold wasn't all mine—we hadn't divided it yet—and I wasn't saying anything. He told me its history. Offered me three Shambit figurines to go with it, still nine thumbweights. Y—" Lurk wasn't listening closely, getting bored.

Some things you say because they'll be understood later. "I already knew nobody could force me to buy without actually drawing a knife. So I was entertained. He showed me everything he had, and I smiled and admired and watched him go from nine thumbweights to two and a half. Willow loved it. And I told Fighting Cat what he'd done wrong a year later."

PART THREE

The Year of Two Burnings

CHAPTER
71

They left Firewoods Town at dawn of the third day. At noon they came to a side road that led steeply downhill and off to the west.

A score of locals had been overjoyed to find there was suddenly employment in the Feathersnake wagon trains. Where the road forked, they watched in astonishment as four wagons were separated out.

Fallen Wolf had been hired to replace a guard who was going with Whandall. "That's where you came up from the river, twenty years and more ago," he said. "You'd felled some trees. Big ones."

Whandall remembered. Two trees had blocked the wagons. It had taken all day to cut them, and he'd been much younger and stronger then. "I'd hate doing it again," he said.

"My Uncle Badwater found them," he said. "You'd already started a road in. Uncle logged them out, and that's been a logging road ever since."

Whandall frowned. "Does it go all the way to Tep's Town, then?"

"Great Coyote, no!" Fallen Wolf was horrified. "Down and along the stream, up the other side of the hill, then the creepers start. Creepers and vines, and stuff that wants to kill you!"

"And no one has explored farther?"

Fallen Wolf looked from Whandall to Saber Tooth and back. Thinking. "Okay, you hired me, you hired what I know. When I was about sixteen, maybe nine years ago, there was a lot of smoke out of the Valley of

Smokes. A lot more than usual. Me and three friends put on leather stuff, took axes and food, and tried to get in.

"The creepers were bad enough; they'll be worse now. We hid from three armored men who were coming out. Four days we cut our way through, chopping tangled crap you'll be glad to find gone. Then we saw a wall. Big stone house. Masked men in leathers, spears. Saw them just in time. We ran. They came after us. We brushed some stuff we'd avoided going in. Got away, but I sure wouldn't want to go back! We were a month getting over the itch."

"Want to come with us now?" Whandall asked.

"You all going?"

"Just four wagons," Whandall said. "With me."

"So it's true."

"What's true?" Saber Tooth demanded.

"Crazy old woman in town, babbling that Whandall Feathersnake is going home," Fallen Wolf said. "Look, all my life I wanted to work in the Feathersnake wagon trains, but if it's all the same to you, I'll stay with the main wagon train. I'd hate to get killed my first trip out!"

Fighting Cat's wagon came by. "Not going farther than the Springs?" he called. "I see you haven't lost your skill."

"Farther *south*. Thank you."

"And good luck. Wish I were going in with you; Mother would love to know."

"I'll visit her afterward."

Fighting Cat went on. He wasn't expecting Whandall back. He'd heard about Tep's Town all his life.

Of thirty-one volunteers, Whandall rejected five. That gave him twenty-eight fighters counting himself and Green Stone, one spy—he'd better not count on Lurk to fight—and one wizard.

They had four wagons. He took leathers, axes, long poles to make severs. Morth gathered herbs to make remedies against touch-me and thorns.

They carried weapons, but not to sell. A mixed bag for trade goods, a sampling of things based on old memories. Memory said that clay and metal pots would be best, but they had few because there were good markets for those along the Hemp Road. Mostly they had anything that should have sold somewhere but hadn't.

Saber Tooth stood by as Whandall's band turned off down the logging road. "Farewell. Good trading."

Whandall waved. Then all his attention was taken with guiding the bison down the old road. When he looked back, Saber Tooth and the Feathersnake wagon train were gone.

They reached the stream by evening and made camp high. "It reached you in three days last time," Whandall told Morth. "How long until it finds you?"

Morth shook his head. "There's no knowing. But I wouldn't stay here very long."

"I don't intend to."

At dawn he sent Lurk and Hammer Miller ahead to scout out the old route up the hill, then a crew with axes and brush hooks to clear the way. They were moving up the stream by noon, the wagons jouncing along the old streambed.

"A big flood cleared out many of the boulders," Whandall said. "I suppose that was your flood, Morth?" There was no way to know, but bison moved up the streambed as fast as the boneheads had taken them down. By nightfall they were ready to climb up the embankment, and Whandall had torches lit. He would not let them camp until they were high above the water.

And he remembered what he had learned while he was eldest in the Placehold: everyone complains to the Lord, and they do it all the time.

They found the first of the touch-me creepers just over the brow of the hill. The trail Whandall had burned through the forest was clear of big trees, but vines had grown into it. One rustled slightly as the bison approached it. The bison stopped. Could it sense danger? Or did it feel Whandall's thoughts?

But the way didn't seem too bad. There was more creeper than anything else. Here and there were the bright flowers of lordkin's-kiss and the duller lavender of creepy-julia, but the plants mostly defended the big trees. The road they would take wound through those. A few redwoods had sprouted up and were now a dozen years and more tall, still small among the giants. Small armies grew around their bases.

It would be tedious but not impossible.

Whandall halted the wagon train and drew everyone around.

"I've told you of touch-me before. This is what it looks like."

"Does it strangle you?" Lurk asked.

"No, but the poisons can make you wish it had," Whandall said. "And it doesn't just lie there; it can come after you. That's lordkiss over there. Stay away from it. Lizard, serve out the tools, and lash blades to the poles we brought. I'll show you how to deal with lordkiss.

"All of you, I don't know what this stuff will do to a bison, but I don't think we want to find out. We certainly don't want to brush up against a bison who's got the oils on his coat. Remember that when you're clearing the path.

"*This*"—*whack*, his palm against a slim trunk—"is an apple tree. You can eat the fruit. There's other stuff you can eat, trees and bushes and patches of brambles, but most of them are poison. Ask Morth or me. Morth can see poison."

"Yes, Father—"

"Burning Tower, you were supposed to go on with Saber Tooth!"

"Did I say I would?"

Of course she had never agreed, and it was too late to send her back now. Whandall looked into her triumphant smile, remembering Willow's nightmares.

That first year he'd grown used to waking in Willow's grip. Coming out of a nightmare, she would wrap herself around him for reassurance. *Yes, you're here; I'm out of the city, I'm free.* The nightmares faded over the second and third years . . . and she faced the old terrors when she named her third child.

If something happened to Burning Tower, Willow would be long getting over the loss. So would he.

"Use rakes," Whandall said. "Never touch it with your hands, and use the yellow blankets we brought to clean tools. Wear leathers, and don't touch the leathers when you're taking them off or putting them on. When you do begin to itch, see Morth, and don't put that off."

"Don't forget, we may want to come out fast, with heavy loads and enemies behind," Green Stone reminded them. "So make the way smooth *now*. Now let's get to it."

It felt good, at first, to swing an ax again. He left the creeper to the younger men and women, and took Greathand to attack the first tree to bar their way. It was a small redwood, no more than ten years old, perhaps less. They used severs to clear away the defending brush. Greathand stepped forward with his ax.

"Wait," Whandall said. He approached the tree and bowed. "I'm sorry you're in our way," he said. He bowed again. "Now."

Greathand chopped through the arm-thick trunk in one blow.

When Burning Tower found a patch of redberry brambles, she called him. He was unspeakably relieved. "Drop all your weapons here," he told the assembled workers. "Yes, the knives too. Now go look." They walked cautiously closer to the brambles. Then the magic reached them and they surged forward. They gorged, fighting like children for the berries, and left only twigs.

Hours later he held them back from a darker bramble patch. "Poison," he told Burning Tower, raising his voice so others would hear. "The creepers'll wind around your ankles and hold you while you die. They want your body for fertilizer. The only thing that can eat those berries is a kind of bird. Those." Little and yellow, with scarlet wings, fluttering among the brambles. "Watch for the flushers. Flushers and thornberries, they made a deal, long ago. The flushers swallow the seeds and carry them—"

"Father? How do you know?"

What *was* he remembering? "Coyote," he said. "Coyote made the bargain. He can eat thornberries too." Would that protect Whandall? Not bloody likely, he decided.

They made camp in the wagons, in a wider area they had cleared. It was not wide enough to allow them to unload the wagon boxes. Whandall was hungry. Chopping wood and vines was harder work than he was used to.

But dinner was delayed.

"Father!" Burning Tower called. "All the fires are out! I can't light the brazier."

"Curse. Of course you can't," Whandall said. He called for Greathand. "You'll have to strike fire for us. Keep it outside. From here on, fire won't burn inside a house or a home, and our wagons must seem too much like houses to Yangin-Atep."

"It may be more than that," Morth said.

"You have a vision?"

"No. But does Yangin-Atep? I've lost most of my perception, Whandall."

The Toronexti were waiting for them.

Just after first light on the fifth day, the wagon train rounded a curve to see a thick wedge of grass cleared of creeper and brush, leading like a funnel to a brick gatehouse. Seven men in leathers, wearing fancy hats with tassels perched ridiculously above their leather masks, stood in a line in front of the brick gatehouse. More were on the roof, and Whandall thought there were others concealed in the thick chaparral on both sides of the road. The seven were armed but their weapons were sheathed. Whandall couldn't see the men in the gatehouse. Beyond the gatehouse four men tended a big cook fire with an iron pot suspended over it.

As the last wagon rounded the bend, Lurk dropped away from the wagon train.

"Sure you can find us?" Whandall asked.

"I know the language. How can you hide a wagon train?" Nothing Was Seen asked reasonably. "Tonight or tomorrow."

"I don't remember their acting like this," Hammer said. He had come up to walk beside Whandall as others drove their wagons. His sling was barely concealed and he had a bag full of rocks.

"Nor I. Don't show our strength yet."

The Toronexti seemed to be engaged in a ritual. One came forward holding a leather strip. Something was wrong with the hand that held it. Two fingers were missing right to the wrist.

Because he was hidden beneath the masks and leathers, there was no other way to identify him at all.

He unrolled the leather strip and held it in front of him as he spoke. "Greetings, strangers to our land. This is Tep's Town. We are the Toronexti, spokespeople and servants to the Lord's Witnesses of Lordshills, Lord's Town, and Tep's Town. You are welcome here. Your trade goods are safe here.

"We regret that there is a small charge for this protection, and another for passage through our territory. Our inspectors will assess the charges depending on what goods you are carrying.

"Do you submit to the authority of the Lord's Witnesses?"

"You have some proof of your authority?" Morth asked dryly.

The Toronexti spokesman beamed. "We do! We have a charter from the Lord's Witnesses."

"Ah." Morth seemed boundlessly amused. "May I see it?"

"Whatever for?" Whandall demanded.

Morth shrugged.

Half Hand turned to his colleagues. They huddled. Finally the spokesman emerged and said, "One of you may approach the charter. It is kept inside the gatehouse."

"Inside," Whandall said to Morth. "So it won't burn? I'm guessing."

"A reasonable guess," Morth said. "Note the cook fire, to placate Yan-gin-Atep." Louder he said, "I will approach. I am Morth of Atlantis, wizard to the wagon train of Whandall Feathersnake, whose fame is known to the four winds."

Morth went inside. Whandall conferred with Hammer and Insolent Lizard. "Did anyone see them last night?"

Lizard said, "I thought I heard something up the road, but nobody came close, and I'd swear no one came through the forest."

"So they knew wagons were coming, but not how many," Whandall said. "Maybe they didn't bring their whole strength—"

Greathand was shouting. "Hey, harpy!"

The wagon train boiled with activity. Every armed man turned out. The women slammed the wagon covers closed. Hammer and Insolent Lizard were already running toward Greathand's wagon before Whandall could react to the traditional shout of a wagonman for help.

Two Toronexti stood menaced by Greathand and his hammer. Four more had drawn swords, and another held a spear. Greathand was shouting, the Toronexti were shouting, and no one understood a word . . .

"What is this?" Whandall demanded.

"We are Toronexti inspectors, and this man is resisting," one of the Toronexti said.

"Hold off, Greathand," Whandall said. "If you please." To the Toronexti: "Our wizard is inspecting your documents. Surely you can wait for this? Please go back to your guardhouse for instructions from your officers!"

Interestingly, they did.

"Not Lordkin," Hammer said. "Not as I remember Lordkin, anyway."

"It's an old puzzle." Lordkin wouldn't acknowledge any authority of officers and wouldn't worry about charters in the first place. But he knew Toronexti only from the Lordkin's viewpoint.

Whandall drew his wagon owners around him. "This could be tricky. Watch me, and be careful. We *do not* want to fight. Stone, go see what's keeping Morth."

Green Stone returned a few minutes later. "He's looking at an enormous pile of parchment," Stone said. "They won't let him touch it, but one of them, a crazy-looking guy in a robe and a funny hat, is spreading out the stuff on a table. One of the sheets has huge writing that says 'witnesseth' and then some other stuff I wasn't close enough to see."

"You can read it?" Greathand asked.

Willow had taught all the children to read the languages of the Hemp Road, but—

"Sure, it's in that language Mother and Dad use when they don't want us kids to understand them," Stone said. "Morth taught me that speech. And the letters are the same as we use."

"Did Morth say how long he'd be?"

"He said give him a quarter hour, but it wouldn't make much difference. Whatever that means. Dad, there was something else scrawled across the ceiling in big black letters. 'I killed Sapphire my wife. I burned my house to hide her corpse, but Yangin-Atep's rage took me and I burned more. Fire surrounded and killed me. But I am not Yangin-Atep's! I am kinless!' "

Some old memory was knocking at his skull, demanding entry, but there just wasn't time. "All right. Time to get ready. We'll have to let them inspect the wagons," Whandall said. "The only thing we have to hide is gold, and that's hidden as well as it can be."

"Those bottles aren't hidden," Hammer said. "A whole wagonload!"

"Leave those to me."

Morth returned chuckling. "It's a charter all right. And regulations. What they can collect, what they can't. In theory they're limited to one part in ten, except they can collect up to nine parts in ten of any tar being imported."

"No one would bring tar into Tep's Town," Whandall protested.

Green Stone said, "One part in ten isn't all that bad—"

"*Then* there are the exceptions," Morth said. "Whandall, that document seems to have grown over the fifty years or so when there was still trade from outside into Tep's Town."

"I don't remember there ever being any land trade," Hammer protested.

"Neither do they, nor does anyone living," Morth said. "But there are still regulations and rules, and what it amounts to is they can take anything they want if they read it all closely enough."

"And they're sure to have read it," Whandall said.

"Well, no, they haven't," Morth said. "They can't read. Except for that one, the odd one with the robe, who keeps babbling about old crimes. Egon Forigaft."

"Forigaft." A Lordkin name. Again, the old memory would not come.

"He appears to be their clerk. They treat him with an elaborate respect that he does not deserve, but Whandall, he is the only one of them who can read. They don't care what that charter says, I think. They will take what they believe is in their best interest."

"Maybe that's why these costumes, and showing us the charter," Whandall mused. "They've never seen foreign trade. Let's find out."

He strolled rapidly up to the gatehouse. "Noble Toronexti," he said. He'd learned long ago flattery was cheap goods. "We are the first of our kind in many years. Others will come, bearing many goods, cook pots, pottery of the finest make, skins of exotic animals. Furs and feathers and gems to adorn your women, all this can we bring, but none will come if we do not return happy."

The Toronexti officer grinned behind his mask. "And what do you bring this time?"

"Little of value, for this is an exploration. But we do have these, as gifts for your officers." He waved, and one of the boys brought a cheap carpet, laid it down, and unrolled it. Three bronze knives lay there, with half a dozen showy rings with glass stones, the kind that Whandall was accustomed to giving Hemp Road children as trinkets.

The Toronexti scooped them up eagerly, carpet and all. The officer eyed Whandall's knife. "Yours is even more elaborate—"

"Take it if you like." The Toronexti was already stepping forward as Whandall said, "That's how I got it."

The Toronexti officer stopped. He eyed Whandall's ears, then his tattoo. "You have been here before."

Whandall said nothing.

"A good way to get a knife," the Toronexti said. "What more have you brought?"

"There will be more of value when we leave," Whandall said.

"If you trade well."

"We will." Whandall sighed. "I show you the most valuable thing we have." He waved again, and Green Stone brought another cheap carpet.

Curse, Whandall thought. *I should have realized they have no real carpets here. They'll all want them!*

Stone unrolled the carpet. Twelve black glass bottles were nested in wood shavings.

"I know the people of Lord's Town will pay well for these," he said. "Let's think, now. The Lord's Town kinless will give me more for these bottles than they'd give you. A *lot* more. Because I don't work for the Lords." Whandall watched the tax man's face: was that still an insult? And would the man see past it, to see that Whandall was right?

"With," the tax man said. "Work with. Show me those two." He pointed to the smallest bottles.

"The little ones?"

"They're finer work."

Whandall's face didn't change as he realized the Toronexti had nothing like glass bottles. They were common enough outside, but he had never seen a glass bottle in Tep's Town! They must not be in the sea trade.

And they liked the smallest ones. Whandall remembered Green Stone's tale of the spirals of bottles made by Morth's magic. They'd left *thousands* of bottles smaller than these! What might they be worth here?

Later. Carefully Whandall lifted out the two tiny bottles. As he put one in the Toronexti's hand, he winked at Morth.

The wizard did nothing Whandall could see, but the bottle broke into a paste of sand and putrid liquid that ran on the officer's fingers.

"Curse!" Whandall exclaimed.

"Curse indeed. What *is* that?" the Toronexti demanded.

"Extract from civet cat glands," Whandall said. "It is used to make perfume."

"Perfume? That?" He reached for the other bottle. It too broke into putrescence.

Whandall stared, bug-eyed, and cried out as if strangling. Then he put a third bottle in the tax man's limp hand. Again the glass crumbled into sand and stinking liquid. The Toronexti flung it away with a curse. The other tax man broke into wild laughter. "Magic? Magic doesn't work here, you fool!"

Morth said, "I'm sorry, Feathersnake! These magic bottles will disintegrate at the touch of anyone in this cursed town. They'll have to be emptied over a basin!"

"You say the kinless of Lord's Town will pay for this? To make perfume?" the Toronexti officer demanded.

"Well, they do in Condigeo!"

"Then let them do it! We certainly don't want that stuff. The bottles now—"

"Another time," Morth said. "They can be made without magic. I had not realized the backwardness of this place."

"Backward? *Us?*" But the Toronexti guard was laughing. "So what else do you have?"

"Little, for we thought those the best things to sell."

"Why'd you think that?" the Toronexti asked craftily.

"We speak to ship captains," Whandall said. "We learn. What, would you know all the secrets of a master trader?" He smiled broadly.

Behind him his wagoneers had arrayed themselves. Greathand leaned on a two-handed sword, point down. Hammer and some of the younger kinless idly held slings and rocks. Green Stone held an ax and wore a big Lordkin knife. They all smiled and listened to their wagonmaster. And stood with weapons ready.

Whandall had no trouble reading the Toronexti leader's thoughts. The wagoneers might be telling truth—there were more and richer trains to come if this one came out whole. There were thirty armed men, more than the strength the Toronexti had brought today. The wagon train would be more valuable coming out than going in, and it would come at a time when they could bring their entire strength.

"Do you have more of those rings?"

"A dozen, as a gift," Whandall said.

"Food?"

Whandall threw down a box of dried bison meat.

The Toronexti grinned. "Pass, friends."

CHAPTER
72

The trail crossed the Deerpiss a final time. "Now," Whandall told Green Stone. "We'll see Tep's Town as soon as we've got around this grove."

The town lay ahead, down a gentle slope. Thirty men armed and wearing Lordsmen armor blocked the road. They stood to attention, not menacing, but there was no way around them.

"Bandits," Green Stone shouted.

Whandall stood on the driving bench and gestured violently at the following wagons, both hands out, flat, empty, pushing down. *Put down your weapons!* Green Stone saw the urgency in his father's face. He rushed back to the others, urging calm.

Whandall dropped from the wagon. He stepped forward, the big engraved knife prominently sheathed. "Hail."

"Hail." The spokesman was elderly, his face hidden in the Lordsman helmet and armor, but the voice sounded familiar. "Whandall Feathersnake. We have heard the stories." He turned to speak to someone behind him, a man hidden by the ranks of guardsmen. "It's him, Lord. Whandall Placehold, returned." He turned back, looked at the caravan, and turned again. "Come back rich, he has."

"Peacevoice Waterman," Whandall said.

"Master Peacevoice Waterman to you, sir!" There was some amusement and no malice in the voice. "Not surprised you remember me. Sir."

"Is that Lord Samorty in command, then?"

"No, sir, Lord Samorty is dead these five years, sir."

Somehow he was surprised. But Lords *did* die; they only seemed to live forever. "May we pass? We come to trade," Whandall said.

"Up to the commander, sir!"

With patience, Whandall said, "Then let's talk to the commander—"

Waterman's face didn't change. He turned and shouted, "Whandall Placehold wishes to speak with the commander, Lord!"

The hidden Lord said something in a low voice. "Lord says a quarter hour, Master Peacevoice!" a guardsman shouted.

"Quarter hour, sir!" Waterman said. He returned to a position of rigid attention. When it was clear he wasn't going to say or do anything else, Whandall went back to the wagons.

Morth was grinning. "Interesting."

"Why?" Whandall demanded.

"Look." Morth pointed. A small cart drawn by one of the big horses the Lords used had pulled up behind the ranks of guards. Three workers had taken a small tent from the wagon and were busily setting it up. Another set a charcoal burner down. It was clear from the way he handled it that it held a live fire, and sure enough, he put a tea kettle on top of it. Another worker brought a table, then two chairs, went away for a while, then returned with a third chair.

The kinless workers were dressed all in yellow and black shirts. Whandall remembered Samorty's gardeners, but those weren't the same colors. Morth frowned. "Quintana," he said.

"Say?"

"Those are Quintana's colors," Morth said. "And it appears from his age that that's Lord Quintana himself. He must be seventy years old now, and no magic to help. And he came himself. Whandall, they are certainly taking you seriously."

"Is this good?"

Morth shrugged.

A corporal came up to them. "Whandall Feathersnake, Lord Chief Witness Quintana requests your company at tea," he said formally. "And asks that you permit the sage Morth of Atlantis to accompany you."

Morth's grin turned sour, but he said, "We will be delighted. Come, Whandall."

It was Whandall's turn to grin.

A servant stood behind Quintana and held his chair as Quintana stood. "Whandall Feathersnake, I am delighted to meet you. Morth of Atlantis, it is good to see you again. You look younger than the last time we met."

"Indeed, I am younger, Lord Quintana."

Quintana smiled wryly. "I don't suppose you can sell me anything that will do the same for me?"

"Not so long as you insist on living in that blighted area you call the Lordshills," Morth said.

"Ah. But elsewhere?"

"Nowhere short of the distant mountains," Morth said. "I've found a *wonderful* place half a hundred days' walk west by north—"

Quintana nodded. "Hardly surprising. Please be seated, Wagonmaster, Sage. I can offer you tea."

Weak hemp tea with a smoky flavor of tar. Morth sipped and made appreciative noises. Whandall smiled: the Lord wasn't trying to drug him.

"May I be blunt?" Quintana said. "Wagonmaster, what are your intentions?"

"We bring trade goods," Whandall said. "Some fit for Lords. If we have reason, we will send in more wagons with more goods. I had hoped to make camp at Lord's Town."

"There is no suitable accommodation for all of you there," Quintana said. "We can offer lodging for you and the Sage in Lord's Town, but there is no place for all of you, and I am certain you would prefer to remain together."

"Oh, yes." Get separated, *here?*

"So. Welcome back to Tep's Town," Quintana said.

Morth chuckled.

"You are amused, Sage?"

"Mildly so," Morth said. "And curious as to why the chief witness would come personally to greet a trader."

Quintana's expression didn't change. "We are not often visited by wealthy caravans."

"Even so, I would wager this is the first one you have met."

"It is also the first I have seen, as you must know. And I grow old; I grow bored." Quintana said. He stood abruptly. "I grow frail. Master Peacevoice Waterman will escort you to a suitable camping ground. Perhaps I may visit you there. Welcome to Tep's Town."

Whandall invited Waterman to ride on the wagon with him.

"Don't mind if I do, sir," Waterman said. "Not getting any younger."

"Beaten up any boys lately?" Whandall asked conversationally.

"A few," Waterman said. "Comes with the job. Didn't fancy you'd have forgotten. Sir."

"Truth is," Whandall said, "that was nicely judged. Here." He pulled the sleeve from his left arm. "I can't forget, no, but I can still pick things up. I wonder if you've seen the teller Tras Preetror lately?"

"Not for ten years. He doesn't come to Lord's Town, of course, but I keep·track. Why?"

Whandall told the tale as they drove. "So I've been on both sides of that fence, Master Peacevoice."

They drove in silence for a few minutes. "There was something Lord Quintana wasn't saying," Whandall said.

"Yes, sir, there was," Waterman said readily enough. "You're still not welcome in Lordshills."

"But—Lord Samorty's dead?"

"Oh, yes."

Waterman—Quintana—the Lords were keeping a promise made to a dead man. Because he was dead, the order could never be changed. Lords were strange. Whandall had not guessed how strange.

"Them Toronexti," Waterman said.

Huh? "What about them?"

Waterman said nothing. Why had he brought up the subject at all? "Do you work for the Toronexti?" Whandall prompted.

Waterman sucked air through his teeth, an ugly sound. "Why ask that?"

"Not to offend. The Toronexti had to send you a runner," Whandall said. "He must have waited just long enough to see"—he brushed his tattooed cheek—"*me,* and then run like the wind. And you came. With Lord Quintana and most of your army."

"Not most," Waterman said. "Some. As to the Toronexti, what you think you know about them is likely wrong."

"Please do go on. We like to trade stories."

"And it's my turn?" Waterman grinned. "Most Lordkin think they're just another band. A few think they work for the Lords."

"Don't they?"

"Used to," Waterman said. "Used to collect taxes, and keep some, of course. They kept the kinless from running away, looked after trade stuff for the Lords. But my father's father told me trade stopped coming through the woods, and then there were *more* Toronexti, and they kept more of what they took." Waterman spat over the side. He said, "Gathered. I guess maybe they still keep to some of their tasks. Some goods get through from the forest. They did send a runner to tell us about your wagons. But mostly they work for themselves now."

"We never knew where they lived, how they lived, what they did with all that wealth. Who their neighbors were. If they were Lordkin, where's their turf? If they're kinless . . . are they kinless?"

"I know how they started," the Master Peacevoice said. "Our forebears burned their way through the forest and took Tep's Town. You know that. But Lords and Lordkin didn't want to live together. When things had settled down, there were . . . I'm told . . . exactly sixty boys and girls who had a Lord for a father and a Lordkin for a mother."

"Never the other way around?"

"No."

Silence could often be the essence of tact.

Waterman said, "A place had to be found for them. They were set to guard the way through the forest. Kinless must not escape, you see; they might bring allies. But the tax men lived on site and built their homes along the Deerpiss. It was their duty."

"No homes there now," Whandall remembered. "Just that guardhouse and the barrier. That big center section is stone; must have been built by kinless. The wings are crude work, more recent. They *didn't* become kinless."

Waterman said nothing.

Whandall asked, "What do you wonder, when you wonder about the Toronexti?"

They'd passed the edge of town and were moving through Flower Market territory. The streets looked empty until Whandall's mind adjusted. Then . . . here was the snapdragon sign crudely painted on a crumbling wall. Motion along a roof: a clumsy lurker . . . a whole line of them. Motion in window slits. An audience was watching the parade.

Waterman hadn't answered.

Whandall asked, "Why tell me?"

Waterman stared straight ahead.

They rolled along in a silence that might have been companionable. Whandall waited. Some secrets must be hidden, but some may be traded. . . .

The caravan skirted the edge of Serpent's Walk, along the road between Serpent's Walk and Flower Market. Whandall remembered the road. Lordkin came out of houses to stare at them. No one was going to try gathering from wagons escorted by marching Lordsmen.

Over there was an empty lot. A large square building must have covered that, and another behind it, now both gone. Ahead was a ruined wall, remains of a burned out building, and ahead of that—

A field, once paved with cobblestones. Grass and mustard stalks grew among the stones. All the walls around the field were ruins, buildings long burned out.

A fountain stood in the center. Water trickled from it—

"But this is Peacegiven Square!" Whandall shouted.

Waterman nodded, his expression unreadable, amused? Wry? Whandall couldn't tell. "That is it. Sir. It's where Lord Quintana said you was to make camp. Good roads from here, room to set up a market, not much water but more than most places. He thought it would be a good place."

Whandall stared at the ruins. "All right, he has a point. This will do. Master Peacevoice, it strikes me that you could have told me about *this*. Where we're to set up our market, and why, and what happened here in the twenty-two years I've been gone. But you decided to talk about the Toronexti. Was *I* supposed to know something? I never came anywhere near the Deerpiss until—"

Until Wanshig got involved in making wine.

There's a question; he's waiting for it. Whandall asked, "Did Lord Quintana ask you to mention Toronexti?"

"Wouldn't say yes; wouldn't say no," Waterman said.

"What would the Lords do if the Toronexti just . . . disappeared one day?"

"Find someone to take their place," Waterman said. "Someone more reasonable, and a lot fewer. I think me and ten men could do their job."

"Sons? Nephews?"

"There's a notion."

CHAPTER
73

Whandall raised his hand above his head and brought his arm around in a wide circle. "Circle the wagons," but with only four they made a square.

There were wagons—small flatbeds, with no roofs, in the kinless style—at the far end of the square. Waterman went over to them. Whandall was just unhitching the bison when Waterman returned leading a young man. He was shaven clean, no tattoos, and no more than twenty, perhaps less. It was difficult to tell his age because of his clothing. He wore a dark robe and a close-fitting cap that came down over his forehead and was low enough to cover his ears.

"Witness Clerk Sandry," Waterman said. "I present you to Wagonmaster Whandall Feathersnake. Wagonmaster, Clerk Sandry is here to assist you. Any questions you may have, any requests, he'll help you."

"Thank you, Master Peacevoice." As Waterman went back to his troops, Whandall inspected the younger man. He was taller than Whandall remembered any Witness Clerk as being, and of course Whandall had been younger and shorter then. Most of his body was hidden by the loose robe, but where his arms showed they were more muscular than any clerk's. His cap wasn't new, but it didn't fit him very well. Whandall's expression didn't change. "Welcome, Clerk Sandry."

"Just Sandry will do, sir."

"Very well. I presume you can read."

"Yes, sir, I can read and calculate."

"Good. Find us a place to corral the bison. Then find where we can buy fodder for them. Bison eat a lot, Clerk Sandry. More than you would expect. We'll want a full wagonload of hay or straw."

"As you wish, sir," Sandry said. He inspected the trickle of water from the fountain. "Might I also suggest a water wagon? Sir."

"What will that cost us?"

"I'll find out, sir. But not so much if it's river water. Only for animals, of course."

Whandall remembered the stinking water of the rivers in Tep's Town. He'd been glad enough of it at one time. Now he was used to better, and the memory of that water choked him. The fountain water wasn't good, but it had to be better than river water.

"Please arrange it."

"Yes, sir."

Green Stone came up to watch Sandry walking across the square. Whandall explained.

"Who do you think he is, Father?" Green Stone asked.

Whandall shook his head. "I never knew that much about the Lords and Witnesses and their clerks. He may be just what he says he is, but I doubt it. Remember that he can read. Don't leave anything around he shouldn't see."

"I never do," Stone said.

"Of course you don't."

"Handsome boy," Burning Tower said from behind him.

"Too old for you, Blazes," Green Stone said.

"Well, maybe," Burning Tower said. "And maybe not."

"Don't you two have work to do?" Whandall Placehold Feathersnake asked.

At the far end of the square kinless workmen set up a camp for Waterman and his Lordsmen guards. One of the kinless, a boy about fifteen, came over to Whandall. He took off his cap and shuffled from one foot to the other. Whandall stared in confusion, then embarrassing memories returned. A kinless who wanted to speak to a Lordkin but was afraid.

"Talk to me."

"Master Peacevoice Waterman said I was to ask if you need workers to help setting up camp."

"No, thank you. We're used to doing it ourselves."

The kinless boy watched as Whandall's people unloaded wagon boxes. He seemed astonished.

Of course. There was Green Stone, with a Lordkin's ears, carrying a box with one of the Miller boys. The Millers all looked kinless, except for those who looked like Bison tribesmen, and Mother Quail, daughter to a Bison man and the younger Miller girl, an exotic mix whose beauty edged the supernatural. Burning Tower looked like a slim young Lordkin girl. And they all worked together.

"Firewood," Whandall said. "We'll pay for firewood."

The kinless boy nodded. "We can get you some." He seemed hesitant.

"Spit it out, lad," Whandall said.

The boy flinched.

"Come on—what is it?"

"My name is Adz Weaver."

"Weaver. Ah. You'll be kin to my wife, then?"

"It's true? You *married* Willow Ropewalker?"

"More than twenty years now," Whandall said. "Stone," he called. "Green Stone is our second son. Stone, this is Adz Weaver. He'll be some kind of cousin."

Stone held up his hand in greeting. Whandall nodded approval. It was a Hemp Road gesture not used in Tep's Town, but then in Tep's Town there wasn't any gesture a Lordkin would use to greet a kinless.

Adz Weaver glanced around, obviously aware that a knot of Lordkin were watching from the Serpent's Walk side of Peacegiven Square. "You're welcome here," Whandall said. "But it might be best if you come back after we have the walls up. No sense in gathering Lordkins' attention. And we do need firewood."

"Yes, sir," Weaver said. Whandall smiled to himself. Adz Weaver had used the tone that kinless used when addressing an older relative, not the more obsequious falling tone used to address Lordkin.

Progress.

Well before the Lordsmen guards' camp was up, the wagon boxes had been offloaded, carpets unrolled, awnings erected, and the bison corralled in a nearby vacant lot. Sandry appeared with kinless driving a wagonload of hay and another wagon with a water tank. Whandall recognized one of the fire prevention wagons kinless used. More kinless brought firewood. When Stone offered a kinless the smallest fleck of gold they had for a heap of wood, it was obvious that they'd paid far too much. Whandall negotiated for shells and was pleased: they bought several bags of shells, too many to count, for one gold nugget.

Trading would be good here.

Whandall's travel nest was divided into two rooms. The inner was more ornate than most, as befitted a wealthy merchant prince. Willow worried about that, so the outer sides of Whandall's wagon boxes were scarred and unfinished, and the outer room was plain. In the inner room the wood was polished, rubbed with the shells of laq beetles until it shone. Two mirrors hung so that they faced each other, making a magical display the children never tired of. Wool for his carpets came from highland sheep sheared after a hard winter, and his cushions were filled with wool and down. Outside was poverty, but inside the nest everything said "I can afford to ignore your inadequate offer."

Dinner was locally bought chicken stewed with local vegetables. Between what the Toronexti took and what they'd sold here, there wasn't any more bison jerky or fruit. Whandall had just filled his bowl for a second helping when Stone came into the nest. "There's an old man wants to see you."

"You should be specific," Whandall said. "Kinless, Lordkin, Lordsman. Witness. Lord even. Not just man."

"I can't tell," Stone said patiently. "He has a knife."

"Lordkin," Whandall said. "Old?"

"A lot older than you, Father. No teeth, not much hair."

"I'll come out."

Old described him. The Lordkin still stood erect and proud and wore his big Lordkin knife defiantly, but Whandall thought he'd better have sons with him if he wanted to walk far in Tep's Town.

Whandall held out his hand, Lordkin to Lordkin. They slapped palms. The old man's eyes twinkled. "Don't know me, do you, Whandall?"

Whandall frowned.

"Know anything about wine?"

"Alferth!"

"That's me."

"Come in; have some tea," Whandall said. He led him into the outer nest. No point in giving too much away—

Alferth looked around and laughed. "Tarnisos said you took a kinless wagon, and I heard you married a kinless. Now you live like one?" He grinned. "You must be rich."

"I am," Whandall admitted. "How is Tarnisos?"

"Dead. Most everyone you knew is dead, Whandall."

Lordkin killed each other. Even men who lived here forgot.

"Something I've wondered about all these years," Alferth said. "Tarnisos said you really were possessed by Yangin-Atep. Burned a torch right out of his hand! Was he lying?"

"No, I did that." Whandall tried to remember that time. Alferth and the others beating a kinless man—Willow's father!—into something unidentifiable. The rage that filled his mind and flowed through his fingers . . . was gone. "I burned our way through the forest."

"I always hoped it was true," Alferth said. "Never happened to me. I mocked Yangin-Atep, pretended to be possessed when I wasn't." He shrugged. "Too old now, I think. Why would Yangin-Atep be interested in an old man?"

He looks twenty years older than me, Whandall thought. *But it can't be more than five.*

"Hungry?" Whandall asked.

"Nearly always," Alferth admitted.

Whandall clapped his hands. "Stone, please ask Burning Tower to bring dinner for my friend. Alferth, this is my son, Green Stone."

Alferth stared.

Son, Whandall thought. *I said son, and Alferth isn't kin.*

Alferth came to himself and nodded greeting. He'd been studying Green Stone's ears. Of course he would. Well, the Lordkin could just damned well get used to it!

Burning Tower brought in a pot of stew. Alferth took a carved wooden cup from his belt and held it out. She filled it, not bothering to hide her curiosity about this strange man who sat as a friend in her father's nest.

"Things have not been good?" Whandall asked.

"Not good, not since the year we had two Burnings."

"In one year?"

"Yeah. Nine years ago now. First Burning, that was *fun,* but the second was bad. We burned things we needed. That's when Peacegiven Square went, with half the city."

"How did it start?"

Alferth shrugged. "I never did know, Whandall, because I never really believed in Yangin-Atep. But that time, that second Burning, *everyone* was possessed! They ran around pointing and fires roared up, and we all went damn near mad gathering. I went right into a fire and came out with an armload of burning bath towels! Took me half a year healing from the burns. I'll never have a beard again, this side. Pelzed smelled roasting meat and ran into a burning butcher shop and staggered out hugging a side of ox. His heart quit."

"Lord Pelzed is dead, then?" Whandall wasn't much surprised.

"Sure—hey, Whandall, your brother is Lord of Serpent's Walk now."

"Shastern?"

Alferth's face wrinkled. "Shastern? Oh, him, naw, he's been dead what, fifteen years? No, the old one, Lord Wanshig, he's Lord of Serpent's Walk now. Matter of fact that's why I'm here—be sure it's really you."

And see how the land lies, Whandall thought. "Tell my brother—tell Lord Wanshig I'm delighted. And I would like to see him again, here or anywhere he'd like."

Alferth's face twisted into a grin. "Thought you would be." He looked around the plain boxes. He leaned close and dropped his voice. "I could help you find a better place to feed him."

Whandall stood. "Let me try first," he said. He pushed aside a tall man's height of boxes that turned out to be nailed together, and led Alferth into the inner nest.

"Yangin-Atep's eyes! You do live fancy," he said. "So those stories are all true—you went off and got rich!"

"There's a lot more," Whandall said. He gestured eastward. "Out there. I can bring more in. Except I can't."

"Hmm?"

"Toronexti. They took a lot of what we brought. They'll take more going out." Testing, Whandall said, "I'd kill them all if I could." Alferth had felt that way once.

"Thought of it myself," Alferth said. "I hired Toronexti to guard Lord Quintana's grapes and move his wine that he put in my charge. They let some Lordkin gather one of our wagons, *just* what they was supposed to stop, and two of them dead and the rest screaming *at me*. That was you and Freethspat, wasn't it, Whandall?"

"Sure."

"And we all took our lumps, Quintana and the Toronexti and me, and let it go. But, you know, strong as they were supposed to be, they shouldn't let go so easily. I should have known. But I kept my Toronexti guards, and paid them high out of what I was getting, and when that *wave* of gatherers came out of Tep's Town, they ran. They let that mob into the vineyards and the vats. Some of 'em were in the mob! Quintana had a price on my head for a year, and he never spoke to me again. Sure I'd like to kill the Toronexti, but you can't fight Lords."

"Lords protect Toronexti? *Which* Toronexti?"

"All. Whandall, everyone knows that. They *collect* for the Lords. Well, maybe you don't know it," Alferth conceded. "But everyone who ever tried to make anything of himself knows it. If you nose around their territory, the Lords take a big interest in you."

"Toronexti have a *territory?* Is this something everyone knows too? We only knew—"

Alferth held out his empty cup. Whandall clapped and waited for Burning Tower to fill the cup again. He said, "We only knew about the Deerpiss and the gatehouse. We never knew where they lived."

Alferth said, "They don't talk. But I *knew* they had a territory. They *must*. They hide their faces. The leathers they always wear, that must hide a band mark. There *had* to be a way to hurt them. What else could I think about while I hid? I asked around, and I thought. Then the search got hotter and I had to stop looking. I had to leave Serpent's Walk. I live on the beach at Sea Cliffs, and nobody knows anything there."

"That sounds—"

"But before they shut me down, I learned some. Foot of Granite Knob. That's theirs."

"*Them?* Alferth, no. The Wolverines don't live near the Deerpiss."

"I'd bet my patch of dry sand on it, against the rest of this stew."

Not a heavy bet. Whandall thought back. He'd never been on Wolverine turf. Children were told to avoid it. It was over toward the forest, backed up against a chaparral-covered granite hill, not isolated but easily defended, near two hours' walk from the Deerpiss. No one ever went there uninvited, and there weren't many invitations.

You saw Wolverines raiding, but rarely, and in big packs. Funny, nobody ever wondered . . . nobody but a merchant *would* ever wonder how bands that big could gather enough to share. Like they did it just to fight, just for practice. . . .

Wolverine territory. "You're pretty near guessing," Whandall said.

"Whandall, do you remember those crazies who could *read?* At your party they got too much of your powder—"

"Got into a graveyard. Heads full of ghosts. Pelzed traded them to the Wolverines for a wagonload of oranges. That used to *itch* at me. How did he get anyone to take them at all?"

A slow grin, four teeth in it. Alferth asked, "Why would Wolverines want readers too crazy to remember secrets?"

"Forigaft."

"Right."

The brothers Forigaft. Egon was the youngest, sold to the Wolverines and now clerk to the Toronexti! I owe you, Alferth. "Have an orange? Show your belly some variety."

"Yeah!"

"Does my brother live in Pelzed's old house?" Whandall asked.

"He let Pelzed's women keep it," Alferth said. "Lord Wanshig lives in that big stone place you come from. I think his lady Wess didn't want to move."

Wess. Whandall felt a twinge in his loins. Wess was alive. She'd be the first lady of the Placehold. Alferth wouldn't know about that.

They talked until well after dark. When Alferth left, Whandall noticed that four young Lordkin were waiting under a torch. He merged with them; they doused the torch and all merged into the shadows.

Then one of the shadows became Lurk.

Lurk glided in almost supernatural silence, but slowly, sideways and twisted over. One arm was swollen into a red pillow streaked with purple. Whandall knew those marks. He didn't touch them. He set him down on a burlap sheet and sent for Morth.

Morth looked ancient, worse than Alferth. He came leaning heavily on Sandry's arm. The wizard examined Nothing Was Seen without touching the boy. He muttered words in a language none of them knew. They watched, fearing to interrupt.

Morth snarled, "I sold ointments for plant poisons for near thirty years! Now I'll have to make more on the spot! Clerk Sandry, I need *any* breed of belladonna. Tomato, bell pepper, potato, chilis—"

Sandry was slow to react . . . as if he weren't used to taking orders. Then, "At once, Sage."

They could hear him speaking rapidly to someone outside. Morth moved them out of the nest. Under the awning outside he tended a firepot, set water to boiling, added chipped dried roots and some leaves from the forest, soaked a clean shirt. "Wash yourself, if you can stay awake. What were you doing in the chaparral, boy?"

Lurk looked to Whandall. *Speak in front of the wizard?* Whandall said, "Go ahead."

"Whandall set me to watch the tax men." Lurk's voice was slurred. "A wagon came out of those low woods, a tiny wagon with a tiny pony driving it. I tried to follow it home. They went straight into the woods. There was just a trace of path. I *know* that wagon was wider than I am, and *it* got through, but it wasn't trying to hide too." He scrubbed his arm, tenderly. "When my arm swelled up I was deep in the woods and getting dizzy. Here, something scratched me here too before I could get out." Three puffy parallel lines along his hip. "I swear it *reached out.*"

"Wash that too, idiot!" the wizard snarled. "Get your clothes *off.* We'll have to bury them."

Whandall said, "They reach. You remember what I told you going through the forest? It's the same stuff. It *wants* to kill you. You were smart not to go in very far."

"Lucky, too," Lurk said. "But I lost them." He sounded disgusted.

Sandry was back with a double handful of bell peppers. Morth went to work.

"They were carrying a big pile of stuff, that stack Morth was looking at in their gatehouse," Lurk said. "They loaded it in that wagon, and maybe ten of them went with it, like it was the most valuable thing they had."

"What did they do with it?" Whandall asked.

"Don't know. I told you. Got away." Lurk's voice was fading fast.

"What do you think they were doing, Clerk Sandry?" Whandall asked.

Sandry's face was a mask to match Whandall's trading face. "No idea, sir. None at all."

"I see." Whandall turned back to Lurk and said, softly, "Maybe I found them at the other end."

Lurk looked less puzzled than dizzy. But Whandall was making maps in his head. Do it on parchment later, check it out. . . .

No one had ever walked it, really, but it must be near two hours from Alferth's grape fields down the Deerpiss and across to Wolverine turf . . . by the streets. Those streets curved around a knob of hill covered with chaparral thickening to dwarf forest. But as the crow flies—

How could he have seen Staxir's armor and Kreeg Miller's leathers and never made the connection? *They go into the woods. Kinless woodsmen can do that, and so can I. The Toronexti have to, to move what they take!*

"Which way did they go?" Whandall asked. "Show me on a map." He called for lamps and parchment.

While they waited, Morth wrapped paste-covered cloths around puffy red blotches on Nothing Was Seen's arm and lower belly. "And drink this."

Lurk sipped. He protested, "Man, that's *coffee!*"

"Sorry. If I had honey . . . oh, just drink it."

"I will send for honey," Sandry said.

And we were speaking Condigeo, which Sandry hasn't admitted knowing, Whandall thought. "Thank you."

With Stone and Morth and Sandry at his elbows, Whandall drew maps of Tep's Town. Whandall gave his attention to Wolverine turf and the Deerpiss, and the streets that curved around a peninsula of forest. Through the forest was much shorter, but slower too if a man didn't want to die horribly.

But Morth was concentrating *his* efforts from the Black Pit west toward the sea, sketching in detail on a path that evaded the Lordshills, otherwise following the lowlands.

When Sandry refused to help them work on Lord's Town, Morth protested. "These have to be accurate. I'll need them later. And at least twenty of your Lordkin, Whandall—"

"I tire of your hints. Maps won't help," Whandall said. "Morth, no Lordkin knows maps." He turned to the kinless boy huddled at the outer edge of the band. "Adz Weaver, do you understand maps?"

"No, sir; I never saw anything like that," the young kinless said. "But I've been watching; I think I have the idea. You're making a picture of where we are?"

Whandall was startled. "Yes! Come here; help us mark this."

They watched Adz draw detail into kinless territory.

And it was all filling in nicely. "If he can learn that quickly, so can others," Morth said.

Whandall nodded. If kinless could learn, Lordkin could learn. Lordkin were smarter than kinless. He said, "Nothing Was Seen."

Lurk stood with difficulty. He leaned on his arms above the map. "Is this the big stone gatehouse that blocks the way to the forest? They went along here, up the Deerpiss. About here they went off the road and uphill, and I last saw them here, bush getting thick—"

Whandall grinned. "Good."

"Good? I lost them!"

"Up and across!" Whandall's fingertip ran through the mapped forest to the suburb of Granite Knob.

"I'll go see."

"Wait for dawn."

"No," Lurk said.

Stone would have stopped him, but Whandall shook his head. It would be a matter of pride with Lurk. Let him go. . . . "*Not* into the forest, understand? I only want to know where they come out."

Lurk nodded, then faded.

They worked on maps all night.

CHAPTER
74

Master Peacevoice Waterman and two men came to Whandall's wagon when the sun was an hour high. "Message, sir!" Waterman said. "Lady Shanda wishes to see you, here, at the sixth hour today, sir."

Shanda. "Who is Lady Shanda, Master Peacevoice?"

Waterman's expression changed only slightly. "First lady of Lord's Town, sir."

"She's married to Quintana?" Whandall asked.

Waterman was shocked. "No sir. She is married to Lord Quintana's nephew, and Lord Quintana being a widower, she is the official hostess for his household, sir." His voice held reproach, as if Whandall should know better.

"You like her, don't you, Master Peacevoice?"

"Everybody likes Lady Shanda, sir. That right, Corporal Driver?"

"Yes, Master Peacevoice."

Interesting. Sixth hour. Five hours from now. She must be partway here already. "Please send word to Lady Shanda that we will be delighted to have her join us at the sixth hour," Whandall said. A conventional phrase, but he found that he meant it. Shanda.

They set up the market before noon. A tightrope, high the way Burning Tower liked it. Hammer Miller and a kinless boy stood under to catch. Neither Lordkin nor Lord would do that in Tep's Town, and for the moment it was better if Whandall Feathersnake kept his dignity, even if he didn't like it.

Nothing went wrong. Burning Tower's act was flawless. And Clerk Sandry stood, mouth open, watching her in fascination as she wheeled and spiraled halfway down the pole, then deftly climbed, feet on the pole, back up it again.

"Smitten," Whandall heard Green Stone say behind him. "With my sister."

"And well he might," Whandall said softly.

"With Blazes? But all right, she's good on that rope."

"That wasn't the entire reason I had in mind," Whandall said.

It was only after Burning Tower finished her act and went to the changing tent that Sandry went to negotiate for another wagonload of hay and another of water for the bison. As Whandall had guessed, no one in Tep's Town would have dreamed that animals could eat so much.

Or make so much waste for the kinless to clean up . . .

Shanda arrived in a small wagon drawn by four Lord's horses. A teenage girl rode with her. Two chariots, one in front and one behind, clattered along with her. Each chariot held an armored man. If they were trying to convince him that Shanda was important, they succeeded.

He knew she was younger than he was, but she looked Whandall's age. He would not have recognized her. The self-assurance he remembered was there, but the little girl had become regal, desirable, attractive rather than beautiful, but extremely so. She wore a short skirt of thin wool, belt with ornate silver buckle, a brooch with blue and amber stones. Her hair was coiled atop her head, and although she must have been traveling all day in a wagon, she looked cool and fresh.

The girl with Shanda carried a large pine cone. Shanda smiled faintly. "What's it like outside?" she asked.

It took Whandall a moment to remember. "Don't they let you go outside yet?" he asked.

She laughed. "You do remember." She pointed to the pine cone. "And keep your promises too."

"Is that really the same one?"

"No, of course not," she said. "This is my daughter, Roni. Roni, greet Whandall Placehold Feathersnake, merchant prince and a very old friend of your mother's."

Whandall bowed. "And this is Green Stone, my son, and Burning Tower, my daughter. I think the girls will be about the same age. Will you come in, Lady Shanda? We have tea." He led her into the inner nest.

Shanda marveled. "You have done well. Two mirrors! And I'd love to know the secret of how you get wood to shine like that." She stared admiringly at the carpets. "You have done well indeed, Whandall Feathersnake."

"Thank you, Lady. And have things been well for you?"

"Not as well as we would like," Shanda said, serious for a moment before her smile returned. "But well enough."

"Did you ever finish the new aqueduct?"

Her smile faded again. "Not yet. We keep hoping."

"Peacegiven Square," Whandall said. "I was shocked."

She nodded, waited until Burning Tower poured tea, sipped, and nodded again. "Thank you. Whandall, it shocked us all, that second Burning."

"What happened?"

"Lord Chanthor always hoped to buy dragon bones," Shanda said.

"I remember. We were hiding on Shanda's balcony," Whandall said to his son. Green Stone and Burning Tower knew the story, but Roni *looked* at her mother. "Some captain sold Chanthor rocks in a fancy box. He had the man killed."

"Yes. And another promised but couldn't deliver, but he didn't take any money. Chanthor kept trying. One day it came. Dragon bones! In an iron box. Terribly, terribly expensive.

"We really couldn't afford them, but, well, we planned to do so much for the people!" Shanda said. "Make rain in just the right places to clear out the waterways, wash all the filth out to sea. Repair buildings. Heal the sick. Finish the aqueduct! It would have been worth what we paid." She was talking as much to Green Stone as to Whandall. Maybe it was the ears? Green Stone could absolve her, speaking for the kinless? Forgive her for the crushing weight of taxes to buy this disaster.

Resalet had opened a cold iron box. . . .

"Back there, at that building, the Witnesses had an office." Shanda pointed through the doorway to where no building stood. Dark ground, charred. "Lord Chanthor brought the box there to be registered. Then they set up by the fountain for the ceremony," she waved at the fountain, blackened and split by heat and near waterless, "with our wizard. We tried to find Morth of Atlantis. He'd gone like smoke in a Burning. Years later we were told he left with you, Whandall! So we hired the wizard from the ship that brought the dragon bones, and on the fountain he opened it . . ." She fell silent.

"And the last thing his eyes ever saw?"

She stared.

"Yangin-Atep took the magic," Whandall prompted.

Shanda's daughter Roni jumped. "Yes!" she said. "He's right, isn't he, Mother? We were home waiting. Mother was so excited, all the good we could do, and she was watching for dark storm clouds, for rain, and suddenly black smoke was pouring up everywhere. Burning," Roni said. "We'd just *had* a Burning!"

"It was horrible, Whandall," Shanda whispered. "They burned so much! The square, the new ropewalk we'd paid so much to build after we lost the Ropewalker family! To you, they told me! You took the Ropewalkers out of Tep's Town. I don't think I ever quite forgave you for that."

"I didn't know who they were when we started through the forest," Whandall said. "Or what Ropewalkers do. But, Shanda, I'd have freed those children anyway."

"What? Yes. Yes, of course," Shanda said, and blushed violently. "Whandall, I almost went outside. My stepfather thought of marrying me to a Condigeo merchant prince, and I'd have lived in Condigeo. But he didn't—maybe the man lost his nerve—and then I met Qu'yuma." Her voice and expression changed and for a moment Whandall envied Qu'yuma.

Green Stone asked, "Yangin-Atep took the dragon bone manna to himself. Like with new gold?"

"And came violently awake," said his father. "And possessed whoever he could."

"And the city has never been the same," Roni said.

He thought, *Really?* He remembered better than that.

Shanda brightened. "But now you're here! You can help."

"How?" Whandall asked.

"Trade. We can use more trade," Shanda said.

"It's hard for wagons to compete with the sea captains," Whandall said.

Roni started to say something, looked to her mother, and kept silence. Whandall let the silence stretch on. It was painful, but he was Whandall Feathersnake, and his son was watching. Better to win the bargain and then be generous than to let anyone think he could be cozened.

"There aren't so many ships, now," Shanda said, trying to keep it light. She sipped weak hemp tea. "They came for the rope, of course," and the words were escaping, slipping free. "It was *all* that brought them. Father explained it to me. When the Ropewalk disappeared, we had to import another system, and that evil captain screwed us against a wall—sorry. Sorry. But he took every coin we could find, and then the Ropewalk was gone in the two Burnings! Ships still come for tar, but now the harbor is silting up," she said. "It's hard to get in, and worse, we don't have as much to trade as we used to. There's only the little Ropewalk now, so there's not much rope for the ships."

"Tar," Whandall said. "Tar is always valuable."

"And we have lots, yes," Shanda said. "But I may as well be honest. They found tar somewhere south of here, some lagoon between here and Condigeo. It's hard to get to, but if we charge what we need, the ships will go there instead. But you'll help, won't you?"

"Why should he?" Green Stone demanded.

Whandall gestured. This was not the time to play roles in the game of negotiation. Was it?

"It's his home," Shanda said simply.

"No, Lady," Green Stone said. "Not anymore. Whandall Feathersnake lives in the New Castle at Road's End. Everyone along the Hemp Road knows that!"

Burning Tower looked admiringly at her brother.

And it's all true, but this was *my home,* Whandall thought. *Good or bad, it was my home.* "I'll do what I can," Whandall said. "We'll look to see what's plentiful here and valuable on the Hemp Road. There must be something. And however easy or hard these new tar fields are to get to by ship, this place is easiest for me. Decide what's your price for tar. It'll tell me whether I come back."

A pony nickered outside. Whandall's expression didn't change as he thought how valuable a bonehead pony grown into a one-horn stallion would be. He said, "Ponies, maybe; there are places along the Hemp Road that might buy a pony. There must be other such things, magical items and animals stunted by Yangin-Atep. We'll look.

"But there's a problem," Whandall said. "The Toronexti make it very difficult for traders."

"We've spoken to them about that," Shanda said. "But I'm afraid they go their own way, much as the Lordkin do. And they have a charter."

"Scraped-off skins?" Whandall asked. "Covered with black marks?"

"I never saw it," Shanda said. "Writings, yes, witnessed by Lords in every generation, granting them privileges. Promises made long ago."

"By dead men."

She shrugged. "Still promises, written and witnessed. Written and witnessed."

Summon them up and ask . . . but this is Tep's Town. "If they lost that charter?"

Her eyes twinkled, just a touch, like the young girl he'd known deviling her governess. No one else saw it. "They'd never do that. It would be like—like it never was, wouldn't it?"

"How is Miss Batty?" Whandall asked suddenly.

"She married a senior guard," Shanda said. "But I didn't know for years. Samorty dismissed her after we . . ." She glanced at her daughter, then said it anyway. "Spent the night in the forest."

"They keep a shop in Lord's Town," Roni said. "Her daughter is learning to be a governess. For my children after I'm married." Roni was very serious.

"And Serana?"

Roni smiled. "She's chief cook, which means she doesn't do any work and orders everyone around."

"Even me," Shanda said.

"Good. Tell her I remember her puddings. Wait. Here . . ." He found it tucked under an Owl Tribe basin. Rosemary in a little parchment bag. "Tell her to crush this and rub some on red meat before roasting. Bison or goat or terror bird. And I'll send her some spices with the next caravan I send in here."

"Oh, good. You will be back?" Roni asked.

"If this works out. Shanda, I will need some help. Chariots. I'll need at least two—three would be better—with drivers. Lord's horses, not ponies! If I send my clerks around to look for trade goods, I want to know they can outrun gatherers." And because he'd seen Morth mapping out a path a day-walk long!

"I'll send for drivers," Shanda said. "The kinless hire out, but it will be better if your people are with a Lordsman. Fewer problems—I know. Roni, your cousin Sandry and his friends. Do you think they'd like to do this?"

"Sandry?" Whandall asked.

"We know a Sandry," Green Stone said. "Master Peacevoice Waterman brought him. To assist us. Said he was a clerk."

Shanda smiled thinly. "I hope you're not angry?"

Whandall grinned. "I'd guessed he was more than a clerk," he said. "What of the others? Will they be drivers?"

"Sandry will," Roni said. "I'm not sure about all the others."

"We'll send several," Shanda said. "Whandall can choose those he likes best. I'll have them here in the morning. And I'll speak to Master Peacevoice Waterman about deceptions."

And what will you say to him? "*Be more clever next time?*" "Thank you. Now, who sells me tar?"

"Us," Shanda said. "The Black Pit belongs to the Lords. A kinless family takes care of that for us. Roni, see to that, please. Find out how many jars Whandall will want, and arrange for them to be filled and sealed and brought here. It's time you learned some of that aspect of city management, I think."

"It's a man's job, Mother."

"Of course it is, but if women don't understand these things, how can we make sure the men do them right?" She grinned at Whandall, the old Shanda again for an instant. "I'm sure our merchant prince understands," she said.

"And if I don't, Willow will explain. My wife," he said, in case she'd missed it earlier. Both of us married, with children. Right? Right.

He was ready for bed when Morth came in. "I walked up Observation Hill," he said. "I used to go there a lot. Those ruins at the top, that was an old kinless fort. I can see the ocean from there, way off. I couldn't *see* anything, but with my talisman I perceived the elemental."

"Talisman. Another doll?"

"Yes. It won't last long. Whandall, the elemental perceived *me*. I should go out to look for myself. Sea Cliffs."

"Take a fast chariot. I'll have chariots tomorrow."

CHAPTER
75

Two hours after daybreak, seven chariots clattered into Peacegiven Square and drew up in a line in front of the Lordsman camp. An earnest young driver in Lordsman armor stood beside each one. One was Sandry, no longer wearing a clerk's cap. The horses were big grays, matched pairs at each chariot. They were well groomed and well fed. The chariots would hold two adults. In each chariot was a leather sheath holding a long thrusting spear and two shorter throwing spears ready to hand between driver and passenger.

They were smaller than Whandall remembered. He'd imagined Lords' chariots big enough to hold half a dozen men. They looked that big coming at you, but of course that was silly. Not even the big Lord's horses could pull such a load.

Master Peacevoice Waterman walked up and down the line examining each horse and driver. He muttered something and one of the drivers flicked dust off his gleaming armor. Another tightened the harness of his horse. When Waterman was satisfied, he strode briskly to Whandall's tent. "Chariots and drivers waiting inspection, sir!"

Morth and Whandall crossed the square to the waiting line. Whandall moved closer to Waterman. "I'm not used to chariots," he confided.

"Not surprised at that," Waterman said. "Trick is to spread your feet out, brace one against the sidework. There's a brace built into the floor to wedge your other foot against. Bend your knees so there's some spring in them; otherwise, you'll bounce right out when you hit a bump. Chariots are fast, but they tire the horses fast too."

"Are these horses tired?" Morth asked.

"Not too bad, sir; they led these in at first light, no load. The horses that pulled the chariots here from Lord's Town are resting up. They'll all be fresh come tomorrow morning."

"Good. Who's the best driver?"

"For what purpose, sir?"

Morth considered.

Finding the right questions wasn't easy here. "Speed. Distance," Whandall said. "We might have to cross most of the city. Maybe fighting."

"Best *fighting* driver would be young Heroul there."

Whandall regarded the charioteer. Young, clear eyed. Armor polished. He stood impatiently. "Is he reliable?"

"Depends on what for," Waterman said. "He'll take orders just fine. And he's got the fastest horses in the corps."

"Who for just speed and distance and a passenger who can't fight?"

"That's not Heroul. He likes to *win*," Waterman said. "You can depend on young Sandry there. Lord Samorty's grandson, he is, and best officer cadet in the corps."

"Lord Rabblie's son?"

Waterman looked at him oddly. "Reckon they called Lord Rabilard something like that when he was a lad. Yes, sir, that's his father."

And the Lords still talk about family to strangers. Brag, even. Not like Lordkin. Like *us*.

"He'll be steady, then?"

"I'd trust him," Waterman said. "You needn't tell him I said that. Cadet's head doesn't need more swelling."

"Thanks. You won't need to introduce us."

"Reckon I won't, sir," Waterman said.

"Morth, you take Sandry, then—"

"No, I want speed," Morth said. "You said that one is fastest?"

"Yes, sir."

"I'll take Heroul. And put some handhold lashings in that chariot. If you don't know how, I do. I had one of these in Atlantis."

Whandall stood uncertainly in Sandry's chariot. It was hard enough keeping his footing on streets. The potholes rattled him around inside this bucket on wheels. It would be a lot harder going across country. If Sandry noticed Whandall having difficulty keeping his footing, he didn't say anything about it.

"Can you carry an old man in one of these?" Whandall asked.

Sandry nodded. He needed all his attention to avoid a young Lordkin who had darted into the street. Then he answered. "Yes, Wagonmaster. We can strap a chair where you're standing, strap a man into the chair. But you're doing fine." *For a beginner,* he didn't add.

"Not me," Whandall said. "Morth."

"He didn't seem that old."

"He can get older fast."

"Oh. Aunt Shanda says she's known you a long time," Sandry said.

"Yes, more than thirty years." He looked at Sandry and made a decision. "Did you ever know of a servant girl named Dream-Lotus? Kinless, from the Ropewalk area."

"No, but I can ask," Sandry said. "Is it important?"

"Not very. I'd just like to know. Turn right just ahead there."

The streets were in worse repair, and there were more burned buildings than Whandall remembered. "Now left." Ahead lay the Serpent's Walk meetinghouse. Curse, it had a roof now! And a new fence. Oversize cactus plants grew against the fence. Two kinless were raking the yard, although it didn't appear to need raking. *Neat,* Whandall thought. *Wanshig always was neat after he came back from the sea.*

The Placehold looked neat too. In Whandall's time there was a half-ruined house down the block. That was gone, its lot planted with what looked like cabbages tended by kinless, and a small cottage stood behind the cabbage patch.

Whandall pointed to the front door of the Placehold. "Stop just there and wait for me. You won't be allowed inside."

Sandry nodded. He looked glad of the armor he wore. "Sure you'll be welcome?"

"No," Whandall said.

"What's the best way out of here?" Sandry asked.

Whandall chuckled. "Straight ahead, left at the end of the block. And stay in the middle of the street."

"You know it."

Boys lounged at the doorway. That hadn't changed. "Tell Lord Wanshig that Whandall wishes to speak with him." He lowered his voice so that Sandry wouldn't be able to hear. "Whandall Placehold."

Two of the boys ran inside. Another stayed in the door staring at Whandall's tattoo.

The doorway stood invitingly open. Whandall grinned to himself. At least one, probably several armed Lordkin adults would be in there, one behind the door waiting for anyone to come in uninvited—

A girl about fifteen came to the door. She wore a bright dress, too fancy for housework. "Be welcome, Whandall," she said, loud enough that everyone near would hear.

"Thank you—"

"I'm Firegift, Uncle Whandall. My mother is Wess."

And calling me Uncle says I'm accepted as one of the men of the Place-hold, not that she's Wanshig's daughter, Whandall thought. She could be, but she won't claim that. Just her mother. The Lordkin ways were coming back to him, but as a half-remembered dream.

"Lord Wanshig is waiting upstairs."

Wanshig sat at one end of the big meeting hall. It seemed full of people, none Whandall could recognize. Except Wess. She stood in the doorway of the corner room. The room that was his, with her, for a while, when Whandall Placehold was the eldest man in the Placehold. A lifetime ago.

She was still pretty. Not as pretty as Willow, but to Whandall no woman ever had been. But Wess was a fine woman still! Firegift went to stand by her mother. They looked more alike, side by side, than they had when they were apart.

"Hail, brother," Wanshig said.

"Lord Wanshig."

Wanshig laughed hard. Then he got up and came to Whandall, slapped hands, hugged him in a wiry embrace that showed Wanshig hadn't lost his strength. Neither had Whandall, and they stood half embracing and half testing for a minute.

"Been a long time," Wanshig said.

"That it has. You've come up in the world."

Wanshig looked at the ornate knife Whandall wore. "So have you."

"That's nothing," Whandall said. He took off the knife and sheath, revealing a plainer and more functional blade underneath. "A present," Whandall said, and held out the ornately decorated knife. "Among others. I'm rich, brother."

"That's nice—"

"I can make the Placehold rich," Whandall said. "I'll need help doing it. Actually, I'll need Placehold and Serpent's Walk together."

"After lunch you'll tell me," Wanshig said. He gestured, dismissing the men and women who had crowded around. "You'll all meet Whandall later," he said. "Give me time to talk with my brother."

Brother. We had the same mother. Not necessarily the same father, and in our case certainly not the same. Lordkin!

The others went away or settled in corners of the big room.

"We'll eat in here," Wanshig said. He led Whandall into the big corner room. A table had been set up, and Firegift was bringing food and tea. "You'll remember Wess. She's my lady now. First lady of the Placehold," Wanshig said.

Whandall didn't say anything.

"What? Ah. That's right; you'll remember Elriss," Wanshig said.

"And Mother."

Wanshig nodded. "Dead, brother. Dead together, with Shastern. Fifteen years ago—"

"Sixteen," Wess said. "Firegift is fifteen."

"Sixteen years ago. The Burning started by Tarnisos."

"Tarnisos killed our family?"

"No, he started the Burning. It was a Mother's Day; the women had gone to Peacegiven Square. The Lords still gave Mother's Day presents there. You remember?"

"Yes."

"Shastern went with them. They had collected the gifts, were coming back, when the Burning started." Wanshig shook his head. "We went looking for them. Found them dead, two Bull Pizzles dead with them. Everything they had was gathered, of course. Later Pelzed and Freethspat went looking for Pizzles to settle the score, but the Pizzles claimed their people were killed helping Shastern. Could have been, even. Could have been."

"Who did they say?" Whandall demanded.

Wanshig's expression was bleak. "You think you'll get even, now, after sixteen years when you weren't here, little brother? You think I haven't tried?"

"Sorry. Of course you did."

Wanshig nodded grimly.

"What happened to Freethspat?"

"He tried too. Mother was his woman; he was really close to her. Closer than I was to Elriss by then, I think. He went looking one day. Never came back."

"And Wanshig became eldest in the Placehold," Wess said. And didn't say that Firegift was born a few months later, but that was clear enough.

"So. How can we help you, little brother?" Wanshig asked.

"Two ways, if you can work with me," Whandall said.

"It's possible," Wanshig admitted. "What two ways?"

"First, burn out the Wolverines."

"That's hard, little brother. Hard. You know who they are?"

"I hope I do. I've got no quarrel with the Wolverines. But Alferth says they're the Toronexti. I have reasons to think he's right."

"So do I," Wanshig said. "And the Toronexti work for the Lords." He looked thoughtful. "And you? You have a chariot and a Lordsman driver. Have the *Lords* told you you can burn out the Toronexti?"

"Pretty close," Whandall said. "They won't help, but if it happens they'll be happy enough to take credit. There won't be a blood war. If there's a blood price, I can give it back to you."

"I need to think on this. What's your other task?"

"Morth of Atlantis needs help. We'll explain later. But it needs reliable people. He needs a truce with Sea Cliffs, at least to take a chariot there. And Wanshig, I can use some help outside, out of Tep's Town, if there's anyone who wants to go."

Wanshig stared at him. "Out?"

"There's a whole world out there."

"Twenty years ago I'd have come with you," he said. "Not now, and I need all the men I have, in Placehold and in Serpent's Walk. These are hard times, little brother."

"We like it here," Wess said possessively. "But I have a son, Shastern." She nodded at Whandall's look. "Named for your younger brother. He's a wild boy. I don't think he'll live long here. Take him with you."

"How old?"

"Ten," Wess said.

"He can come. But Wess, if he comes with us, he won't be a Lordkin anymore. He'll learn different ways. I doubt he can ever come back."

"You did," Wess said.

"Whandall, there are some who'd like adventure," Wanshig said. He sighed. "And I'm still Lordkin, and they'll never let me go to sea again. Unless you own ships, little brother?"

"That's not the route I took. Let me show you, big brother. Did you learn maps while you were sailing?"

"Maps? We knew about maps. Never saw them. They were locked up in the captain's cabin."

"The idea is to make a picture of where you are and where you want to be and things you see on the way. Landmarks." Whandall began drawing on the table. Tep's Town as a little black blotch, Firewoods in dried chili seeds, the Hemp Road in charcoal. Wess watched the mess being made, looked at Wanshig, and decided not to interfere.

"This is where we went, me and a wagon with children hidden like wine. Wildest battle of my life, *here*. My tattoo lights up when I kill, out there where there's still magic." By First Pines, he'd run out of room. "I have to draw it smaller."

"So that's how it works."

"May I teach this? In the courtyard? It would be something to give back," Whandall said. Anyone who worked the caravans would have to learn maps eventually. Who could he take? Best find out who had the knack! Best find out—

"Big brother, do you remember when I tried to teach you about knives?"

Wanshig grimaced. "Yes."

"May I try again? Teach them all? Tomorrow. Maps today."

Wanshig looked into his face.

"You're older and smarter. I'm a better teacher. Line up your best knife fighters. Watch me. Watch them. This time you'll get it."

"You meant it."

Whandall made no answer.

"Yes. I want to watch that," Wanshig said. "We'll listen to your wizard and I'll send a gift to Sea Cliffs. Give me a day or so to get the word out— Whandall of Serpent's Walk is back and is welcome at the Placehold. Your woman too, of course."

"She's not here." Whandall thought of Willow coming into a Lordkin castle. "She's outside."

They returned to Peacegiven Square to find Morth raving.

"He's a madman!" Morth shouted. He pointed to Heroul, who stood grinning on his chariot. It looked odd with no horse hitched to it. Then Morth turned jubilant. "But it's *there!*"

"The wave."

"Heroul drove me out to Sea Cliffs. The wave stood up and came at us, way too low, of course. Hit the cliff hard enough to shake our shoes! Then this maniac drove us right down into the lowlands!"

"Heroul, are you all right?" Sandry asked.

The young charioteer's grin was wide. "It was wonderful!" he burbled. "The water just humped itself and came right at us! Real magic! Nothing like Qirinty's dancing cups—"

"And this madman *toyed* with it!" Morth said. "He stayed just ahead of it, all the way—"

"—along Dead Seal Flats. It slowed when it started up the ridge," Heroul said. "I could see it was slowing, and I didn't want to founder the horses! So *I* slowed, and it came on almost to the top. Then it slumped and ran back down toward the ocean. Ran like water, I mean, not fled."

"You were teasing it!"

"Maybe a little, sir. And we still exhausted the horses." Heroul waved to indicate two chariot horses being groomed by some of Waterman's men. "I'll get new ones for tomorrow, let these rest up a day."

"Not for me, you won't, you maniac!" Morth said.

Whandall grinned. "Younglord Heroul can drive me tomorrow," he said. "Sandry, if you please, shepherd this ancient wizard around the city."

"Certainly, sir."

Morth gave them a sour look. "That water sprite has chased me half my life, and today was as close as it ever came to catching me."

"But it didn't," Heroul said. "Sir."

PART FOUR

Heroes and Myths

CHAPTER
76

A t dawn the next morning a half dozen kinless came to Peacegiven
Square and began work on the ruins of an adobe house at one corner. Whandall remembered the house as belonging to a Bull Pizzle
Lordkin. Or was it Flower Market? But the big Lordkin who came with
the kinless wore a serpent from left eye to left hand.

In an hour they had cleared out the front yard and set up a cook fire. In
another they had set out tables and chairs and hung up a sign painted with a
cup and roasted bird's leg. A tea shop, at Peacegiven Square. Another sign
went up: a serpent, but this was set at the edge of the lot, right at the corner. The
sign in front of the shop bore a palmetto fan to indicate peace, all welcome.

Pelzed had dreamed of taking another side of Peacegiven Square, but he
had never dared. Of course now it wasn't worth as much. . . .

Whandall went over to inspect. Sandry—Younglord Sandry—followed.
The kinless waitress was in her thirties, well dressed, elaborately polite.
"Yes, Lords. Welcome."

Whandall lifted his hand in greeting. It was a useful gesture, a way to
be polite without losing status. The big Serpent's Walk Lordkin came out
of the house. He was young and hadn't had the tattoo long. "Lagdret," he
said. "You'll be Whandall. Welcome." He pointed to the back of the house.
"I'll be living here until the Bakers here get the house next door fitted up.
Lord Wanshig says if you need me, call." He went back into the shop without waiting to be introduced to Sandry.

"Polite," Whandall said.

Sandry looked the question.

"He hasn't anything to say to you, and he won't take up your time. He came out here to tell me only because Wanshig asked him to. His job—never say *job;* it's just what he's agreed to do—is to protect this place. What he gets out of it is a new house kept up by the kinless he protects." Whandall smiled thinly. "Probably his first house; now he can attract a woman of his own."

"I should learn more about Lordkin," Sandry said.

Whandall smiled. "Our custom, it is, to swap information and stories."

"Ah."

"I never knew much about Lords," Whandall said. "No more than I could learn watching from a distance."

"Sometimes you were closer," Sandry said. "What do you want to know?"

"There are bandits on the Hemp Road. Sometimes enough of them get together to set up a town and collect tolls. Now, all towns collect tolls, one way or another, but most of them give something back. Keep the roads up, provide dinners, drive away gatherers, keep a good market square open. Bandit towns just take. When that happens, all the wagon trains get together and go burn them out.

"Sandry, your Aunt Shanda wants us to bring wagon trade into Tep's Town."

"We all do."

"So tell me about the Toronexti."

Sandry looked surprised. "I distinctly remember Lord Quintana telling Waterman to talk to you about the Toronexti."

"Maybe he didn't tell me enough."

"They have a charter," Sandry said. "Promises made over the years. Some of them were bad promises, stupid promises, but they've kept the decrees, every one of them, and if we try to do anything about them they can produce a promise, signed and sealed, saying we can't do that."

"Lords are big on keeping promises?"

"Formal, written, signed, and sealed? Of course."

"Did you promise to help them?"

"Against all outside enemies," Sandry said.

"Not against Lordkin?"

"No! They'd never ask. At least they never have, and if they did now, well, it would take three full meetings of all the Lords even to consider extending the Toronexti charter. But it wouldn't happen. The charter says *they* protect *us* against revolt."

Whandall sipped tea. It was good, root tea, not hemp. The shop wanted three shells a cup, a high price, but prices always went up when the wagon train was in town. "Sandry, are you afraid of Master Peacevoice Waterman?"

"Wouldn't you be?"

"Well, maybe, but by that light I should be afraid of Greathand the blacksmith," Whandall said. "But Waterman's a Lordsman and you're a Lord."

"Younglord," Sandry corrected. "Apprentice, if you like to think of it that way. Waterman would take my orders, if I were dumb enough to talk back to him. Then it would get back to my father. Wagonmaster, you tell your blacksmith what to make, but you don't tell him how to make it."

"I wouldn't know how."

"And I wouldn't know how to train men."

"Or get them to fight," Whandall said.

"That part's easy. It's called leadership," Sandry said, and blushed a little. "Getting them to fight together, to do things all of them at once, not one at a time, that's hard."

Like learning knife fighting, Whandall thought. *But if you learn one thing at a time, you can put it all together.* He thought about battles they'd had with bandits. Kettle Belly had taught him to get as many men together as you can, make them stay together and fight together. Twenty on three always won, and usually with none of the twenty getting hurt.

And the Lords knew all that, and the Lordkin didn't, and—

"So what shall we do today?" Sandry asked.

"I'll send you with Morth, but hold up a breath or two." Whandall considered. "You can't tell me how to fight the Toronexti." He got a confirming nod. "But what can you tell me about dealing with the Wolverines under Granite Knob?"

Sandry smiled. "I asked about that after last night. Fights between Lordkin are not my concern. I won't help you fight them, but I can tell you anything you want to know about Wolverines."

And Whandall was sure, now. The Toronexti were the Wolverines. But what good did it do to know that?

It was known that he intended to take a few people out of Serpent's Walk, out of Tep's Town. Some were willing to help him choose.

Several Lordkin tried to extract promises from him. Take my nephew, he doesn't fit in . . . my daughter, she's sleeping with the wrong men . . . my son, he's murdered someone powerful . . . my brother, he keeps getting beaten up. Whandall didn't promise. Nobody can force you to buy without actually drawing knife . . . and that happened only once.

Fubgire was one of Wanshig's guards, in his late twenties, brawny and agile. Whandall retreated from the room where Fubgire confronted him, into the courtyard, and there he turned it into a knife fighting lesson.

Kinless and Lordkin came to him, driven by distaste for the ways of the

Burning City. He would make an offer to a few of these. He set some of
the kinless to working on maps.

Yesterday the courtyard had been covered with maps sketched in saw-
dust. Today Morth and Wanshig and a few visitors from other turf were
making maps inside.

Lured by the fight with Fubgire or by Wanshig's wonderful new knife
or by rumor and curiosity, nearly forty men waited at dawn to be trained in
knife fighting by Whandall Placehold. Too many by far, of course. One
was Fubgire, older than most of these, but bandaged and determined to
learn from his mistakes. Try him on maps too?

Whandall began to teach. More drifted up, until there were sixty in the
Placehold courtyard.

Many felt that they already knew how to fight, that no outsider had anything to teach them. They spoke this truth, or it showed in their sneers.
They began to drift away.

Some stuck to it. Some stayed to laugh at the rest, and they had a point.
That was why he had practiced in secret, because it did look funny. When
Wanshig finally emerged around noon, the numbers were down to thirty.

The essence of knife training, as Whandall taught it, was to practice
each of several moves separately until the mind turned to jelly. Whandall
looked for those who could stick to it for an hour, perfecting one move, and
move on to the next, and end the day without screaming in anyone's face.

To them, and to those who could work with maps and still not scream in
anyone's face, he would make an offer.

There were too many. He had no confidence in most of them. The
cursed trouble was that you could not set tests for a Lordkin, because he
wouldn't put up with it. You learned what a Lordkin was made of by
watching him, sometimes for years.

Whandall didn't have years.

His bed was waiting, but so was Morth. The wizard asked, "How are
you feeling?"

"Worn out. I've been training Lordkin in knife fighting. How would you
feel? Want some tea?"

"Yes, please. Whandall, do these Lordkin make you angry? You've been
away a long time."

"Embarrassed. I used to *be* them. I kept my temper all day."

"I expected you to lose your temper with the Toronexti."

"Morth, it's a dance. They're clumsy at bargaining. That bottle trick
was fun."

"Has anything made you angry lately?"

"Is this about anger, Morth?"

"Yes."

Whandall considered. "Not angry. Shocked. This . . . wilderness was Peacegiven Square. It wasn't just the place where our mothers gathered what our families needed to live. It was . . . order. Order where we lived, like the houses in the Lordshills."

"You're shocked but not angry."

"Well, I—"

"I wasn't asking. Whandall, Yangin-Atep hasn't even looked at you these three days, not a flicker, I can *tell,* and that's why. You don't get angry. If I threw a calming spell at you, I'd have to tell you about it later. But can you keep it up?"

"Merchants don't get angry, Morth. Good merchants don't even fake it."

"Then . . . it could work. Here's what I need."

Whandall listened. Presently he asked, "Why?"

And presently he asked, "Why should I?"

"Oh, make up your own cursed motives. What has a water elemental ever done for you?"

"It gave me water to drink when I was a boy."

"I thought that was me, but all right. Yangin-Atep?"

"Burned . . . burned my family. Yes, I see. Morth, this is the craziest idea I've ever heard, even from you, but I . . . I think I see how to use this. I mean, for the caravan. For my family. For Feathersnake. If you'll do it *my* way."

"Yes?" And Morth listened.

The next day's mapmaking went on in the dining hall behind locked doors. Whandall spent some time in the courtyard supervising knife fighters at their practice, and some time with the map.

The Gulls at Sea Cliffs hadn't seen Morth dancing on the cliff above them. They knew only that a tremendous wave stood up and smashed four houses before it washed against the cliff. Three housed kinless, but in the biggest house three or four Lordkin lived in every room. Two were killed. Nine were homeless.

Now came word from Wanshig of Serpent's Walk. Their people were drowned, their stronghold smashed and washed away, by a water demon. Wanshig's runners told the Gulls what had hurt them, and who could kill it, and what was needed.

The sprite's route inland would begin there.

"So we hold Sea Cliffs, and they brought in those that hold Dead Seal Flats. Now, you want to put people all along here," Wanshig said. "If you don't want them attacked, nobody had better know what you're giving them, and we still need truce for the whole length. This is Ogre turf here. They're crazy. We can't get truce and we couldn't trust it. Why not go around?"

· "We'd never get a moving wave up here. Too high."

"Lord Wanshig?" That was Artcher, one of Wanshig's entourage, likely a nephew. He'd shown some skill with maps. Now he asked, "What if we ran the line along here? It's Long Avenue. The road runs this way because deer followed the low route, and it's Weasel turf from here all the way to here. They keep their truce too."

"They take cursed big gifts to make truce!"

"I think I hear my secret name," Whandall said. An ornate knife, some glass jewelry, honey candy, and half their route was secured right there.

As they nailed down the route, Wanshig sent out runners. The blades Whandall had brought for Lords were all going to Lordkin, but that was all right. The Lords wanted him much more than he had expected.

"That's a nice low run. Dark Man's Cup?"

"Bull Pizzles," Wanshig said.

"Don't tell me that!"

"Freethspat was good, little brother, but he didn't keep other people's promises. It's a garbage dump again too. Look, Dark Man's Cup is perfect if those Pizzles will trust me not to snatch it back."

"Offer to scour it clean for two coils of hemp. Say we've got a wizard. If they've heard the rumors, they'll know it's true. Say they can pay on delivery."

Runners began flowing in with answers. Long Avenue was under truce. Bull Pizzles would deal if Serpent's Walk would wait half a year for the hemp. Now send a credible messenger to get the kinless out of Dark Man's Cup. No details could be given, as they might leak, but *get out!*

Dirty Birds were easy, still allies after all these years.

Silly Rabbits would not make truce. They *had* to have that stretch. Send another offer, but count on sending guards to protect Whandall's chosen.

That evening Whandall gathered his chosen in the banquet room, now map room. He spoke briefly, and he passed out bottles.

"Anyone who wants to leave Tep's Town: here is a cold iron-glazed bottle. Don't open it tonight!"

Knife training and mapmaking gave him men who could keep their temper. Millers and Ropewalkers he gave special consideration. This woman could read. This one cooked a stew from random gatherings. Green Stone watched children pulling weeds on the Placehold roof garden, and chose three. Freethspat's boy, Whandall's last half brother aged thirty, was worth a look. He'd rejected the maps and the knife practice, but he got a bottle.

Any of his chosen might take a mate when they left.

None were told what would be done. Yangin-Atep might take anyone's mind.

Back in Peacegiven Square, Whandall went to Morth's quarters to choose his running gear. "Pick something colorful, something distinctive. Don't you have anything that isn't gray or black, Morth?"

"I've seen your motley crew. None of them dress like any other! Those Flower Market Lordkin make Seshmarls look diffident! And you want distinctive?"

Whandall sighed. "Sandry, doesn't your cousin Roni know a seamstress?"

"Likely enough, sir."

"Green Stone, write. 'Roni, Morth must have a wizard's robe by *tomorrow night*. Something anyone can see from a mountaintop on a cloudy day. Please carry my word to your seamstress. This is her price.' " Whandall chose a swath of the finest cloth in the caravan, lavender with highlights in it, then sheets of bright green and bright gold. "And this for Morth."

CHAPTER
77

The bottles had been given out the previous evening. This day was given to more knifeplay and mapmaking. After dinner all gathered to be given their final instructions.

Morth wore robes in blazing green patched with huge golden stars. Whandall stared. The cursed robe was perfect, just perfect. From a mountaintop on a cloudy day. He'd said that. It would be bad to laugh, but . . . "Morth, you *really* look like a *wizard,* Morth."

"Oh, shut up!" Morth hurled the pointed cap at the floor. "How was that supposed to *stay* on? Did you think—"

"This is Morth!" Whandall bellowed, and waved grandly. *"Look at him! Know him when you see him again!"* There was laughter, none of it muffled. These were Lordkin. "Good. Morth, now I need you to ferret out every bottle that has been opened."

Laughter died as Morth moved among the giggling horde and pointed, pointed. Wanshig's musclemen moved after him and saw to it that certain men and women went away.

"I only had it open for an instant!"

Morth took the stopper off. "Nothing. Refined. Keep it, but go."

Another complained. Morth pulled the stopper out and back fast. "Still some power left. How long did you have this open?"

"Long enough for Tarcress to finish cooking sand dabs. Just time to pour a bit out, to think that that was gold and . . . put it back."

"Keep your place." Morth opened another bottle. "No gold. Fool! Keep the bottle and get out."

"Gathered by my brother!"

"Fool!"

Wanshig asked above the noise, "You're sure? They keep the bottles?"

"If they go quietly. Fifteen of my heroes are clean missing, bottle and all, but these came," Whandall said.

"I count eleven missing."

Morth tapped five in a clump of six. The sixth boy watched them depart. Whandall asked him, "What happened?"

"We all live in a room at the Placehold. Last night Flaide opened his bottle and poured out a handful of gold. He told the rest of us."

"Why didn't you open yours?"

Silence.

"Good. Your name? Sadesp, were you all six stationed next to each other? Curse. Whandall, all of these other bottles stayed closed."

"Hold up, Morth. I don't know some of these people." Fifteen gone but four replaced by strangers. The woman was looking at him. "Did I give you that bottle?"

Pride and terror. "No, Feathersnake. I'm taking Leathersmith Miller's place."

"Where is he?"

"Smitty slept beside me last night. I'm Sapphire Carpenter, and I know more about love than any woman in the inner city."

Wanshig said, "She speaks the truth. Sapphire, you're *leaving?*"

"Morth, look her over."

"She's clean. No diseases, no curses. A few fleas. She's left the bottle stopped. Sapphire, can you throw?"

"Yes. Smitty showed me his place. I have his map."

She'd kept the bottle unopened for several hours.

"Take your place," Morth said. "And, Sapphire, if you think you know every pleasure that may pass between a man and a woman, we should talk."

Three more carried black bottles Whandall hadn't given them. Three men had backed out, or gotten high or drunk, or—face it—been killed for their places. Too late to tell. Whandall sent one away, with a gold nugget and no bottle, because he didn't like his look. He would risk the others.

He nodded to Wanshig. Wanshig unbarred a door and they trooped in. "Watch your step," Whandall called, then followed with Green Stone.

They had been all day working on this map, using charcoal and props.

Whandall said, "Green Stone, take over." The boy had been familiar with the general plan for months. He believed, where Whandall didn't quite. And—Whandall should not fully concern himself. A curious fire god might still look into Whandall's mind.

Traders were trained to project their voices above rushing rivers, storms, bandit raids. Green Stone used his caravan voice. "You're the chosen. In your lives you have seen just enough magic to know that it's real. You are going to witness and be part of the most powerful wizardry this city has ever seen. Those who stay behind will never see the like again. Play your part and you will leave Tep's Town and see sights you've not yet had the wit to dream.

"Those of you who understand maps will recognize what's going on here. This," Wanshig's gold saltbox, gathered long ago, long emptied, "is the Placehold. Here, the Black Pit"—a dark pool on the floor, ancient blood. They'd started their map there. "Here, the Lordshills. Forest. Deer-piss and the Wedge, and the Toronexti here"—a brass coin.

"These jagged lines way out here are shoreline, here at Sea Cliffs, here at Good Hand Harbor. We got some help on these from a Water Devil. We don't know what's between them. More shore.

"Off beyond Sea Cliffs is ocean and a water elemental. Morth of Atlantis can tell you more about it. It's been trying to kill Morth since Atlantis sank.

"Morth intends to kill it. That has never been done before.

"The elemental will show itself as a mountain of water. It will chase Morth. Morth—see these paired lines? One red, one green, all the way across the map? Morth will follow the green line from Sea Cliffs across Dead Seal Flats, uphill here, down along Long Avenue to Dark Man's Cup—see? And on inland. The wave will follow the lowlands. We'll be strung out all along the red line, above it all, watching.

"We want to throw bottles ahead of the wave. When Morth is past, take the stopper out and throw the black bottle. Throw it at something hard, like a rock! It has to break!" Take the stopper out *or* break it—both would work—but these were Lordkin; they might forget.

"Yangin-Atep takes the magic, all in an instant, if they break too soon. You—Sintothok?—you opened your bottle, but not long enough for Yangin-Atep to gather all the manna in the gold. But break it just in front of the wave, the elemental will take it.

"And that's the point of all this. The wave will sink and flow back to the ocean if we don't give it the power to go on. The wild magic will keep it moving until it gets *here*. *Here* at the Black Pit is where Morth will trap it, with no manna to move it and no way to get more, and here Morth will kill it.

"Afterward, gather at Peacegiven Square. . . . Questions?"

Lordkin don't raise their hands and wait. They bellow. Green Stone pointed and said, "Hey! Hey! You."

"I've seen waves. They're fast. Your wizard is *nuts*."

"Morth can outrun lightning. I've seen it. You will too. If you miss it you'll regret it the rest of your life. *You—*"

"You want to move the wave *uphill?*"

"Here and here we'll have the wave going uphill, yes. I'll bunch you up a little there, because we'll *really* need the gold."

And because some of these won't throw, Whandall thought, *but you can't tell* them *that some of them can't be trusted.* "Corntham? What?"

"How do you kill a water elemental?"

Morth said, "That's the tricky part."

Green Stone said, "Morth has made gifts to us for our part in this. Our gifts to you will be freedom from Tep's Town, just as you've been promised. You'll have a place in the caravans on the Hemp Road, or you may find better lives than that. Whandall Placehold was one of you. What he is now brought him back as greater than a Lord. My father." Green Stone watched them flinch at that word, and he grinned.

CHAPTER
78

S ome of the bottle throwers, those with the most distant posts, must be
sent off that night in a protected band. Sea Cliffs would house them.
The rest dossed down in the Placehold for what remained of the
night. The caravan would have to take care of itself. Whandall and Green
Stone needed their sleep.

The sale at Peacegiven Square would have nearly emptied out the kinless
quarters. Lordkin who knew nothing of Morth's plan wouldn't be interfer-
ing with Morth's route. They'd be burgling empty houses while the kinless
were away, or trying to profit from the fair . . . or so Whandall hoped.

Morth and Whandall boarded their chariots behind Sandry and Heroul.

Wanshig hadn't caught the hang of mapping, and at his age, no wonder.
Two sisters' sons had. They rode Wanshig's chariot, placing bottle throwers from Dark Man's Cup southeast to the Black Pit.

Whandall moved west.

His chosen were not standing beside friends to hold them steady. Each
could just see the next to either side, not too far for a voice to carry.
Except . . . that yawning gap. Five of six boys gone, and Sadesp standing
alone. Whandall slowed to space them more regularly.

Now Morth was far ahead. His chariot slashed through the weeds that
lined Dark Man's Cup, while Whandall and Heroul followed him along
the ridge. Whandall couldn't see deep enough into the chaparral to pick

out kinless houses or the warrens of the hemp growers. They'd been warned. They'd got out, or they hadn't.

The beach was in sight. Sandry stopped his chariot on the ridge above Dead Seal Flats, and Morth got out and went on.

The last runner, a woman of Sea Cliffs, had slowed to a walk and was checking her map to find her place. Her man had already taken his. Whandall had Heroul pull up between them. He walked to the edge.

He would have driven on to the bluff above Sea Cliffs Beach. He'd see it all from there. From here, Morth was already out of sight. But Whandall's chariot would need the head start, if what he remembered was no hallucination.

A wave rose up and rolled forward, crested in white, climbing as it came. Where was Morth? Already gone?

There, a green and gold dot, unmistakable—*look* at that man *move!* The wave came after him too slowly, losing ground, but higher every second. *Throw,* Whandall thought, but he wouldn't speak. This was how he would know his own, if they threw or if they didn't.

Whandall jumped aboard. "Go. Go!"

Heroul used the reins. Horse, then chariot lurched into motion.

Delirious laughter rose above the wave's roar, and Whandall wondered why the sound was so delayed when Morth was halfway to the first rise.

The woman threw. Her man threw too. Bottles arced down and shattered, and a mountain of water rolled past, raising thunder and spume just below Whandall's whirling wheels.

The big horse looked terrified. Heroul was elated. The wave so far down was no threat to them. Morth was nearly out of sight, disappearing in chaparral, where Dead Seal Flats rose uphill.

Morth stopped as if he'd hit a wall.

The wave rolled on. Whandall rolled past an elderly kinless man curled up with his hands over his ears, crying, bottle abandoned. Wrinin of Flower Market hurled her bottle; it bounced unbroken and rolled but left a trail of yellow gold. Sapphire Carpenter waited until she was in his full view, then threw beautifully; the bottle smashed just under the wave.

Morth was in a tottering run, and the wave was closing. Bald scalp, thin white fringe. Teeth showed in a snarl of effort as he turned back, just for an instant, and grinned at the showers of gold and glass splinters. And the wave rose to hide him, but Sandry was waiting with the chariot and was helping Morth to board.

Now the wave was moving uphill, losing water, losing mass. Whandall's chariot was pulling ahead of it. Below, the wizard and Sandry came back into view. The Lord's son drove like White Lightning twisting a gob of molten glass, carefully, aware of danger, not hurrying, doing his job.

Swabott's mother was first lady of Flower Market. They'd *needed* truce with Flower Market to post their bottle throwers. Whandall had prepped him. Swabott knelt with bottle in hand, the stopper already out, as the wave came toward him.

Even from far away, Whandall could see him shaking with terror. When he stood to throw, the bottle jittered in his hand and gold showered all about him. The wave was ahead of Whandall here . . . and now it was passing Swabott, and he hadn't thrown.

He turned toward Whandall, and a serene joy was in his face. He wasn't shaking at all. He took it all in; his smile widened to a manic grin. . . .

Before Whandall could twitch, Swabott was running alongside Whandall's horse! The horse was running full out, but when Swabott swung onto its back the horse screamed and surged faster. Swabott dug his heels into its sides and yelled. Whandall was ready to jab a spear into him when he threw.

The bottle dropped neatly in front of the wave and smashed.

Whandall turned the spear around and rapped Swabott smartly on the back of his head. "Get off my chariot!" Swabott leaped from the horse, rolled, and was on his feet and running, laughing like a madman. Gold fever . . . and he'd earned his place.

The low path turned here and became Dark Man's Cup.

Padanchi the Lop still had one good arm. His bottle shattered ahead of the wave. Then the wave turned to follow Morth's chariot, and the foamy crest slapped Padanchi off the cliff.

Kencchi of the Long Avenue froze at the sight. He didn't hear his woman screaming at him to throw. Nor did Whandall; he only saw her wide mouth, straining throat. But when the time came, she threw. Kencchi didn't.

Decide later.

Morth's properly terrified horse was pulling him nicely through Dark Man's Cup, following its own trail of smashed vegetation. The wave rolled on, no less monstrous, feeding on the wild magic in the smashed bottles.

Here several of his chosen were missing . . . the wave began to slump . . . and there was fighting ahead.

Four of Whandall's bottle throwers had managed to reach each other and were fighting back to back against six men of the North Quarter. North Quarter had broken truce! Whandall signaled Heroul, who pulled toward the ring of Lordkin around the four survivors.

They saw him coming. Running wouldn't help; his first target braced himself to duck aside. Whandall outguessed him and punched his blade deep into the man's torso. His grip on the long haft twisted the man halfway around, and then Whandall could pull the blade free, all in a background of screaming. The ring of gatherers was broken and running. Whandall reached out with the long shaft and stabbed another.

Heroul was looking for another target.

"Keep it moving," Whandall shouted. The wave was gaining on Morth. Its dark green face had crosscurrents in it, interference patterns.

The ground leveled off ahead. Whandall's advantage of altitude was dwindling. He had no reason to think that this mindless water elemental would take an interest in him, but . . . *but.* Whandall's path had grown rougher; the wave was past him; behind him he could see its wake of black wet ground.

Morth might die in this crazy project. Whandall would not mourn long. His promise bound him, but this was also his chance to choose whom he might rescue from the Burning City. *If* Whandall could survive. He might *die* rescuing the idiot wizard.

Morth was almost under the wave, already beyond rescue.

Morth opened a black bottle and showered gold all over himself. Sandry turned in surprise. Morth's hair flashed brick red and he was *moving.*

The chariot was left behind, horse and all, swallowed by foam in the next instant. But Morth was running on the vertical cliff with the charioteer held wriggling above his head. He dropped Sandry on the lip of the crest and veered back into the valley, leaving a wake of mad laughter.

The charioteer was on hands and knees, coughing, then vomiting. Whandall waved at Sandry but didn't slow. Then the horse stumbled and Heroul *had* to slow.

Horse and driver, he'd get no more out of either.

Whandall jumped out and ran, wobbling from the beating his sense of balance had taken. Heroul followed, shouting, "Where? Sir, where are we—?"

"Follow Morth!" He was passing the last bottle carrier—Reblay of Silly Rabbits, sitting spraddle-legged, his bottle thrown. Running on flat land now, past a broken chariot and three men on their backs gasping for air. Wanshig and his two nephews—

Those weren't the nephews he'd started with.

Whandall ran. If he lived, he'd hear the story. The Black Pit was ahead. Whandall could see its ripple and gleam: water covering black tar, a death trap shining in the sun.

Morth was slowing again, gray with fatigue. He looked back, and from the look in his eyes, what he saw was his death.

Manna in raw gold had energized the water sprite and driven it mad. The wave had followed Morth, and a trail of wild magic, deep into the heart of the Burning City. Now it was stranded in a place where the magic was gone; and now there was nothing behind it but refined gold. It still stood higher than any building of that age. White-crested, with weird ripples rolling across its green face, it rolled toward the staggering, gasping wizard.

Reblay was *not* the last bottle carrier. *Here* was where Freethspat's son should have been, where lay a black bottle no bigger than Whandall's fist. Whandall scooped it up and kept running. He neared Morth, pulled the stopper and threw.

Gold and glass sprayed around the wizard's feet. Morth whooped and ran, over the fence in a leap, across the dark water too fast to sink into it, to the far side of the Black Pit and over the far fence.

A mountain of water rolled into the Black Pit, absorbed the pond water, and grew.

The tar burst into flame.

Whandall barely felt his hair and eyebrows singed to ash. For an instant that seemed to last forever, he perceived what Yangin-Atep perceived. . . .

CHAPTER
79

Yangin-Atep, Loki, Prometheus, Moloch, Coyote, the hearth fires of the Indo-European tribes, uncountable fire gods were one and many. He, she, they had the aspect/powers of bilocation and shared minds. Pleasure or pain seeped from lands where a lord of fire and mischief might be worshipped or tortured.

Every cook fire was a nerve ending for Yangin-Atep. Whandall could feel the god's shape, the terrible freezing wound at his heart, the numb places where parts of the city were abandoned and no fires were lit, the long, trailing tail through the Firewoods. He felt sensation where Lord and Lordkin armies had passed, the path of Whandall's escape and return.

Yangin-Atep stirred rarely. It was only his attention that moved . . . but where Yangin-Atep's attention fell, things happened. Fires went out when Yangin-Atep took their energy. He put out forest fires. Cook fires he allowed to burn. If he snuffed them too early, they were of no use.

Fires indoors went out. Yangin-Atep in Whandall's mind remembered why. An ancient chief had bargained with Yangin-Atep, had woven a spell to prevent his nomad people from settling in houses.

Cook fires gave him his life.

But there was not enough magic even in fire. Every several years, Yangin-Atep fell into deathlike sleep. Then fires raged unchecked, even indoors. Yangin-Atep's famine-madness would fall on receptive worshippers, and people called that the Burning. In his coma Yangin-Atep might not respond to the Burning for days, yet his chosen would feel the easing of his hunger, his growing strength. Their own grief was eased by the fires.

When Yangin-Atep revived it was all in a surge. He took fire where it was hottest, and though some fools might continue to throw torches, the Burning was over.

But now the trickle of life in Yangin-Atep was trickling away, and a line of bleeding emptiness crawled toward him from the sea. It was water, water come to challenge him. The manna that kept a water elemental alive was the life of Yangin-Atep.

The fire god's attention moved across the Burning City and centered on the Black Pit.

Tar and oil.

The pond water that covered the Black Pit had been rolled up into the greater mass of the sprite. Tar lay naked and exposed. Yangin-Atep's attention set it afire. Flames cradled the sprite. The sprite danced like a bead of water on a skillet, trying to withdraw from the fire.

Ancient dead animals played in the flames. Sabertooth cats pawed at the air, swatting at the water above them. Great flaming birds circled. A mastodon formed, then *grew* until it loomed above the sprite. Behemoth stamped down with both forefeet ... and was gone, and the sprite was unharmed.

The child Whandall had seen these ghosts as holes in fog. Now they were flame ... but Whandall's perception saw more. Yangin-Atep was summoning them to absorb their manna. The fire god was eating the ghosts.

Morth lay limp on the far side of the Pit. Whandall made his way around the fence toward Morth, his haft and blade forgotten in his hands. It was a long way around. He could barely see, hear, feel, with the fire god's senses raging in his head.

The elemental knew what it wanted, and Yangin-Atep felt it too. Yangin-Atep raised fire to block the elemental from its prey, from Morth of Atlantis. The elemental countered with a blast of wild magic, gold magic, nearly its last. If Whandall couldn't feel magic, the fire god could. Yangin-Atep's attention snuffed out, then snapped back.

And Morth, half dead beside the Black Pit fence, snapped awake and strong, awash in manna. He spilled his pack, stripped to the waist, and smeared his arms and chest with white paint, all in great haste. He faced the Pit and his arms began to wave.

To Whandall it looked like he was conducting music or a dance. Indeed, fire-beasts danced in response, even as they winked out one by one.

The war was half seen, half felt, half hidden. Whandall wasn't perceiving it all. In flashes of clarity he made his way to Morth.

Morth's back was turned. "Just stay clear," he said without turning around. Gold rings glittered on every finger.

"Can't I do something?"

"Clear!" Morth danced on.

Then Whandall's only senses were Yangin-Atep's.

Water wanted to cool fire. Fire wanted to burn water. Yangin-Atep wrapped the elemental like an eggcup around an egg. Water sizzled. Fire dimmed. Both were dying.

Some power remained in the Black Pit to feed the ghosts of the ancient animals, and that power was being used now. Yangin-Atep reached out for more and was blocked at the fence. But there was enough.

The sprite died in a blast of live steam.

Whandall covered his face with his arms and fell to the tarry ground. Heat scalded his hands. Morth's arms never missed a beat, but Whandall heard his howl.

Yangin-Atep hunted. If there had been a trace of the water elemental, Yangin-Atep would have eaten the manna in it. But the water thing was dead, myth, gone. Yangin-Atep reached farther.

There was *nothing* outside the Black Pit.

Now Whandall felt claustrophobic terror, a sudden shrinkage. From occupying the valley's vastness, enclosed by forest and sea, fed by cook fires, Yangin-Atep was numb and paraplegic beyond the border of the Black Pit. Some enemy was weaving—*had* woven—a wall!

Yangin-Atep twitched to the rhythm of the spell and sought a new enemy, and found him too late. Whandall recognized Morth of Atlantis, his dancing arms and fingers, but the wall was complete and Morth was outside, untouchable. Manna streamed thinly from the stars, but Yangin-Atep couldn't feel it. Morth had woven a lid to the box.

Yangin-Atep pushed against it. Whandall heard Morth's bellow of agony, dimly, but he *felt* the fire god's agony. The magical barrier was pitifully thin, but it was water magic.

Yangin-Atep hunted with the ferocity of a Lordkin, and found . . . a Lordkin.

Then Whandall and Yangin-Atep were two aspects of the fire god. The fire god reached down and picked up his haft and Lordkin blade.

Whandall Feathersnake let it fall.

Yangin-Atep stooped to pick up the spear, stooped and reached, bent his knees and reached, desperate to make this body move. *Move!* Why wouldn't the Lordkin *move?*

Morth danced like a marionette, his back turned. Whandall Feathersnake stood at peace with himself and the god raging in his mind. Whandall was familiar with the hard sell. Every merchant in the world thinks he can make you buy, but he can't. Listen, nod, enjoy the entertainment. Offer tea. At the right price, buy.

Whandall felt the fire fill him, running down his arms. Little flames licked his fingernails. Fire lit his mind. *The Toronexti! We'll burn them out! Houses, gatehouse, forest paths, men, we'll burn them all! Take the children hostage to hold the women. Next, the Bull Pizzles—*

What you offer has value, of course, but how can I risk so much? If I lose, my people starve, my family, all who trust Feathersnake. No, your price is too high.

Flame licked his fingertips. *Rage!*

Frivolously high. Fire, you can't be serious.

Burn!

Control. Relax. Stand. Smile. *Breathe.*

There was no manna left. Yangin-Atep faded to a dying spark.

Not here on the surface, but deep down beneath the tar where no wizard could ever have been, the last trace of the fire god found a last spark of manna. The fire god sank, faded, and was myth.

Yangin-Atep was myth.

Whandall's face hurt. Clothing had covered the rest of him, but his hands and the left side of his face and scalp were hot with pain. His hand found no eyebrows, no lashes, no hair on that side.

Morth was a stick figure, bald as an egg. Clothing charred black across the front of him, and his arms waved, conducting unseen musicians. Whandall dared not interfere. There was no trace of ancient animal ghosts now, and every fire was out.

Morth lowered his arms, bowed, and fell on his face.

Whandall rolled him over. Morth's eyes were half open, seeing nothing.

Whandall said, "The sprite is dead, Morth."

Morth sucked air. *Alive.* "Can't know that."

"Morth, I strangled it myself and ate every trace of it. It's *dead.* Excuse me, did I say? I was being Yangin-Atep."

"Feathersnake Inn."

"All gods welcome. I want no more of it, Morth."

"Won't happen again. What's left of Yangin-Atep, I wove deep into the tar. Whatever the fire god has been doing to this town, it's over. Ten thousand years, maybe more, maybe forever, Yangin-Atep sleeps below the tar. Maybe you can make something of that. I'm burned. Get me to the sea, for the manna. Wash me with salt water. Wait. You sure the sprite is—"

"Dead."

"Good."

PART FIVE

Feathersnake

CHAPTER
80

Sandry and Burning Tower clattered up, horses lathered. Heroul was just behind him with Green Stone.

"Father!" Burning Tower shouted.

"I'm all right."

His children began to inspect him. They looked to be caught between horror and laughter. Whandall said, "It's Morth who needs help. Sandry, can you get him to the sea?"

"He doesn't look strong enough to ride in a chariot," Sandry said.

"I'll get a wagon," Heroul said. "Coming?" he asked Green Stone.

"See to it," Whandall said. "Get Morth *into* the water."

"I will," Heroul shouted. He wheeled away and lashed the horses, dashing across the uneven ground.

"We'll stay with you," Whandall said.

Burning Tower knelt beside the aged wizard.

"Stay there," Morth said. "Some say there's magic in a young girl's smile. Whandall! We did it!"

Heroul was back with a kinless in Quintana colors driving a four-horse wagon. Whandall and Green Stone lifted the wizard into the wagon and laid him on the blankets that filled it.

Whandall demanded, "Morth, how long?"

Morth smiled with no teeth. "Get me into the sea," Morth said distinctly. "The sea is magical everywhere. Quick enough, I might live."

The wagon moved away with Heroul's chariot as escort.

"Shouldn't we go with him?" Burning Tower asked.

"He's in good hands," Whandall said. "I'm more worried about the caravan now. Sandry, can this thing carry three?"

"If one is as light as she is," he said.

"I can ride the wagon tongue," Burning Tower said. "See!"

"Blazes—Burning Tower, that isn't safe," Sandry said.

"Safer than a tightrope. You just drive."

It was the final-day sale for the caravan. Pitchmen were shouting it. "Last day. Everything goes! Never be lower prices."

Burning Tower leaped from the chariot before it stopped. She raced to the sign outside Whandall Feathersnake's market pitch, snatched up a charcoal from the fire, and began to scrawl huge black letters across the neatly scribed sign. Nothing Was Seen came out of the nest to stare as if he could read.

"Lurk, are you all right?"

The bandit boy looked nearly healed but still swollen in spots. "Feathersnake, they're working me like a kinless." He must have learned that from a customer. *See, I speak your language!* "You look half fried, and where's the wizard? Tell me a story!"

"Later. Back to work." Sandry was half strangling on his own laughter. Whandall had never seen him do that. He demanded, "What does it say?"

Sandry looked at Whandall. It was clear what he was seeing: a tattooed man with every hair of his body singed off, burn spots and blisters on his arms and hands and on one cheek. Sandry struggled with laughter and lost. "Sir, it says *FIRE SALE*."

"I should never have let her mother teach her to read," Whandall growled. "I want a new shirt. Then let's see if I can sell something."

The sale was a roaring success, kinless and Lordkin alike come to see what the traders from Outside had brought, what they could buy.

Heroul and Green Stone returned in late afternoon. Whandall was selling a carpet out of his own travel nest. He'd run out of stock early. Two Lordsmen were paying a manweight of tar and some jewelry; the Lord waited silent behind them. Whandall asked, "Is the wizard dead?"

"Morth is well," Green Stone said.

Whandall looked around. "You left him alone?" Abandoning an ally was much different from leaving one's dead.

"He's not alone." Though it was half killing them, they both waited for Whandall to complete the sale. Then Green Stone babbled, "We ran straight to Good Hand Harbor. Some Water Devil gatherers would have stopped a wagon, but not Heroul's chariot. They followed us. There's a boat bigger than *all* the boats we saw at Lion's, and there were seamen all about. But there's a beach. We didn't want to move him, so we ran the wagon right down into the water. I got in and held Morth's head up.

"There were seamen and Water Devils all wanting our story. They saw the same thing we did. Morth lay there looking drowned, grinning with no teeth and bragging in a guttural whisper about what we'd done. He's got deep burns, meat burns, but some blisters healed while we watched. He grew some hair, just stubble in patches where he was burned least, but it's *red* stubble. He grew teeth. He started to laugh."

Heroul said, "Last I saw him, he was up to his neck in sea water asking the crew for food. Said he could pay. Wants to know if the ship needs a wizard. A crewman was going for the captain."

"A wizard in his element," Whandall mused. "Did he say when he was coming back?"

"Father, he won't even try to stand up," Green Stone said. "He said he can't leave the sea, not for weeks."

"We can't stay weeks!"

"Father, he's done his part!" Green Stone said.

"You look worried," Burning Tower said.

"Oh, Stones is right, Blazes, but now we have to fight our way out past the Toronexti without a wizard!"

"Oh. But we've got Sandry."

"We'll escort you out," Sandry said.

Burning Tower caught his tone. "Sandry? You won't *fight?*"

"We can defend ourselves if they attack us. *Maybe* they're that stupid."

"And maybe that will be enough," Whandall said.

Green Stone was looking out at the crowd. "Good business," he said.

"Yes, but Stones, none of them seem to know," Burning Tower said. "Yangin-Atep's gone mythical and they don't know!"

"Morth said it would take a while," Green Stone said. "Manna is low, and there aren't any wizards. They've been gone for centuries. How will anyone know magic works here?" He rubbed his hands together. "Father. We get out. We join up with Saber Tooth and come back with Clever Squirrel and every shaman we can hire! Think what they'll pay here just for rain! We'll clean up."

"You're thinking like Saber Tooth," Burning Tower told her brother.

"About time," Whandall said.

Peacegiven Square buzzed like a hive, and trade was brisk. A few Lordkin were to be expected, and Whandall had counted twenty or so. They were looking, not gathering much. The merchants must have educated them early . . . but Whandall was keeping his eye on a cluster of Lordkin, seeing them as trouble, wondering when they'd split up and begin gathering.

Serpent's Walk would have *filtered* in, not come in a bunch. Others had noticed. Merchants and customers were all beginning to bristle.

Whandall wondered if it might make sense to pay off the Toronexti. Get out, then return in two weeks with weapons and magic . . . and plant poison rubbed on sever blades . . .

No. Too late in the year. After the tax men stripped them, they wouldn't have wealth to show outside. They wouldn't get enough fighting men to bring back, and winning a few battles wouldn't help if they had to stay the winter. *No.*

The knot of a dozen Lordkin he'd been watching had crossed the square to Hammer Miller's wagon. They began gathering goods. When Hammer came out to collect, one backhanded him with a laugh.

"Hey, harpy!"

The whole square glittered for a moment. The cry of "Hey, harpy!" rose in a chorus. Whandall jumped the counter, knife in hand.

He was surprised to see Sandry and Heroul wheel their chariots around and leave the fight, rolling at top speed toward the Lordsmen camp. But the rest of the action was familiar.

Kinless took cover.

Most of the Lordkin decided it wasn't their business and took cover too. A few, enraged at having their fun interrupted, readied to fight. But the harpies were behaving like Wolverines: clustered back to back in the open square, giving themselves room to fight, allowing nobody near.

Caravaners armed themselves and moved toward the gatherers at a trot. The flurry of slingshot missiles surprised the harpies. They didn't notice what else was going on among the Lordsmen. Whandall barely saw it himself, but, running to test his knifework against Tep's Town harpies, he slowed.

Waterman had been watching. As the two chariots neared the camp, they were joined by three more.

"Riders mount up!" Waterman shouted.

Men ran from their tents to take places beside the charioteers. "Go get 'em! Sir!" Waterman shouted.

Sandry waved toward the knot of harpies. "At a walk! At a trot!"

He took the long spear in his right hand. The other drivers were doing the same. The riders held short spears at the ready.

"Charge!"

Five chariots in line hurtled across the square. "Throw!" Five short spears arched out, and four of the intruding Lordkin fell. The others ran, dropping their loot, dropping everything else they carried. Only one turned to raise his Lordkin knife in defiance. He got Heroul's spear dead in his chest for his effort. The charioteers came to a halt.

Across the square Waterman was still forming up his infantry troops, but there was no need. Heroul set his foot on a corpse and wrenched his spear loose. Three of the gatherers were dead. Two others probably wouldn't live, not if *that* was the care they were getting.

Whandall went to a dead harpy and turned him over with a foot.

A stylized long-nosed animal was tattooed on the upper arm. The style had changed in twenty-two years, but—"Wolverines," Whandall said.

"Glad that's over," Burning Tower said. She stood half fascinated by the dead men, every now and then glancing up toward Sandry. Sandry looked both pleased with himself and astonished that all his training had paid off—it worked just the way his teachers had said it would. . . .

"It's not over," Whandall said. He pointed.

Lagdret of Serpent's Walk lay dead in front of the Miller tea shop. The pretty waitress behind him was bleeding from a knife wound to her shoulder.

Wanshig arrived half an hour later. He sent two of his Lordkin to wrap Lagdret's body. "Carry him home," he said.

Wanshig inspected the dead Wolverine. "These?"

Whandall said, "These, or the ones that got away. Wolverines, anyway."

"Doesn't matter."

"No?" Whandall was astonished at his brother's cold voice.

"Doesn't matter," Wanshig said again. "Wolverines killed my man. Killed a Placeholder on neutral ground. Never make half a war. Whandall, is it true? We've put *Yangin-Atep* to sleep?"

"Yes."

"I had to try it. I took a torch indoors. Of course that would work . . ." Wanshig looked around him; Lordkin and kinless were coming out from cover, watching each other warily. Wanshig said softly, ". . . during the Burning."

"Ten thousand years, Morth said."

"But a torch burns indoors, and the Wolverines don't know it," Wanshig said. "Well, they'll know it soon enough. By noon tomorrow every damn one of them will know it."

"Do you have enough men to attack the Wolverines?" Whandall asked. "They're strong."

"So are we," Wanshig said. "Whandall, I've done my best to stay out of wars. Build alliances. Do favors. Now I'm calling in every favor I have coming. Flower Market and Bull Pizzle won't want to send anyone, but they can't keep me from asking, from spreading the word that we're going to gather in rich territory, got room for anyone who wants some loot.

"Can I tell them the Lordsmen fought Wolverines when I talk about gathering?"

"They fought *here,* yes, but they may not carry it farther. Don't promise anything. We'll be leaving in the morning," Whandall said. "The Toronexti are sure to be watching. We can't get to their gatehouse before noon."

"They'll want a lot of their strength there," Wanshig said. "You'd be rich pickings. Like nothing they've seen in their lifetimes! And they won't expect me to be looking for them right away. They sent a man to offer blood money."

Whandall looked at his brother.

Wanshig grinned. "Never found me. Can't find me. He went to the Serpent's Walk clubhouse. At the clubhouse, they said I was gone back to the Placehold; Placehold will send him to Pelzed's old place. He's always just missed me. Curse, you did bring some excitement, Whandall! I never quite found the right time to take back Dark Man's Cup. But I contracted to clean it, right? It's as clean as a river bottom! And the Bull Pizzles don't want to pay."

"So when will you go into Wolverine territory?" Whandall asked.

"Was planning on first thing in the morning, but it's even better at noon. About the time they see you, their turf will be burning." Wanshig laughed. "Never fight half a war. I taught my people—"

"I taught mine."

"Whandall, Wess will bring her boy over in the morning. You take care of him."

"I will. Wanshig? The gold is still down there, you know, under the water, all along the Long Avenue."

"Ah." Wanshig stood. "It's been instructive, Dall. And maybe I'll see you again, maybe not."

"You too, Shig. I'll be back."

"I think you will. Maybe I'll be here too."

CHAPTER
81

It was barely light when Wess came. Wess's son looked nothing like Shastern. He was a small boy, big eyes, a thoughtful look. "Like I remember you were," Wess said. "But he's smaller than you were. Take care of him, Whandall."

"Things will be different here," Whandall said. "Maybe—"

"Not that different that soon," Wess said. "Please."

"He can come with us, Wess, but we have to get past the Toronexti. If that goes bad—" He thought for a moment. "If that goes bad I'll send him home with one of the Lordsmen. Sandry has been to the Placehold. He'll take him."

"All right." Wess kissed her son. He stared with big eyes at her, then at Whandall. "Good-bye." She turned and ran.

"Burning Tower, this is Shastern," Whandall said. "Keep him out of trouble. Shastern, you stay with her." *And just maybe,* Whandall thought, *that will keep both of you out of the fight.*

Thirty-seven of Whandall's tested bottle throwers came at dawn. Ten were kinless. All carried large sacks, all the possessions they would be taking outside. They chattered eagerly of a new life.

"Who's missing?" Whandall asked. "I thought everyone would come."

Fubgire had endured the knife lessons and thrown his bottle. He said, "Wanshig was persuasive. They went to gather at Granite Knob. The rest of us are here, Lord."

"I'm not a Lord. We have no Lords. I'm Wagonmaster."

"Close enough for me, Lord." But Fubgire was laughing.

"All of you, stay together," Whandall said. "Green Stone will tell you what to do."

A couple of the Lordkin muttered.

"Get used to that!" Whandall snapped. "Working with us means following instructions. The way to win in a fight is to stay together and act together. Green Stone knows your language. Listen to him!

"I ask you to walk alongside the last wagon. Keep your weapons ready, don't hide them, but don't threaten anyone. If you have to raise a weapon, use it. We're going to see if the Lords can talk us past the Toronexti. I don't expect them to do it."

"We'll have to fight, then?" Hammer Miller asked.

"I think so, Hammer. Don't you?"

"Yes." He turned to the ten kinless who were coming out with them. "You all have your slings." It wasn't a question, and they all did: the ceremonial nooses around their necks came off quickly.

"Be sure you have a good supply of rocks."

The Lordkin frowned. Kinless without nooses, kinless with weapons.

The wagon train left as soon as it was light enough to see, but Waterman had his men on the road first. The Lordsmen marched on ahead. Whandall glimpsed Lurk and Shastern in the last wagon and thought no more of it. He had larger concerns.

There were seven chariots, Sandry and his friends. Every chariot held a driver and a spear thrower. The charioteers tried to stay with the wagon train, but horses hated to match a bison's pace. They learned to hang back, then dash ahead to catch up.

It was enough of an escort that no one wanted trouble. Word had spread: Wolverines had attacked the wagons, and the Lordsmen had killed Wolverines. Leave the wagon train alone! Even the stupidest of Lordkin could understand that. The bison moved at their slow pace through streets deceptively quiet.

Near noon, an old man hobbled out of the shade of the biggest tree. He leaned heavily on a giant. The giant was elderly, gone to fat, and his smile was more goofy than challenging. Still, a giant. They approached without fear. Bent and twisted as the master was, Whandall wondered at his equally goofy grin. Like a Lordkin springing a trap?

Then Whandall recognized him. "Tras!"

"Whandall Feathersnake. Always surprising. I much prefer this to your last surprise."

"I—"

"Shall I tell you how I got myself off your land alive? After I crawled back into the crypt, I fainted. When my man Hejak—"

"Hold up, Tras. Arshur?"

"Arshur the Magnificent," the giant confirmed. "Not sure I remember you. Got a drink?"

"I was with Alferth when you got your first drink here. You getting beaten up, that started the Burning twenty-odd years back. I thought you'd be leaving on the next ship."

"I like it here."

They rounded the last bend. The Toronexti were ahead.

The caravan moved toward them. Whandall's merchants moved to the tailgates, ready to jump down. The new recruits huddled around Green Stone. They would be at the gatehouse in minutes.

Hobbling along with his stick in one hand, the other on Arshur's arm, Tras was still keeping up with the burdened bison. "Hejak gave up on me and was leaving when I crawled out, but I—"

Whandall said in some haste, "Tras, I'm just too busy right now, but can you climb a tree?"

Tras Preetror gaped. "Do I look—?"

"He can climb a tree," Arshur said. "Or I can throw him up a tree. Should I do that?"

"Both of you." Watchman had pounded Arshur's head with sticks. The treatment seemed to have done some permanent damage.

Now Tras Preetror saw the armored Toronexti ahead. "That officer—I know how he hurt his hand."

"I've stopped caring."

"Three Lordsmen wanted out of Tep's Town, with their armor. The tax men tried to stop them. They wanted one suit of armor."

"Tras, you two are about to see a really good story happen right in front of you."

"They're more careful now. Do you mean . . ." Tras was finally seeing the danger. "Story. May I call it 'The Death of Whandall Feathersnake'?"

"If that's what you see, that's what you tell, but see it from a height, Tras, and in hiding. If you live, *you owe me.*"

The kinless bonehead ponies were getting larger, horns growing as they approached the forest. That hadn't happened this close to Tep's Town last time, Whandall remembered. Yangin-Atep was myth. Whoever saw the implications first would make fortunes.

Waterman was ahead of them, his band grown to nearly fifty men drawn up in three ranks. An officer's tent was set up behind them. Whandall didn't recognize the Lord, but Sandry rode up alongside the wagon. "My father," he said. He whipped up his horses to go to his father's tent.

The wagons reached the Toronexti gate.

The big Toronexti officer with the injured hand was waiting. There were more of the masked and armored tax collectors, fifty that Whandall could see, more in the tollgate building, probably some behind the building. Whandall waited.

Sandry brought his chariot up. "Let them pass."

"Now why should I do that?" Half Hand demanded.

"Orders from the Lord Chief Witness. This wagon train passes without taxes."

"Now does it? Chief Clerk!"

The shuttered door on the second floor of the brick gatehouse popped open. There stood Egon Forigaft, and a glimpse of dark ancient tapestries behind him. He leaned far out over the ten-foot drop to put daylight on the sheet of parchment in his hands. A Toronexti guard held his sash.

"Decree of Lord Chief Witness Harcarth: the Toronexti shall have the right of taxation on all goods departing through the forest. There is more."

"Enough, I think," the scarred officer said. "Younglord, we have a charter. Witnessed and signed, Younglord. Witnessed and signed."

Sandry shrugged helplessly. Toronexti moved forward.

Whandall said, "Hey, harpy!"

The fighting men of the wagon train leaped down to join the Lordkin and kinless walking alongside the wagons. Together they made a formidable band. Women took over the reins, closed the gaps in the wagon covers.

"You want our goods? Come and take them!" Whandall shouted.

"A decree!" Egon Forigaft shouted. "The Lords will assist the Toronexti when they are attacked by outsiders."

"Who's an outsider?" Whandall jumped to a wagon roof and stripped off his shirt. "I am Whandall of Serpent's Walk! Who dares say I am not Lordkin?"

No one moved. Sandry laughed. "What does it say about Lordkin, Clerk?"

Egon found it. "The Toronexti shall protect the Lords and their agents from civil unrest."

Sandry said, "We owe you no protection from Lordkin. *You* protect *us,* you misbegotten goblins!"

One of the Toronexti threw a stone. It struck Sandry's spearman in the stomach. The spearman bent over, retching.

Sandry gave a wide grin and lifted his spear.

"A proclamation of Lord Qirinthal the First!" Egon shouted from his upper story. "There shall be truce between Lords and Toronexti so long as this charter endures. If Toronexti shall strike a Lordsman, that Toronexti shall be liable for double the injury in blood, two eyes for an eye, two limbs for a limb, two lives for a life, and this be paid, the truce shall endure!"

"We pay!" the Toronexti officer shouted. "Bring me that man!" He pointed to the window, though the man who had thrown the stone had vanished. Two Toronexti dragged him over. The officer hit him in the stomach with all his strength, then again. "Do the Lords demand another man be punished?" he shouted.

Sandry turned away in disgust.

"It's that stack of old parchments, isn't it?" Whandall said.

Sandry nodded.

"What if it were to burn?"

Sandry grinned.

"Go! Stone! Distract them while I get that paper!" Whandall shouted. The Toronexti wouldn't understand the language of the Hemp Road.

Stone led his band toward the Toronexti. Whandall charged forward to dash inside the gatehouse, but someone inside saw what he intended. The gatehouse door slammed shut with a crash.

"Greathand! Break the door!"

Greathand had a sword in one hand and a hammer in the other. He ran forward. Whandall ran with him, his cloak wrapped around his arm to protect them both. He blocked a slash, felt his cloak yield to a sharp blade. A Toronexti moved toward them, then fell to Hammer Miller's sling. Now a dozen slingers were in action, and stones fell among the Toronexti. They held up their arms to protect their heads. Two more fell.

Twenty of the tax men came around the building. They held shields and moved in behind them in a rattle of stones from the kinless slings. They got between the other Toronexti and the slingers.

Whandall's Lordkin stalwarts rushed forward, but despite all Stone could do, they didn't stay together. They came in ones and twos, and in ones and twos they were cut down. Whandall saw a dozen of his men on the ground to half that many enemies.

"Smoke!" One of the Toronexti gibbered and pointed. A black cloud of smoke rose over Granite Knob. "Smoke! That's our *homes!*"

Whandall smiled grimly.

"We have to protect our homes!"

"Stand fast!" Half Hand shouted. "It's a trick! It's just smoke to draw us away! Stand fast!"

Greathand pounded on the door with his hammer. The door did not yield. "I need an ax!" he shouted.

Hammer Miller ran to a wagon and got an ax. He ran toward Greathand with a tax man behind him. Hammer swung the ax. The Toronexti ducked and lashed out with his Lordkin knife. Hammer fell in a shapeless heap.

"See, Younglords, how we protect you!" The Toronexti officer gestured to send ten armored men to face Whandall, Greathand, and four others at the door. One of the newcomers took the ax from Hammer Miller, started forward, and went down under a Toronexti knife. Greathand shouted defiance and moved toward the ax. The battle surged around him. Four men charged. Greathand turned and struck two men with his hammer before he was beaten to his knees. More Toronexti moved toward Whandall, moving together, carefully and slowly—

Whandall's wagon curtain opened, and Burning Tower ran out.

Right. Whandall had foisted Shastern on her, but she'd passed the boy on to Nothing Was Seen, and now she was free to run at the Toronexti line with a torch in her hand. She leaped onto the back of one of the bison, over his head, and down to the ground. Before laughing Toronexti could catch her, she reached the flagstaff in front of the building and climbed it. From the top she leaped across to the open doorway where Egon Forigaft stood. She waved her torch in triumph.

The Toronexti officer roared in laughter. "Torches inside, here, on Yangin-Atep's spine!" His laughter turned to horror as Burning Tower put her torch to the thin parchments Egon Forigaft was holding. They blazed. She whirled the torch about, and ancient ceremonial tapestries were burning, flames everywhere.

"There!" she shouted. "Where's your charter now? Read it now!" She kicked blazing parchment out of the doorway. "It's gone. Sandry!" Then she was out of the doorway, climbing toward the roof, two Toronexti chasing her.

Sandry shouted. "Waterman!"

"Sir!"

"Clean out these vermin!"

"Sir! Lock shields! Spears high! Forward!"

The line of Lordsmen moved toward the Toronexti.

Sandry grabbed the throwing spear from his crippled spearman. It arched high. The Toronexti on the roof screamed and fell. Burning Tower stood on the roof and shouted. "Good throw, Sandry!"

And six more chariots were charging the Toronexti line. Javelins flew, and now there was only Whandall and the Toronexti leader with the ruined hand. Half Hand backed away. Whandall feinted high, then drove his knife point just below the line of the man's leather armor. It went in to the hilt.

He turned to see everyone staring at him.

* * *

"Your face," ten-year-old Shastern said in awe. "It lit up!"

"For the last time," Whandall said. "I hope." What did they *see?*

There were eleven dead, four from the wagon train. "Six more probably won't make it," Green Stone said. "Three times that if we don't get out to a healer pretty quick. Too bad we don't have Morth."

"We'll go," Whandall said. "The way's clear. Get loaded up."

"Shall I come with you?" Sandry asked.

"Aren't you needed here?"

Sandry looked at the piled bodies. "It will all be different now. Yes, sir, I may be needed. But—"

"She'll be back," Whandall said. "In a year. If you still remember her—"

"He will," Burning Tower said from behind him. "I will!"

"We'll know that next year," Whandall said. "Stone, are we loaded?"

"We are."

"Move them out." Whandall looked back. Tep's Town wasn't visible from here, but there was dark smoke over the hill below Granite Knob. Not many of the Toronexti would be going home to defend Wolverine territory.

Smoke rose elsewhere too. Wanshig hadn't done that, and the time of Yangin-Atep's Burning was over. But . . .

Tep's Town was only now discovering that fires would burn indoors.

Given their lack of faith in the fire god, kinless didn't have the habit of leaving flammable trash about. Lordkin did. Sailors didn't. A few days from now, the Placehold might be the last stronghold unburned.

And it wasn't Feathersnake's problem. "Move them out, Stone. It's your wagon route. Not too soon for you to take charge of it. I'm going home."

AFTERWORD

Over millennia the Hemp Road spread from Condigeo south through the isthmus and deep into the southern continent. When the caravans died out, the feathered serpent remained a symbol of civilization.

The "Native" Americans who invaded the American continents from Siberia fourteen thousand years ago found that they could use the native mammoths and horses as meat. These creatures they ultimately exterminated. When the Americas were later invaded from Europe, there were no suitable riding beasts from which to fight.

The *Los Angeles Times* says, ". . . redwood fossils discovered in Pit 91 [of the La Brea Tar Pits] indicate that the big trees, now generally seen only in the mountain forests of Northern California, grew along what is now Wilshire Boulevard" (July 28, 1999).

When the redwoods were gone, the truce of the forest died too. California chaparral has lost much of its malevolence, but some plants still maintain their blades, needles, and poisons. Hemp still soothes, distracts, then strangles its victims at any opportunity.

The killer bees of Tep's Town ultimately armed every hive on Earth with poisoned weapons. Bees no longer negotiate worth a damn.

* * *

Foxglove—digitalis—has lost much of its power. The pretty little flower is still a euphoric and a poison.

The madness that comes of touching river gold is still remembered in Germany, in *Die Nibelungen,* and in the United States, in such movies as *The Treasure of the Sierra Madre.*
The legend of a madman's lost gold remains current.

Parents continued to tell the tale of a charismatic man who contracted to resolve a town's infestation of vermin. When the Lords refused to pay him, he led away not just the vermin but all the youth of the town. Ultimately his tale became that of the Pied Piper of Hamelin.

The story of Jispomnos's murders, which spread with the tellers from Tep's Town to Condigeo and then returned to Tep's Town as an opera, spread farther yet. Ultimately it fell into the hands of the playwright William Shakespeare, to become *Othello.*

Yangin-Atep lay mythical for nearly fourteen thousand years, entombed in petroleum tar, until two men came to dig for oil in the La Brea Tar Pits.
Their names were Canfield and Doheny. Yangin-Atep's call and the lust for precious metal played a resonance with the gold fever in their brains. At the La Brea Tar Pits they tried to dig an oil well with shovels! They didn't stop until they were one hundred and sixty-five feet down, a few inches above death by asphyxiation. Bubbles of unbreathable gas crackled under their shovels. Fumes made them dizzy and sick. At last they went to find a partner who knew about pipes; and then they woke the fire god and built an empire on petroleum.

In 1997 the authors found Pinnacles National Park to be exactly as described. Sage, rosemary, thyme, and pallid dragon nip still grow there, and the giants' fingers and dragons' rib cages are still in place.

Yangin-Atep feeds the fires that move a billion automobiles and a million airplanes everywhere in the world.
Not cook fires alone but also automobile and diesel motors are each a nerve ending for Yangin-Atep. The god's nerve trunks reach along freeways, paths that once ran through forest, then and still Yangin-Atep's tail. From time to time the fire god's attention shifts, and then the Burning comes again.
Some people like to play with fire.